Untold Paranormal Police Stories

By
Ronald R. Schmidt

Order this book online at www.trafford.com
or email orders@trafford.com

Most Trafford titles are also available at major online book retailers.

© Copyright 2011 Ronald R. Schmidt.
All rights reserved. No part of this publication may be reproduced, stored in a retrieval system, or transmitted, in any form or by any means, electronic, mechanical, photocopying, recording, or otherwise, without the written prior permission of the author.

3 prior books published.
1. The Lorelei, 2. The Undelivered and 3. The Mountain's Ghostly Secrets

This is a work of fiction. All of the characters, names, incidents, organizations, and dialogue in this novel are either the products of the author's imagination or are used fictitiously.

Printed in the United States of America.

ISBN: 978-1-4269-4389-8 (sc)
ISBN: 978-1-4269-4390-4 (hc)
ISBN: 978-1-4269-4391-1 (e)

Library of Congress Control Number: 2010914776

Trafford rev. 12/14/2010

www.trafford.com

North America & international
toll-free: 1 888 232 4444 (USA & Canada)
phone: 250 383 6864 • fax: 812 355 4082

Contents

Untold Paranormal Police Stories

PROLOGUE:

From the beginning of time, all of the world's dedicated peace officers have laid their lives on the line time and again to protect the citizens that they are sworn to serve. In America, our various law enforcement departments have evolved into professional organizations of men and women that are so highly educated and trained, that virtually nothing they could encounter is uncontrollable or able to escape their technical knowledge or training capabilities. Without exception, they are all literally ready to handle all situations and adversities that might come their way during their normal working schedules. Yet, based on their training and education what do they do if and when something occurs that is so bazaar, or so far outside of their normal common sense or logical world that there is no reasonable way to explain, let alone rationalize it. What do they do when they cannot explain something they experienced that was beyond logic or normality, because they know in discussing it with others, they would be criticized, or believed to have lost their minds, or maybe even their courage? Is it possible in their day to day contact with criminals, evil doers or just lost souls, that something so bazaar could suddenly present itself to them that it would cause these champions of law enforcement to question their own eyes, common sense and physical capabilities? Could there ever be an instance where they simply felt that it was best to turn away and try to forget what happened, hoping that no one would ever know what occurred, because they know whatever it was, could never be explain to anyone that did not personally witness it?

This story is about two highly decorated, respected and well trained Los Angeles Police Officers with many years of service and experience who firmly believed that there was literally nothing that they had not already encountered before. Yet, on one very quiet evening something so strange and unexplainable occurs that neither of these two men can explain it, let alone rationalize what happened, causing them to doubt their own senses.

Our story will show what happens when two long-time partners are literally touched by an event that literally changes their entire perception of the world we live in, and leaves them with a dilemma of not only how to report the facts in a believable way, but to also accept it for what it was and be able to move on with their own lives. As you follow this story, you will see what happens when a paranormal world collides with the logical day to day world of people who deal with facts. You are about to read about two heroes that are forced to deal with things in reality that no one is ready to accept, believe in, let alone talk about. And, how each deals with it, and what eventually happens to each man is the basis of *Untold Paranormal Police Stories.*

CHAPTER 1; *The Awakening*

On a cool fall Friday evening in mid October 2005, two Los Angele's police officers are on patrol in an unincorporated city named San Pedro, in Southern California, which is serviced by the city of Los Angeles. San Pedro is a former fishing community, which is now home to The Port of Los Angeles. Its population is approximately one hundred thousand people. Patrolling in the north western part of that town, the police remain especially alert to one residential area known for its on-going gang activity. Two very experienced police officers were assigned to that area and warned to be alert for any sign of trouble.

The lead officer, George Newton is a forty-year-old Caucasian male with twelve years experience on the force. During his time as a policeman, he believes that he has seen it all. After earning two Medals of Valor for heroism while on the job he knows that he truly loves his work and the risks associated with it. Recently divorced, he is now content with driving his police cruiser and basically spending as much time as possible on the job, so that he doesn't have time to dwell on his financial and personal problems associated with his failed marriage and court ordered payments to his estranged wife. Cruising slowly, they look up and down each street and alley for any signs of gang activity. George is a large man at 6' 3," weighing over 225 pounds. He has a shaved head, neatly trimmed mustache and a tan, toned body, George enjoys working out at the police gym before and after his shifts and believes he is physically strong enough and formidable in stature that provides him with some assurances that in most cases, gang members would not be very anxious to tangle with him. Sitting next to George is his partner of two years, Gene Wilson, a Caucasian with six years police experience and also a man in good physical condition. Although somewhat shorter at 5' 10", Gene has curly blond hair and is also well built and strong. Single, Gene is thirty-two years old, never married and attends Long Beach State University during the day while working as a policeman at night to pay his bills. Gene dreams of someday becoming a criminal lawyer and feels with a police background he will be able to join a prestigious law firm after graduation, which is still at least six months away. Often studying law books as they patrolled in their squad car, he is constantly teased by George for his choice of wanting to be a lawyer.

On this night, the men have been alerted that two rival gangs were in the area and trouble was believed to be immanent. Yet, by 10:00 pm., the rumored rumble had still not yet materialized and all had been quiet so far, allowing the two officers to simply enjoy a quiet Friday evening. But, as experienced as the two men were, they realized that violence could occur at any moment, anywhere, which made them both alert and aware of their surroundings at all times and more than prepared to arise to that evening's challenge if necessary.

While the two officers cruise the area, their patrolling efforts continue to increase into an even wider circle, but always returning back to the same main streets where the trouble was expected. However, by 11:00 pm., with no activity reported anywhere, the two decide to stop for dinner at their favorite café on 7th Street, in downtown San Pedro. Departing from their cruising rout they radio in to advise of their anticipated food break and upon receiving approval, they begin heading towards the restaurant. Deciding to take a shortcut, they cruise through a more affluent neighborhood of San Pedro where there are many nicer, older Spanish type homes with well-manicured yards.

Driving through one quiet neighborhood on Walker Lane, they pass several well cared for older homes that were all likely built in the 1920s. The street is lined on both sides with large Elm trees. They comment as they drive on the how nice the lawns were and how well cared for all the homes appeared to be. As they travel towards their destination, Gene suddenly spots something unusual on the opposite side of the road and asks George to turn around. Doing as Gene instructed, George did not know what was wrong, but didn't question his request. Gene asks George to pull up and stop behind a newer black Ford Pickup truck that was parked at the curb.

Stopping where he was instructed to do, George asks, "Gene what the Hell did you see and why are we stopping here?" As George asks the question, Gene steps out of the vehicle and approaches the driver's side of the Ford truck. Obviously, he saw something and knowing that he had to back up his partner George gets out and cautiously approaches the rear of the vehicle from the passenger's side.

Inside the truck, they see a middle aged Caucasian man sitting at the vehicle's steering wheel staring straight ahead.

"Sir, can you tell me what you are doing," asks Gene?

The man sits there not moving but staring straight ahead. He is totally silent for a moment, and then he slowly turns to face Gene, and responds, "I was trying to push this vehicle in front of me forwards a little bit, in order to allow myself adequate room to pull away from the curb." He continues to explain that this particular vehicle in front of him is way too close to his truck, and he fears the vehicle will cause him difficulty when he tries to go to work Monday morning.

As the man talks, George is sizing him up and trying to decide what if any danger he presented to the two officers.

Gene then says, "Sir, I turned our vehicle around upon seeing you pushing this unoccupied white Toyota sedan in front of you forward with your truck, because it appeared that you might be inflicting damage to it. Please step out of your vehicle and come over here to the curb so we can talk easier and determine why you are doing this and what must be done about it."

Slowly and almost in a stiff jointed manner the man exits the truck. George makes a note of both the Toyota's and the Ford's license numbers as he waits for Gene to tell him what was happening. Complying with Gene's request, the man steps out, closes his truck door and walks around, then steps up and onto the curb. Standing between both officers he waits for their questions. The man is estimated to be in his late fifties and was well dressed in a business suite and tie. Standing at about six foot, he was thin, and balding. However, his necktie was loosened around the neck and it was obvious from the strong odor of alcohol in the air that he had been drinking and was likely drunk.

George asks, "Sir, do you have any identification?"

Reaching into his back pocket the man pulls out his wallet and removes his driver's license and hands it to George. Taking it, George returns to their police car, where he calls in to see if the man had any outstanding warrants.

As George departs, Gene asks, "Sir, I smell a strong alcoholic odor on you, how much have you had to drink tonight?"

Before the man can answer, George returns and signals to Gene that he had no warrants. Looking at the drivers license George asks, "Are you Bill Balsam?"

Without saying anything the man nods affirmatively, indicating that he was Bill Balsam. Gene then says, 'Mr. Balsam, don't you know what you were doing is illegal? Pushing another person's vehicle like that is not only wrong it is dangerous. Even if the vehicle was yours, it is still dangerous, since there was no one at the vehicles controls. I would like for you to take a seat on the curb while my partner and I discuss what we should do."

Looking at Gene the man says, "Yes it is dangerous, but you have to understand that this Toyota is dangerous too. It gets very close to me. So close that I can not get out of my own vehicle. I was just pushing it a little forward so I would have room to exit when I have to use my truck Monday."

The two officers begin talking. Gene tells George how the man is likely intoxicated and being behind the wheel, regardless of not actually going anywhere is theoretically drunk driving. However, George is more tolerant and says he agrees, but the man was in front of his own home, and was not intending to go anywhere. Plus, he can easily see how such anger could arise from someone parking so close to the front of ones vehicle that it could cause him to try and push it away. He also adds, that the man was cooperative and likely not a danger to anyone. In addition, he explains how hungry he was and if they did arrested the man, it would require a lot of paperwork and he really wasn't interested in doing that at this time.

George then says, "Follow me Gene and let me take over the lead here." George returns to Mr. Balsam at the curb and says, "Sir, we could arrest you right here and now for drunk driving. However, we will not do that, under the condition that you place a hand written note on the windshield of that vehicle indicating what you did here tonight. That way, if there is any damage to that vehicle, the owner will know whom to contact. I want you to leave that note on the windshield now, and do not remove it, as we will be driving back and forth here a couple of times tonight to be sure you did as we asked. And, you need to know that if it is gone, we are going to come to your house here and arrest you for drunk driving. Do you understand?"

Mr. Balsam nods his head in agreement. He then asks if they wanted him to do that right now? The two officers indicate that yes they did., The man then explains that he would have to go into his house to obtain a piece of paper and pencil in order to be able to write the needed note. He asks for their permission to do that. George looks at him and agrees, but indicates he must return quickly, in order for them to see him personally place the note on the vehicle's windshield. Upon receiving permission to do that, the man slowly walks into his garage through his already opened garage door. Inside he turns right, to enter his house through the door leading from the garage into his home.

Gene looks at George and says, "I guess you are right. He certainly didn't intend to drive in his condition and he was definitely very cooperative. But, I'll guaranty that he was also very drunk, regardless of how cooperative he was. Did you notice how rigid he was and how he walked as though each step he took hurt. He also spoke weird, like he was having difficulty forming words?"

The two officers stand outside for a longer period than what they felt was necessary to allow the man enough time to go inside and find a pen and paper in order to write out the note. Soon, they begin wondering what was delaying the man? George is hungry and wants to go eat. He looks at Gene and says, "It shouldn't take him this long to find something to write on." Wondering what was wrong, George tells Gene that they needed to go check on him. Without responding to that, the two men approach his front door, instead of entering through the open garage. They knock on the door, and an attractive middle-aged dark haired woman answers the door. Seeing who it was, she is slightly startled and responds, "Yes officers, can I help you with something?"

George begins by explaining what had occurred moments earlier in her front yard and then explains that they were waiting for Mr. Balsam to come back outside with the note for the vehicle he had pushed with his truck.

The woman looks at the two officers very oddly and asks, "Is this some type of a joke? Why are you saying that to me?"

Gene then speaks up and reiterates George's comments. He asks the woman's name and discovers her to be the man's wife, Betty Balsam. Continuing, he says, "Your husband, Mr. Balsam, just asked us if we would allow him to go into his house and write out a note and return with it. We agreed to allow him to do that. We watched him enter the garage, and then go inside the house, where he was to write his note." As he explains this he stops talking and asks to see the woman's identity, in order to verify she was truly the man's wife.

The woman retrieves her purse which was lying close by on a telephone table. She reaches inside and pulls out her wallet and takes out her driver's license. Handing it to Gene, he can clearly see that she was Betty Balsam and the picture on the license proved her identity.

Looking at both officers, Mrs. Balsam says, "Bill Balsam, the man you are talking about was my husband. But, there is definitely something wrong here with what you are claiming occurred. You two gentlemen are wrong and must be mistaken about who you spoke to out front, because it could not have been my Bill."

Gene is somewhat mystified by the woman's comments and repeats her claim back to her, asking why it couldn't have been him?

"Officer, my husband, Bill Balsam is dead. He was killed right outside here, on this very street as he exited his Ford truck, exactly one year ago this very night. A drunk driver in a small white Toyota hit him and fled the scene. So you can see, there is no way the man you spoke with could have been my Bill. And, there are no other persons living here with me. So, you have to be mistaken about someone coming into my house. I have been here since 5:30 pm., and I am definitely alone," explains the lady.

Looking at each other the officers turn back to her and ask if they can come inside to obtain more facts, and look around to see if an intruder might be hiding in her house?

With nothing to hide, the woman opens the door and invites them in. The two men enter and stand in her entryway while George repeats back to her exactly what she claimed happened. As he talks, the two men see many photographs in frames sitting all around the living room. Picking up one nearest them, he sees it to be a picture of the man they just spoke with.

George asks, "Mrs. Balsam, who is the man in this photograph?"

The woman responds, "That was my husband, Bill."

George shows the picture to Gene, the two men look at one another and wonder what she was trying to pull on them. By now they are assuming that Mr. Balsam had entered the home, told her what happened and was hiding somewhere and she was trying to cover for him.

To that Gene says, "Mrs. Balsam, we are certain a man, looking very much like this man (as he shows her the photograph) spoke with us out front about twenty minutes ago and then came into this very house. For your safety, would you mind if we searched your home? Possible this man is an intruder who resembles your husband, and if so, we need to find him if he is hiding somewhere in here. He may be dangerous"

The woman looks at them as if they were crazy, but shrugs her shoulders and says, "Please, be my guest. But I assure you, no one has come into this house tonight, except you two gentlemen."

Searching, the two men look everywhere and find no one. The house was empty, just as she had said it was. It definitely appeared to Gene and George that she was telling them the truth. And, if anyone was hiding in there, they couldn't find them.

George looks at Gene and says, "I am going back out to the car and check this out. I want to verify her claim that this man was killed out front here a year ago. You may as well stay here and take her report, in case the guy we are looking for shows up, we can arrest him."

Gene nods in agreement, and asks Mrs. Balsam to start at the beginning and explain in more detail how her husband died.

The woman again repeats her story and explains how he had been working late, was tired, got out of his vehicle door and was immediately struck by the Toyota. The other driver was drunk and claimed that he didn't see him.

Outside, sitting in the police car, George finds that he still had Mr. Balsam's driver's license tucked into his left side shirt pocket, as he had not returned it to him.

Inside, Mrs. Balsam continues by explaining how her husband was a long time insurance broker in town and was working late on Friday night. Arriving home around 9:00 pm., he came inside, greeted her and then remembered that he left his briefcase in his truck. She said he exited the house through the garage, as he had wanted to retrieve a limb trimmer in there in order to thin out the bush by their front door. He claimed it was getting to thick and he intended to trim it before coming back inside. She explained that he returned to his truck, entered it through the driver's side, looked around and found his briefcase. He then opened his driver's side door again and exited the truck. Unfortunately, the drunk driver in the small white vehicle was too close to the curb and ran him down. She says, "I heard the squealing of his brakes, then a crashing sound as he hit my husband while he stood along side his truck. The driver continued moving forward several more feet and then hit a second vehicle that forced him to stop. My husband was tossed several feet into the air, landed on his head and died within seconds of the impact. The driver of the other car was trapped inside his own car. When I heard the crash I went outside, but quickly ran back in and called 911. When the police and ambulance arrived, the driver was arrested, as the odor of alcohol on him was so strong, it could be smelled ten feet away from his vehicle. The ambulance loaded my husband up and took him away. As I said, that was one year ago this very night, at about this time of the evening. Also, I need to tell you, I have never had the courage to move my husband's truck away from where it currently is parked or even sell it. It is exactly where he left it. I locked it up and no one has been in it since."

"Wow, that is certainly a terrible story. I am very sorry for your loss. It had to be very hard dealing with something like that. But please, I have just one more question Mrs. Balsam, and that was, had your husband been drinking that night," ask Gene?

"Oh no sir, Bill was a bad diabetic and he rarely took a drink. He was particular about that. He only had a glass of wine on special occasions. Otherwise, he never drank alcoholic beverages at all. No, he was late coming home from a business meeting and he had telephoned me to ask if I would hold his dinner in the oven? He most definitely had not been drinking that night. Plus, I am sure the corner's report would have shown that fact too," explains Mrs. Balsam.

Upon her saying that, George re-enters the house. He hands Mrs. Balsam her husband's drivers license and asks if that picture was her husband's?

Mrs. Balsam looks at it and says, "Yes, this is Bill's license, how in the world did you get it. I am sure that I had it stored away in this drawer. (She goes over to a small desk by the phone and looks inside.) Oh my God, it is gone. How did you find it?"

George looks at Gene and says, "I guess we have disturbed you enough tonight Mrs. Balsam. I am sorry to have intruded on you and have caused you to relive these old memories. Please have a good evening." He turns and motions for Gene to follow him outside.

Getting in to the police car George says, "I have no explanation for what we experienced tonight partner. First of all, a man named William Balsam was struck and killed right here on this very spot one year ago tonight. The victim fits the description in every detail of the man we interrogated and who walked into his garage. Also, the driver's license he gave me and I had in my pocket was definitely his. The toxicology report showed the victim to be sober, but the man driving the vehicle that struck and killed him was a twenty-two year old man that was so drunk, he couldn't even walk. And, he was driving a white 2002 Toyota, with the same exact license number that was just now parked in front of the man's truck, which he was pushing away. Please, note, the Toyota vehicle he was pushing is no longer there. And, in the impound report it was said the Toyota was totaled. Also, I walked over to the Ford truck and it is now locked and the door and glass on this side is extremely dirty. It looks like it has been sitting there for a very long time and definitely not entered by anyone recently."

Gene looks at George and says. "Yes, Mrs. Balsam says it has been there, locked ever since her husband died last year. What is going on here George? Who did we interview? Are you somehow saying we interviewed a dead man?"

George starts the police car and begins driving away, and says, "Gene, I cannot explain what we encountered. But, I'll tell you one thing, I thought by now I had seen it all, yet, I apparently hadn't, because this is something totally new. I absolutely have no explanation for any of it. I am just happy you were with me and saw it too. Otherwise, I would be sitting here thinking I have gone totally crazy."

The two are silent as they drive to the restaurant for dinner. Parking, they exit their vehicle, enter the building and are only half aware of their surroundings as they order and eat their food. Neither man says anything to the other throughout their meal. Their minds are fixated on what they had just encountered.

Getting back into their car, they check in and are told to continue their patrolling at the same neighborhood that they had been in before.

Gene quietly asks, "George, how do we fill in our report about what we encountered? We have done all this checking on that man and we need something to backup our time and efforts. What do we report?"

"I guess it will have to be brief and we must leave out who we encountered. Maybe I had best do it myself after I think about it more. But, we definitely can't say what really happened, that is for sure. We would be laughed out of the station," explains George.

The rest of the evening is quiet. They patrol until their shift ends. Without much discussion about the incident, they returned to the police station, park their vehicle, go inside and change their clothes. The two then head home without any further comment about the incident.

Arriving home, Gene is not able to study any of his law books. His mind is totally obsessed with what they encountered. He knows there are no such things as ghosts. So, how can he explain to himself what he saw and experienced. The man seemed so real. They even talked with him. He answered their questions and was very lucid. Yet, he just disappeared into that garage. Also, the vehicle he was pushing was the one that killed him. And, it too disappeared after they went into his home. What was the explanation for it all?

When George and Gene's shift was about to begin the next day, the two men meet at their police cruiser. Loading their equipment in and looking at one another Gene says, "George, I couldn't sleep at all when I got home last night. I am so confused by what we encountered last night that I feel like I have to find a logical answer to it, or I am going to go crazy. I have never believed in anything paranormal before and frankly it is just too odd of an encounter to simply forget about."

George is quiet as they depart the police station in their cruiser. Eventually, he responds by saying, "Gene, there are things in this world that we know nothing about. There are things we will never know anything about. This has to be one of those things. My suggestion is to forget it. Otherwise, it will consume you and you won't be any good to me, or yourself. Just drop it. I do not think that we should discuss it anymore. It was what it was and no amount of talking about it or thinking over what happened will make the experience any better or easier to understand."
Gene thinks about George's comments and understands where he is coming from. Yet, this just wasn't something a curious person like him could reasonably let drop. He knows George is serious and that it is not a topic that the two need to dwell on. However, he also knows he must dig into it on his own and try to resolve what happened. Possibly he could try to see if anything like that has ever happened before, and if so, how was it resolved. Maybe there was an easy explanation?

As the night progresses, it too is uneventful. A couple of traffic stops and two calls for loud partying noise ended an otherwise quiet evening. Returning to the station, the two men had not spoken much about anything, as it was obvious something was definitely eating at them both. Exiting their vehicles, and standing side by side in the locker room as they changed their clothes, they remain unnaturally quiet. Finishing dressing, they say goodnight and they both get in their vehicles and drive home.

While driving, George's thoughts remain on the events of their meeting the ghost. And, it definitely affected him. Like Gene, he had never thought about anything paranormal before. However, might this be proof of an afterlife? Might there be more to life than anyone knows? In some respects it was comforting to know that maybe life didn't end when one's mortal soul was finished here on this earth. If it didn't end, what was death like? This man interacted with them as any normal person would. So, do ghosts have a life among themselves? It was a fascinating idea, and one he was beginning to feel comfortable with. People die and enjoy another life after their time here on earth. It was definitely something he needed to think about and become comfortable with. Yet, he knew it was a question he would never obtain an answer to.

Gene too is thinking about their encounter as he drives home. But, his ideas and questions are more technical and he wants to know how he can find the answers. He knows there has to be a lot of information written about the paranormal world and life after death. Maybe something is available at his university library? There may even be people at his college that are knowledgeable about the paranormal that he could discuss this whole thing with. He decides that tomorrow at school he will talk to a counselor after class and see what help he might be able to find. Meanwhile, he knows George is a private type of guy and he realizes that it would be best for them to concentrate on police work and stay away from any subject that lead to any type of paranormal discussion.

At 9:00 am., Gene is up and driving across town for his early morning class in Long Beach. He knows this will be a short day and he will have ample time to speak to a counselor and maybe get some ideas where he can begin his search about the paranormal world. Arriving at the college at 9:30 am, he goes into the school's Administrative Office and signs up to see a counselor as soon as possible. At 12:30 pm, he was finished with that day's class and goes back to the Administrative Office to inquire about his request to see a counselor. He is told that he can see Dr. Amelia Valenzuela at 2:00 pm, in her office at the Student Center. Looking at his watch, Gene decides to have lunch and then head to the campus library to see what information might be available there. He enters the student center at 1:50 pm., and advises the counter person he had an appointment at 2:00 pm.

Sitting down to wait for a few minutes he is escorted into Dr. Valenzuela's office. After a five-minute wait, Dr. Valenzuela arrives, greets Gene and introduces herself. He is surprised at seeing her, because she is very young, and extremely attractive. Feeling almost embarrassed, he is somewhat shy over what he seeks information about. He fears because of her youth, she is likely not experienced enough to know anything about paranormal issues. He doesn't know why, but he thinks she will likely think he is joking or not serious.

"So, Mr. Wilson, I am sorry I was late, but hopefully you still have time to tell me why you needed to see a counselor. I have reviewed your student file and see that you are entering your final semester of law. And, I have also noted that you are currently working as a Los Angeles Police Officer. So, how can I help you," asks the counselor?

Shyly Gene looks at the beautiful woman and momentarily is more interested in impressing her than he is in trying to find out about ghosts. Stammering a bit he finally says, "Well, something happened to me and my partner a few nights ago, as we were patrolling the streets of San Pedro, and it has really been bothering me, to a point that it is even affecting my concentration at work and my classes here. So, I thought it would be in my best interest to research the issue and see if I could find some helpful information that might get me back on the right track."

Looking at Gene the young woman is very interested in his comments. Waiting for him to say more about his problem, she finally asks, "So, your question is what Mr. Wilson?"

"I know that you are going to think I am crazy, but I assure you that I am not. I had something very strange happen to me two nights ago and both my partner and I cannot explain it and neither of us really wants to talk to one another about it either. I know there are issues with what I need to know, but if you could point me towards someone who may have an in-depth understanding about the subject, it would really help. And, I would be greatly appreciative," explains Gene.

The woman looks rather oddly at Gene and says, Mr. Wilson, you are being very vague here about what it is you need my help with. I really cannot direct you to anyone, if I don't know exactly what it is you need help with."

Gene stammers a bit more as he can begin feeling the frustration the woman has with his invasive comments . He is seriously tongue-tied and doesn't want to just blurt his question out, but realizes that unless he tells her more, she will simply end their discussion and ask him to leave. Taking a deep breath he says, "I encountered something paranormal and there is no way what happened to me, could have happened. My partner and I both experienced it, and what happened is really hard to talk about. But, I need to know if the school has any expertise or are their any individuals working here that have any experience or knowledge about the paranormal world?"

Smiling, the counselor asks, "Are you wondering whether or not I know of anyone here at school who has any knowledge about ghosts?" Looking off out of the window as she says that, she does not want to make direct eye contact with Gene.

Sheepishly, Gene lifts his head up, and shyly nods yes, as to indicate that was exactly what he was asking.

"Mr. Wilson, looking at your scholastic record and realizing that you are a policeman, I would think such pranks are a bit juvenile for someone like you. What is it you hoped to accomplish with this story?" Hesitating for a moment, she then says, "Wait a minute, did some of my faculty workers here put you up to this? Are you pulling some kind of a joke on the College's newest counselor?" I'll bet you are," asks Amelia?

"Absolutely not Miss. Valenzuela. I know it sounds like a joking type of question, and I can see why you would think that. But believe me when I say something extremely disturbing happened to me and my partner the other night and unless I can figure it out, I fear I will truly go crazy wondering about it. Please believe me. I am serious, and I assure you this is no joke," begs Gene.

The woman looks long at Gene, obviously trying to decide whether or not she believed him. Looking out of the window at the campus, she also looks around her office to see if anyone was spying on her, which would be proof that a joke was being played out. Finally, upon seeing no one she says, "Mr. Wilson, if you are pulling a joke on me, I promise you that I will make the remaining days of your education here extremely difficult. So, if this is a joke, now is the time to admit it. Are you telling me the truth," she demands?

Without hesitating, Gene says, "Absolutely I am. There is no hidden agenda here. I truly need to find someone to help me. I have no idea where to turn to. I tried before coming in here to research information at our campus library, but there wasn't anything useful anywhere to be found in there. I need help, I promise you I am serious."

"Ok, as you may be able to guess Mr. Wilson, I am new to this campus and my job. For ten years I taught History at San Pedro High School. I decided to complete my education and obtain my doctorate two years ago by going back to UCLA. I just graduated last summer and this is my first assignment. Now, you come to me with this question. Hopefully, you can appreciate why I am reluctant to believe you. But, let me first say, I have no idea where to send you. I do not know who can help you. I know of no one here on campus with expertise in what you seek. Now, that doesn't mean there isn't anyone here, it just means I don't know about them. So, if you can give me a couple of days, I will ask around and try and see what help I can find for you. Can you wait until next Monday and return back here again after lunchtime, and maybe by then I will have been able to find more information for you," responds Amelia?

Smiling as he realizes that maybe she was truly trying to help him, Gene says, "Yes, of course. Monday will be just fine. Please know how much I appreciate your assistance and be assured I am not joking with you in the slightest way Amelia," says Gene.

"Ok Mr. Wilson, I will ask around and see what people, classes or information that might be available to you. I'll see you Monday," comments Amelia.

Gene gets up, shakes her hand and thanks her for anything she may be able to do for him. As he walks back to his car, he wonders what if anything she can accomplish? She is definitely young and likely has no experience in such matters. He even wonders if anyone will listen to her if she does seek help for him. He assumes he has no choice but to wait and see what happens.

That evening, as he and George are on patrol, they talk about many things, but primarily the upcoming football season and other non-serious issues. Gene gets the distinct feeling that George is purposely staying away from the Balsam incident and wants nothing more said about it. This decision saddens Gene somewhat, as he thinks George is likely a smart guy with street sense and he really felt like he needed to talk about it to someone that wouldn't laugh. And, given the nature of their work, he also knows that they cannot afford to get distracted in any way. As the two men patrol in south San Pedro, they field several calls during the evening. One was about domestic violence, two were complaints of loud music and one was about a possible burglary of a downtown warehouse, which turned out to be a faulty alarm. All are handled timely and there were no major issues with any of them. Stopping at a fast food restaurant for dinner they sit quietly and enjoy their food. Obviously, the two men were still thinking about their 'ghostly' encounter as their normal feisty interaction and camaraderie had slowed to a point that they were now barely communicative.

Gene, is the first to say, "George, you seem awfully quiet, is there anything bothering you? Are you Ok?"

George eats his hamburger and sips his soda, and then looking up at Gene he responds by saying, "Yes, I am fine. But, I guess our strange encounter a few nights ago is still weighing heavy on my mind. You think you have it all figured out and then something like that happens and destroys everything you believe in. It can't help but make you wonder about everything you have been taught or felt throughout your life. It just instantly changed my realm of reality and take on life. And, it does no good to dwell on it or discuss it because it isn't anything we can prove or resolve. It isn't anything you can explain to anyone. Plus, if you could, no one would belief us anyway."

Gene thinks about George's conflicted feelings and says, "I understand and agree. But, I did meet with a college counselor today and asked her for guidance and assistance in helping me find someone who could better explain it to me. And, it took all I could muster up to convince her I wasn't crazy or trying to pull a super bad joke on her."

"So, what did she say? Is she going to help you," asks George?

Gene smiles and says, "Yes, I believe she will do what she can. But, to be honest, she is young, and this is her first college job. Plus, she just started and I seriously doubt that anyone there will know her, or be willing to confide any paranormal information to her. But, who knows, I'll wait and see what she uncovers next Monday."

As they finish eating, they get a call to investigate a traffic accident where multiple vehicles are involved at the intersection of 7th and Gaffey Ave. Finishing, they get up and rush to the site. Already on the scene were two other police cars and one fire engine. Four vehicles were involved and three people were seriously injured.

Arriving at the accident, George and Gene are instructed by a senior officer to take reports form one of the drivers of the primary vehicle, as well as the occupants, while other officers will talk to everyone else. As they take the information two ambulances arrive and begin extricating the injured people. Two hours later they are back in their vehicle patrolling the city, while discussing the reason for the crash. Gene comments on how senseless the accident was. George agrees and they finish their shift without any more calls.

Back at the station, the two men change their clothes. George inquires whether or not Gene would like to visit an after hours bar for a beer? Gene thinks about it, but tells George that he would like to, but he has a test early in the morning and needs to study before going to sleep. To that, each man gets in his own vehicle and they depart the police station. As Gene enters his apartment, he checks his phone messages and is surprised to find that he has one from Counselor Amelia Valenzuela stating she had some information for him and he could stop by the Student Center tomorrow and pick it up.

At noon the next day, Gene walks out of his class, having finished his test. Feeling good about what he knew, he hopes he had a perfect score. He then walks over to the Student Center where he asks to see Counselor

Valenzuela. Surprisingly, she was in and had a few minutes to spend with him. Greeting each other, Gene follows her into her office and sits down.

"Mr. Wilson, I am not sure what exactly you hope to discover, as I was unable to find anyone here at this campus that you could meet with in order to aid you in your endeavors. I did find a couple of people for you to talk to who are not academics, but have a lot of experience in the paranormal world. I do hesitate to mention this to you, because I am not sure what it is exactly you want to accomplish, or find out about. However, assuming it is something to do with ghostly activity, maybe what I have arranged for you is what you are seeking. I do not know if you are aware of a very famous paranormal 'haunting' case that has been well documented which took place in San Pedro? I was a college student at UCLA when it first began in 1986. 1 recall learning of it when my little sister was telling all of us one night at dinner about a classmate of hers at San Pedro High School whose family was being haunted and attacked by a ghost. Of course we all thought it was a big joke at first, but my sister swore it was true. It turned out to become a very well documented story and was even filmed by a couple of psychic researchers who investigated the haunting from its beginning to the end, over a three year period. It originally began in San Pedro. Apparently, the entity attached itself to the family and stayed with them even when they moved to Northern California. At one point the researchers were able to actually make contact with the entity and it told the investigator that it had been a fisherman who was drowned at the hands of someone in San Pedro's fishing village. The entity was very vindictive towards one of the researchers, as it actually communicated with him that he looked very much like the person who killed him in 1930. I have the name and address of the woman who lived through it all, and she has since moved back to San Pedro, and is no longer haunted by the murdered seaman. I have known this woman and her family for a long time. I called her last night and told her a bit about you and she has agreed to meet with you. She also has the name and address of the people who investigated the incident and she is willing to supply you with those names if you want.

She will likely have the answers to many of your questions, but there is no doubt that those who helped her will have more. So, here is her name and address. Call her and maybe what you need to know can be found there. Otherwise, I really do not think I can help you find anyone else that can or will be willing to help you."

"Oh, this is a perfect start. I am sure her contacts can help me, or at the least they can point me in the right direction. I really appreciate your assistance Ms. Valenzuela. Thanks very much," exclaims Gene.

Smiling, she says, "Good, I hope this is what you need, and if it is, maybe some day you can explain it all to me? But please, let me know how your visit with her goes."

Gene gets up, shakes her hand and says, "1 will be happy to do that." He then departs her office and heads home. Arriving at his apartment he wastes no time in calling the lady in question. The phone rings and a woman answers. Gene asks, "Is this Gloria Ramos?" The woman affirms that it is. The two chat a while and she invites him over to her house on Saturday afternoon, when she is free and able to talk with him longer and describe in depth what happened. Meanwhile, he asks and she gives him the address of the property where she lived when the activity started in 1986.

Later that night as they are patrolling, Gene asks George to cruise by the haunted address. George asks why and Gene explains his conversation with the counselor and the haunted tenant. He explains he is just curious to see what a haunted house really looked like. The two find the complex and can easily see that it was currently occupied. Parking in front of the property, Gene explains what happened and that he will meet with the woman this Saturday afternoon who lived there and experienced it all. As they sit and talk, they see nothing that would indicate the home was ever haunted or that anything paranormal ever occurred there.

George looks at the place and says, "Gene, I sincerely hope you are not going to get yourself into any trouble when you begin researching the subject of ghosts. I fear such an exercise will only screw with your head and it could have long lasting consequence. I fear you will become obsessed with such stuff and your mental state as a policeman will be affected. You know as well as I do that you have to be completely alert at all times in this job. And, anything that distracts you from that could be deadly for either one of us. And, by God, I don't want it to be me. Do you understand what I mean?"

Gene understands what George is saying and knows he is right. He thinks about it and says, "I am never going to let you down. I will always cover your back and I'll be there for you no matter what. Yet, for me personally, I need to just understand a little better about what we encountered. You know as well as me that what we experienced is likely something neither of us will ever run across again. And, it is likely something that very few other people will either. I just want to know a little about it. When I do that, I'll be done with it, I promise. I just need to have answers to a few questions. So, don't worry, I'll be careful and stay focused on us, that you can be assured of."

As George starts the car, and pulls away from the curb he says, "Good, I hope that works for you. But I cannot help but fear the more you learn the harder it will be to let it go, causing it to become some type of obsession for you. And, if that happens, you have to know that I can no longer rely on you as a safe partner."

Gene understands George's concern and tries to assure him again that it is only a curiosity and he is sure his interest will be satisfied once he knows more. Yet, he knows himself all too well and just as he has so often done in studying for his law degree, he will read about some case law that makes him crazy and causes a need within him to know more. He worries that delving into the paranormal world will be just as exciting and maybe addictive too. He prays not, but he knows how obsessive he can be over certain events and things. He tells himself this will be different.

Saturday morning arrives and Gene gets up early in order to get ready for his meeting. He is very excited and cannot wait to make his prearranged meeting. He realizes how anxious he was and worries about what George had warned him about. The morning drags on as he cleans his small apartment and does his laundry. Eventually, the time to go is near and he gets ready for his meeting with Mrs. Ramos. Driving to her address he thinks about what he wants to ask her. Finding her is easy and he parks his car. Walking up to the door, he knocks. Within a few moments a woman answers. Gene introduces himself as does the woman. In fact, two of the woman's adult children, Bob and Leticia are also home, who were present during the entire haunting episode that plagued the family for five years from 1986 to 1991.

Upon entering, Gene is offered a seat. The four exchange pleasantries for a few minutes until the woman inquires about what exactly he wanted to know and why. Explaining that he recently had an encounter with a spirit himself and that he needed to try and understand more about it in order to stop himself from dwelling on the event. He explains that he hoped she might be able to explain her experiences and provide some professional contacts for him to talk to. The woman smiles and says she understood his feelings and she is happy to tell him everything that the family knows about the paranormal world that they were introduced to. Listening closely, the women and her two children, Bob Ramos, a college student and Leticia Perez, a young married woman, recount for Gene the entire sequence of events of their daily haunting, and how they finally had to move away. She also states that the entity eventually disappeared. She then shows Gene a home movie of much of the haunting that was caught on film by the investigators, including scenes of an attempted murder upon one of the research assistants who was up in her attic examining it during a period of high activity. She said he was apparently choked around the neck with a cotton clothesline cord by the entity while he was up there. She explains how they eventually used an old Ouija Board game to determine that the entity was a San Pedro fisherman murdered in 1930. Gene is favorably impressed with the woman's detailed account of what occurred as well as the obvious depictions shown on the film. Gene concludes in his discussion that the woman and her children were legitimate victims of something, which was likely a true haunting encounter. He considers how hard such an ordeal must have been to experience and wonders out loud how anyone could have endured such a long-term attack. He then asks for and receives the names and contact information of the men who did the research and experienced the events she described. The woman had not talked with the researchers in a couple of years, but felt confident they would be more than willing to meet with him. After a period of time, Gene thanks the woman and her children and departs.

Driving home he is fascinated at the terrifying encounter the family endured and wonders how he would have dealt with such a thing? Certainly, had he of heard this story prior to his own encounter he would have simply laughed at its absurdity. Yet, now, after what he experienced, there is no doubt that he believed them. So, what does that say about his need to listen better to people that he encounters on the job when they try to explain their side of a story? Does this help or hurt him as a police investigator?

Obviously, not everything he hears is true, but maybe more of it is than what he has been trained to believe? He quickly can see how his mind could become conflicted over what a victim was trying to explain. As a policeman, he knows he has to be rational and take the course of action that appears most prudent. Yet, knowing what he just heard, he would have been laughing at such a story only mere days ago, where now he knows that there is much more to the paranormal world than he ever dreamed possible. What lesson is there in all of this for him?

Gene arrives at his home and goes into his apartment and sits on his couch to think about it all. Later, he gets ready for work, and still wonders how much if any of what he discovered should be shared with

George? Maybe it would be best to say nothing to him, and only answer direct questions if asked. Recalling George's warning over him becoming too involved in these events, it is possible the less said the better. While dressing, his mind is busy thinking about what he still wanted to know and how to phrase it with the paranormal investigators when he calls them.

To aid him in asking everything, he thinks making a list of questions would be good. He also wonders how best to phrase those questions? Realizing that the investigators are far more knowledgeable about the paranormal than he is, he concludes that even though it is a difficult subject for him to discuss, it likely would not be for them. Therefore, he decides not to worry about how to ask his questions. He will just say what is on his mind and what comes up as they talk. Looking at his watch, he sees he is now running late and he needed to be going to work.

The night begins as all others do. First there is a briefing as to what the officers should be alert for, and an on-going warning of potential gang activity. Then, as always when the briefing ends, they head to their police car, where George drives. The evening was cooler than normal and rain appeared to be likely. Therefore, George wants to be sure their rain gear was in the trunk. When their shift begins, Gene can sense something was wrong with George, as he is more quiet than normal. After about thirty minutes of driving and enduring George's silence, Gene asks his partner what was wrong.

Slow to respond, George says, "Oh it is a personal thing. My ex-wife is causing me more problems. But it isn't anything to burden you with. So, what is going on with you? Did you make any progress on the San Pedro ghost house?"

Thinking about how to respond he says, "Yes, in fact today, I met the family that lived in that house we saw last night. They are nice people and they have an entertaining story to tell. It is possible that they are a real case where something paranormal did occur, but who can say for sure? I would definitely not have believed them last week. But today, who knows? Anyway, I think the less I worry about it the better. Let's just drive carefully tonight partner. I think we are going to see some bad weather and that will mean some slippery streets and a lot of traffic accidents."

The evening begins slowly. They cruise their normal route and carefully watch out for any signs of problems. At 10:15 pm, they are ordered to investigate the sound of shots fired at a residence. They are close by and respond quickly. Arriving at the address within minutes, they are at an area where several old two story apartments are located on Centre Street, which is an old section of town. The address given is easy to find. Parking in front with their cruiser lights on, before they exit their vehicle, they spot a man and woman shielding themselves from the rain under the eves of an adjoining apartment. Upon seeing the police arrive, with umbrellas open the two forms dart towards the police car. Rolling down the window on George's side, he listens as the couple describes how they heard arguing, followed by what sounded like three gunshots.

George asks them if they knew the names of the occupants of that property, and are told they had only recently moved in and they didn't know their names. He inquires about their age and if they had any children. They are told the couple is in their mid twenties and there didn't appear to be any children in the family. Thanking the couple, George and Gene get out of their car and slowly approach the front of the property. With their backs to the front of the unit they try to peer inside. But, the blinds are closed and no movement can be seen inside. Knocking loudly on the door, they announce themselves as policemen and demand someone open the door. Waiting, there is still no activity or response to their demand.

Gene asks, "Shall I kick the door in?

"Yes, but be careful. Kick it hard and then move away to the side quickly. I will enter first and you follow in behind me," instructs George.

Standing back about three feet, Gene raises his right leg and kicks open the door. As he does so, the light in the front room goes off, and nothing can be immediately seen inside the apartment. Using their flashlights they call out, announcing again that they are the police. Slowly moving through the living room, then the kitchen, they see a light on further down the hall, which they assume is a bedroom. Slowly, the two men move towards the light, while also observing everything around them. Being sure that no one had come up behind them, they searched the house carefully one room at a time. Approaching the lighted bedroom, the door is slightly ajar. George kicks open the door, and to their greatest fears, a woman is lying on the bed, face down and the mattress is blood soaked. Feeling for a pulse, a slight one is felt. Immediately George radios for backup, a supervisor and an ambulance.

George turns to Gene and says, "Be careful partner, whoever did this may still be in here. As he says that, he sees the closet door move which is also partly open. Pointing to it, George signals Gene that he is going to look inside. He slowly walks over to it, grabs the doorknob and thrusts it open.

George immediately sees legs and shoes hiding behind a row of clothing. Knowing they have cornered the shooter, he yells to Gene, "Look out, the shooter is in here."

As he says that the man exits the closet and begins shooting at them with a handgun. One bullet strikes Gene in the left side of his forehead and also his right shoulder. Instantly George returns fire and places three shots into the man's chest, dropping him where he stood. Removing the man's weapon from his left hand he feels for a pulse and cannot find any. George immediately handcuffs the shooter. Turning to attend to Gene, he surveys his injuries. George quickly takes his portable radio and calls in that shots were fired and an officer was down, he asks for more ambulances.

Within mere minutes the house is full of police and paramedics. Gene and the woman are immediately taken to Little Company of Mary Hospital in San Pedro, which is only a mile away. George stands by as he describes to a supervising sergeant and two forensic investigators exactly what happened.

When the two victims arrive at the hospital the woman is pronounced dead, while Gene is quickly evaluated and taken into surgery.

An hour later, George is in the waiting room anxiously trying to find out how his partner was. He and several other officers were pacing the floor and waiting. George is determined to stay and wait for some word on Gene's condition. Eventually, one of the doctors from the surgical team comes out and says, "Mr. Wilson has suffered a serious head injury. We were forced to put him into a drug-induced coma while we assess his injury. The second shot to the arm was less serious. However, it will likely be at least twenty-four hours before we know anything for sure."

While George is standing there, his co-officers all come up and offer him their condolences and assure him there wasn't anything he could have done to prevent the shooting. After doing that, they all slowly leave to return to their duties. George is still in shock. In his entire career, he has never had a partner shot or been forced to use his weapon to apprehend a suspect. Now, he has experienced both and he does not know what to do. Soon, a supervisor from his unit arrives. George updates him and admits he was lost in his resolve and was worried for his friend. The sergeant understands George's emotional state and orders him to head back to the station, drop of his patrol car and go home. He says that a full report will be needed tomorrow and he would file it with Internal Affairs. Meanwhile, he tells George to take three days off. Lost in his own thoughts, George leaves the hospital and as he was instructed to do, he returns his police cruiser and goes home.

George sits in his darkened living room while his mind was in a fog. He can think of nothing but Gene and how the night's events play out over and over in his head like a slow running movie. George realizes where he was in that apartment and wonders what he could have done differently to avoid the shooting. Suddenly, his phone rings which forces his mind to snap back to reality. He answers it and no one was there. Angry, he slams the receiver down and goes back and sits down, this time turning on the television. He sits there and watches whatever was on the station, but really can only think about Gene. Within minutes, George falls asleep in his chair. He is woken up some time later to the sound of his phone ringing again. He opens his eyes and sees it is now daylight outside. He looks at his watch and is surprised to find that it was 10:00 am. Staggering to his phone he answers it. For a moment there is no response. Then, just as he was about to hang up he hears a familiar voice say, "Hey George, it's me, I just thought you might like to know that I am Ok." Then there is no further comment heard from Gene.

George is so elated and excited to here Gene's voice and to know he was Ok. Gathering up his composure he finally says, "So, are you really Ok? It is great to hear form you partner. I was really worried about you, as the doctor said your head injury was serious. But if you are able to call me you must not be as bad as he thought?" Waiting for some response, George expects to have Gene confirm that he was fine, but instead the line is dead. Assuming that Gene may have fallen asleep, he looks up the hospital's phone number and calls them back. Reaching the hospital receptionist, he asks for Gene's room. However, he is told that there are no phones in the Intensive Care Unit where Gene is, and since he is in a coma, he couldn't talk to him anyway. George is now confused. He responds to the nurse by saying, "I do not understand, Gene just called me a few minutes ago."

"Sir, you must be mistaken. There is no way he could have done that as he is in a coma. He hasn't moved and there is no phone anywhere close to his bed," states the nurse.

Now, totally confused, George hangs up without saying anything more. Thinking that maybe he was out of his mind, he wonders if he could have just imagined the call? He then thinks that Gene may have actually called but the hospital didn't know it. Maybe Gene was trying to reach him for some serious reason, and if so, George worries that Gene might need his help. Should he head over there now and find out what was happening?

Without changing the clothes he fell asleep in, he jumps back in his vehicle and races to the hospital. Parking and going inside, he asks to speak to someone in authority. Soon, a nurse comes out and George identifies himself and tells her what happened. He explains that he was worried that Gene needed him and maybe whomever he talked to on the switchboard was wrong about Gene being unable to call him.

A nurse arrives and says, "Hello Mr. Newton, I am registered nurse Lana Hansen. If you would follow me, I will show you that Mr. Wilson is being well cared for and there is no way he could have called you."

The two walk back deeper into the hospital where he is escorted to a window. From there he can see through it, into an area where Gene was lying. Looking at him, there was definitely no doubt that he was in a bed, with many tubes coming out of different parts of his body. Also, he was asleep and there were no telephones in that room. Just the sight of the machines and monitors all around him was proof he hadn't gotten up or was able to call him. As he and the nurse look at him she asks, "So, Mr. Newton is that your friend Mr. Wilson?"

"Yes, it definitely is," says George.

"Well then Mr. Newton, as you can clearly see for yourself he isn't awake and definitely didn't have the ability to call you," says the nurse.

Looking at him George must admit she was right, as he was totally incapacitated and unable to make a call to anyone, even if he had a phone in there.

Then, just as he was about to ask her a question, she exclaims, "What the Hell," and immediately leaves him and runs into the restricted Intensive Care area, and over to Gene's side. Watching her, she bends down and picks up something and reconnects it to one of the monitors attached to Gene. This causes an alarm to sound and soon three people are at Gene's side. He watches as the nurse he was talking with becomes very angry about something and begins giving the other nurses in the unit her verbal admonishment over whatever was disconnected. After a few minutes all seemed resolved and she rejoins George outside the ICU.

Looking at her, George asks, "What happened? It looked pretty serious to me. Is he Ok?"

"Yes he is, but in layman's terms, if I had not seen that the sensor connecting the main monitor and his breathing tube were somehow pulled out and lying on the floor, he could have easily died. That is because our hospital nurses that monitor Intensive Care patients were watching his stats from a central monitor in a different location. And, what they were watching was not his actual body information, but just a normal rhythm pattern caused by the machine. So, to be honest Mr. Newton, it is a good thing you came here and caused me to bring you back to this area. Otherwise, we may not have discovered the problem in time."

George is now even more perplexed and doesn't know what to think. Who or what called him? What if he hadn't come here after being hung up on? Could it have been a problem for Gene? If Gene didn't call, then who was on the phone? He is now seriously troubled and this newest event just adds to the mystery of the phone call, which makes everything that much more weird. Obviously, his visit here at this time saved Gene's life.

Heading to the parking lot, he quickly finds his car. George begins to realize something unnatural may be at work here. Did somehow his unconscious friend know he was in trouble and mentally call him? Yet, there is no way he could have done that. Plus, if he had not come down here to check on him, might the disconnected equipment have been fatal. Was Gene somehow beaconing him to come here in order to find the disconnected equipment? Is it remotely possible that was the reason for the mysterious phone call?

As George drives back home he doesn't know what to think and it was likely that he would never know the answer. He soon realizes that worrying about it and trying to find the answer could cause him serious problems if he continued to dwell on it too long. Arriving back at his apartment, he takes a beer from the refrigerator, sits in his easy chair and watches a college football game.

Meanwhile, back at the hospital a nurse that was instructed to closely watch Gene to be sure his monitors remained in place and to try and determine how they could have come out and fallen to the floor like they did, notices a lot of sudden eye movement from Gene as she attends him. She assumes this means that he was either dreaming or maybe about to wake up. Leaving to summon a doctor, they both return to find Gene's entire body moving and flinching as if he was dreaming that he was running or maybe chasing someone.

The doctor looks at Gene's pupils and states that this was a good sign, since it denoted that he was having some kind of brain activity, which suggested that he was most likely dreaming and his brain was functioning to some degree. The two wait and monitor this movement and make a full accounting of what was happening on his personal chart.

CHAPTER 2; *Gene's Epiphany*

While Gene lies in a state of unconsciousness, his mind is far from being at rest or asleep. Scary scenarios are playing out in his mind, which cause him to dream strange things and it makes him extremely afraid, causing him to silently shout out for help, in order to escape the demons that are attacking him.

At first he sees himself lying in his hospital bed. He looks down and there are entities of some kind all around him. They are acting as though they are waiting for him to wake up and join him in doing something. However, they all have both of their hands on his head and he can feel them pushing down on it very hard, which is almost crushing him. This eventually causes him to fall asleep and begin dreaming of different places in time.

His first vision is that of a dark place, very hot, where naked bodies are lying everywhere on the ground entangled amongst themselves like pretzels. The bodies he sees are both male and female who are lying together, twisting and turning and obviously in pure agony. Screams of pain and despair are heard, as no one can escape its torture and confinement. There are thousands of these people on the ground and strangely he can hear each one individually screaming out in agony. He senses that they are confined there like prisoners because of their own making, sentenced for all eternity to dwell in their current state of evil existence and tortured awareness. The pain being felt and called out by each person is very real and frightening, as he desperately knows that he wants nothing ever to do with this place. Begging his mind to leave, he seems somehow stuck there in a state of limbo, with only this vision of pure evilness to look at. Gene is aware of the fact he was dreaming, yet, it was more than that. He felt as if it was a message and a glimpse into something that was real and definitely in his future. Squirming in his own skin he continues to tell his mind to move away and seek a place of more tranquility or at least something better. Yet, the visions he witnesses only intensify as he suddenly feels himself lying down amongst the masses of bodies on the ground. Their pain is now his, and he feels their skin touching him. He then immediately begins to feel the heat of the place they were in, as well as the sudden despair that was coming over him, to where he no longer had the ability to control his thought process or emotions. It then suddenly occurs to Gene that he must have died and somehow he entered the real 'HELL.' He knows for absolute sure that this must be what death in 'HELL' felt like. But he also knows that he must be there in error, as he has never harmed anyone or tried to be anything but a decent man in his life, serving as a police officer hoping to help everyone. So, why was he experiencing this? Is this where he was destined to be? It is nothing like what he had ever imagined before. In fact, he knows that in life, he really never believed that a real 'HELL' truly existed. Yet, here he was, and now he realizes he was wrong and that this place was exactly as everyone described it as being. He tries to break free to escape the heat, pain and desperation of where he was. He realizes that he no longer cared for the pain and discomfort that the others he saw were experiencing, as all that mattered now was how he could save himself. He begins to hate everyone around him and all he can think of is escaping this torturous agony. Soon, like everyone else he is lying amongst, he begins to wither and yell out in the pain and despair. He was now just like everyone he first saw and heard. He was now among them and likely here to stay. If he is dead and in 'HELL,' he was doomed just like them. All he can think of is his self, and how to stop the torture he was experiencing. He tries to concentrate and pray to God to help him, but he cannot do anything except to feel his own pain and selfish desire to escape this terrible place. His ability to think and fight back is slowly slipping away and he realizes for sure he must have died, and this is where his soul will now dwell for all eternity. The feeling is so bad and the hate, fear and total sickening emotional state of being there was like nothing anyone could ever imagine, let alone read about or describe to others. He cries to himself and knows that whatever he did, this was now his fate. He is lost and his soul must have been dammed to be here by God, left to dwell here for all eternity. He tries to pray, and is actually able to verbally beg God for forgiveness, but all he hears is himself and everyone around him screaming for help. Lost and now a part of this huge mass of anguished souls, he is forced into accepting his future of despair and pain that is here. Yet, he still knows that in his short life he tried to be a good person and his being here had to be a mistake. Might his being here be just a test, one which all mankind must endure for a brief period before moving on? As he thinks about that possibility, suddenly a bright, white light totally obscures his mind's vision and his pain and agony immediately ceases. Again, Gene is fully aware of this light being a different place in time, and wonders if maybe God did hear his prayers? Could he be spared the terrible pain and agony he was currently enduring? And, if he is dead, might he be able to go to a better resting place?

Soon, his pain and agony subsides, as he tries to force himself into seeing where he currently was. Eventually, he begins experiencing a feeling that was overwhelming to him. It was a feeling that he could only describe as being in a restful state of existence. Here, nothing seemed bad and he feels nothing but happiness all around him. The white light is slowly going away and he is left with a warm and definitely very tranquil sense of being. Soon, his vision begins centering in on what he believes are visions of human shapes that are far away in the reseeding white light. Slowly they all begin coming forward and start to approach him from their distant location. Within seconds they are all in his immediate location. As he senses them approaching him, he also realizes he is being surrounded by familiar bodies. Love surrounds his entire sphere of being. Then, faces are readily identifiable and close. He is shocked to realize that they are dead loved ones. They approach him and gently let him know that they are there to guide him and to care for him until he has assimilated in this new state of being. As he marvels at their faces and the wonderful feeling he has of seeing his relatives. However, as he starts to reach out and touch them, a black figure approaches from behind, causing the friendly figures to quickly begin pulling away from him. The black figure isn't anyone or anything he can identify, nor does he know if it is friendly or not. But, he senses it to be evil.

Quickly, all of the figures that had surrounded him are drawn away and fade totally out of sight. The bright white light once again begins to return. Now, left with only the bright light to look at, although the warm and happy feeling is still with him, even when everyone was gone, Gene wonders if this could be 'HEAVEN?" It is possible that he went to 'HELL,' by mistake. But if that was so, why did the black figure appear and pull him away from all of his loved ones? Then, within seconds the white light encompasses him again and all Gene feels is sadness and a sense of unawareness. The bright light is suddenly gone and it is dark again all around him. He feels as though he is no longer anywhere, but possibly just asleep in a bed somewhere.

Slowly, Gene is aware of noises and activity that are occurring all around him. Yet, he is unable to open his eyes to see who or what it was. He tries to concentrate on the noises and sounds. One sound he detects is the voice of a woman calling his name. She says, "Mr. Wilson, can you hear me? Can you open your eyes?"

Gene is quickly aware of more noise around him and senses the woman calling to him, now, someone has a hold of his right hand. However, he still cannot open his eyes to see who the person was. He tries, but they just won't open. He then tries to speak, and let her know he did hear her, but his voice will not work either. Then, realizing that someone had a hold of his hand, he tries to squeeze the hand. He tries several times and as he was about to give up, the voice says, "Yes, please squeeze my hand again."

He knows she was talking to him and immediately squeezes her hand for a second time. Again he tries to open his eyes and speak but he cannot.

"Mr. Wilson, that is good. Please rest now, you will be awake soon. Just rest and I will talk to you later," says the voice, as she lets go of his hand. Upon doing that, Gene immediately falls back asleep.

Some time later Gene wakes up again. Now, he is able to see all around and realizes that he was in a hospital bed, in a room hooked to monitors and he was alive. Instantly, he recalls his terrible dreams and the desperation that he experienced. He wonders why his mind would play such a trick on him, yet he is extremely grateful to be alive and in a hospital. Then, he realizes that he cannot remember why he was there or what happened to him. He does know his own name and that he is a Los Angeles police officer. But he has no recollection of the events leading up to his being in this hospital bed.

Gene wonders why he was there, when suddenly three people flock around him. "Hello Mr. Wilson, how are you," asks one of the ladies. Another one begins to listen to his heart through a stethoscope, while the third is checking his pulse. One voice was familiar and he soon remembers his hand-squeezing event.

In a low and raspy voice he asks. "Are you the woman who was calling may name earlier?"

Looking at him, the woman identifies herself as Nurse Lana Hansen. She explains that she was the person holding his hand and was trying to wake him up yesterday.

She tells the other two nurses to go and find Doctor Hocson and tell him that Mr. Wilson was awake. After the two other nurses leave, she says, "You are a lucky man Mr. Wilson. I was fearful that we lost you a couple of times last night after discovering that some of your monitors and feeding tubs were accidentally disconnected from you three days ago. At first you seemed fine. Then you went into cardiac arrest three different times. Once, the last time, the doctors gave up on you and actually pronounced you dead. Then, within mere seconds of that event, you let out a gasp and your heart began functioning properly again. But, you did give us a scare that is for sure. Today, you look much better and even somewhat rested."

As she finishes talking, a doctor arrives and introduces himself as Dr. Peter Hocson. He tells Gene how well he appeared to be and begins examining him. Upon finishing, he explains that he would be moved from the intensive Care Unit to a private room in a day or two. He then asks Gene if he had any questions he could answer.

Smiling, Gene looks at the doctor and says, "Yes I do doctor. Can you tell me what happened to me? Why am I here? I do not recall anything."

Looking back at Gene, Dr. Hocson says, "Well sir, first of all it is quite common for people not to remember serious head injuries, even auto accidents where there is trauma involved. In your case, I understand that you and your police partner were investigating a shooting here in San Pedro, when a man hiding in a closet came out and shot you. I am sure your partner can fill you in better, but that is really all I know." The doctor then departs and leaves Gene alone with the nurses.

While one continues to adjust Gene's feeding tubes, the others survey other monitors. Nurse Hansen says, "Mr. Wilson, I think you are a lucky man. When you first arrived, we all feared that your head injury was more disabling than it has turned out to be. Your partner, Mr. Newton has been in several times and sat here with you. In fact, upon his first visit he insisted you had telephoned him right after your injury. It was so real to him that he actually made me show him that you were not awake and that there was no way you could have called him. But, it was a good thing he came here, because it caused me to discover that some of your monitoring and feeding tubes were disconnected. It might be that he saved your life by making that visit. In any case, I am sure he will be here again this afternoon, as that seems to be his pattern before going to work. You can ask him all of your questions then."

Gene looks at her and then asks, 'Is George Ok? I mean he wasn't injured or shot in the confrontation was he?"

The nurse smiles and says, "No, he wasn't hurt. He is fine."

Happy at hearing that comment, he watches as the nurses leave to tend other patients. Left alone, his mind quickly recounts the terrible encounters he experienced in his dream when he saw people standing around him pushing in on his head. He then recalls the place he believes was 'HELL.' He also thinks about the white light and the good feeling he had following that evil encounter, in what may have been a glimpse of 'HEAVEN.' He wonders if his brush with death is the reason he visited those two places? However, if he did die, if only for mere moments as the nurse said, maybe what he experienced was not simply two dreams at all, but maybe it was the real thing? Was the dark figure that pulled him away from his departed loved ones, possibly an angel, or some type of messenger sent to bring him back to this life? Regardless of whether the two encounters were real or not, the first one was definitely an evil experience that he can only hope that he would never have to endure again. He becomes almost consumed with the feeling that somehow he truly was shown what the real 'HELL' is, and he knows what it would be like to dwell there, which isn't anywhere he would ever want to end up being. Yet, why was he shown this? He knows that there is no way he could have just imagined such a place on his own, because he isn't that creative. But for what purpose would he be shown this place? He believes that he is a good man and certainly not deserving of having to go there if he died. Or, was this maybe a sign that he is bad? Might this be God's way of letting him know he has a second chance to change his life and become a better person? Or, was this a glimpse of what he actually had to look forward to? As he closes his eyes to think about it, he quickly falls off into a deep sleep again.

Asleep, Gene suddenly sees himself in a different type of hospital. It is a bright day and he is now confined to a wheelchair but wide-awake. Yet, he realizes that in this chair he cannot move. He immediately realizes that he is 100% paralyzed. He cannot control any of his normal motor functions. In this place he has been pushed off into a corner where normal people casually walk by and ignore his presence, or possible needs. He tries to get their attention but no one looks at him or notices his begging eyes. He feels totally abandoned and lost in his own grief. He wants desperately for someone to talk to him or at the least acknowledge his presence, but they never do. Why is he here in this place? Why is he in this chair and totally unable to care for himself? Was he injured as a policeman? Is this what a person who has suffered a stroke or heart attack may be forced to endure? Might this be how people in convalescent hospitals exist until they die? Why is this happening to him? In his mind he is screaming for help. He needs desperately for someone to see him. As he silently calls for help and attention he slowly feels a strange sensation coming over him, which he thinks is how it would feel if his life was slipping away and no one cared, or would come to his aid. Soon, in this dream he is falling asleep. He sees his head slump forward and he realizes that he has died. He sees his slumped body sitting there, while no one notices or attends to him. Soon, he sees the day's bright sun shine turn into twilight, which causes the hospital's lights to come on. People like him in wheel chairs are now being pushed past his slumping body. As this happens, still no one looks in his direction. Many wheelchairs pass, until eventually some caregiver comes over to him. They casually lift his head, feel for a pulse and then wheel him away.

Sweating and angry, Gene wakes up and opens his eyes. He immediately feels himself all over and realizes that this too was just another bad dream. He is still in the hospital and he is not paralyzed. He looks around and sees that it was beginning to get dark outside. For a moment he fears this might be his time to die. He cannot help but to be scared and nervous. Could that possibly be a glimpse as to what was in store for him? Being confined to a wheelchair until he dies in a place where no one cares? As he panics a familiar voice is heard coming from behind him.

"Well it is about time you woke up and were able to see me. What has been keeping you asleep so long partner," asks George?

Gene strains his neck by looking first right then left and then down where he sees sitting in one of the room's visitor chairs, his friend George. Also, Gene notices he had been moved out of the intensive care unit into a private room. He looks at his friend and says, "Believe me George what I have been going through these past couple of days in here was anything but pleasant. This head injury has caused me to have some terrible dreams, and I just now experienced one heck of a nightmare."

George stands up and approaches Gene's bedside and says, "Well, I can appreciate what you have gone through. You have had a rough time of it, for sure. The doctor says you actually died a couple of times and luckily they were able to revive you. But, it looks like the worst is over, as they believe you should be getting better, a lot faster now."

Looking at George and knowing what the doctor said, he asks, "George, I do not remember anything. The doctor and nurse told me that I was shot. Looking at my arm, it looks like I took one there and one in the head. Can you explain exactly what happened?"

George smiles and explains every detail to Gene. He omits some of the gory information as to how bad his head wound was but otherwise tells him step by step what happened, including his being furloughed for three days to try and get over Gene's injury.

Gene shakes his head in disbelief and knows he just didn't remember any of it. He then asks George how long have I been in this hospital?

Continuing to smile, George says, "Well, lets see, I think the shooting went down on October 16th And tomorrow is Thanksgiving. So, it has been quite a long time. In fact, the hospital was anxious to get you out of ICU, so they could get you into rehab as soon as possible. Apparently atrophy has set in with your limbs and they fear if you don't get up and move around soon, you could become permanently paralyzed and confined to a wheelchair. So, I think they will be working on you aggressively and pretty quickly now."

Hearing this he immediately recalls the dream where he died in a wheelchair. He knows that it is a fate he would never allow to happen. He quickly tries to move his arms and legs as he lies in bed, and discovers how very painful it was to do so. Worrying about the dream he swears to himself that will not be his future. He then asks, "George, how badly am I hurt? Were there any discussion by the doctors over the fact that I may not be able to return to work?"

George legitimately doesn't know the answer to that and doesn't know what to say exactly. Seeing how badly Gene was hurt, being put on disability in his mind is definitely a possibility. Thinking quickly he says, "Gene, I haven't heard anything like that. As far as I know you are now on the road to a full recovery. However, I think that is something you need to ask your doctor. You definitely have a lot of physical training ahead and I know it is going to take awhile, but I definitely hope that you and I can partner again."

Looking at George he realizes that he has been in the hospital a long time, and will likely be here a while longer. Therefore, it is probable that George has already been assigned a new partner. Worried about that he asks, "So, George, do you have a new partner yet?"

"Hey Gene, don't sweat it. Yes, I have a temporary ride along, but he is a rookie and when you are able to return, he is gone, I promise you that," says, George.

Smiling Gene knows he must be worse than he originally thought and easily recalls all his nightmares and especially the last one about dying an invalid, alone and homeless. He then says, "George, you are my friend, if you learn or hear anything that affects me, at work or here at the hospital, promise you will let me know."

George understands where Gene is coming from and he promise. Meanwhile, it was getting late and he needed to go. He therefore says, "Look partner it is almost time for me to be at the station and I don't want to be late. But, you hang in here and I will see you Friday. I am going to my sister's in Burbank for Thanksgiving tomorrow afternoon, so I won't be able to be back here until Friday. I know tomorrow you will likely get some turkey from the hospital kitchen, so try and enjoy it. Ask a lot of questions of your doctors and nurses, and I will too. Hang in there, I am really happy you are finally awake, and I'll see you later." George then turns and leaves.

Watching George depart, Gene begins to worry that maybe he is in worse condition than he had anticipated. Maybe his bad dreams were signs of things to which he would eventually be introduced to. What did it all mean? He firmly believes that he has truly seen a glimpse of 'HELL' and maybe even a sign of what 'HEAVEN' might be like. But, what about his view of how his life ended in a convalescents hospital? Will he end up alone, afraid and unattended? Is it possible his current injuries are that serious? He knows he is a single man with only a few living relatives. So yes, in a few years he could be that pathetic person he saw in a wheel chair. No wife, no children or anyone who cared enough to visit and see that he had proper nursing. He prays to himself that such a fate was not possible and he also prays that if God would help him now, he will promise to be a better person going forward and try his best to help others.

Gene closes his eyes and tries to move his arms and legs. He wanted desperately to prove to himself that he was not paralyzed in any way. First concentrating on his arms, he moves his left one first. He raises it, makes a fist and opens and closes his hand several times. He then does the same with his right, followed by both legs. He thanks God he can move them. Now, for his head, can he turn his neck? Yes, he can in both directions. Even though he develops a slight headache, he says out loud, "Oh thank you lord." Opening his eyes, he immediately sees the face of a woman staring down at him. He recognizes her face, but it takes a few moments before he realizes that it was the college counselor he had been talking with, Amelia Valenzuela.

She smiles and says, "Mr. Wilson, how are you?"

Looking at the woman, Gene says, "Well, hello Ms. Valenzuela. I am much better now that I am able to be awake and see such a beautiful face looking down at me."

Obviously happy to hear him respond to her questions that way, she says, "Mr. Wilson, I am happy to see your now awake and able to converse so easily. I stopped in a few days ago and was told you were still in a coma and in ICU. And, the nurse I spoke to was beginning to worry that you wouldn't wake up at all, because you were out for so long. I have to say when I read in the paper of your being shot, I was very afraid for you. It is really nice to see you are doing so well and will obviously recover."

"Ms. Valenzuela, "I am very pleased that you cared enough to go out of your way to stop in and brighten my day. Yes, I have really been out of it, but seeing your beautiful face and smile really perks me up, and please call me Gene," he asks.

"Thank you, and please feel free to call me Amelia. I wasn't sure what I would say to you when and if we spoke. But, I can assure you that I feel less awkward now after seeing you so improved. So, did you ever go see Gloria Ramos," asks Amelia?

Gene thinks a moment and then says, "Oh yes. We had a nice visit. Her two grown children were there too and I have to say her explanation of the events they all endured was really fascinating. I was very happy to meet her. She also gave me the names and phone numbers of the three men that helped her. So, when I get back on my feet, I definitely plan on calling on them."

Feeling a bit awkward at visiting Gene, and not knowing really what else to say, Amelia, comments, "Tomorrow is Thanksgiving Gene, I didn't know if anyone told you that or not. I am sure it doesn't seem like you have been in here that long. But, it has been several weeks."

"Yes, my partner George just left here and he said the same thing. He also said he was going to visit his sister tomorrow. And, you are right, I really am confused, as I do not feel like I have been here long at all," exclaims Gene.

"Well, I guess I had best be going and let you rest. I have to go to the grocery store for some last minute items for tomorrow's gathering. So, I hope you are up and around soon and back to school. I fear you have missed a few tests and you will need to make them up when you can. So, rest for now and I will see you later," comments Amelia. She smiles touches his hand and turns to leave.

Before she departed Gene asks, "So, when exactly will I see you again Amelia, you are definitely good therapy for me."

At hearing that Amelia turns back around to face him, and moves back to his bedside. She kind of stutters a second, as she says, "Well, I am not really sure. I didn't know whether or not you would really like to be visited again, especially when you are laid up like this. But, if you want, maybe I can come back again this weekend, if that is something you would like for me to do?"

Upon listening to her, Gene responds, "I would love to visit with you more Amelia. Your beauty and warm smile is excellent medicine. I am just sorry it will take you so long to come back. But, I guess I can wait until this weekend, as I am sure not going anywhere soon. So, yes this weekend would be wonderful."

She nods in a manner letting him know that she will be back. She then asks, "Do you like pumpkin pie Gene?"

"Oh yes, most definitely. That is one of my favorite desert. Why do you ask," inquires Gene?

"Well, I was thinking that maybe tomorrow evening I could sneak you in a peace after my family has finished eating at our house. Maybe I could return tomorrow evening if you would like," says Amelia.

Gene smiles broadly and says, "I'll be right here waiting for you Amelia, and it would be very nice to see you tomorrow. It would be a Thanksgiving I'd never forget."

After Amelia departs Gene wonders how he could of have been lucky enough to have her visit him in the first place? After she left, he realized that he was very attracted to her, beginning the moment he first met her at school. And, for her to visit him this way must mean she felt something for him too? He then wonders if she was married? He realizes he never asked her that question. He prays she isn't. He knows that he will definitely ask that question the first thing tomorrow when she returns with the pie. As he thinks about her and maybe a possible love connection, he closes his eyes and falls asleep again with her on his mind.

Gene wakes up an hour or so later. As he lies there he hears someone next to him. Turning to look, he now sees that there was a second person in the bed next to him. The man was young, and likely was just brought into his room. He looks at the man and says, "Hi, how are you? My name is Gene, who are you?"

"Hello Gene, I am Roger Stern. I was just brought in here. I am going to have my appendix removed in the morning. Damned, I hate being here over the holiday. This isn't how I planned on spending Thanksgiving that is for sure. So, what is your story," asks Roger?

Gene explains that he is a policeman and was shot while investigating a reported shooting. He tells the man how long he was out and when his accident occurred.

Responding back, the man tells Gene that he had read about the shooting and was happy he was recovering so well. He goes on to explain he is a building contractor, and he has been having severe pains in his side for a week now.

When Roger speaks, a doctor enters the room. Gene smiles and says, "Hello." He recognizes the doctor as one of a couple that had attended him off and on while he was there. The doctor smiles at Gene and then immediately goes over to Roger where the two men converse. Gene cannot hear any of their conversation. When done, the doctor approaches Gene.

"So, Mr. Wilson, how are you feeling? I am pleased to see you are now awake and talking. I would like to take a few moments to look you over, if that is all right with you," explains the doctor.

"I do not mind at all doctor. And, I do have some questions myself, as I have not really had any answers given to me that I can recall. Can you tell me how I am doing," asks Gene.

As the doctor looks into his eyes, takes his pulse and listens to his heartbeat he says, "Well, sir, you have a serious head wound. Your arm was also injured but to a much lesser degree. We were all worried about your motor skills being diminished, but it does appear now as if you are not going to suffer any ill effects at all. So, I think it is safe to say you are out of the woods, so to speak. In fact, Friday we are planning on getting you up and out of this bed to begin your physical therapy. You have been on your back a lot longer than we like to see. But, as I check your heartbeat now, and your pulse, I would say you are definitely strong enough to begin getting up and moving around."

Gene is happy to hear all of that and asks, "In you opinion doctor, given my current condition when might I be able to get back to work?"

Thinking about it the doctor is careful in his answer. He says, "I really cannot say. You need to understand that when you disturb the brain in any way, it can take a long time to heal. And you definitely had a serious injury.

Minor in nature, but all the same it was damaged. Once we begin physical therapy and are able to administer a battery of mental and physical skills tests we will know more then and exactly how much, if any permanent damage your brain sustained. Once we know that, we can figure out what exercises you will need to get back to how you were before the accident. So, you just need to remain patient and realize that it will take time, and there isn't anything we can do to rush it along."

Worried somewhat over what was being said Gene asks, "Doctor, are you saying that there is a possibility that I will not be able to return to work?"

"I didn't say that, but yes, it is possible after you are healed as much as you are going to be, it won't be enough. Today, we have no idea as to how much your motor skills or mental capacity has suffered. But, as soon as we start your treatment, we will know more. Therefore, again, as I said, be patient and above all do everything your therapist tells you to do. The harder you work, the better it will be." As the doctor concludes those comments he tells Gene he has other patients to see and he had to go. As he says that he exits the room.

"I wouldn't worry too much Gene. You sound and look pretty normal to me. I would say going back to work will not be an issue, but I also suggest you 'milk' it for as long as you can. Take it easy and get rested as much as possible. Remember, those mean streets will always be there," says Roger.

Early the next morning Gene is awakened by Roger's moans. He was suffering from pains in his side and the nurses were already there to aid and get him ready for his operation that morning. Eventually, he is wheeled out of the room and once again Gene is alone. He sees the clock and notes it was 9:00 am. He immediately begins thinking about Amelia visiting him later that day, and realizes how excited he was over that meeting. He wants to get cleaned up and shaved so he looks better for her. Pushing his call button an orderly arrives and Gene tells the man what he needed help with. By noon, Gene is cleaned up, shaved and his teeth are brushed. He had also combed his hair as best he could, given his prone position. Food is served and they turn on his television so he could watch a football game. Being Thanksgiving, most employees are polite and stop in to wish him well. As Gene watches his television his mind wonders off and he cannot get into the game. He worries about his brain damage. What if he is handicapped? How much money would he be able to receive on disability? What if it is worse and he needs to hire someone to attend to his needs? What if he eventually does become paralyzed? Suddenly, he begins to panic and has to force himself to calm down. He tries to relax and tell himself he will be fine and he will make a 100% recovery. Yet, he worries and fears the worst.

While trying to take his mind off of his worries, he tries again to watch the football game.

Then, when he least expected it, Amelia peaks around the door and into his room. Spotting her beautiful smile, Gene quickly smiles back and motions for her to come on in to his room.

Looking at him she says, "Gene, happy Thanksgiving. Did you get any turkey today? I brought you a 'dogie' bag from my family dinner. I have turkey, potatoes, stuffing and green beans. Are you hungry? I hope it is Ok for me to be in here with all this stuff?"

"Hey, don't worry about it. You are a wonderful sight to behold. You are really dressed nicely and I could care less about the hospital's food policy. Just seeing your beautiful face is all the nourishment I need. I was getting really depressed and full of self-pity for myself. Earlier today I spoke with a doctor who kind of scared me. He left a lot of questions for me to think about," says Gene.

Amelia sees that Gene was upset and asks, "What did he say to upset you the way he did?"

Gene tries to explain what he said and how worried he became after dwelling on what could go wrong and tells her how he fears over being on disability.

"I do understand your fear Gene. I can only assume all brain injuries will cause problems to some degree no matter how minor they are. However, when I speak with you, I sense no hesitation or any type of problem with your speech or thought process. That being said, I think your fears are unfounded. I'll bet you will make a complete recovery and I will also wager it won't take very long for that to happen. In fact, I brought you a book from your law class and it is likely a smart thing for you to be reviewing it while you are laid up here. Reading should be good for your motor skills too," explains Amelia.

"I have an important question for you Amelia," asks Gene?

Amelia looks at Gene and says, Sure, what is it? What is it that you wish to know?"

Sheepishly, Gene looks at Amelia and then asks, "Are you married?"

Responding back quickly, Amelia says, "What? Of course not. Why would you think I was married?"

Gene smiles and replies, "Well, it was just something I hadn't asked you before and it was a question I really wanted an answer to. When you left here yesterday I realized that was something I really needed to know."

"If I were a married woman, I doubt that I would be visiting you without bringing him along too. I am not the type of woman to be flirting with men if I were married. I was not raised that way," says Amelia.

Gene quickly responds, "Oh I didn't know that you were flirting with me. Is that what you call it?" Laughing, Gene then asks, "How is flirting different from talking?"

Amelia blushes and tries to correct her comments and finally says, "Gene, you know what I mean. I wouldn't be here alone with you if I were a married woman."

Still smiling at her he says, "I am just joking with you Amelia, but seriously it was a question I needed to ask to be sure I wasn't wasting my time fantasizing over you, and wondering if maybe when I get out of here we could enjoy a real date together?"

Quickly responding, Amelia says, "No one has ever fantasized about me before, that I know about. And, I wouldn't be here if I didn't hope you would someday ask me out on a real date."

The two spend the next hour talking about themselves and their families. By 6:00 pm., Amelia looks at her watch and says she needs to be getting on home. She explains that there was a lot of cleaning up that needed doing and she was responsible for doing that as well as cooking. She makes Gene promise to try her Thanksgiving dinner and she kisses him on the forehead and leaves.

Time slowly passes and one week later Gene sits in an outer office waiting to meet with a therapist who has a battery of mental tests to administer to him. After a few minutes he is surprised to find that his therapist, Dr, Cathy Allen was a young attractive woman, who was very friendly. Standing at her office door she invites Gene to come inside and sit down. She explains that her job was to evaluate his mental condition and to assess his overall skill level progression as his therapy continues to evolve. She explains this is how they will determine if there is any impairment to his brain in any area.

"So, Mr. Wilson I understand that your physical therapy is going well. I am told that you are now moderately exercising twice a day and your coordination and dexterity seem to be improving at a rapid rate. So, you need to know that this conversation with me today is part of your therapy as well, and it is going to be conducted in much the same way. Here, we will be testing your mental capacities and trying to determine whether any special testing or exercise is needed before letting you go home. So, do you have any questions," she asks?

Gene thinks about it and is confident that none of his motor and mental skills have been damaged in any way, and he looks forward to getting through all of her tests. Responding to her question he says, "No, I understand it is necessary and I look forward to getting everything addressed and assessed."

The two then spend the next hour discussing history, literature, religion and other daily topics of conversation, which Gene seems to glide right on through. After answering the majority of questions and looking at pictures the therapist thanks him and says, "You did very good Mr. Wilson and I will look forward to our next encounter tomorrow. When we finish this week, I can complete my report and hopefully get you ready to leave here. Do you have any questions?"

While thinking about it he asks, "I guess I am curious as to what all of these tests I took so far have told you about me? And of course I am very anxious to hear you say that I can return to work. So, is there anything that you have discovered that would cause me to worry about achieving that goal?"

Dr. Allen smiles and says, "To that question Mr. Wilson, I fear I must refrain from responding until I finish all of our tests here, but rest assured that you are doing much better than anyone ever anticipated. Go on back to your room and get a good nights rest, I will see you tomorrow."

Nodding in agreement Gene heads back to his room, where upon entering he finds Amelia sitting and waiting for him.

Seeing her immediately brightens his day. He hugs her and the two walk out into the hospital waiting area and sit down on a couch, where they begin talking. Gene tells her what has been happening and explains how he is hopeful of getting out of there in a couple of days, assuming all goes well.

Amelia tells him that was great news and she reminds him of his promise to take her to dinner someplace nice when he is out and able.

Responding back to her comment he says, "Pretty lady, a date with you would be the best off all medicines or therapies I could ever hope for. I definitely am looking forward to that, and I promise that it will happen very soon."

After and hour of chatting and discussing everything imaginable Amelia tells Gene that it was time for her to be going home. Standing up, Gene works up his nerve and reaches out and grabs her by the shoulders, pulls her body into his and seriously kisses her for the first time

After finishing, Amelia says, "Well, it sure took you long enough to accomplish that first kiss. I was beginning to worry that you might never have the nerve to do that. I thought you policemen were aggressive and considered yourselves to be big ladies men. I am finally happy to find out I wasn't wrong." She then kisses him back, turns, picks up her purse and departs without another word, leaving Gene to think about their first encounter and her actions.

Gene slowly returns to his room where he undressed, crawls into bed and turns on the television. He realizes that he likes Amelia a lot. She was also smart and pretty. But, based on their cultural difference, (her being a Catholic and he, a Methodist) he worries about anything romantic developing long termed between them. Deciding it was too early in their relationship to worry about that, he is satisfied for now to just enjoy her companionship.

Three days later after all psychological test had been completed, Gene is asked back to see Dr Allen, where she wanted to discuss the results of his overall motor skills tests and let him know what if any future tests would be needed.

Sitting in her waiting room, he reads a magazine and realizes for the first time his ability to concentrate was poor, he finds it hard to concentrate on what was being reported. He begins to worry about that, when Dr. Allen comes out and invites him into her office. Complying, he sits down and eagerly waits for her comments.

"Well, Mr. Wilson, I have studied all of the tests that I administered to you and it would appear the likelihood of you making a full recovery is good. I also have the results of your physical rehabilitation and that too appears to be going well. Therefore, I think it is safe to sign your release papers and let you get out of here. You will still need to spend three days a week with a physical therapist for probably another couple of months before you are considered to be back to normal. But overall, I see no problem with that occurring. What do you think, do you have any issues you want to discuss," she asks?

Anxious to leave, he hesitates to ask her about the reading problem he just experienced. He worries that it might be a problem, since he was unable to concentrate on the article. But, wanting to know everything, Gene tells Dr. Allen about his concerns.

Listening, she thinks about that and retrieves yet another test and asks him to be patient as she sets it up. It was designed to make him concentrate on shapes, colors and sizes, as an overhead projector instantly comes on and shows them on a large movie screen at one end of her office. After the film is over, she turns off the projector, hands Gene a sheet of paper and asks him to write down as many of the shapes and colors and sizes as he could remember. Finishing the test, Dr. Allen looks at everything and says, "I think you are fine. The test I just administered suggests that your injury and concentration problems should improve a little bit every day. One thing that would help immensely would be for you to immediately begin reading novels, newspapers and anything that requires you to think and concentrate about what has happened. Let's plan on redoing this same test again in forty-five days. But, it is my opinion that eventually you will be just fine and, yes able to return to work. So, other than your concentration, is there anything else at all you would like to know about or discuss?"

Gene would really like to ask her about the weird dreams he experienced but he feared that she might not think given such thoughts he was well enough to return to work. He was also tempted to ask her what she knew about the paranormal world as he would dearly love to talk to her about his and George's experience with the dead insurance broker. However, being anxious to get away from the hospital and be released in order to return back to work he says, "No, Dr. Allen, I think I feel pretty good and I want you to know how much I do appreciate everything you have done for me here."

Standing up, she extends her hand and says, "Well, if you ever want to talk about anything, I am always here for you. I will make an appointment on my calendar to see you in forty-five days to retest your concentration ability. Meanwhile, please do as I ask and read everything you can. And, if you need anything, please do not hesitate to call me." She then hands Gene one of her business cards.

The two then shake hands and Gene returns to his hospital room, where he quickly packs his personal items and checks himself out of the hospital and catches a cab home.

Walking into his apartment after being away for so long, it seems like someone else's house. He sits on his sofa and looks all around. He admits to himself it appeared somewhat different than what he remembered. He goes into the kitchen and opens the refrigerator and is bowled over by the smell of rotting food. He forgot what he had left in there and obviously, a lot of it did not withstand the length of time he was away. He grabs a plastic garbage bag and loads everything rotten into it. He hauls it downstairs and is greeted by his landlady who eagerly welcomes him home. Back upstairs in his apartment he sits back down on his couch and thinks to himself that he didn't remember her either. Was this poor memory normal, or was it a sign of something more serious. As he wonders about his poor memory his phone rings. Answering it, he is pleasantly surprised at hearing Amelia's voice asking how he was. The two talk for a long time. Before ending their conversation, they set a date for dinner the following night. They decide to meet at a popular Greek Restaurant in downtown San Pedro.

The next evening, after enjoying a nice Greek dinner and an evening with Amelia, the two begin to leave the restaurant, when Amelia suggests that they walk down to the Port of Los Angeles and watch the container ships entering and leaving the harbor. Doing as she suggested, while standing by the edge and watching the ships, Gene looks at Amelia under the bright lights that are illuminating the area, and marvels at her beauty. He then puts his arm around her shoulder and pulls her near. She dips her head onto his shoulder and lifts her left arm up to Gene's cheek. She pulls him down to her face and kisses him passionately. Returning her kiss, they hug and squeeze one another. After a few minutes of kissing, Gene suggests that they return to his apartment for a nice warm brandy.

At noon the next day, wearing the same clothes as the night before, Amelia departs Gene's home and the two kiss and make plans for their next date in two days.

CHAPTER 3; *Life, Back on the Street*

Two months later Gene is released by the hospital and fully reinstated back on the job. George quickly arranges for Gene to once again be his partner. Their first night on patrol, they drive and discuss Gene's injury. George tells Gene how bad he felt the night when he was shot. Gene assures George that he did not blame him and he felt fine now, and was completely ready to assume all of his normal duties. However, one thing Gene has never been able to forget was the visions he had of seeing 'HELL,' and 'HEAVEN,' as well as maybe his own future, as he died all alone in that convalescent hospital.

For the first two hours they talk a lot, as George brings Gene up to date on everything that has happened on the force since he has been away. The night is quiet and there are no calls or requests for anything. It was almost like it was planned that Gene's first night back would be subdued and boring. As they patrol, Gene sits quietly thinking about his good fortune and how happy he was to be back beside George cruising and looking for whatever might happen. Yet, his nagging dreams continue to play over in his mind like a movie. He worries about it so much George notices and eventually asks what was bothering him.

Gene looks over at his partner and says, "Oh, I was just thinking about stuff. You know, this is a new year, and I seriously hope it means I can finish my law studies by summer and take the bar exam. I guess what worries me most about that is the reality that once I do that, I will no longer be here and away from police work. Plus, I feel that I must confide in you about something else that is really on my mind and bothering me."

Looking at Gene, George smiles and says, "Don't tell me partner, you are in love, aren't you?"

Gene is blushing all over and with an extremely big smile he says, 'George, Amelia is everything I could ever want. She is smart, beautiful and so very passionate. Yes, I am in love with her, but I really do not know what to do about it."

Laughing out loud George says, "Well, if it is that serious, there is only one thing you can do, and that is to marry the girl, you dummy."

"Yes, I know that you are right, and believe me I want to. But there is the issue of our religions. She is a devout Catholic and I am not. I can't attend church with her and to be honest I do not know what I would want for our children. She would want to raise them under her religion and I do not think I would like that. It might sound stupid, but it is a big issue for me," explains Gene.

Departing from their current conversation George says, "Well, I have to admit partner I am seriously happy that you are back. My temporary partner, Henry, was a good kid, but I guess I became use to having you sitting there and he just wasn't as much fun. Besides, he was way too serious. Everything for him had to be done by the book. That just isn't any fun for me. But now, here you are getting all serious on me, telling me you are going to be a lawyer and maybe a husband. What happened to the non-serious playboy I use to know?"

Gene is a little bit embarrassed but admits to himself that he wanted to tell George about Amelia from the first. He therefore begins, "Amelia Valenzuela is a very nice and extremely great woman. It began when she first visited me in the hospital. It went then from good to great. In fact, we have actually discussed moving in together to see how we get along."

"Well, that is great. I hope she is someone you can enjoy. And, if she is that great, I wouldn't think a religious difference would matter at all. You know Republicans marry Democrats and blacks marry whites, so if it is really love, it will work out some how and I see no problem with it. But, quitting the police force, now that is a different issue."

Gene is quiet for a while and eventually says, "Yes, I know you are right. Love should overcome a lot of differences. And I have been telling myself all that too. So, I guess we will just live together for a while and see how it goes. I just thought you should know what I was up to."

"Look Gene, what you do with your life is up to-you. If she is as good as you say, then I wish you the best. But, back to your leaving the force and becoming a lawyer, are you sure that is really something you want to do," asks George?

Looking at George, Gene says, "Look partner, I have been going to law school now for over four years. Did you never once assume I might really be serious about being a lawyer? Let me tell you something, when the actual time comes for me to make that decision, I honestly do not know what I will do."

George listens to Gene's comments and suddenly remembers something he wanted to bring up and discuss. "Say, changing the subject, speaking of you being in the hospital, did I ever tell you about the phone call I got from you while you were unconscious? I swear you called me and said you were fine and not to worry. Then the line went dead. I later verified that you were in ICU and couldn't possibly have called me even if you wanted to. How do you think something like that could happen," asks George?

Gene did recall George telling him that earlier, but he really didn't remember the event again until now. He thinks about it and says, "George, so many strange things happened to me in that hospital while I was unconscious. Your call is just one more oddity that happened that I can't explain. My time there at the beginning was like an 'Epiphany' or something close to it. I do not want to freak you out, so stop me if I do. But I know that I died once or twice while I was in a coma. And, when it happened, I am convinced that each time I saw both of the other sides. Maybe somehow in my state of being unconscious, I was somehow able to reach out to you and physically make a mental phone call or something. I admit I don't remember ever thinking of calling you, but that might be what I did? Believe me, nothing that happened during that time would surprise me at all. Otherwise, I have no explanation for any of it. But, if what you say-happened, did happen, I can't explain it."

As George drives he is quiet for a while. He then has to know and asks, "What exactly are you talking about? What is an 'Epiphany,' what the Hell are you saying?"

Gene knows how George thinks, and he fears if he tells him of his dreams of HELL and HEAVEN he may think something is wrong with his brain and maybe he won't want him as a partner any longer. Thinking how to respond he says, "George, it is all really fuzzy, but when I was out, I had seriously bad dreams. They might have been as a result of being zapped by those electric heart paddles each time my heart stopped. Who knows? But, I am back now and my mind is awake and clear. It was something I want to forget. So please just let it pass, I beg you."

Before George can respond they get a call of a domestic disturbance. Gene picks up the radio and immediately responds and they head off to the address given.

Arriving at the location within three minutes, they pull up to the curb and jump out of their car. It is an area full of older two story wooden apartments. Gene looks around and is surprised to see several people standing off on both sides of the apartment more or less hiding behind the bushes that are along the street. Gene assumes that they heard the commotion and were standing by just to see what was going to happen.

Suddenly, George motions for Gene to stand near the unit's front door. George draws his weapon and knocks on the door. Standing to the side of the door, George shouts out, "Police, open the door, now."

At first there is no response. George repeats the order. Soon, a young woman answers and is crying. Standing outside, both men peer into the house from two different locations. George then asks the woman, "Are you hurt?"

The young woman is crying and shakes her head no. But both men can see that she does have a slight cut to her bottom lip and left cheek. Both were bleeding and swollen.

Gene steps closer to her, as George kicks the door open and rushes inside. Gene looks quickly at her to be sure she had no weapons, and he too enters the residence. Stopping and shielding their bodies from the rest of the apartment's rooms, George asks the woman who hit her and where were they?

The woman points down the hall and says, "He is in our bedroom hiding. He didn't mean to hurt me, please don't arrest him."

Slowly the two make their way to the room's door and knock on it. They order the man out. Within seconds he exits the room and places his hands in the air, showing that he was not armed. He is ordered to the floor and instructed to lie face down. The man was somewhat older than the girl and appeared to be slightly drunk. He is ordered to immediately lie still where he is checked for weapons and then handcuffed. Determining he was not carrying any weapons and claimed that there were none in the house, they are both escorted into the living room, where George interrogates the man and Gene the woman. Ending the conversations, they compare their two stories and find them both to be very similar. Sitting both down on their couch, George lectures them about fighting and his hitting a woman. They nod in agreement and the woman begs the two men not to arrest her husband. Thinking about it and discussing their options, they remove the man's handcuffs and leave after giving them both stern warnings.

Back in their vehicle they wonder if they did the right thing. Gene asks George if he knew who called in the complaint, as it would seem neither of them did. George says, "Well someone did. Maybe it was a neighbor.

Gene responds, "Yes, that may be right. Lord knows there were a lot of them standing around outside when we pulled up. Maybe we should have asked them some questions. They might have given us more information."

George hears Gene's comment and slightly turning his head towards his partner while driving he asks, "What people are you talking about? There was no one standing outside anywhere. Are you joking?"

Gene is dumbfounded and responds, "What do you mean? I saw at least six people standing on both sides of their apartment door."

George just laughs and says, "If I didn't know you better I would swear you have been drinking. Believe me partner, there were no bystanders anywhere around there."

Gene knows that George wasn't joking at this point. Yet, he knows what he saw. How was it he saw them and George didn't? He concludes that maybe George was just too occupied on watching the door and getting inside and simply didn't see anyone. Gene decides to let the subject drop.

Later, as the two men are sitting in the Gaffey Street Diner, eating, George once again asks Gene about his dreams at the hospital?

Gene smiles and says, George, I really don't think they would be of interest to you. I am sure it was a result of the medication and me being out of my head. Besides, it is really fuzzy now."

Eating for a few minutes and being quiet, George finally says, "Well, I am certain that I got a call from you, which caused me to go back to the hospital and check on you. I was told it was fortunate that I did, because some stuff that had been hooked to you came off and it could have been serious. Driving home later, I actually concluded to myself that your call was real because you knew that something was wrong and that was your way of asking me for help. So, let me ask again, what did you see in your dreams? Regardless of what you might think, I am seriously interested. I know there is no logical answer to explain how I got your call, and maybe, just maybe your dreams might help me to understand it better."

Gene is afraid to tell George what he believes he saw, but he can also see that unless he does, George may become even angrier at him and will likely press him harder until he does talk. Gene begins by describing the place he calls, 'HELL' and then his glimpse of the place he calls 'HEAVEN' and how he was pulled away from both places, but only after actually experiencing how they both felt for short periods of time. He then finishes by telling George about dying all alone in that convalescent hospital.

George is shocked at Gene's account of the two places he describes as being 'HELL' and 'HEAVEN,' as well as the convalescent hospital and says, "Gene, I have to admit that sounds really strange. Why do you think you experienced those three dreams? They sounded like they were really vivid to you. Has that experience made any difference to your beliefs or ideas about living your own life?"

"That is a really good question George. Immediately after experiencing them, I was really wondering why it happened? Was it some type of a sign of what was ahead for me? And, I admit that I am still not sure. But, I would be lying if I said it hasn't changed me somewhat. I admit the feeling I had being in 'HELL' was awful. Also dying all alone was a bad experience. If either of them were a true glimpse into the way death can be, I guaranty you that 'HELL' is no place any person would want to be. Thinking about it, I do not believe I am an evil person. I truly want to help people and I would give up my life if necessary to save another person. So, unless I am bad and destined to go there, why show it to me? It was a real eye opening experience, I'll guaranty that," explains Gene.

The two finish eating and begin the second half of their shift. They drive around until 11 pm., when they receive a call instructing them to investigate an automobile roll over on an isolated road, where some teenagers had been drag racing. With lights and siren on, they head to 25th Street in South San Pedro. Arriving at the site of the accident, three cars are parked and one is lying on its side, up against a hillside. The two officers get out and rush to the rolled over vehicle and find two teenagers trapped inside. One was dead, but the other, a female was alive but badly hurt. Fearing a fire might occur as fuel was leaking out, George calls for back up to include a tow truck and an ambulance. Meanwhile, Gene is trying desperately to get the passenger side door open, but it is badly jammed. Approaching the vehicle, George picks up a large rock lying nearby and begins smashing the front windshield. Gene also realizes that was likely their best method of getting into the vehicle and he too does the same thing. Within a few minutes they had the front windshield broken out and immediately extract the woman. Gene drags her far enough away that she would be safe in the event of an explosion. He then returns to where George was working on unhooking the driver. Together they extract him within a few minutes. They drag his body close to the girl's and then tell everyone to move away from the vehicle. Once again as he looks around, Gene sees several strangers just standing off in the distance, almost hiding behind the bushes and brush watching his every move. Meanwhile, Gene takes reports from bystanders who had stopped to render aid, while George attends to the woman, they learn that the dead man was racing another car when he lost control and rolled over several times. The witnesses say the other car kept going. They give a description of the other vehicle and the occupants. It appeared to be a case of teenage stupidity as they both tried to beat the other to where ever it was they were going. Seeing the accident these three vehicles stopped and tried to render assistance, but were unable to open either door.

As the ambulance and fire trucks arrive, upon getting their statements Gene thanks the bystanders and tells them that they can go. George walks over to him and shakes his head and says, "What a waste. I don't think she is going to make it either. Here we have two young lives just suddenly gone, and for what? I just cannot understand why anyone would race on this narrow and winding highway. It was suicidal." Meanwhile, the fire truck sprays down the vehicle and the ambulance departs. By now two more police cars are on scene and Gene tells George that he was going to interview the other bystanders who were off of the road standing over by the brush.

Looking around, George doesn't see anyone and asks Gene who he was referring to? He says, "I do not see anyone over there."

Gene looks back at George and asks, "You do not see the four people standing over there?" As he says that, he looks back towards them, and now they too are all gone.

George doesn't really know what to say to Gene's claim of seeing people off in the brush here and at the previous call. Looking at Gene, George comes to the conclusion that he wasn't joking.

Gene walks up to him and says, "I swear partner, I saw four people standing over there, and now they are gone."

George asks, "Did they look a lot like the people you saw earlier back in town?"

Thinking about it, they were similar. I did see six people at the earlier call and four here. And, in both cases George clearly didn't see any of them. Was something paranormal happening to him? Or, more likely, maybe he was loosing his mind? In any case, he decides to shut up about it and maybe try and figure out what was happening to him.

The two men pull into the police station after completion of their shift. They are both quiet as they park and exit the car. Locking it they head inside where George turns in their reports and Gene heads directly to the locker room to change his clothes. Before he finishes getting dressed, George returns and they sit silently together for a while.

George than says, "Gene, we certainly had a busy night and for your first shift back after three months away, you were pretty sharp. But, these mysterious people you claim to see hiding off to the side of those two locations is puzzling to me. Possibly you should find that therapist woman you had been seeing in the hospital and see what she thinks about it? Maybe talking to her would help? I am concerned for you. I fear that you are just not ready to be back to work yet? Since we are off the next two days, I seriously recommend you try to make an appointment to see her during that time."

Gene listens and agrees something was wrong. He had never seen things like that before and maybe his mind was playing tricks on him. He responds to George's suggestion by saying, "Yes, you may be right. I will set an appointment with her as soon as possible. In any ease, I'll see you later."

Gene then leaves the building and starts his drive home. In his car he wonders why he is seeing these things and definitely agrees it wasn't anything he had experienced prior to his being shot. He wonders if his head injury was the cause of what he is seeing? Or, maybe worse, could he now be mentally impaired from that injury? As he pulls into his parking spot and exits his vehicle, he locks it and heads up to his apartment. Opening the door, he goes in and sits down in front of the television and for a while simply stares at its darken screen. Eventually he realizes that he wasn't watching anything. He then gets up and turns on the set. Sitting back down he watches his favorite law enforcement program until he falls asleep in his chair. Waking at 3:00 am, he gets up, looks around and checks his watch. As he does that he senses movement on both his right and left side. Looking in both of those directions he sees nothing. Deciding he was sleepy and only seeing things, he turns off the television and goes to bed. As he begins to relax and fall asleep, he suddenly realizes that his blankets and sheets are being slowly pulled off of his bed. This wakes him up causing him to realize he was holding onto everything in order to keep them from falling off of his bed. Getting out of bed he turns on a light and looks around. Definitely his blanket and sheet had fallen onto the floor, in a way that let him know something had pulled them off.

Gene searches for whatever it was that was pulling at his bedding. He looks everywhere, in his closets, the bathroom and even under his bed. Yet, he finds no one. He is totally puzzled as he looks at the heap of blankets and sheets on his floor. Could he have been dreaming and simply kicked them off as he slept? Getting back in bed he puts everything back where it belonged. Again just as he was about to fall off asleep, his bedding once again begins moving down towards the bottom of his bed. This time he gives everything a hard yank and yells, out. "Dame it, leave my bedding alone." After he says that, the tugging stops and he hears a loud swishing sound, similar to what you would hear when opening a large can of coffee. It sounded like what ever was pulling at his bedding quickly departed his room. And, he didn't experience the sensation again.

CHAPTER 4; *Gene Discovers Something New About Himself*

Gene wakes up at 10:00 am. Lying there, he immediately recalls his and George's conversation the night before about the shadow people that he thought he saw plus his bedclothes pulling episodes he experienced. He knows theses are all weird experiences and something he needed to figure out. He even wondered if somehow they were connected? Possibly, George was right, suggesting that he should try and contact Dr. Allen, and discuss what was happening to him.

Getting up he makes a pot of coffee and sits in his kitchen thinking about everything. He wonders if he truly does have a problem. Obviously, to see people where none exist and feel covers being pulled off by invisible hands isn't normal. He worries about being on patrol and maybe seeing someone who wasn't really there or even harming someone real, or worse yet, letting George down and causing him to be injured. Considering the consequences, he looks up the therapist's phone number and calls her.

Answering her phone, the therapist talks with Gene for a while and upon sensing something was wrong, sets an appointment with him for later that very day. Hanging up, Gene thinks how best to describe to her what he has been experiencing. Considering the facts, he decides the best way to handle it is simply to tell her directly what was happening.

Later that day, Gene goes to the hospital and arrives on time. He is greeted by Dr. Allen. Entering her office, he sits for a few moments and discusses routine events and how his first two days back to work felt. Then, he begins talking about George's suggestion that he see her again, explaining why. Gene describing the mysterious people that only he could see. Interested in his comments the therapist digs in deeper and finally hears about Gene's three dreams while in the hospital.

"Mr. Wilson, I am really disappointed to know that you experienced these things while we were in therapy and you never shared them with me. These are serious issues and they tell me more about you than you can imagine. I realize how badly you wanted to be normal and return to work, but those dreams were crucial facts and now these people you claim to see are telling me a valuable story about you," explains the doctor.

Gene is embarrassed and responds, "Well, I honestly felt that what I dreamed was merely subconscious anxieties due to being in a hospital. And, they were really just weird dreams, nothing more or nothing less. However, I am worried about my seeing these people who are hiding behind bushes that are only visible to me. Plus, feeling something pulling at my blankets and sheets."

The doctor thinks a moment and then says, "Gene, it is a proven fact that the human brain is an extraordinary thing. You likely know that we humans only utilize a very small portion of its overall capability. I venture to guess, if mankind survives long enough, people will increase their capability by using more of it over time, and what they may be able to do in the future would only be considered science fiction today. So, what if somehow a brain was disturbed by say a gunshot wound? Could that slightly alter the personality and capabilities of its user? Could it increase ones awareness of other dimensions, realms, time, space and reality? Who can say? The fact is, you did suffer a brain injury and whether it enhanced your overall capabilities by enabling you to see things that no one else does, is anyone's guess. You could be seeing and experiencing real phenomena activity, or you may be damaged and not functioning properly. That is what we need to find out."

"So, how do we get to the bottom of it and find out what is wrong with me, "asks Gene?

Doctor Allen looks at Gene and says, "I want to get you to a place where we can take brain scans and have you work with specialists who understand how to assess your psychic abilities. I know UCLA medical school has such a program and maybe so does USC. So, let me make some inquiries and I'll set an appointment for you."

"Ok, that sounds like a plan. But, meanwhile can I keep working," asks Gene?

"From what I sense in talking to you today and from your admitted ability to perform your work last night, I see no danger to you or your partner if you continue working. However, if you think you are not capable, say so now, and I will see to it that you are placed on paid medical leave, pending the outcome of your upcoming tests," explains Dr. Allen.

Gene thinks about it and concludes he is performing at proper standards and except for the sighting of those mysterious people, he had no other problems and believes that he is fit for duty. He therefore says, "No, I think I am fine to work. I will just have to be aware of the existence of these mysterious shadow people."

The doctor stands up, and says. "Then that is settled Mr. Wilson, work it is, and I will call you later today to let you know when and where your appointment will be set up."

Gene gets up, shakes her hand and departs her office. As he walks away he wonders what they will find. Might he some how have developed new higher awareness caused by his brain being injured, or is it more likely that he is just crazy? He is afraid to find out, yet anxious too know. He thinks about his need to perform his job with George and concludes that he is capable of doing that. And, other than his problems with the shadow people, he is otherwise fit for duty.

Later that evening Gene receives a call from Amelia. The two talk, and Gene tells her about his returning to see Dr. Allan. He tells her about seeing the hiding people and Dr. Allen wondered if his head injury gave him any accelerated powers to see or sense paranormal entities or events. Amelia tells Gene how fascinating the idea was and then the two plan a dinner date.

After hanging up, Gene sits back and relaxes while thinking about Amelia and how much he enjoyed her company. Suddenly, his phone rings again. "Hello," says Gene.

"Mr. Wilson, this is Dr. Allen. I have good news. I was able to schedule an appointment for you in the neurology and science facility at UCLA Medical Center, for next Wednesday at 8:00 am."

Gene thinks about that and knowing he will be home sleeping then he says, "Ok Doctor, that will be fine. I will need to get up early, but I can definitely make it." He then gets the name and address of who and where he must be. He asks how long the tests would take and how soon they would have any information.

Dr. Allen responds, "Mr. Wilson, I would plan on spending at least two hours with them. And, I would also assume the results shouldn't take that long. Maybe four or five days at the most. I'll be sure to contact you just as soon as the results are sent to me."

Two days later Gene and George are back on patrol, where Gene is wondering how much he should tell George. As they drive, the night was quiet and the two discuss sports, women and other miscellaneous topics, but George never asks if Gene made an appointment with his psychiatrist, as he suggested. As they drive, Gene wonders why the subject never came up. He thought George was worried about it and assumed that he would have asked that question first thing?

After a while Gene decides to mention it. He says, "By the way George, I did take your suggestion and I went to see Dr. Allen."

"Who," asks George?

Gene chuckles to himself. He then wonders if maybe George was only joking all along. Might he have seen those people all along and was just pulling a prank on him? He says, "Remember, you suggested I go back and see that shrink that I was working with at the hospital."

George acts as though he didn't know what Gene was talking about and says, "No, 1 do not recall discussing that with you, refresh my memory."

Gene then explains, "George, on our last patrol I told you about seeing people hiding behind bushes that you didn't see. You were worried and said I needed to go see the person I was working with at the hospital before being discharged. You thought maybe she discharged me too early"

"Oh yes, I know what you are referring to. So, have you called her yet," asks George?

Gene thinks to himself about what the doctor said and wonders how much he should tell him. He then responds by saying, "Yes, not only did I call her, I saw her too. In fact, she was quite impressed with what I told her I saw. She believes the bullet wound to my brain, may have somehow enhanced my physic abilities, which allows me to see things that exist on different levels or plains that not everyone else can see." Gene knows that isn't what she really said, but it was a plausible conclusion and he thought he would mention it to see what George would say. If he were joking about not seeing those people, he would now have to admit it. And, if he wasn't, it was a way to see what he thought about his partner having psychic powers.

George is a bit shocked to hear Gene's comment. He thinks a minute and asks, "Are you and her saying that the gun shot you received in the head has done something to your brain which now allows you to see ghosts?"

"Well, that is a bit more than what she said, but she hinted it was a possibility. In fact, she has me scheduled to take a battery of tests with brain doctors who can evaluate those tests and determine exactly why I am seeing these strange people that you can't see. She explained that what I claim to be able to see, might be real. And, that could only happen if somehow my brain injury caused this to occur. She says as humans, we only utilize a very small percentage of our brain capabilities and maybe the injury woke up an area not normally used. She says that the experts I will be seeing will hopefully be better equipped to make that assessment."

George doesn't know what to say to Gene's comments and is definitely worried for Gene's mental stability. Yet, he was afraid to say exactly what he believed the truth was, which is, he has suffered extensive brain damage. He says, "Well, that is interesting. I will look forward to hearing more after your tests. But, to change the subject, are you still seeing that cute little college counselor?"

Gene can tell that George is uncomfortable talking about what he just told him. Sensing that, he also concludes that George was not joking about not seeing the hiding people that he saw. He decides to drop the topic all together and he says, "Oh yes. Amelia and I are seeing a lot of each other. We spent the day together yesterday and I admit I am really beginning to enjoy being with her." After he says that they get a call of gang activity with shots fired and are told to proceed cautiously to Main and 12th street to meet a citizen with information. Within five minutes they arrive at the location. The buildings are an older four storied housing project containing forty smaller apartments. At first they see nothing, but are quickly approached by two young women. Rolling down their window, one liens in and whispers that they heard gunshot coming from upstairs and a sound like someone was being hurt. They said the building was a known drug hangout, where gangs sold dope.

George quickly radios in his information and requests backup. He exits the vehicle and motions for Gene to do the same and check the north side of the building while he would check the south side for anyone lurking in the darkened alleys. George also had decided not to enter the building until backup arrived. He orders the two young women to step away and take shelter behind the police car.

The very second that Gene walked around the north side of the building, he comes face to face with three of the mysterious shadow people he had seen before. They then quickly squat down behind the alley trashcans. Not knowing for sure who they were, he immediately investigates their location. Walking over to them he demands to know who they were and why they were there?

Meanwhile, George begins to move around the south side of the build to check for anyone hiding there. Just as he does that he sees Gene running to his location yelling for him to hit the ground. Instantly doing what he heard Gene yell, he falls to the ground just as three young men come out from behind a large utility poll and begin shooting at them. Both officers immediately return fire, striking all three youths and dropping them where they stood. As this happens the two girls instantly run away.

Shocked to know he was only seconds from death he is seriously grateful that Gene appeared and saw the attackers. As they cautiously approach the three men on the ground, two more police cars arrive and immediately converge around them. One of the three men was dead, and two were seriously injured. Two officers then place handcuffs on all three men, Gene calls for an ambulance. Within a few minutes the ambulances arrives and hauls the two injured men away. Meanwhile, the Los Angeles County Coroner was on the scene and investigating the one death.

Both George and Gene are beside their police car waiting for their debriefing from a superior. As they wait, George looks at Gene and says, "Well, if I had any concern about you covering my back, I sure have none now. Thanks for saving my life partner."

Gene smiles and starts to respond to George's thanks, when two Los Angeles investigators from Internal Affairs Division arrive to question them. The two officers are immediately separated and vigorously questioned about what had happened. Also as their questioning begins, George and Gene's sergeant arrives and acts as a defense for his men. He tells George and Gene that until a decision was rendered that they should return to the police station and wait for further orders. Upon being released by the IAD detectives, the two men get in their police cruiser and start the drive back to police headquarters.

George and Gene sit silently for a few minutes as they head away. George then turns to Gene and asks, "How was it you saw those guys when I couldn't? Don't get me wrong, because I am grateful. But, I am wondering why I didn't see them? But again thank God you did."

Gene does not respond immediately. His mind is wondering about who's bullet killed the young man. He knows that he did fire his weapon at the man. And, if he is the one who killed him, he would like to know that fact. Obviously, they had no choice as those two women had obviously set them up for those three men, who were out to kill cops. But, it is still something he wanted to know. He then looks at George and says, "Yes George, you can thank God, because he is the one that saved you, not me.

I know what I am going to say will spook you, but you need to know the truth. The fact is, when I started to inspect the north side of that building, I immediately saw those shadow people again, hiding behind the building's trashcans. Thinking at first that maybe they were gang members, I chased after them. When I found them hunkering down behind the trashcans, I asked them who they were and what they were there for."

George looks at Gene as he is talking and immediately interrupts him and asks, "Are you joking with me?"

Gene quickly responds and asks, "Do you want to hear the truth or not?"

George is grateful to Gene and realizes that he is being rude and needed to hear what Gene has to say. He quietly says, "Yes, please continue."

"When I first encountered the three shadow people, I immediately could tell that they were not gang members and it was equally as obvious they were not flesh and blood entities either. In fact, I was immediately scared by their presence, but I still knew I had to confront them. This was the third time I had encountered them, and I wanted to face my demons, so to speak. Anyway, to my surprise one stood up and said that I need to immediately go to your aid as three gang members were hiding and waiting to lure you into that alley so they could gun you down. They told me to go immediately. I turned away for just an instant to look at the two young women behind the car, when I turned back the three shadow people were gone. Not waiting or looking for them, I ran to your side of the building and told you to hit the ground. That's when the three gang bangers came out from behind the utility polls and began shooting. My gun was already out and I began shooting at them the second I yelled at you. So, say what you want, but those shadow people saved your life and maybe mine too."

George is in shock and doesn't speak for a long time. He is even having difficulty driving the car. As they pull into the police parking garage he parks, turns off the engine and says, "Gene, please wait. This is more than I can accept. I do not doubt you. But, how can shadow people be waiting around for you? What logic is it that such things would follow us and do what you say they did? Policemen have encountered bad-guys for centuries and no one has ever had the aid of shadow people. How can you explain it?"

Gene too is serious, and turns to respond to George. He waits a few seconds and then says, "What makes you think those shadow people were not close to all of those other lawmen fighting bad guys? Not seeing them didn't mean they weren't there. Have you ever heard the term, Guardian

Angels? I can't say for sure, but maybe that is what they are and I am able to see them? Otherwise, I have no other explanation for their appearance."

George takes the keys out of the car, opens the door and gets out. As he walks towards the station, he turns back to look at Gene and says, "I am totally blown away. What you are saying is certainly an explanation, but can it really be true? If it is, then my take on this world is totally screwed up. And, if you are right, maybe it was one of them that called me that night you were shot. Maybe they gave me the warning to go to the hospital? "

Gene smiles and says, "Yes, maybe they did call you. But, now, nothing surprises me. Because when we first ran across the spirit of Mr. Balsam in his truck, that changed my thinking right then and there about everything in this world. This latest sighting is just one more piece of evidence that there is so much more to life and death that we know nothing about. And, I am sure there is still a lot more for us to learn."

The two continue walking into the building where they are separated and placed into interrogation rooms, waiting to speak further to IAD investigators. As each man sits quietly waiting, they search their own beliefs. For Gene, he is becoming a big believer in life after death, angels and likely other non-godly entities. For George, he has always been strong and never let religion or God enter into his thought process. Yet, he now wonders if there was any truth at all to what Gene says he encountered? There was no denying that Gene's warning saved his life this night. Could that just be good luck or was something more biblical responsible?

Within two hours, the two men are cleared and are informed that the shootings were justified as they would have definitely been victims themselves if they had not reacted as quickly as they did. They are congratulated for their quick reaction to a deadly situation. And, as the two men are about to leave the station, their Captain shakes each man's hand and says, "You are either the two luckiest men I have ever known, or something special from above was watching over you guys tonight."

Smiling at their Captain, the two men leave the station without any further discussions between them.

The following morning they both receive calls and instructions from the personnel department to visit the department's psychologist, indicating such a meeting was mandatory after a shooting where deadly force occurs. And, they would not be allowed to return to active duty until they had completed the appointment. For George, this would be his second visit, as he had to do the same thing after Gene was shot.

Gene was scheduled first, which as luck would have it, was with Dr. Allen. Upon entering her office and explaining what happened, she is totally shocked. She was not expecting to hear anything like what Gene claims happened. She was briefed on the shooting, but his seeing the shadow people was more than her training had prepared her for. Taking it all in, she decides to think about it. And to aid her in that process, she begins her discussion with Gene by determining what his current state of mind was over the shadow people and the killing of the young man. And, in his opinion, was he able to return to work? Or, was he likely going to freeze and not be able to defend himself if another deadly confrontation occurred? After an hour, she does detect some concern and the grief over his killing the man, but it did not appear to be something he could not deal with. As they talk, Gene asks Dr. Allen what she knew about shadow people.

Dr. Allen knows that she isn't knowledgeable enough to explain what he said he saw. Yet, given his comments about what happened, she has to believe him. Yet, that didn't help her at all to explain any of it. She looks at him and says, "Mr. Wilson, what you have told me is short of a miracle if it is true. I do not doubt you, but I cannot explain it nor am I prepared to discuss it with you right now. Let's save that topic for later. Meanwhile, I need to give you some tests and then when the results come in, I will know more. And, when we next meet, maybe I will have some better information and ideas to share with you. Meanwhile, I think you are fine to go back to work, just be careful."

The next evening Gene is sitting in the police station briefing room waiting for George. As he sits there he wonders what this evening will bring. Might there be more encounters with the shadow people? Can he truly believe they are there to help him? What if instead of being angels, they are evil. Maybe all their past kindness was just a ruse to fool him. Maybe all they really want to do is harm him and George. It is all just too much to try and deal with. As he begins to realize the many questions that are possible and need resolving.

George then arrives and walks over to Gene and says, "Come on partner, let's roll. I hate those IAD people and those shrink questions stink. It is as if we are the bad guys. What about our rights? Do we have none? I need to get out of here and start patrolling so I can clear my head and feel like a useful police officer again."

Gene stands up and follows George without saying a word. Taking his normal place in the squad car, they buckle up while George starts the vehicle and pulls out into traffic. The two ride along quietly for a while when after about ten minutes, George says, "I am having a real problem trying to come to grips with your comments about those shadow people and how they told you about the hiding gang bangers that were waiting to shoot me. I know what you said and that you firmly believe it, but I just cannot accept it. So, please Gene, let's talk about anything else tonight, but not shadow people, is that all right with you?

Knowing how George feels, Gene understands and frankly wouldn't know how to explain their presence anyway. And, given the fact he isn't completely sure they are good or bad, he would rather not discuss them either. He responds to George by saying, "George, I agree. Since I can't prove their existence to myself, I sure can't do it for you. So, yes, let's just patrol and keep the conversation to things we both know are true."

The night passes quietly without any incidents. Stopping only three times to ticket routine traffic violators, eat dinner, they end their shift and are both home by 1:00 am.

Entering his home, Gene sees that the message light on his phone was blinking. Checking his messages, there is one call from Amelia wanting to get together for dinner and one from Dr. Allen asking him to meet her in her office tomorrow morning at 11:00 am, in order to discuss some information she has found after his recent visit with her.

Gene is tired, confused, worried and totally afraid of what is happening to him. He is anxious to visit Dr. Allen to hopefully get some answers. Rising early the next day, he quickly cleans his apartment and then dresses for his meeting. Gene drives to the hospital, gets out and begins walking through the hospital heading for Dr. Allen's office. As he does that, he passes the Intensive Care Unit where he had spent so much time and is mysteriously drawn to the sight of a young woman asleep in there who is also hooked to several monitors and fluid bags. As he begins to leave, he then hears her call his name and ask for him to wait. Looking back, she now has her eyes open and is sitting up and looking directly at him. Startled that she would know his name, he stops and watches as she calls to him again. Standing there he looks at her and responds by saying, "Yes, what is it, what do you need?"

The young woman says, "I am confused, I don't know why I am in here, and I don't remember my name. Can you help me Officer Wilson?"

Looking at her he responds by saying "Yes, I'll see what I can do for you?"

Still looking at him she says, "Oh thank you. I don't know why, but when you passed by I sensed you were a good man and would know what to do. I most desperately need to know what has happened to me and why I am here. I would also like to know who I am," explains the young woman.

"Ok, I will go see what I can find out about you and I will come right back and tell you what I discover." Gene then departs and starts to look for a nurse. After a few minutes he spots the unit's head nurse sitting at a desk reviewing her reports. He immediately recalls her as one of the people who helped him when he too was in that unit. Stopping her, he reintroduces himself to her, causing her to instantly smile at seeing how well he appeared to be.

"Wow, it is good to see you Gene. I am very happy to know that you have recovered so well, "says Nurse Hansen.

"Yes, I feel pretty good. There are some occasions where I feel a bit tired or even sluggish, but overall I am doing well. Say, I was wondering about the condition of the young lady back in the ICU? She seems very confused and asked me to see if you could tell her why she is there and even what her name is," asks Gene.

Looking quite strangely at him, she says, "Are you referring to the young blond woman in ICU? What do you mean she asked you why she is there? Are you saying she is awake? As she asks that question, she instantly turns and runs towards ICU.

Gene Follows directly behind her. Arriving at the unit, the young woman is not only asleep, but Nurse Hansen tells him that she is in a coma and believed to be brain dead.

Gene turns to the nurse and says, "That can't be so, because I spoke to her just minutes ago. She was awake, sitting up and very lucid. She couldn't remember her name or how she got here, so she asked me to seek out someone who could help her. I know what I saw," says Gene.

Looking at him, Nurse Hansen says, "There is no way you spoke to this girl. She has been here for over 5 days, and she has been tested very thoroughly and our doctors say she is definitely clinically brain dead. They are currently awaiting the arrival of some relative from Texas who will determine when we turn off her respirator."

Knowing what he experienced he has no way to contradict what he was told, but he knows she is not brain dead as he definitely spoke to her. Looking at the nurse he asks, "So, what happened to her and what is her name?"

Nurse Hansen looks at him and says, "Well she was involved in a traffic accident in Wilmington. A drunk driver ran the car she was in off the road and down into a drainage ditch. She was a passenger and went head first through the windshield. Also the driver died on the scene. That is about all I know. Her name is Nancy Wainwright." She then explains that she is busy but says again how happy she was that he looked so good. She then turns and departs the unit.

Standing there he stares at Nancy. How could he have conversed with her? If she truly is in a coma and brain dead, what did he experience? Is there any way they connected mentally? But if that was so, her brain couldn't be dead. What if they are wrong? Looking at her he asks out loud, "Nancy, can you hear me?"

Receiving no response, he turns and begins heading towards Dr. Allen's office. As he begins to leave, once more the young woman calls out his name. Stopping and returning to ICU, she is awake and calling out to him. Excited he rushes back and responds. Looking at her through the large window he tells her, her name and what had happened to her.

Seemingly relieved, the young woman smiles and says, "Oh thank you sir. I don't recall any of it, but it is a relief to know the truth. And, I am happy to know my name. You are a kind man." She then closes her eyes and falls fast asleep.

Gene watches her for a few moments then turns and begins looking for Dr. Allen's office. Finding her office he enters and speaks to her receptionist. Being aware of his appointment with Dr. Allen, the receptionist, Rita James explains that Dr Allen was out, but would be right back. And, as he sits down to wait, in walks Dr. Allen, as she eagerly greets him.

"Hello Mr. Wilson, you look really good. I am happy you got my message and was able to come in," comments the doctor.

"Well to be honest Dr. Allen the timing is good, that is because since I left here strange things have been occurring with me on the job that causes me to wonder about stuff, and I would really like to tell you about it," explains Gene.

"Sure, come on in and let's talk," says the doctor.

Gene jumps right in and quickly explains everything to her again, including the strange people he still sees and the various warnings he continues to experience from them. He also mentions the young woman named Nancy that he just ran in to in the ICU.

The doctor listens intently, but isn't sure what to say. After a few moments she says, "Mr. Wilson, there are definitely a lot of things in this world that we psychologists do not fully understand. And one of those things is how the average human brain works. Surprisingly, as I explained to you before, the average human uses only a very small percentage of their brain's capacity. The likely reason for that is if a person was able to use more, life as we know it here, would basically seem real boring and likely not worth the trouble. So, I now think it is possible that when you were shot, the bullet stimulated a new portion of your brain which had not been used before. I cannot say for sure, but you may now have abilities and senses that were dormant before. The reason I wanted to see you to day was to ask if you would be interested in visiting with a colleague of mine, named Dr. Samuel Mendenhall, who specializes in ESP and other special psychic phenomenon activities that the majority of us simply do not understand. In any case, I think meeting him would help you a lot. And, I think he will be out here for a seminar next month. If he is, let me arrange a meeting between you two here in my office."

Gene listens with interest and agrees that he wants to know what is wrong with him. He then says, "Yes I would really like that. Please do set me up. But, will he be more conclusive in his diagnosis than those doctors were at UCLA? After taking all those tests, they still couldn't tell me anything for sure."

He is told by Dr. Allen that Dr. Mendenhall is an expert and she was sure he could help him. She then says that he would be contacted in about a week to schedule the appointment.

Upon departing Dr. Allen's office Gene again walks past the ICU and is surprised to see the young woman he had been talking with was no longer in there. When he reached the nurses station, he asks about her and is told she had been removed. Upon more questioning he learns she had in fact died only moments earlier and was taken down to the hospital's morgue.

Wondering what really happened, he thinks she couldn't be dead, because as he spoke to her, she seemed fine. But, he wonders if maybe he didn't really talk with her at all, but instead he somehow was able to communicate with her mentally. Maybe he really didn't physically speak to her, but heard in his head what she wanted to know? He is baffled and even more confused now than ever before. What is happening to him? Is he somehow different after being shot in the head? Might Dr. Allen be right? Is he now using a different part of his brain? If so, what will become of him? How can he work effectively as a policeman? How can he assure his partner he is capable of performing his duties and assist him when it is necessary? Might his brain just be wondering off into who knows where? Maybe the people he sees are not really there at all, but just an image coming from his brain?

Approaching his car he begins to unlock it in order to get in and head home. However, before getting in he hears his name called. Turning around, there behind him, stands the young blond woman. She is now fully dressed and appears completely healed. She is definitely not dead, as the nurse reported.

"Hello sir," I wanted to thank you again for your help. When you told me what happened and my name, I felt better almost instantly. However, I am somewhat confused right now as I don't know why I am dressed and out here. I do not seem to have any injuries, but if I was in the hospital, I must have been hurt somewhere. Also, I feel kind of lost."

Gene looks at the woman in wonderment. He knows inside they all said she died, yet here she is right in front of him. And inside she had a head bandage, but now she is fully healed. Might she be a spirit? He wants to touch her but is afraid to do so.

As he looks at her, a blank look comes over her face. She smiles and begins to turn away from him, just as if he wasn't talking to her. Watching her, she begins walking towards the hospital entrance, when suddenly, right in front of him she slowly vanishes into thin air.

Completely mystified, Gene just keeps staring at the spot where she disappeared from, completely unable to believe his own eyes, while still wondering if she might reappear. However, after a few minutes with nothing happening, he opens his car door, gets in, and begins driving towards his apartment. As he goes along, he cannot begin to explain to himself what occurred this day. Did he see and interact with a genuine ghost? Did he actually communicate with the woman as she lay in her bed in the ICU, dying? He knows both times that he saw something and communicated with it, but what was it really? He knows that no one would believe what he saw and experienced, not even Dr. Allen. So, how can he begin to understand it?

Arriving at his home he notes the time and figures he has about four hours before he is on duty. He therefore decides to stretch out on his bed and try and catch a short nap. As he sleeps, his mind mulls over the activities of the day. Yet, even asleep he cannot make any sense of it. As he sleeps, the face of the mysterious woman continues to persist in his mind.

Eventually waking up, he is sweating profusely and realizes how disoriented he felt. He assumes the constant dreaming of the woman was what was causing his uncomfortable condition. Noting the time, he gets up, showers, shaves and dresses for work.

Arriving at the police station about twenty minutes early, he changes his clothes and relaxes with a cup of coffee, before meeting his partner for their evening patrolling activities.

Soon George is looking for him and upon finding Gene, motions him over to join him as he too is ready to begin work. In their cruiser George asks Gene how his day went and did he visit with Dr. Allen?

Responding yes, he tells George how she has set another meeting, but this time with a different specialist that she personally knows and feels will be able to help him. Gene says how much he is looking forward to meeting this new man. He also briefly mentions to George how she now does believe that the gunshot wound he received has slightly altered his brain's thought process.

Upon hearing all of that George tells Gene how he too was anxious to hear more once he meets the specialist.

The evening progresses without any calls or incidents. Soon they break for their dinner and upon returning to their vehicle, almost immediately receive a call about a two vehicle accident in the Wilmington area. Proceeding with lights and siren, upon arrival they are the first unit on the scene and immediately must secure the area and keep on-lookers back. They could immediately see where one vehicle was run off of the road by another. Upon a quick review it was noted the driver of that vehicle was drunk. Both vehicles were badly damaged and its occupants were injured. George looks over the first vehicle while Gene walks down the embankment where the second vehicle came to rest. He immediately sees the driver that was behind the wheel had a head injury and was bleeding profusely from the impact with the windshield. However, the passenger apparently did not have her seat belt on, as she was thrown through the windshield and was partially lying on the vehicles hood. As Gene approaches her and checks her vital signs he looks in the woman's face and is instantly shocked to recognize her as the woman from the ICU, who he had encountered earlier in the day. Jumping back, he cannot believe his eyes. Was this morning simply a preview of what was to latter occur? Using his radio he instantly calls up to George to inform him of his discovery and the need for multiple ambulances. As he waited, he feared for the two occupant's lives and decided it was best not to touch or move either one of them. He does see the woman's purse in the vehicle's back seat and removes it in order to establish her identity.

He slowly opens her purse and takes out her wallet. There it was, her driver's license with the name showing Nancy Wainwright. And there was no doubt that the picture he is looking at is the very same woman he encountered earlier that day in the hospital. How can any of this be real? How could there be two accidents occurring the exact same way with two identical woman with the same name? It was impossible.

Two hours later as their shift was about to end, the two men are back in their vehicle heading towards the police station. They are both quiet as the gruesome sight of the accident affected them both. Pulling into the station they exit the vehicle, and go inside to complete their reports.

Later that evening as Gene arrives home; he first checks his phone messages, and hears a call from Amelia, asking why she had not heard from him. Considering the lateness of the hour he decides to call her in the morning. Taking off his clothes he goes directly to bed. Laying there, his mind races wildly as he sees the images of the day's events unfolding. How could this woman he just saw look and have the same name as the person he encountered earlier in the hospital? How could her injuries be exactly the same, and inflicted in the same location as the first Nancy? It just wasn't probable that such a scenario could happen. Yet, it has.

Waking up at 10:00 am, Gene finds his bedding once again pulled off of him and lying in a pile at the foot of his bed. Realizing he had to do something to find out what was happening he decides to once again visit Dr. Allen in the hospital and seek her advice. He was also interested in the condition of the second Nancy. Therefore he decides to visit her too and verify her condition. Hopefully, he could find the same nurse he spoke to yesterday and see what she thought about this new patient. Dressing quickly, Gene departs for the hospital.

Entering the hospital, he quickly goes to the ICU, where he sees Nancy # 2, laying in the same bed as Nancy #1 was in yesterday. In fact, her head injuries even looked the same as the one yesterday. Bewildered he waits a moment before seeking out the nurse to see what this Nancy's prognosis was. Gene wonders if maybe this Nancy would also communicate with him in the same manner as the first Nancy did. However, when she does not, he turns around and goes to the nurse's station. There, he encounters a different nurse. Introducing himself he explains how he and his partner found the young woman last night and how he was interested in her condition.

The nurse explained that she was in very serious condition and was in a coma. She also said several neurosurgeons were scheduled to see her that day and they would know more after that.

Gene then comments to the nurse on the similarity of this woman's injuries and the Nancy who he encountered yesterday.

To Gene's amazement, the nurse says, "Sir, I am confused. We have not had anyone in ICU for over a week. We definitely didn't have anyone die in there yesterday. I fear you are mistaken."

"What? I was here myself yesterday and saw her. In fact, when I spoke to nurse Lana Hansen about her, she said the woman was brain dead," explains Gene.

Looking even more puzzled now at his comments, the nurse says, "Sir, Nurse Hansen has not worked here for over two months. So, there is no way you could have seen her in here yesterday, as she moved to Colorado. And, to my knowledge, no one has even heard from her since she left."

Now totally bewildered, all Gene can say is, "Wow, I guess I am hallucinating or something. But, thanks for your help." He then turns and makes a bee-line for Dr. Allen's office. Entering her office the same receptionist, Ms. James, is there.

"Hello Mr. Wilson, I am surprised to see you here again so soon. Is there any problem," she asks?

Looking at her, he is almost afraid to ask, but he knows that he must. Working up his courage he inquires, "Was I in here yesterday and did I see Dr. Allen?"

Smiling at him, the woman cocks her head to one side and says, "Yes to both questions, why are you asking?"

"Is Dr. Allen in? I really need to speak to her, it is very important," he asks?

"Yes she is, but she is currently with a patient. If you wish to wait, maybe she can see you before her lunch appointment," says the woman.

Gene has to only wait a few minutes when the door opens and Dr. Allen and a man exit. She shakes his hand as he leaves and says he would see her again next week. Turning to see Gene, she comments how surprised she was to see him and asks what he needed?

Standing up and approaching her, Gene says, "I really need to see you right now Doctor. I think I am having a nervous breakdown and I fear if I can't talk to someone about it right now, I will explode."

Opening her door she says, "Sure, come on in." Sitting down she invites Gene to tell her what was bothering him.

He begins by telling her about the woman he saw in ICU just before coming to her office yesterday. Then about her being gone when he left her office. He then explains how he talked to Nurse Hansen yesterday and how she said the woman was brain dead and had in fact died while he was in her office. He then proceeds to describe the ghostly image that approached him in the parking lot to thank him for getting her name and telling her why she was there. He then explains how she just turned away and disappeared. He follows that up with describing in complete detail how he and his partner were called to the traffic accident last night and discovered the exact same woman who was now in ICU with the exact same name and injuries. He ends his discussion by explaining his current conversation with the nurse on duty, and how she said Nurse Hansen, who he spoke to yesterday was not here yesterday and that she has been gone from this hospital for over two months.

Dr. Allen looks at Gene and says, "That is one Hell of a story. I do recall the conversation yesterday about your communicating with the ICU victim. But, I never looked for myself to see what or if she was really there or not. But, I can guaranty you that Nurse Hansen was not here yesterday, and did leave a couple of months ago. What very few people around here do not know is that three weeks ago she too was killed in a head-on traffic accident in Denver. Nothing was reported to our staff because she left here under strange circumstances. Apparently the hospital had numerous complaints from patients and their relatives about her lack of professional care. And, she and the nurses working under her never got along very well. So, management felt it best to not tell the employees of her death. But what you are telling me is extraordinary. The only thing I can say or suggest is that somehow when you walked past that empty ICU yesterday, you had some type of a mental telepathy event occur. Your mind sensed something and it conjured up this accident victim, who was someone you had never met before. It is extraordinary, for sure. What I would like to do tonight is contact my associate, Dr. Mendenhall, the person I want you to meet. I will tell him everything you have said here yesterday and today. Maybe I can get some advice from him, or better yet, maybe he will make a special trip out here to meet and talk with you."

"Dr. Allen, is it possible that I am crazy? Is it safe for me to be working as a policeman? I fear something serious might happen and I will not be able to control my self. What should I do," asks Gene?

"That worries me too. To be honest I have no helpful answer for you, because what you are experiencing is way over my educational level. If everything you say really happened, you are breaking new ground and experiencing things I have never heard or read about before. But, maybe for your own safety and those working with you, I should recommend more therapy and get you placed on administrative leave? Otherwise, I fear for your safety, that is for sure," explains the doctor.

"Yes, I too agree with that. I know my partner is worried over my recent actions and I think he fears I am not up to the task of backing him up. But, I don't want anyone at the station to hear about what I just told you, as those guys will definitely think I am completely nuts," explains Gene.

Smiling, Dr. Allen says, "I will inform your Captain that in my opinion you need time off of patrol to get more rested, as I found you to be working too hard and given your brain injury, it has proven to be too soon for you to return to daily patrol work. That is all anyone needs to know. Does that sound Ok to you?"

Shaking his head affirmatively Gene says, that will be fine. Yet, I do not want anyone to think I am not capable of making a full recovery. Everyone at the station likes to talk and rumors about me are bound to surface."

Dr. Allen sits down and writes out a note, signs it and hands it to Gene. She says, "This will do the trick. And, it is vague enough that no one will take anything from it. I have simply said that your injury is not healing as rapidly as we had hoped and you still need at least thirty more days of light duty. So, with that, maybe they can find you something inside to do that won't cause you to be out on patrol. Then, once my colleague sees you, we can decide after that what is best for you. I will call you tomorrow after I speak to him tonight. I'll let you know when he can see you."

"Do you think there is anything wrong with me? What could possibly cause me to experience something like what just happened? I am scared and worry that I am going crazy. It is a terrible feeling and I really must know what is wrong with me. Please help me to find the answer, please," begs Gene.

"We will get to the bottom of it Mr. Wilson, I promise you that," says Dr. Allen.

Taking the note, Gene leaves the doctors office and walks out of the hospital, stopping for moments to look at the woman in ICU. Pausing, he marvels at how much she looked like the first Nancy. What was happening to him? Was she really only something he conjured up in his mind yesterday and was never actually there? Was it somehow just a glimpse into the pending accident of last night? How did he conjure up Nurse Hansen?

He doesn't know what to think, but knows something in his brain wasn't right. Continuing on outside to his vehicle, before entering he hesitates and looks around, kind of wondering if he would see this new woman's spirit? When nothing appears after a few minutes he gets in his vehicle and drives home.

Arriving at his apartment, he goes inside and calls his partner George to let him know that he will be unable to join him on patrol for awhile. He explains how the doctor wants him to remain on light duty until the other doctor can assess his progress and get to the bottom of the visions he has experienced.

George listens and says, "Gene, I think that is good advice. To be honest, I have worried about you too, and given all the strange things you claimed to have seen, I feared you returned back here to quickly. Don't worry, I'll find another temporary replacement while you concentrate on getting well. Then, when you are better, everything will be as it was and we can partner again. The two then chat about non police issues and eventually end the conversation with George telling Gene that he would see him later at the station.

Later that night Gene gives his Captain his note. Upon reading it, he advises the Watch Commander, who places Gene on desk duty at the station. The work load would be light, basically consisting of answering the phone and filling out reports. He is also assigned to front desk duties for walk-ins and must be available to facilitate answering citizen questions.

The first night passes quickly and without any distractions or problems. The shift ends and Gene heads home. Upon entering his apartment, he checks his messages and finds one from Dr. Allen, who says her colleague, Dr. Mendenhall is very anxious to meet with him and perform some physiological tests to see what is going on. She asks for him to call her in the morning as he will be here in two days. Also, a second message from Amelia was there and he realizes he had not called her as he planned. Gene knows she is anxious to know what he is doing, but had no idea about his current experiences. He promises himself that he will most definitely call her in the morning at the college.

Excited at hearing Dr. Allen's comments, Gene jots down the number she left and then goes to bed. Laying there he wonders what the second doctor will say about his stories. Will he believe him? And, if so, what would he do? Or, might he just think he is a phony or maybe crazy. Tossing and turning, sleep eventually occurs and once it does he doesn't wake up until almost 11:00 am.

Remembering the need to call Amelia, he places a call to her first. Finding her to be in a meeting he leaves a message. He then places his second call to Dr. Allen's office. Speaking directly to her, she tells him Dr. Mendenhall will be in town in two days and wants to spend as much time with him as possible. Since Gene was normally off work on that day, an appointment is scheduled and everyone agrees that they will meet at her office at 1:00 pm in two days.

After hanging up, the phone rings and it is Amelia. She sounds worried and angry at the same time that he had not called her. Gene tells Amelia that bazaar and unnatural things were happening to him and he had been placed on light duty. She expresses her concern and asks to see him.

Knowing how his mind was, he prefers not to see her until his meeting with Dr. Mendenhall was over. He explains how his head was so twisted, he really was poor company for any one, let alone her.

Verbally disagreeing, Amelia knows it was no use to try and convince Gene otherwise, so she makes him promise to call her after his meeting with Dr. Mendenhall.

For the next two days, Gene patiently waits. Working one shift, he is off on the second day. At home he eagerly waits for his 1:00 pm appointment with Dr. Mendenhall.

As he dresses, he wonders what this new day will produce. Is he going to know something new or is this second doctor just going to treat him like an experiment? Will he truly be able to diagnosis his condition?

Arriving at the hospital early, Gene first goes to look into the ICU to check on Nancy # 2. Seeing her still there and still asleep, he wonders what her condition was. Standing there he watches as she sleeps and waits to see if she will mentally communicate with him. However, after several minutes, he sees nothing and heads on over to Dr. Allen's office. Inside, he is greeted by the office receptionist. Smiling at him, she asks Gene to please sit and wait, as both Dr. Allen and Dr. Mendenhall are together in her office going over his files. Within ten minutes her door opens and Gene is invited in. Dr. Allen introduces him to Dr. Mendenhall. A tall thin man in his early sixties, with thick gray hair, supporting a nicely groomed silver goatee, Dr. Mendenhall looks very much like a psychiatrist, and for some reason Gene feels immediately comfortable in his presence.

"Please Mr. Wilson sit down and make yourself comfortable. My colleague here has been telling me some very fascinating facts about you, your injury and subsequent strange encounters. So, please, if you wouldn't mind, in your own account, could you tell me everything that has happened since your injury, and please, do not omit anything," asks Dr. Mendenhall? As he says that he takes out a small recorder and turns it on, and picks up a large tablet to write on.

Settling into the doctor's easy chair, Gene makes himself comfortable and then starts at the very beginning, including a complete description of all of the strange dreams he had while he was in the ICU. He describes in detail his vision of Hell and Heaven. He also discusses watching himself die in a convalescent hospital with people walking past him and ignoring his obvious distressed condition. He continues with talking about the man he and his partner first encountered inside his truck, which later proved to be a paranormal event. Then, upon returning back to work after the gun shot, the strange dark figures hiding in the surrounding bushes. He recounts his warnings he got from those figures about saving his partner George's life as the gang bangers lay in wait for him. He concludes with the most bazaar of all, the encounter he had with the first Nancy and Nurse Hansen, who was apparently not only long gone from the hospital, but recently deceased as well. He explains in detail how Nancy # 1's ghostly image appeared to him in the parking lot and how she thanked him. Then, he describes how she just dissolved into thin air.

During all of this Dr. Mendenhall says nothing but takes careful notes and checks his recorder a few times to be sure it was working properly.

Gene concludes his story by explaining how he and his partner were called to a traffic accident in the exact place where Nancy #1 was said to have had her accident. He describes seeing her and the driver and how the crash was identical to what Nurse Hansen said happened to Nancy #1. Then, as he investigates the grizzly scene, he explains how he sees it is the exact same woman he thought he saw in the hospital the day before. He explains how he checked her identity, and found her to have the exact same name as the woman he encountered before.

Sitting quietly after hearing everything Dr Mendenhall is writing furiously and doesn't speak for several moments. He than looks up, smiles and says, "Wow that is quite a story and very interesting. What I would like to do next is perform a series of tests on you to see how your extra sensory perception is working. Is that Ok with you?"

Gene nods in agreement and asks, "Are you referring to ESP? I never have considered myself a Medium or a Psychic in any way before doctor. Is that what you think is happening to me?"

Smiling Dr. Mendenhall says, "Well, in order to eliminate various ideas we need to perform some tests. One is to have you guess what I am hiding behind a solid screen. So, let me try a few tests and I can eliminate items as we test them."

The doctor then asks Gene to wait while he sets up everything. He opens several bags and extracts items. He eventually says he is ready to begin. The first thing he does is to draw something on a small chalk board, while being sure that Gene does not see what he drew. He then holds up the board, with the drawing facing the doctor and away from Gene. He then asks Gene if he could describe what he drew on the board.

Closing his eyes, Gene thinks for a few moments. He then opens his eyes and says, "I believe that you have drawn the shape of a skeleton key."

Completely startled, Dr. Mendenhall turns the board around and shows both Gene and Dr. Allen that yes indeed that was exactly what he had drawn. Everyone is shocked. However, not sure if maybe somehow Gene might have seen what he drew, he gets up goes into the receptionist area. He returns and once again asks Gene to describe what was now on the other side of the chalk board.

Again Gene closes his eyes and after a few seconds, opens them and says, "You have drawn a tree, with a lot of foliage."

Dumbfounded, Dr. Mendenhall shows them the drawing of a tree, which indeed had a lot of foliage. Everyone looks at each other with a shocked look on their faces. Dr Mendenhall performs eight more tests and each time Gene correctly states what was drawn on the chalk board. That series of tests is followed by another that requires Gene to identify pictures on placards that were prepared in advance by the doctor. These pictures ranged from images of kids playing in sandboxes to mountains and other picturesque locations all around the world. Out of ten photos, Gene correctly identifies seven.

Upon completing the tests, Gene looks at Dr. Mendenhall and asks, "Doctor, what does it all mean? Can you deduce anything from these tests that might explain my strange encounters?"

Putting his tests and equipment away, Dr Mendenhall looks at both Gene and Dr. Allen and says, "Without a doubt the gunshot wound you sustained has caused something in your brain to awaken which has enhanced your psychic and mental awareness, which allows you to see things and images that are not visible to most other people. There are several other tests I would like to perform. However, they are more difficult, but they will allow me to assess exactly to what degree your psychic powers have developed to. And, if the results are favorable, it might lead me to knowing exactly what area of the brain is being stimulated. Earlier today, I viewed the x-rays that were taken when you were first admitted to this hospital. And, from where your injury was, I would not have anticipated anything like this occurring. It was a simple head injury and your recovery should have been without any side affects. But, obviously, something was disturbed and I am seriously curious to find out what that was. The added tests are not with me today, and I doubt that you would care to travel to my office to allow me to perform them. With that being said, let me first assure you that you are not crazy in any way. I know you feared that was possible. Also, what you are experiencing could be temporary or it could be a permanent event. I just don't know and I do not think there are any tests that I could give you that can determine how long this phenomenon may last. Let me also say, I would greatly appreciate it if we could all stay in touch with one another and when I am next in this area, I would like to see you and I will bring those more detailed tests with me. Maybe then we can figure out exactly what has happened. Would that be acceptable to you?"

Gene smiles at him and says, "I truly appreciate what you have done today and explained to me. It is a relief to know I am not nuts and something physical is allowing me to experience these things I am enduring. I can at least cope with it better now, knowing that I am not crazy. And, yes, I will make myself available to you when and wherever you want."

Departing Dr. Allen's office, Gene feels so much better and knows that Dr. Mendenhall can and will help him. Happy, Gene is suddenly very anxious to share his good news with Amelia.

CHAPTER 5; *The Truth about The Shadow People Surfaces*

Adjusting his mind to the fact that not everything he will see or experience is seen by others, he tries to reconcile his life as a police officer accordingly. Within three weeks after his session with Dr. Mendenhall he is back on patrol with his old partner George. He also signs up for and begins attending his final law class at Long Beach College. He and Amelia have moved in together and life is good. For two months all goes well and nothing unusual occurs to cause him to worry about his special and unique gifts.

Patrolling late one March evening the two men discuss Gene's completion of his law courses and his plans of someday becoming a lawyer. George asks him what his timetable is and what he was doing about finding a law firm to work for once he passed the bar?

Gene confides in George and says, "I haven't really thought about all of that yet. I guess I need to, but I do enjoy this work so much, I fear I will miss it if I leave. Plus, Amelia and I are talking about marriage. So, a good paycheck is really important right now."

Hearing the marriage comment, George says, "Look partner, I know I am no example of what marriage should be for a cop, because I have done it twice and neither one worked out. You have to know, this business has its drawbacks. Late hours, the physical risk we endure and the grizzly things we see every day makes it hard to go home every night and be a loving spouse. It is very hard on a marriage. So, please understand that. On the other hand, being a lawyer might make it all a lot simpler and provide for a better foundation to build a family around."

Gene knows George is right and all of that has weighed heavily on his overall thoughts about marriage. He responds to George's comments by saying, "Yes, I know all that, and you are right for sure. Having a normal 9 to 5 job and going home with a positive attitude every day, plus having weekends off would definitely improve our chances for success, that is for sure."

While talking they receive a call to proceed to an address where a 911 caller said some type of disturbance was occurring. The caller's message was said to be vague, making the actual events sketchy. They are warned to proceed with caution. As they begin to respond, Gene realizes the address given was either close to, or the same one where he went when he met Mrs. Gloria Ramos who was the lady that had experienced the San Pedro haunting. Curious as to what they would encounter, he says nothing to George, as they quickly proceed to the address.

Pulling up and stopping at the home, they immediately see the place was quiet and dark inside, leading them to wonder if the address given was correct, or if it was just a prank call.

Gene looks around and realizes that this indeed was Mrs. Ramos's home, where he visited her and discussed her former haunting experiences. Knowing they had to at least check it out, to be sure no one was in danger, they exit their vehicle and slowly approach the front door. Then, as they are about twenty feet away, the lights inside suddenly flash on and off about ten times, as if someone was inside playing with the light switch. George knocks on the door, and announces that it was the Los Angeles Police. No one immediately answers. Then, from inside voices are heard as the lights once again go through a series of flashes. Again they knock and demand that someone open the door. As they say that, the door slowly opens and there stood Mrs. Ramos, who was the same person he had met months earlier.

"Mrs. Ramos, it is Officer Gene Wilson. Remember me? I was here to talk with you a few months ago about your haunting experiences. Please tell us what is wrong," demands Gene.

Looking at him, it was obvious that something was bothering her as she was trying to remember him. Suddenly she exits the house, just as a chair is thrown at her, hitting the doorway and almost striking her. Definitely scared she bolts out and says, "It's them again. I fear it is back and this time much more violent. Please help my grandson. He is hiding inside in a closet in the kitchen."

George asks, "Who is here and trying to harm you?"

Turning to Gene she says, "I don't know for sure who or what it is, but it is something evil. It entered my house as my grandson and my daughter were playing with a Ouija Board yesterday. When I saw what they were doing I ordered them to stop immediately. But it was too late, it was here and it has been here ever since. But tonight, it became angry and began throwing my dishes and pots around. It messed with the lights and both my grandson and I became very afraid of it."

Looking oddly at her, George asks "What are you talking about? Who do you think is here? What's a Ouija Board? What are you saying?"

Gene looks at his partner and says, "George believe me, I understand what she is saying. I will explain it to you later. But for now, I am going to go inside and find her grandson." As he says that he opens the door and enters the house. At first he sees nothing as he approaches the kitchen door to look for the grandchild. Entering the kitchen, he turns on the light and stops in his tracks, as standing straight in front of him by the sink, is the most hideous looking thing he has ever seen. It is tall, with pointed ears, red eyes and a large gaping mouth full of very large fang like teeth. It looks intently at Gene and then grotesquely starts to smile, as it realizes Gene can actually see it. Standing there, it is not only very tall, but its entire body is covered in a brownish green fur like substance, with large areas of rough skin exposed.

Gene remains still as he stares at the entity for several seconds fearing what it might do to him. Staring back at Gene the entity grotesquely starts to laugh wildly. It then turns and darts out of the kitchen and into the dining room. Looking in the room where it went, Gene is astonished to find that it has now totally disappeared. As he looks around outside for the beast, he hears the muffled sounds of a sobbing child inside the kitchen pantry. Upon inspection, he finds the little boy hiding in there. Taking the child by the hand, the two quickly exit the house. Outside, the child runs into his grandmother's open arms.

Standing next to her, George asks Gene what was going on? What was this nuisance call all about and who was it in there that threw the chair at the woman when she exited the house?

Looking at Mrs. Ramos, Gene approaches her and whispers, "I actually saw it in your kitchen. I know what you experienced was bad, but I can tell you the evilness in there is something totally different than what you experienced at your former home. This thing was never human, I believe it to be demonic in nature, and I have no idea why it is here or how you can deal with it. I think you need to immediately seek the help of your church's priest. I fear if you just leave here it will follow you."

"Oh Officer Wilson, I know you are right. And, I am certain that the Ouija Board is what attracted it to us. I am really scared, as it is so different from my previous encounters. Did you really see it," asks Mrs. Ramos?

Looking at his partner and at Mrs. Ramos, George asks, "What are you two talking about? What are we looking for?"

Trying to calm Mrs. Ramos and her grandson down, Gene turns to his partner and says, "I know you will think us both crazy, but believe me when I say Mrs. Ramos here is being pursued by some sort of demonic entity. I fear it is here for some evil purpose and if I am right, no one in this house will be safe. But worst yet, I think it has attached itself to these people and not the house. So, their leaving this place won't likely help them to get away from it at all, unless they seek shelter in a house of God."

Looking at his partner as if he were totally nuts, George says, "Gene I thought you were cured of those foolish feelings? I had hoped all this ghost stuff was behind us. But it seems as though it is not. You are once again acting weird and I just cannot handle this any longer, something has to be done. I need a partner who isn't always seeing shadow people or ghosts. I just don't know what to do, that is for sure."

As he says that, from inside the house, the lights once again begin going on and off. It was as if someone was in each room and every light gets turned on and off at exactly the same time.

Looking at his partner Gene asks, "Do you see that? Does it look as if I am making up some ghostly story? What do you think is causing that? Go inside for yourself and see what you find. How can every light in that house be going on and off at exactly the same instant? Go on in, if you think I'm crazy. Because if I am, you certainly have nothing to fear from what is in there."

George just stands there for a moment and watches the light show in amazement, as they seem to be going on and off inside in every room by themselves, and, at intervals that would seem to be in time with some sort of a musical tune. Definitely, he knew something was deliberately causing it, but he had no idea who it was or why. Cautiously, he removes his revolver, turns to Gene and says, "Stay here with her while I do go inside to see who is doing this." He then slowly enters the front door. As the lights flash on and off inside the home, they come on often enough to allow George enough light to see clearly, enabling him to step over and around furniture, and/or see anyone that might be there. Cautiously he moves from room to room, but no person is seen. He investigates each room carefully, and eventually concludes no one was in there, and possibly the entire event was the result of some sort of electrical short, and nothing more. Holstering his pistol he begins to exit the house when suddenly something big and smelling very bad is standing directly in front of him. As the lights continue to go on and off, it is easy to make out the shape as that of a very large man, yet its physical outline was also bulky and its head was not in proportion with its body size. Being only inches away, he reaches out to touch the image. As he does this, it instantly disappears. George is dumbfounded because he knew for sure something was definitely there in front of him. Again, he removes his pistol and starts searching for the intruder. He slowly approaches each room again, when suddenly something grabs his arm and knocks him to the ground. When this happens, his pistol flies out of his hand and he is instantly lying on his back looking upwards. As the lights continue to flash on and off he tries to see whatever it was that pushed him down. However, he sees nothing. Scared that whoever it was, now had his weapon, he tries to crawl for cover behind a sofa.

Meanwhile, waiting outside, Gene is becoming concerned for his partner's safety as he figures that George has been inside far too long. Telling Mrs. Ramos to wait outside Gene draws his pistol and slowly enters the house. The lights are still going on and off in an uneven manner, but he too can see well enough not to trip over anything. As he enters each room he calls out to George.

Once in the living room, George answers, "I am over here Gene, I am behind this sofa. Something knocked me down and I have lost my weapon. Be careful, whoever it was that hit me is in here somewhere."

Just as George says that, Gene steps on something. Looking down to see what he had stepped on, there it was, right on the floor. Bending down he picks up George's pistol and responds, "I found it. Come on out, I have you covered."

Slowly George stands up and sees his partner. Looking around for what he encountered, he still sees nothing. Moving towards Gene, George takes the pistol from his hand. He then says, "Come on, let's get out of here." As he says that the two men head for the front door. Exiting the house, George turns and looks at Gene and says, "Thanks for coming in. I have no idea who or what I encountered in there, but it was strange." He then explains how he saw it first in front of him and when he reached out to touch it, it disappeared. Then, as he was searching for it, something grabbed his arm and knocked him to the ground. He explained that not knowing where his weapon was, he feared whoever knocked him down had picked it up and was waiting to use it on him. That was why he crawled behind the sofa.

Gene smiles at his partner and says, "Well, my friend, what you likely encountered was something you do not believe exists. And, in my opinion, there is no way you could have contained or captured it anyway."

Confused, George asks, "Well, if that is so, who do you think it was? It was strangely proportioned, but it was definitely a big man."

Before responding, he suggests to Mrs. Ramos that she needed to spend the night elsewhere. Upon saying that, the lights go back on and stay on.

Looking at one another, the two men motion for Mrs. Ramos to wait while they once again go inside and inspect her home. Entering the house once more, with pistols drawn, they walk together from room to room, searching for anyone who was in there and manipulating the lights. As they inspect every room, they look under and behind everything. Arriving back at the front door, no one or anything was found inside.

Exiting the home, George tells Mrs. Ramos that they found no one in there. Now, with it more calm, she is asked to explain what had happened and what caused her to call the police?

Looking at the officers, Mrs. Ramos pulls her grandson into her grasp harder and says, "It became obvious to me that something was wrong and a paranormal presence was nearby, when my grandson here began crying and told me that when he went to bed last night a strange dark shadow figure crouched down at him from atop the ceiling in his bedroom. He said the figure was on the ceiling like a spider, but it was in the form of a man. But upon his seeing that thing again tonight, he ran to me while I sat in the living room watching television. He jumped on my lap and began describing the large shadow shaped man squatting on his ceiling looking down at him. He claims he could see the figure clearly as his night light was on and it was bright enough to allow him to see the image. He went on to say the specter was very large and crawling all over the ceiling going up and down the wall to the floor and back again. And, each time it was on the floor it walked over towards him and stood erect next to his bedside. He said it scared him when it bent over to touch his head. At that point he climbed out of his bed and darted into the living room to be near me. After listening to him, I went to his bedroom to see what he was talking about. I looked everywhere, but I saw nothing. Yet, since he was so upset, I let him stay next to me watching TV until he fell asleep. When that occurred, I picked him up and put him back in his bed, assuming he had only experienced a bad dream. However, as I was covering him up, I too spotted a creepy looking shadow figure squatting down in the corner of the room next to his dresser drawers. I instantly realized he was right, as there truly was something in his room. I immediately scooped him up and ran into my bedroom where I locked my door behind me. Huddling next to my closet trying to figure out what the image might be, this dark shadow begins oozing into my room, coming out of my forced air vent on the floor. Once out, the shadow began growing in height and soon took on the full shaped body of a large man. It just stood there staring at us. Soon, facial features began taking shape and it started grinning at me with such a horrid smile, while baring its very large fang like teeth. Once again I grabbed my grandson and ran past the beast and headed for the kitchen where I called 911 for help. We then hid in the pantry until I heard you knocking at my door. I left my grandson in the pantry with the door closed and told him to hide. When I opened my front door and saw you two men, the beast then apparently threw a chair at me. And, from there on, you know the rest of the story."

Gene looks at her and knowing what he too had seen, immediately believes her story. George also knows what he saw, but in his mind, there was no way he could believe such a story about a shadow man that crawled on the ceiling. Turning to Mrs. Ramos, he says, "Look Mrs. Ramos, I agree that someone is definitely hiding in there and it is not safe for you and your grandson to stay here tonight. Is there any place where we can take you to stay tonight?"

"Oh, I am so scared, what if this thing follows me? Where could I go and be away from it? I just don't know what to do," exclaims Mrs. Ramos.

The two men look at one another and actually smile as they both wonder at the same time if she could seek shelter for the evening at her church? Looking at her, Gene asks, "Mrs. Ramos, would there be a chance that you could stay the night inside your church? Maybe if we talk to your priest and explain about the intruder here tonight he would be willing to put you and your grandson up for the night."

Upon hearing that, Gloria Ramos nods her head in agreement. Gene then immediately says, "And maybe tomorrow he could return here and perform some sort of an exorcism and chase this thing from your home?"

Smiling and crying at the same time she hugs her grandson and signals the two officers that was likely an excellent option. As she starts to accompany them to their car, she stops, turns and says, "Oh I am sorry, but before I go, I need to get my purse, with my wallet and house keys in it. I must have those items, as I definitely need to lock my front door."

Looking at one another and then at her, Gene says, "I understand, I'll go back inside and get it, where is it located?"

"It is in my bedroom on the night stand. It is a brown bag and it has a long strap handle. Please be careful, as no one knows what that thing is capable of doing," comments Mrs. Ramos.

Without replying, Gene quickly enters the house and rapidly heads to her bedroom. Opening the door, there the purse was. Grabbing it, he quickly runs for the door. He wastes no time looking for the entity and he happily does not encounter it. Opening the door, he closes it and hands Mrs. Ramos the purse.

"Oh thank you I was worried for your safety and it is great you are safe," says, Mrs. Ramos. She then opens the purse, removes her keys and locks the front door.

As she does that, inside, the lights all begin blinking off and on again in the same manner as they had been doing before. Stopping to watch for a few moments, George motions for everyone to get into the police car. Once everyone was in, George asks for directions and then heads for her church.

While they drive, everyone is silent. The two officers are wondering to themselves how they could possibly document this visit and trip to the church in their mandatory report. Looking at Gene, George says, "Well partner, this is certainly one for the books. What did we encounter and who would ever believe this story?"

Gene responds by saying, as he turns to look at Mrs. Ramos, "Well, I know two people that will. And, you have to admit that we both experienced something that was certainly weird. If they don't believe us at the station, there is nothing we can do about it. And, if we are laughed at, then so be it. But, as for me, I know what we saw and experienced was real and we are doing the right thing here in helping these people."

George then inquires from Mrs. Ramos about the grandson's mother. He asks where she was and might she be going back to her house tonight unaware of the entity?

Mrs. Ramos explains that her daughter had come over the night before to leave her son with her while she and her husband took a few days vacation and went up north to visit friends. She tells George that she would call her in the morning to adviser her about what has happened.

Upon arriving at the church, George turns to her, suggesting that Mrs. Ramos wait in the police car while the two of them go in and talk to the priest. The two men exit their vehicle, and enter the church's front doors. Inside, there was no one to be seen. Wandering around they find a janitor who directs them to Father Kelley's bedroom. Approaching the room, they knock.

A faint voice is heard to say, "Come in."

Opening the door, inside, they find the priest. He was in bed reading something. Seeing the two officers he immediately gets up and waits for their comments. "Are you Father Kelley," asks George?

"Yes sir, I am. What can I do for you two men," asks the priest?

Gene immediately jumps in and begins explaining why they were there.

Ten minutes later the trio exit the church and head for Mrs. Ramos who was waiting patiently in the police car. The priest opens the car door and greets Mrs. Ramos.

"Oh my child, I am so sorry for your troubles. These two officers have explained everything and I will do all I can to help you. But for tonight, please accept the sanctuary of our church and come with me, as I will find somewhere for you and the child to sleep where you will definitely be safe. We can talk in the morning and decide what must be done," explains the priest.

Exiting the vehicle, Mrs. Ramos and her grandson walk with the priest towards the church. Before entering, she turns and says, "Thank you gentlemen. I truly appreciate what you did for us and for bringing me here tonight. I'll let you know what happens next."

As the two officers begin driving away, they radio in to inform the station that they were free from the last call and that they were again on patrol. Driving for a while, neither man says anything, obviously seriously troubled by what they saw and encountered.

George turns to Gene and asks, "Ok, what exactly do you think that thing was if not an intruder? How can we ever understand it or even rationalize what occurred, let alone document it in our report?

As they drive, Gene doesn't respond for a few seconds. Obviously trying to decide what exactly to say to his partner's question and how much information he can logically explain to George. He begins by saying, "Partner, let me tell you something. What you do not know about me that happened after my injury is a very bazaar and very strange story. In fact, it can only be described as life changing. I have recently experienced several strange things and because of that, I feared for my sanity. That is what forced me to go see Dr. Allen in the first place, who upon hearing my experiences actually referred me to a colleague of hers who specializes in my type of problems."

Turning and looking at Gene, George says, "Boy, what a lead in, I can hardly wait to hear all this. Should I pull over and stop so I won't miss anything?"

Frowning at hearing that, Gene just looks seriously at George and says, "Look, what I am willing to tell you now, after experiencing what we just did, isn't anything to joke about. If you want to hear what I have to say, based on scientific tests, fine. But if not, that's Ok too. But let me preface everything by saying you must understand, what I am willing to share now is very personal and private. And, I am willing to tell you something that may help you to understand what it was that we encountered tonight. If you are going to make fun of me, or joke about it, then forget it, I am not going to share anything with you, let alone divulge any of my seriously private issues."

"Oh, lighten up partner. You know I'm just joking. I am interested in what you think. Please, go ahead and tell me what you think we encountered in that woman's house tonight? And, I am also interested in hearing about what you have been going through. I know we haven't spoken of your doctor visits, but be assured that I am curious to know what happened. I promise to listen to you and not make fun of anything you say," explains George.

Looking at George, Gene takes a deep breath and slowly describes his encounter with the Nancy woman he first encountered in the hospital's ICU, and then the Nancy that the two of them came upon in the vehicle accident later on. He describes in detail how he and the first Nancy mentally communicated as he stood outside her room and his seeing her later in the parking lot. He also discusses his meetings with Dr. Mendenhall and how he tested him for Physic and other paranormal behavior. He relates the findings and explains how he explained that the bullet he received into his brain somehow altered his abilities to see all types of unnatural things that others can't see.

George listens with interest and tries to formulate in his own mind how much of this he could believe. He also wonders if maybe Gene was seriously mentally ill. In response, he asks, "Ok, I understand what you are saying here, and assuming everything is as you say, then what do you think we encountered back there?"

Without any hesitation, Gene says, "A demon of some sort, I imagine. It certainly wasn't ghostly in nature, because I feel it had never been human. Therefore, it could only have been demonic in nature. Plus, as Mrs. Ramos described how it hovered on the ceiling looking down, I would only conclude it was something very evil and menacing."

Choking back the natural urge to laugh, George tries hard to contain himself, and after a few moments he says, "Wow partner, that is really something. It sounds to me like you have no doubts at all about what you think that thing was. But, since we never saw it on the ceiling nor did we actually see it in any clear visible manner, I'm not sure I can agree with you."

Not hesitating Gene says, "Look George, I didn't mention it earlier, because I knew you didn't believe Mrs. Ramos story. But, you need to know that when I entered that house looking for her grandson, I did encounter that entity, face to face. I was no more than five feet away from it, standing directly in front of him and I saw it very clearly. It was large, well over six feet; it smelled badly, had large pointed ears, red eyes, and an oversize head with a very large mouth full of fang like teeth. It looked at me and laughed at me in a grotesquely hideous manner. Believe me when I say, it wasn't human. It was not of this world. It was something directly from Hell."

Not knowing how to respond to Gene's claim, George can only shake his head in disbelief and continues driving, maintaining his silence. Now, seriously worried about his partner's mental health and his overall reliability in being able to effectively continue partnering with him, he knows that he has a lot to think about.

After about ten minutes of silence, Gene wonders what George is thinking. He then asks, "So, why no response to my comments? What do you have to say about what I just told you, George?"

Remaining silent, George continues driving and doesn't say anything or immediately respond to Gene's question. He knows that anything he says will prompt an argument and he just isn't ready for that sort of confrontation at this time. He respects his partner and can only assume his current condition is related to his gun shot injury, an event he still feels responsible for. Suddenly a broadcast is heard asking for backup at a domestic dispute site in San Pedro. Responding, Gene radios back that they will field the call, as they were likely the closet unit to the scene.

Understanding that George didn't believe his comments, he is angry that he would not at least comment about it. However, Gene knows there is time later on to finish this conversation, and he fully intends to do so. Yet, meanwhile the immediate need is to respond to the call for help from fellow officers who have requested back up.

Arriving at the address they see an empty police cruiser alongside the curb, with the passenger door open. Not knowing the situation or where the cruiser's occupants were, the two men quickly exit their vehicle and slowly approach the home where the original call was focused on. Peering into the living room window, they see nothing. Walking alongside the driveway, they can partially see inside the other parts of the house. Still nothing is seen or heard. Signaling for Gene to go around the other side, George continues walking until he approaches the rear yard. Looking all around there, he still finds no clues as to where his fellow officers were, let alone the home's occupants.

As Gene walks around the other side of the house he stops to look in each window hoping to see something. Finally, just before arriving at the rear yard he looks to his left, and once again the now familiar shadow people are squatting down behind a row of rose bushes. Approaching them, they tell Gene a woman was inside on the floor of the back bedroom. They also said other people were injured in the back yard and in the house.

Listening to them, per their instruction, Gene looks into the last window along that side of the house, which was obviously a bedroom. Looking closely he does see a woman lying motionless on the floor, between the bed and the door. He tries to determine if she was injured or just hiding. As he watches her, there is no movement, causing him to conclude that she is injured or dead. Moving to the rear yard he meets up with George. Afraid to mention seeing the shadow people, he only tells George about what he saw in the bedroom through the window.

The two decide to enter the house from its rear entrance. With pistols drawn, they slowly enter the house. They first walk through the laundry room, where they see nothing. Opening another door, they are in the kitchen. It is large and rather messy. As they slowly separate and examine the room, under the dining room table they find a child crying and trying to hide from them. Taking the child by his hand they coax him out from under the table. The child was likely ten or eleven at most and has difficulty talking. Eventually, he describes how his mother and father were fighting. When asked, he could not say where either of his parents were at that moment, or where the two policemen were. He did say that two policemen came inside and one took his father outside in the back yard, and the other one went forward into the house.

George instructs the child to stay in the laundry room and remain quiet while they continued looking through out the house for his parents and the two police officers. Approaching the back bedroom door, they slowly open it and immediately see the woman lying on the floor that Gene saw through the window. Checking her vital signs they determine she was dead, shot in the chest by a large caliber weapon. Slowly looking around the room and in the closets, nothing more is seen. Upon finishing their search of that room, George radios their dispatch office, informing them of what has been found and requests them to dispatch a supervisor, an ambulance, a medical examiner and another back up unit. As he completes his call, Gene had already moved on to the next door which upon entering discovered it to be a bathroom. He immediately sees lying in the tub was the dead body of one police officer. Joining him in there George checks the officer's vital signs and finds him to also be dead. He also notes that his weapon was not present. Exiting the room they open a door to the second bedroom and carefully inspect it. Again, nothing is found. Moving forward they enter the living room. It was immediately obvious that there had been some type of fight in there as several pieces of furniture were overturned and there was blood on the floor. Looking everywhere in that room, nothing else was found, nor was there any clues readily available to explain what might have happened. As they finish their search, an ambulance is heard approaching the house. Soon paramedics and other police officers are inside the house. The two bodies are quickly located and the detectives begin their investigation.

Meanwhile, still worried over the second missing officer, both George and Gene continue searching all around the outside of the house. Spotting the detached garage at the rear of the backyard, they approach it and raise the large double garage door, where they immediately see two vehicles inside. Slowly circling them they find a pistol lying on the floor and wonder if it belonged to the deceased police officer inside the house. Leaving it where it was, they continue their search. Nothing more is seen in the garage. Exiting the garage's man door, which led outside directly behind the garage, they begin searching again. Carefully looking around they see two bodies lying on the ground. Approaching them, one was the second police officer and the other was likely the husband. They find that the policeman was still alive, although in serious condition. The second man was dead. And, in the police officer's hand was his service revolver, which was likely what was used on the dead man.

Gene quickly returns to the house where he finds the paramedics and tells them of the second officer's condition in the rear yard.

After the wounded police officer was removed and taken to the hospital, the detectives instruct both George and Gene to leave the crime scene and be careful not to disturb anything. Doing as instructed, they return to the house where they find the little boy still in the laundry room. They try to quiz him on what happened, but unfortunately he was too traumatized by the evening's events and totally incapable of giving them any useful information.

While George and Gene sit in their cruiser heading back to the station to end their shift, Gene privately recalls the shadow people he again encountered and now realizes that they are there to help, and not to hinder him. He also recalls how they told him what had happened that evening, giving him a full account of how the encounter with the man and wife escalated into the two police officers becoming involved in the altercation. They tell Gene that the man was beating his wife and how she escaped and ran away from him to the kitchen where she was able to call 911. He then caught up with her in there and shot her. She staggered away, hiding in the back bedroom where she later died. Meanwhile, the police arrived and found the man in the front yard, armed and threatened to kill himself. After a brief scuffle, they disarmed him and put him in the back of their police car. Then, they went inside to search for other family members. Trying to search each room, one officer is jumped in the bathroom by the man who somehow had escaped from his handcuffs and fled the vehicle. In the bathroom, he overpowered the officer and takes his weapon and shoots him. He then leaves him there dying and goes looking for the second policeman. He is tackled by the second police officer in the living room and a fight begins. Within seconds the man runs from the policeman heading out of the house and goes to the back yard where he hides in the garage. Within minutes the policeman finds the man and they struggle again. The man drops the dead policeman's weapon and bolts out of the garage heading to the back yard. There, they fight once more. The man overpowers the policeman and takes his revolver and shoots him. Injured, the policeman is still able to pursue the man, grabs him and once again they struggle. The policeman regains control and takes his pistol away from the man and shoots him. There they both lay until they were found by him and George.

Suddenly, George speaks up and asks, "What in the world do you think happened back there partner? It was very confusing to me. Any speculation on what went down?"

Gene knows what the shadow people told him but he doesn't want to tell George, as he knows what he thinks about the shadow people. Therefore, to cement in his mind the validity of the shadow people, he decides to wait and see what the official explanation is. Plus, if the injured officer lives, he will obviously tell everyone what happened. If the shadow people's account matches the facts, it is obvious he is not seeing things and they are definitely there to help. After giving this his due consideration, Gene responds by saying, "I really couldn't guess. Given the different locations of each body, it's hard to piece together what may have happened. But, if the officer we found recovers, I'm sure he will let us all know." As he says that, Gene decides not to bring up the subject of the shadow people at all, in spite of his earlier conversation that he had with George.

George nods in agreement and the two end their shift, as they drive into police headquarters.

CHAPTER 6; *The Fear of What May Lie Ahead Is Scary*

For the next two weeks all goes well as Gene and George enjoy many good conversations about a variety of issues, but specifically several over Gene's and Amelia's new relationship, as well as Gene's preparation for taking the California Bar Association Exam. Few interruptions occur and Gene never once sees or speaks of the shadow people to George.

One evening, arriving home Gene is greeted by Amelia, where she tells him that Dr. Allen had left a message for him to say Dr. Mendenhall will be in town next Monday and he would like to see Gene in order to administer the last bunch of tests he had spoken of earlier. He asked if Gene could meet him at Dr. Allen's office at 11:00 am.

Happy to hear this, Gene smiles and tells Amelia how much he looked forward to ending his tests. They then talk about each others day and by midnight they go to bed.

As Monday arrives, Gene gets ready for his doctors appointment and arrives at the hospital a little early, hoping to be able to check in on Nancy # 2. Heading to the ICU, he immediately sees the room is empty and there is no one immediately available to ask any questions of. He then goes on over to the nurse's station where a young woman tells him she had no information about the patient named Nancy Wainwright, but the floor's head nurse would be in later that morning, and he could inquire about the woman with her. Being unable to obtain any more information, he decides to head on over to Dr. Allen's office. Walking the short distance, Gene realizes that he is a little early, but if he needs to wait, that's fine. Opening her door, he is immediately greeted by her receptionist, Rita James, who smiles and says, "Good morning Mr. Wilson, please have a seat and the doctors will be with you soon.

After about ten minutes, Dr. Allen emerges from her office with Dr. Mendenhall directly behind her. Smiling at him, she says, "Good morning Mr. Wilson. How are you? Please come on in as Dr. Mendenhall is all set up and prepared to complete your final testing."

Gene gets up and enters the office. He is asked to take a seat and Dr. Mendenhall explains that he has about ten different tests to administer. Signaling that he was ready to proceed, he sits down and listens to what Dr. Mendenhall's instructions were. An hour later, they are done.

"Well, Mr. Wilson, I have to say you did remarkably well on every test. In fact, you scored 100%. There is no doubt about your psychic abilities and extrasensory skills. And, I think I can clearly state that your injury has definitely stimulated an area of the brain that is normally dormant and not used by people in their daily life. I also am willing to state that I do not think it is temporary, because if it were, I feel it would have ceased by now. Also, today, your psychic abilities are even more heightened than they were last month when I tested you. So, don't worry about being crazy, because you are not. What your challenge going forward will be, is to learn how to deal with what you see and experience in your daily life. To most people, what you claim to see and feel will be totally unexplainable and likely not anything they can understand or accept. Therefore, it is my recommendation that when these events occur, keep that experience to yourself. Otherwise, trying to explain it will just cause you more problems. Do you understand," asks Dr. Mendenhall?

Thinking about what was just said, Gene does have one question. He speaks up and asks, "Dr. Mendenhall, one thing you said that really worries me. You said that my psychic abilities today are greater than they were the last time you tested me. If that is so, are you saying it will continue to increase every day of my life? If that is the case, how can I cope with that? Will I eventually become incapacitated and unable to live a normal life?"

"Well sir that is an excellent question. I cannot say with any certainty what will happen or how much more psychic abilities you may gain. It is my professional opinion that you will reach a peak and stop. However, to say for certain, I just don't know. You are making medical history here every day and to my knowledge there are no other cases to which I can compare you to. So, I just cannot give you any definitive answer. However, there are other test that I can perform over time to measure the growth of your physic abilities. And, I can fairly accurately determine if they are continuing to increase, decrease or if they are remaining the same. So, I fear we must stay in touch and maybe every four months or so we need to meet, so I can test you," explains Dr. Mendenhall.

Gene is suddenly fearful of the idea that maybe he isn't ever going to stop increasing his psychic abilities and he will eventually become disabled because of that on-going transformation. The fear causes him to ask, "But, what if it keeps growing inside me? How can I deal with that? What will become of me and will it eventually kill me?"

"Mr. Wilson, I fear you are worrying about something that cannot possibly happen. The damage to your brain was minor in reality, so to worry about your psychic abilities continuing on day after day increasing until you have no control over your thought process is just not a rational scenario. And, I am confident that I can prove that to you when we next meet. Please, trust me, I know it scares you, but I believe in what I am telling you sir," explains Dr. Mendenhall.

"Well Doctor, I hope you are right. It is one thing to be a "little" psychic, but to be consumed by it 24/7 would be unbearable and not a life I would want for myself. I will look forward to our next meeting and for your test results," says Gene.

Dr. Allen adds her thoughts, by saying, "Mr. Wilson, I agree with Dr. Mendenhall, that what you are worried over is highly unlikely, but believe me when I say I understand your concerns. So, let's schedule your next visit now and we will definitely know more then. Meanwhile, try and relax, go ahead and return to full duty. However, what I would also like for you to do is maintain a personal journal, noting in it anything that occurs that you consider paranormal or psychic in nature. Such information will be valuable when it is added to the next set of tests that Dr. Mendenhall will give you. It will help him to better assess your overall psychic capabilities."

Listening, Gene understands what the two doctors are saying, but seriously fears they could be wrong. And, if they are, it is he who will pay the price. And, since it is all just conjecture at this point, he agrees that all that he can do for now is wait. Getting up, he bids the doctors good-bye and leaves Dr. Allen's office with his next appointment date in his hand. Heading to the head nurse station, he finds another nurse on duty. Introducing himself as the officer who responded to Nancy # 2's accident, he asks if the nurse knew anything about her condition.

The nurse introduces herself as Marcie Russell and says, "Yes, I was here when she passed away. That was about two weeks ago. It was a sad case, as she never regained consciousness and was brain dead from the very beginning. Her family made the decision and all gathered around her as the doctors disconnected her from life support. She died very peacefully."

Gene cannot understand what good his connection with Nancy # 1 vs. Nancy # 2 was. If somehow meeting Nancy # 1 could have prevented the death of Nancy # 2 that would make some sense. But, since his meeting had no positive effect on the life of the second Nancy, what good was it for him to meet the first Nancy? It is all so unclear. How can this be a "gift" if it cannot work in a positive way? Otherwise, it is just something that will be there bothering him, and become a nuisance since it is unable to benefit anyone. Thanking Nurse Russell, Gene leaves the hospital and decides to drive by Mrs. Ramos house and see how her situation was.

While driving Gene can't help but worry about his growing powers. If it does, how bad will it get? Can he control the growth by being able to harness the power? Might he be able to actually use it to help law enforcement or maybe other people like Mrs. Ramos? It is all very scary and he absolutely has no idea what he can withstand mentally and physically if it does keep increasing. Soon he is at the Ramos home. Strangely, he sees a for sale sign in the front yard. Getting out he approaches the front door, and starts to knock, but can immediately see inside that the house was empty. Walking around the house he senses nothing evil being present, but sees a lot of trash piled up in the back yard. It was obvious that she had moved. But was the evil spirit they encountered the reason? Was she safe? Many concerns are now coming into his mind and he fears the worse.

Getting back in his car he decides to head on over to the Catholic Church where he and George dropped off Mrs. Ramos and her grandson that terrible night. Arriving at the church, he exits his vehicle and enters the church in search of Father Kelley. After looking through the church and not finding him, he locates the administrative office and sees a young woman inside at a desk typing papers. Entering her office he asks for Father Kelley.

Looking rather oddly at Gene, the young woman says, "Oh sir, I'm sorry, I guess you had not heard, but Father Kelley was killed about a month ago. The news of his death was covered pretty extensively in the local newspaper."

"Oh no," exclaims Gene. "Can you tell me how he died?"

The young woman is obviously very uncomfortable discussing Father Kelley's death with him and says, "Sir, maybe it would be best if you talk to his replacement, Father Sanchez. I think he would be the best person to discuss all of this with. I can set an appointment with him, if you would like?"

Totally bewildered, Gene responds by saying, "Yes, of course, I would be happy to meet him. Can I do so now, or what time works best?"

"Well, I am afraid right now is not possible, as he is currently at a Catholic conference in Los Angeles. But he will be returning tonight. I am sure tomorrow sometime would be fine with him. What works best for you," asks the woman?

Gene thinks a moment and responds, "I guess about this time or earlier would be best for me."

"Ok, then let's say 11:00 am. tomorrow. Can I have your name and say exactly what it is you are interested in discussing with Father Sanchez," asks the woman?

Gene gives the woman one of his police business cards with his name on it and tells her specifically he wants to discuss father Kelley's death and also wants to know if Father Sanchez might know the whereabouts of one of his congregational supporters, Ms. Gloria Ramos?

The young woman makes a note on her calendar and tells Gene she would give the information to Father Sanchez, just as soon as she sees him. She then reconfirms their meeting time tomorrow.

Gene smiles and thanks her for her help. Walking out to his vehicle, he has a strange feeling about how the priest died and prayed it wasn't associated with the Ramos move or her house. He recalled how Father Kelley said he would return there the next day and bless her house, before Gloria and her grandson returned. He seriously hoped nothing evil happened there or harmed him or Mrs. Ramos.

Returning home, Amelia was there, anxiously waiting to find out what he discovered. Surprised to see her there, she explained that she skipped lunch in order to hear all about his doctor's visit. She explained that she came home at noon hoping he would be there. Gene tells Amelia about the tests and his fears of his psychic abilities escalating even more, and never stopping, which could kill him. He then discusses going over to check on Mrs. Ramos and how he found her house empty and up for sale. He then explains how he went to the Catholic Church and discovered Father Kelley had died. Amelia is shocked at hearing that, commenting that she had not heard anything about that before, and being a Catholic she was deeply worried. She also stated that she has friends who attend that church and maybe if she called them they would have some useful information. She asks Gene if she should call any of them prior to his meeting and find out what they might know.

Thinking about that Gene concludes that yes, to know as much as possible before his meeting tomorrow might be useful, especially if this new Father Sanchez was fearful of telling him everything he knew. He therefore says, "Amelia that may be really useful. Also, see if anyone knows the whereabouts of Mrs. Ramos."

Amelia smiles and says, "I will start my calls just as soon as I have the time when I'm back in my office." Upon saying that, she kisses Gene and explains she needed to get back to school.

After Amelia leaves, Gene sits down in his easy chair and closes his eyes hoping to sleep a bit before he has to go to work. Suddenly, visions of Father Kelley fill his mind. He sees him getting out of his car and going inside Mrs. Ramos's house all alone. He is sprinkling holly water from room to room as he says various prayers. As he walks through the house, he suddenly enters the kitchen, where he sees standing there, the same evil presence that Gene saw when he and George were there. It makes itself visible to father Kelley. Totally shocked and scared, Father Kelley is frozen in his tracks. He cannot run away or even move. Watching the beast he tries to communicate with it, but he cannot. Then, the beast slowly reaches out and touches Father Kelley on his chest. This causes Father Kelley to clutch at his heart, and he immediately falls over dead, a victim of a heart attack induced by the evil presence. Then, as if the beast knew Gene was watching him in his dream, he turns to face Gene, smiles and begins laughing grotesquely. Shocked by this last act, Gene immediately wakes up. He knows it was only a dream, but it seemed so real. He is sweating profusely and cannot stop wondering if this was a glimpse of what actually happened to Father Kelley?

Later that evening as he and George are on patrol, George says, "Hey partner, did I tell you we finally got the full story on that grizzly murder of the two people and the one police officer we investigated a few weeks ago. It seems that the injured police officer will survive and he was able to tell the detectives everything. George goes on to describe in detail what the officer remembered. As he sits there listening, everything George says was exactly what the shadow people told him that very night.

Gene smiles to himself and says, "Wow, what a story. It's really fortunate that the officer survived and could tell it. Otherwise, I doubt that any of that could have been deduced from what clues the detectives found."

George then comments about how that was likely the worst scene he had ever been on and he agreed it was good the injured policeman could recall it all. As he says that a vehicle heading south on Gaffey Ave, runs the red light at the intersection of 7th and Gaffey. Hitting the lights they quickly pull over the occupants and find them to be young teenagers who stole the vehicle and were out for an evening 'joy ride.' Checking the registration, they noted that the theft had only occurred two hours earlier. Both young boys were arrested and taken to the police precinct where they were booked on Grand Theft Auto. By the time Gene and George finished filling out their reports it was time to end their shift.

Arriving at his home, Gene quickly notes that Amelia had already turned in. She did leave a note for him outlining her conversations with her various friends about Father Kelley's death and her inquiry about where Gloria Ramos moved to. Basically, all of her friends said the same thing, which was, Father Kelley's death was very suspicious, and no one knew for sure what exactly he died from. And, it appeared that the Catholic Church was not willing to discuss it. They all said he was found dead inside Mrs. Ramos home, while she was out. There was a lot of speculation as to why he was there in the first place, but it appeared that no one Amelia spoke with knew he was there to bless or cleanse the house from that evil spirit. Also, no one knew where Mrs. Ramos moved to.

Taking a beer from the refrigerator Gene relaxes on the couch as he turns on the TV in order to watch some late night news. As he sits there he recounts his dream and wonders if what he saw might actually be what happened to Father Kelley. And, he can easily understand the church not wishing to discuss what he was doing at Mrs. Ramos house in the first place. As he sips his beer, he suddenly recalls the young woman in the church's office saying Father Kelley had been killed. Why did she say that? Did she have inside information that only the people from the church knew about? In his dream, the demon did kill Father Kelley. Is that something the church might actually know more about? Might they have any real proof to substantiate the "killed" comment? He then hopes that more facts can be ascertained at his 11:00 am meeting tomorrow. He also realized that there was a strong possibility that Father Sanchez might not know everything, or even be willing to share everything with him.

The next morning, Amelia accidentally wakes Gene up as she readies herself for work. Anxious to discuss the comments she made in her note to him regarding her friends' discussion about Father Kelley's death, he gets up, puts on a robe and follows her around the apartment as she completes her morning routine. As they talk, it was clear that the Catholic Church had not disclosed anything specific about Father Kelley's death to their parishioners. Gene tells Amelia how strange that was, given what the woman at the church said.

Amelia thinks about that and comments, "Well, it just might be she was not intending to say he was murdered at all. Maybe she was just not communicating to you correctly. It is possible that Father Kelley simply died of a heart attack or stroke. And, there is nothing demonic at all that occurred with him."

Gene responds, "Yes, of course that is always a possibility. Yet, given my vision and her comment, they both make sense to me. And, it wouldn't surprise me at all that the church doesn't want to say what happened, for fear of what the publics response would be. Plus, who would believe them anyway?"

Amelia listens to what he says, and nods in agreement. She then kisses Gene good-bye and departs for her job.

At 10:55 am, Gene enters the church and heads to the priest's office. Entering the office, the same woman he encountered the day before greets him and indicates that Father Sanchez would be right out to meet with him. Five minutes later, the door opens to the priest's office and out steps a young man who asks, "Are you Officer Wilson?"

Standing up and facing the priest, Gene says, "Yes, I am Gene Wilson." He then extends his right arm and the two men shake hands.

Smiling back at Gene the priest says, "Hello, I am Father Sanchez, and I am pleased to meet you. Please come into my office."

The two men enter his office and immediately sit down in two comfortable brown leather arm chairs, several feet away from the priest's desk. Looking at Gene, the priest asks, "So, Mr. Wilson, what is that you wanted to see me about?"

Not hesitating Gene responds by saying, "Father Sanchez, as you know, I am a Los Angeles police officer and consequently a trained investigator. And, one evening not long ago my partner and I responded to a very strange call for help from one of this church's parishioners, a Mrs. Gloria Ramos. She had called us because she claimed a demonic spirit was in her home and she and her grandson were in danger. Well, you can imagine our surprise when upon investigating the call, both me and my partner actually did encounter some type of entity that we both could not explain away. It was so bazaar that we eventually brought Mrs. Ramos and her grandson here to your church for protection. And, that is when we met Father Kelley. We explained to him what had happened and ask if she and the boy could stay here for the night. After hearing what Mrs. Ramos claimed to see and what we saw, he immediately agreed and took them in. He also agreed to visit her house the very next day to bless it and if there was something evil in there, he indicated that he would chase it away. Now I have learned the good Father died in that house and Mrs. Ramos has fled to some other area. I just wanted to hear the official version from someone here at your church as to what really happened to Father Kelley."

Father Sanchez listens with interest and as he responds, Gene could see from the priests facial expressions, that he was surprised by what he was hearing. Thinking how to respond the priest hesitantly clears his throat and then says, "Yes, I am familiar with Mrs. Ramos and her claim of encountering something demonic in her home. However, I was not aware that anybody besides her ever saw any entity."

Responding, Gene says, "Oh there is no doubt in my mind that we saw something evil. It was definitely not human and for a moment I was only a few feet away from it. In fact, it stood right in front of me and smiled in a very grotesque manner. Then, it just disappeared. In addition to that, it attacked my partner a few minutes later and threw him to the ground. Fortunately, no one was actually harmed, but there is no doubt it could have inflicted serious damage to any of us at any time it chose to. That is why we brought Mrs. Ramos here, as we feared taking her anywhere else that thing might have followed her. But we figured it would not enter a house of God to pursue her."

"Well, I have to say sir; I didn't know any of that background on Mrs. Ramos. What I do know is Father Kelley went to Mrs. Ramos home without obtaining permission first from the church. And, we know that while he was there blessing that house, he died from what I am told was a heart attack. Other than that, I really don't know much more," explains the priest.

Realizing this man might be in the dark, and maybe doesn't know more, Gene is sure there has to be someone else within the church that does. He then looks at the priest and says, "Well, I believe there is more to Father Kelley's death than what you are saying, because I have heard one church official here use the word 'murdered' when describing how he died."

Stunned at hearing that comment, Father Sanchez asks who he heard that from. He then tries to assure Gene that was not true.

Gene then asks, "Father, do you or does anyone else here know where Mrs. Ramos moved to? I would really like to check up on her to be sure she is Ok, and find out what she might know about the good Father's death."

Obviously now a bit nervous the priest says, "Oh, I really don't know where she went, and I doubt that anyone here at the church would know her whereabouts either. But, if you will wait a few moments, I will go ask my assistant out front and see if she knows more about Mrs. Ramos."

Returning in five minutes the priest says, "No, as I said no one here knows where Mrs. Ramos may have moved to. But, if you would like for me to ask around, I would be happy to do that?"

Gene realizes that whatever happened in that house and why and where Mrs. Ramos moved to is going to remain the church's secret. And, it was obvious that he was wasting his time trying to gather anymore information here. He smiles at the priest, stands up and says, "No Father Sanchez, there is no need for you to do that. I am sure that through my professional law enforcement contacts we can locate the woman. But, I want to thank you for seeing me and I sincerely wish you good luck in your new position here." Gene then again shakes the priests hand and opens his office door and leaves. As he walks out of the office the woman in the reception area turns away, but not before Gene observes that she was crying. As he departs he wonders if his comments to Father Sanchez may have been the reason for her distress. Might he have known the 'murdered' comment came from her?

Driving home, Gene wonders what to do next. Maybe there was no way to ever find out the truth about Father Kelley's death from the church's officials, but he would bet anything that Mrs. Ramos would know the truth. So, finding her was most important, plus he sincerely did want to know how she was and what had happened in her home that chased her away.

Later that night as Gene and George were on patrol, he tells George about Mrs. Ramos moving out of the house and how the priest was found dead there the day after they dropped her off at his church. He explains how most everyone at the church believed it was a heart attack.

Sitting quietly for a few moments obviously thinking of how to respond, George finally says, "Well, that doesn't surprise me to much that she has left that place. There was definitely something weird going on there. I'm sorry for her. But, for the priest to die there, that is really strange. Maybe he encountered what we did and it simply scared him to death?"

Gene was surprised to hear George's comments and it almost sounded like he had accepted the fact they actually did encounter something non-human while at Mrs. Ramos's home. If that was so, maybe it would make sense to discuss his dream and how the church appears to be trying to cover up what the receptionist woman originally said happened to the priest. Thinking long and hard about it, Gene says, "Partner, I have kept you pretty updated about my various doctor visits and my meeting an out of area shrink that Dr. Allen referred me to. But, what I haven't discussed with you is what the final results were. So, maybe now would be a good time to do that." Gene then describes in detail the various tests and the conclusions Dr. Mendenhall came to.

Stunned at hearing Gene's comments, George is quiet for a few moments and then asks, "So, are you telling me that your recent visions and actions are all a result of that gun shot injury? You are saying that the bullet which struck you in the head somehow penetrated and woke up an area of your brain that is not normally in use? And now, because of that you are able to see strange entities that I can't see, and you are now experiencing dreams about demons and evil entities that kill people, even before it happens? Is that what you are saying?"

Laughing to himself, Gene realizes how unbelievable his claim must sound and knowing George as well as he does, he can easily understand how he would think what he tried to explain sounded crazy. It was likely something totally outrageous and unbelievable to George. To respond, Gene says, "George, you have a way of making the most complicated thing sound so basic, I have to admire that about you. But, let me tell you something. What I have told you is true. And, for me it is a curse, certainly not something to envy. The doctor said my psychic abilities are continuing to increase day upon day, and I seriously fear it will eventually cripple and maybe even kill me. It is very scary for me, so I would appreciate it if you could be a little more compassionate and try to understand what is happening to me and how I am trying to deal with it. In fact, I would be happy to get Dr. Allen on the phone and have her explain it to you."

George listens to what Gene says and responds by saying, "No, I believe you. We have worked together long enough that I know when you are joking and not. But you have to admit such a claim is really hard to believe. Yet, I did say that I believe you believe it. So, let's just let it go at that for now. But, how do we find Mrs. Ramos, that is the question. You say that the house was empty, but do you recall whether or not there was a Realtor sign in the yard? If so, they would know where she went."

Gene thinks about that and did not recall whether or not a real estate sign was posted. Responding, he says, "I'm not sure. There might have been one, but if there was, I did not pay any attention to it."

Smiling, George responds, well that should be easy enough to check out. We are only a few minutes away, so let's drive by there and see for our selves." Driving the few miles across town, they pull up in front of the house. From the outside it looks normal, with the yard nicely mowed and the porch light by the front door on. George parks the car, and the two men exit their vehicle.

Gene looks around the yard and does see a sign indicating the property was for sale. Writing down the company name and phone number they approach the front door. George knocks, but no lights come on from inside and no one answers the door. They then walk around the house and find no vehicles anywhere in the driveway or garage and again no lights are visible from the back yard. Trying to peer into any window, they find that all of the home's shades are pulled down and it was impossible to see inside to determine whether or not any furniture was still there.

Receiving a call from police headquarters they are forced to abandon their investigation to answer a disturbing the peace complaint. Getting into their vehicle they head towards the address which was in south San Pedro. As they drive they do not talk much, obviously each man was wondering about whether or not that entity was still in Mrs. Ramos home. And, also how serious the call they were responding to was.

Approaching the address, they see an elderly couple standing on the curb waiting for them. Stopping their vehicle, George rolls down his window and asks what was going on? The man leans into his window and tells George how this house had been playing loud Hispanic music all day since 8:00 am. It was now well past 11:00 pm, and it was still blaring loudly. George tells the couple that they would quiet them down.

Parking in front of the house, both officers exit their vehicle. Gene takes his place at the side of the front door and George walks up and knocks on the door. Several attempts are made to get the occupants attention, but no one comes to the door. Given the loud music, it was possible they could not hear his knocking. Both men then approach the rear of the house, looking over the back yard gate, they see about six people in the back yard listening to music, dancing and standing around drinking beer.

Reaching over the gate to unlatch it, both officers enter the back yard and approach the occupants. It was obvious that they were all inebriated. One man approaches the two men and asks what the problem was? George tells the man it was late and his music was disturbing the neighbors. Sarcastically, the man says, "Hey dude, this is my pad and I am enjoying it here with my friends, to Hell with the neighbors. I'll party as long as I want."

George immediately grabs the man's hand as he is pounding his index finger into George's chest as he talks. George twists his hand, causing him to fall to his knees. Upon doing that Gene has handcuffs on him immediately. Gene instructs him to lie on the ground. George then goes over to the other guests who saw what was happening and they all instantly stand up and face the two policemen, pretending to be attentive.

George tells Gene to shut down the music, which he immediately does. Meanwhile, the handcuffed man stands back up and approaches the officers from the rear. Seeing the man Gene whirls around and pulls his weapon out and once again orders the man to the ground. Hesitantly the man complies. Meanwhile, George walks over to the other five people and tells them the party was over. He says he was not there to ask them to quiet down, but to tell them to end it. He also says, "Your friend here is going to jail tonight for assaulting an officer. He was aggressive and non-cooperative. Now, he will pay the price. And, if anyone of you do not cooperate, you can accompany him?"

Hearing that, the five guests back away and the two men put their arms and hands up in the air, as if to say, "Not us, we understand and will cooperate."

Gene approaches George from his left side and whispering in his ear he asks, "Partner, do you really want to arrest this fool? It will take us a long time to book him and fill out the necessary reports. Plus, I do not think he intended to be as aggressive as he was. He was just showing off for his guests. What do you think?"

George looks at Gene then at the man on the ground. He walks over to the man and asks, "So, what do you think? Still think the Hell with your neighbors? Are you still thinking you can do what you want?"

Lying on his stomach on the ground, looking up at George the man says, "I'm sorry officer. I was acting stupid. I agree, I need to be more respectful of my neighbors. I will do whatever you say."

"Oh, so you are not acting so tough now. If you would have been this cooperative at the beginning you wouldn't be lying face down in the grass. Do you understand that? Ok, now tell me your name," demands George.

Still looking up at George the man says, "My name is Jesus Rodriguez. This is my home. That is my wife over there. Her name is Kathy."

Turning to face the other five guests, George asks their names, and slowly they all comply with his request. George then looks back down at the man and asks, "Jesus, if I let you go, will you promise not to be so disruptive in the future? In fact, if anyone ever comes here again because of your loud music, I promise you that everyone here will go to jail. Do you understand me?"

Looking up, without hesitation, Jesus says, "Oh yes sir, I promise to be more considerate and you won't ever have to come here again."

With that, George turns to Gene and rather loudly says, "Ok partner, remove the cuffs and let him go. George then turns to the five guests and asks, "Do I have your promise to abide by the law and keep the music down?"

All five shake their heads yes. With that promise, George and Gene exit the back yard and return to their vehicle where Gene fills out an incident report. The elderly couple were no where to be seen. Assuming all was now well, the two men depart the address.

Upon leaving, George says, "I never intended to arrest that man. I just wanted to scare him. And, it all appeared to work just as I wanted. So, it looks to me like our shift is about over. I say let's head back to the station. And, before we leave, I want to know more about your brain injury and what you think we need to do next."

Driving back to the station, they pull into the parking lot about fifteen minutes before the end of their shift. Sitting in their vehicle, George says, "Since we are early, tell me more about what you have experienced and what your prognosis is."

Gene tells George about everything that has happened to date, going over once again the Nancy in the hospital scenario as well as what he experienced when he himself was still confined in there. He pretty much tells George everything that has occurred and about the mental tests he took and how the doctor said he was Psychic, and how his powers were increasing day by day.

George tries to understand what Gene says, but truly in his heart cannot believe it all. He responds by saying, "Look partner, you have been telling me this stuff now for several months. I will admit some really weird things have occurred when you and I were together, but I really find it hard to believe it all. Now, you know me, I am a real skeptic when it comes to paranormal events and it is just hard to understand how such a thing could have happened to you. I have known officers who were wounded like you were and none of them have ever claimed to experience anything close to what you are saying is happening. You just must understand, I want to believe you, but, common sense says it just can't be so. Let's call it a night and go on in and check out, then let's get out of here. We can talk more later on. Ok?

Heading home, Gene considers everything George said, and he could easily understand his reluctance in believing his overall ESP claims. Yet, he was telling George the truth. So, given that fact, he simply didn't know what else to do. Maybe saying nothing more was the best approach to take and for now he should just concentrate all his energy on finding Mrs. Ramos.

As he arrives at his apartment, Amelia was waiting up for him, watching television and laid out half sleeping on the couch. Looking at Gene, she says,"Hi sweetheart, I was waiting up to tell you something."

Smiling at seeing her, Gene bends down and kisses her and then asks, "So, what is it that is so important that kept you up this late?"

Amelia explains to him how one of her friends called her that evening and said she knew where Mrs. Ramos had moved to. And, she said she also had her phone number. Apparently her son and Mrs. Ramos's grandson are friends and he knew where his friend moved to. She then hands Gene her address and phone number. She also said he had a message earlier from Dr. Allen, reminding him of his appointment with her and Dr. Mendenhall next Thursday at 11:00 am.

Gene smiles at getting the news of Mrs. Ramos and tells Amelia how much he appreciated her help and that he would call her tomorrow. He then said he had totally forgotten about his appointment with Dr. Mendenhall, and says, "To be honest honey, going in to see him scares me. I fear I will find out that I am still increasing my psychic powers and it is never going to stop. And, if that is true, then what?" He then concludes his comments by telling Amelia about his and George's conversation this night and how George totally didn't believe him.

Amelia looks at Gene and says, "You cannot be afraid to see Dr. Mendenhall. Whatever the case may be, he can help you. And, as far as George goes, I say stop telling him anything. He is a moron and he will never understand a man with your talents. So, don't tell him anything about your personal life. And, that includes what you and I are doing together. And, speaking of 'doing' things together, I think it is time we went to bed, don't you?"

Smiling at her, Gene stands up, reaches down for her hand and happily escorts Amelia to their bedroom, where he helps her to undress.

The next morning Gene wakes up and immediately sees that Amelia had already left for work. Lying there he thinks about what he needs to do. First thing he wants to do is call Mrs. Ramos. He knows she will tell him everything. Then he needs to confirm his doctor's appointment. Eventually getting out of bed, Gene brews himself some coffee, fries a couple of eggs and reads the morning newspaper. Eventually showering, he dresses and goes to find Mrs. Ramos telephone number. Sitting down he dials the number.

"Hello", says the woman's voice on the other end.

"Hello, is this Gloria Ramos," asks Gene?

At first there is just silence, then hesitantly, the person responds by saying, "Yes, this is Gloria Ramos, who is this?"

"Mrs. Ramos, this is Gene Wilson, the policeman who helped you and your grandson a few weeks ago. Plus, you and I met several months ago when you told me about your ghostly experiences in San Pedro."

"Oh yes, of course I remember you Mr. Wilson. I never did thank you and your partner properly for your help. What can I do for you," asks Mrs. Ramos?

Taking a deep breath and clearing his throat, Gene says, "Well, first of all Mrs. Ramos, I was worried about you. I drove by your house and saw that you had moved. And, upon hearing that Father Kelley died in that house the day following our encounter in there, I just need to know what happened and why you moved."

Suddenly there is again total silence on her end. And, her lack of response causes Gene to ask if she was still on the phone?

"Ah, yes, I'm still here. But, (hesitating again) I cannot talk about any of that over the phone. I fear I'm sounding crazy to you, but I just cannot talk about it, as there are things that can't be explained," comments Mrs. Ramos.

"Mrs. Ramos, if I came to your home, could we sit down together, and would you then be able to talk about everything," asks Gene?

Again there is more silence on her end, when she eventually says, "Oh Mr. Wilson, it has been so distressful, and I live in constant fear of that thing finding me and attacking me again. I really am scared and feel that talking about it will just increase the chances of it finding me. And if it does, I am sure the next time it will kill me. Please, can't we just let it all pass? I do not wish to be rude, but I am seriously afraid of it finding me."

Feeling sympathy for her plight and knowing how scared she sounded, Gene wants to somehow assure her he is there to help and not cause her anymore problems. Quickly thinking about what to say or how to assure her that he wants to protect her he says, "Mrs. Ramos, I am going to tell you something that is very personal and if you can understand how it may benefit you, maybe together we can eliminate your fear and allow you to return to a normal life." Gene then goes on to explain his injury and how it has heightened his mental paranormal abilities and how he now sees 'angels' who are with him and will always point him in the right direction. He tells Mrs. Ramos that if anything negative was to approach him, these 'angels' would warn and protect him. He assures her if they are together anywhere, these 'angels' will protect them both.

Being a religious person, Mrs. Ramos does believe in angels and does take solace in hearing what Gene claims. But, this does not stop her from worrying about the evil entity finding her, even if these angels were around to protect them as Gene says they are. She still fears for her safety. Thinking about it she suggests, "Mr. Wilson, if you want to talk to me at all about any of these issues, the only way I am willing to meet you is through the sanctuary of my church. If you want, I can meet you at the same Catholic Church where Father Kelley was. As for me, I think inside my church, is the best solution and a place where I believe that our souls would be safe no matter what was discussed."

Thinking what a great idea that was, Gene says, "Sure, Mrs. Ramos, that would be fine for me. I can make it any morning or early afternoon, but I have to be on duty by 5:00 pm. So, does tomorrow work for you?"

"Oh yes Mr. Wilson, tomorrow morning would work fine, could we meet in the church at say 10:30 am.? I will be sitting close to the front, in the first seat by the isle. Is that Ok," asks Mrs. Ramos?

Thinking about it, Gene agrees that would be perfect. He therefore says, "That's good for me, so it's a date Mrs. Ramos, I look forward to seeing you tomorrow."

After he hangs up he calls Dr. Allen's office and confirms his next appointment in two days at 11:00 am. The receptionist asks Gene how he was and explains that both doctors are anxious to visit with him.

Arriving home Gene sees his message phone's light was blinking. Checking the message, he is surprised to hear that it was from Captain John Mitchell, his night commander of L.A.P.D.'s police precinct. The message simply asked for him to call the commander as soon as possible.

Dialing the number, a voice answers and asks who was calling. Gene responds and within a few seconds he is connected with Captain Mitchell.

"Captain Mitchell, here," says the voice on the other end.

"Hello Captain Mitchell, this is Officer Gene Wilson, I am returning your call sir," says Gene.

"Yes Wilson, thanks for calling. Look, there is no easy way to say this, so I am just going to state it. Your partner, George Newton met with me earlier today and asked if he and you could be split up. It seems he is worried about your mental state and he really feels he cannot count on you to back him up in the event of an emergency. Now, I have no sides to take in such matters, but it has always been my policy to grant such requests, because teams need to be able to work together, and each person needs to feel confident in their partner's ability to cover their back. And, to be honest, once it is done, it always works out for the best for both parties. So, tonight I have you scheduled to be at a desk here in the precinct. And, when I have time, we can see about finding you a new partner. When you arrive, after changing into your uniform, report to Sergeant Billings. He will be expecting you. Then, I will talk to you later on." explains Captain Mitchel.

Totally shocked at what he just heard, and almost speechless, Gene manages to say, "Yes sir. I certainly disagree with George. But, I do understand what you are saying. I will check in with Sergeant Billings upon my arrival tonight."

Ending the conversation the Captain tells Gene that he will see him tonight and they can discuss George's claims in more detail and he will be happy to listen to Gene's comments as well.

Upon hanging up, Gene is in shock. He sits down and doesn't know what to think. He has only partnered with George and he thought his recent conversations with him were being at least partially understood and accepted. Maybe this was the signal he needed in order to move on and finish getting his law degree. He thinks to himself that he didn't want to be a policeman if he had to start over with a new partner. Gene just sits and thinks about everything and begins to form a plan on when he should take the California Bar Exam. He also plans on how he would go about looking for a law firm to work with. As he sits there, the more confident he becomes over his making the decision that he no longer wanted to be a policeman. So, how and when would he begin his new career? That was what he needed to figure out now.

At 6:00 pm, Gene is at the station, dressed and looking for, and finds Sergeant Billings. After a few moments of commiserating with him the sergeant instructs Gene on what he would be doing. He also says that Captain Mitchell would be around later that evening and talk to him. Meanwhile, until that occurred he was instructed to perform the needed inside duties that Sergeant Billings was responsible for. As Gene sits and works he looks around hoping that George might come in and tell him face to face why he did what he did. Yet, knowing him, he doubted that he would have the nerve to face him. Gene bets that George wouldn't ever say anything to him about it.

At 11:00 pm, Captain Mitchell approaches Gene and suggests they go to his office and talk.

Gene gets up and follows his boss into his office. Captain Mitchell closes his office door and asks Gene to sit down. Looking at Gene he asks, "Gene, how do you feel? Are you back, 100%? What is your assessment of your policing skills?"

Catching his breath he can tell that the Captain seems to know everything that has happened between him and George. He begins by saying, "First of all Captain, let me tell you that I suffered a severe head injury when I was shot several months ago, and to be honest, things are occurring daily that causes me to actually see the world a whole lot differently than I did before. I have been tested by two well respected physicians, and it is their opinion the bullet upon entering my brain, somehow stimulated an area that woke up senses that normal people never experience. I am sure George thinks I am crazy and therefore not reliable or a safe backup. And, probably in his shoes, I might think that too. However, I can prove with letters from these two doctors that I am not crazy and in fact have developed psychic abilities that are constantly growing, which causes me to experience things that I can't fully understand yet, but hopefully, I eventually will. I know this all may sound crazy to you. And, I can only assume you agree with George and might think the only solution is to furlough me. But, if you do, I warn you that I will seek legal advice from my union and I will do whatever I have to, in order to prove I'm telling you the truth."

"Gene, I have already spoken to Dr Allen and she confirms exactly everything that you are saying. I believe that you truly are experiencing something the rest of us can only imagine. I also know that you have a new test pending with her and the other doctor in two days. She says that test will measure the degree of advancement of your new skills. So, let me assure you, I only separated you and George, because he was afraid to serve with you. And, whether or not I agree with him about your abilities isn't the issue. The issue is that each partnership has to feel as though they can count on the other person when there is danger. And, if they cannot, then we need to deal with that. Which is precisely what I did? I do not think you are weak or cannot be counted on. But he did. Therefore, it is now my responsibility to put you where the department can best utilize you. So, in your mind, where might that be?" asks the captain.

Gene is happy to know that the Captain believes him and does not think he is crazy, like George does. But, what can he say to him? If George talks about him to the other officers, it is likely no one will ever want to partner with him. Thinking before he responds he says, "Captain, you may not know it, but I recently graduated from Long Beach State University with a law degree. And, when George and I were together, we often spoke about my primary goal, which was to pass the bar exam and seek a job as a lawyer. Now, given what has happened between me and George, I am sure he has, or will be telling all the other officers around here why he and I are no longer together. As much as I love police work, I just cannot see anybody wanting to partner with me. What would you say if I said I would like inside work for say 30 to 60 days, and during that time, I will schedule the bar exam. And, if I pass it, then my decision about what to do will be very easy for me. I'll quietly resign and become a lawyer."

Looking at Gene, the Captain says, "Gene, I understand your concern. And, like it or not, I agree that George will most likely be talking about you, in order to justify his decision to change partners. You have always been a good officer and I do not think anyone would be in danger partnering with you. But, I do understand and I really do hate to see you go. I can also understand why you would want to be a lawyer. Certainly, it is better pay and decent hours. But as to your suggestion, yes, feel free to stay here doing inside work for as long as you want. Then after you take your test, and pass it, let's talk more then."

"Thanks Captain, I truly appreciate your support and positive comments. I promise I will not let you down. And, thanks for the job offer. I will see you again once I have my test scheduled and I will firm up my termination date.

Without saying anything the Captain stands, extends his hand, the two men shake and Gene returns to his desk. Sitting down he feels better. Everything necessary was said and the Captain understood and sincerely did not want Gene to leave. That was important to him and now he knows whatever happens, he is credible to the senior staff.

Early the next morning Gene rises and begins getting ready for his meeting with Mrs. Ramos. He has several questions and he hopes she can answer without any fear or reluctance of the demonic spirit finding her. He knows her to be a strong and honest woman, but obviously something chased her out of her home and from their last conversation she is definitely fearful.

At 10:30 am, Gene enters the church's front door. Looking around he doesn't see Mrs. Ramos, so he decides to sit in the rear of the church to wait for her. At approximately 10:40 am. Mrs. Ramos enters the church. Immediately seeing Gene she smiles and walks over to him. Gene hugs the woman and asks where she wanted to sit. She explains that before they begin, she wants to say her prayers and talk to God. Understanding, Gene remains in the back of the church as the woman walks forward and kneels in prayer. After about ten minutes, she returns to Gene and sits besides him.

"Well Mrs. Ramos, I was worried about you when I saw your home was vacant. Then, upon learning of Father Kelley's death, I naturally felt that maybe his demise must have had something to do with your decision to leave. But, whatever the story is, I would really like to hear exactly what happened after me and George left you with the priest that night," asks Gene?

With tears forming in her eyes, she takes out a handkerchief and wipes them away. She then takes a deep breath and says, "You have no idea how bad that evil thing is. I left out of fear for my own safety. And as you know, Father Kelley went to my house the very next day with a lot of holly water. He sprinkled it everywhere as he said one prayer after another going from room to room. I sat in his car, as he instructed me to do. After almost thirty minutes, when he didn't return, I began to worry. I decided to get out of the car and go inside to look for him. I found him lying on my kitchen floor. His eyes and mouth were wide open and there was the most awful shocked look on his face. I think that he was literally scared to death. At first I tried to wake him, but he wouldn't respond. I went to the phone and called 911. By the time the police and ambulance arrived, I too had been attacked. The entity made itself known to me. It appeared right out of thin air and was standing no more than two feet away. It stunk so badly and it was laughing at me in a very sadistic way. Its eyes were beet red and its face was wild looking. As it laughed at me it had this grotesque smelly drool dripping down both sides of it ugly mouth. It then began moving closer and closer until my backside was up against the wall. It then pressed its very hot body against me and reached out and put its hairy hand on my head. I immediately began to have the worst pain imaginable in my brain. Without any control over my body, I slumped to the floor like a rag doll. It then bent over and I felt its hot breath on my head as its face came down to my level and looked straight into my eyes, causing me to sense its desire to kill me. Then, just when I expected it to hurt me, the police entered my open front door and that saved me. They claim they didn't see anything attacking me, but I don't know how they couldn't have seen it. That thing was right there, bending over me."

Gene listens intently and says, "I certainly understand your fear. I too saw that thing's face the night we took you to see Father Kelley. And, as you described, it was hideous looking. It was definitely never human and had to be spawned by Lucifer. I have to also tell you about myself and something that is occurring in my brain." Gene goes on to describe his gun shot wound and how it heightened areas of his brain, giving him more in depth insight to the paranormal world. He explains seeing Nancy #1 and Nancy # 2. He tells Mrs. Ramos about the shadow people and how they seem to be there to protect him whenever danger is present.

Mrs. Ramos looks at him and says, "Mr. Wilson, you are truly lucky. There is no doubt that God has selected you for something important. I know you may think this new gift is a curse, but I see it differently. I see it as nothing short of a miracle and something that you need to use wisely. If I had such a gift, I would be grateful and never afraid again."

Gene then explains to her the vision he had of the demonic entity causing Father Kelley's death by touching him, making his heart fail.

Looking at Gene, she says, "Oh my God, that is so strange, I too sensed that entity killed Father Kelley. That was why the shocked look was frozen on his face. And, that is exactly what I explained to the church Bishop and that new priest Father Sanchez. They listened, but did not respond. Yet, I could tell that they too feared something evil had attacked Father Kelley."

"That's interesting to hear. I tried to quiz Father Sanchez about how Father Kelley died, but he refused to respond in any specific way. But, earlier his receptionist had told me Father Kelley was killed. I now wonder if that idea came to her through your commentary, or maybe the church agreed with you and said so verbally to others. I later told the new priest about someone in the church saying that he was killed and he actually appeared to not know anything about that. But when I left his office that same receptionist was crying, which was right after he had exited our meeting to search for information about your new address. It is indeed strange," says Gene.

Thinking about it, Mrs. Ramos says, "Well, I can tell you for certain that Bishop James, who is the head of our church definitely felt that something unnatural happened to Father Kelley, because he too saw the look of fear on the dead priest face. He also realized that Father Kelley was there to cleanse the house of an unholy spirit, as holly water was found on him. And, I also explained why he went there. He told me that Father Kelley had not asked for permission to cleanse the house, which was the normal course of action. He said it was wrong of Father Kelley to proceed on his own. He explained that before any cleansing can occur, the church has to understand what it is dealing with and then decide how to proceed. Often, a specialist might be summoned and Father Kelley could have accompanied the expert, making such encounters with evil entities less likely. So, maybe that's why the church has not wanted to discuss this and maybe they feel it would be best to just let the issue fade away."

After listening to Mrs. Ramos and her explanations about everything that happened, Gene, feels like he now has the correct story. And, he felt no additional need to pursue any more answers from the church. However, he was still wondering about Mrs. Ramos and asks, "So, was the attack you experienced when you found Father Kelley the reason you moved out? Or did anything more occur that forced you to make that decision?"

"Oh, Mr. Wilson, I was scared to death when that thing squeezed my head. I knew then and there that I couldn't ever be safe in that house. So, later that night, my daughter and I returned to pack my suit cases so we could move into a motel until I could decide what to do next. I guess it was about 6:00 pm when we returned. I figured with my daughter by my side for morale support, maybe that thing would leave us alone. All went well for about forty minutes. I had all of my bags packed and hauled out to her car. She had just taken the last suitcase out and I was in my bedroom boxing up my jewelry and family photographs. Suddenly, I hear a scream coming from my daughter in the living room. She had just entered the house after taking my last bag out to her car. She said upon entering the front door the beast appeared to her and physically assaulted her. It pushed her to the ground and was literally pulling off her clothes, and was trying to rape her. When I went into the room and saw what it was doing, I grabbed my bible from the dining table and a large crucifix that was on the wall. I went to them and I immediately began beating it over the beast's head with the small end of the cross. But when I placed my bible flat on its back and began praying out loud to God for help, it stopped attacking my daughter and let out a very loud howl as if it was in pain. It got off of my daughter, stood up, and took a swing at me. It barely made contact, but even so, it knocked me down. Both my daughter and I jumped right up and ran from that house and never looked back. I found a real estate company called Moore Realty and listed it the next day."

"Wow, what a story. Has the Realtor experienced anything when showing the house or being inside," asks Gene?

Thinking about that, Mrs. Ramos says, "Not to my knowledge. I know it has been shown several times and there have been a couple of serious lookers. Yet, so far no offers have been made. I will tell you one thing Mr. Wilson, I am fearful for anyone who buys that house. What if the beast stays there and then harms them. I would be responsible for their injuries because I didn't warn them. Do you think I should tell the Realtor?"

Gene thinks about that and agrees that the Realtor does need to be made aware of what has happened. He knows by law any death in a home needs to be made public to potential buyers, so he assumes the belief that an evil presence is in the home should be made public too. He then says, "Yes, I feel the Realtor needs to know everything. In fact, in California I believe the law requires full disclosure of anything pertinent. That way the listing and selling agents are covered from any potential legal action from a buyer. They likely will not believe you, but that should eliminate any responsibility on your part. And, if you would like, I would be happy to accompany you to their office right now and collaborate the facts on what all has happened in my presence."

Mrs. Ramos is happy Gene made that offer and looking at him she says, "Oh Mr. Wilson, if you would do that, I would be very happy. Being a police officer, I know they will believe you. Otherwise, they would just think me some sort of crazy old woman."

Gene smiles and says, "It would be my pleasure, would you like to go there now and get it over with?"

Looking at her watch she looks up at Gene and says, "If you have the time, so do I. Now is good for me, and if you can go now, lets do it."

Gene stands up and extends his hand to Mrs. Ramos, indicating he was ready to go. She grasps his hand, stands up while Gene says, "If you want I can drive and I'll bring you back here when we are done."

While driving towards the real estate office Mrs. Ramos inquires about Gene's partner. She says, "I never felt he really believed us when you two took us to Father Kelley. He acted as if we were all crazy. I was surprised how different you two are. At the time, you seemed like an odd couple, with you feeling one way and him another."

Listening to her comments Gene responds, "Well, to be honest, George and I did have our problems. Ever since I was shot, and then returned back to work, he and I never really got along like we did before the shooting. As I explained to you earlier, the wound woke up an area of my brain that caused me to begin seeing and sense things that George simply could not see, let along understand. I scared him, and caused him to fear that he could not count on me any longer as a safe partner. And, because of that, he recently asked for, and received a new partner."

Stunned upon hearing that information, Mrs. Ramos says, "Oh, Mr. Wilson, I am so sorry for you. I can't imagine him not feeling safe with you. If anything, added psychic powers would enhance your value to him and likely improve your safety factors. That is really strange."

"Well, it baffled me too when it happened. My feelings were hurt and I was angry. However, over time, I came to realize that as close as we were, we really never knew each other. I now realize that there are people in this world that are non-believers and there is nothing anyone could ever say to convince them otherwise. I fear George is that type of person," explains Gene.

As he finishes his comments, they arrive at Moore Real Estate Company. They exit his vehicle and go inside to talk to the agent that listed her house.

The woman at the reception counter asks if she can help them and Mrs. Ramos asks, "Is Mr. Lawrence Moore in? I need to talk to him regarding the listing he recently took on my home."

Looking at her check out list she sees that Mr. Moore was there, somewhere. She asks Mrs. Ramos and Gene to have a seat while she pages him. They wait about five minutes.

"Hello Mrs. Ramos," says a voice behind her.

Turning around there stood a tall thin man with a neatly groomed beard who was about six feet, three inches tall.

"Oh hello Mr. Moore, how are you? I would like to introduce you to my friend Mr. Wilson."

The two men shake hands and they are invited into a private conference room where Mr. Moore closes the door and invites them to sit down. "So, what is it I can do for you two," asks Mr. Moore?

Gene begins by introducing himself as a friend of Mrs. Ramos, and also mentions he is a Los Angeles Police officer. He begins by saying, "Mr. Moore, I was talking to Mrs. Ramos today and certain events that have occurred in her home that you have listed for sale, are events that I feel are serious enough in nature that she needed to come here to disclose them to you. Then, after you have heard what she has to say you can decide for yourself how you want to proceed. I offered to accompany Mrs. Ramos, to add validity to what we are going to tell you, because I too witnessed these events. Now, let me first say, we cannot prove what we saw and experienced nor can we really explain it either. However, I first met Mrs. Ramos many months ago, but was reunited with her again just recently when my partner and I responded to a call for help at her home." Gene goes on to tell Mr. Moore the complete story, including their experience, their taking her to the church and the subsequent death of the priest. He then continues by discussing in detail the recent attack on Mrs. Ramos and her daughter.

Looking totally dumbfounded Mr. Moore is at a total loss over how to respond. He looks at them both and asks, "Is this a joke?"

Smiling at him, Gene says, "I know what foolishness this sounds like and if I were you, I too would think that. However, we are very serious. Everything I just described to you truly happened. And, knowing a little about California's disclosure laws for selling real estate, I knew we needed to make you aware of these facts to protect Mrs. Ramos and you against any legal action from any potential buyer. So, I think we have now done what was right by coming here and telling you our story. So, it is up to you to judge for yourself just what steps you need to take next."

Mr. Moore looks at Gene and Mrs. Ramos and says, "Well, if this is a joke, it's a good one. But, if you are serious, then I really do need to know about it. Yes, you are right, if anything as you just described was truly there, it does need disclosing. And, I wasn't aware of the priest dying in there either. Therefore, I need to prepare an addendum to the listing agreement, and I need Mr. Ramos to sign it. So, if you are serious, please wait while I get the paper work. This way we are both protected from any problems later on." Within a few minutes Mr. Moore returns and shows the form to Mrs. Ramos. She reads it and without hesitation signs it. She gets one copy and the Realtor keeps one.

Driving Mrs. Ramos back to the church she thanks Gene for taking her there and thinking about that issue. She says, "It would never have occurred to me to tell the real estate man about that evil thing. I would have assumed he would just think I was crazy. Of course with you being a police officer, I think that helped him believe our story. Plus, the fact Father Kelley died there was another event that he needed to know about and disclose."

"Well Mrs. Ramos, you and I know the truth, but you are right, few people have ever experienced such a terrible event and if one is a non-believer in such things, of course they will not believe our story. But, believe us or not, if anyone buys that house, you have at least done what was necessary to protect yourself from any legal action, and you did warn them. Hopefully, Mr. Moore will add that information to the listing agreement whether or not he even believes us." As Gene says that, he pulls up in front of the church. Parking, the two sit in Gene's car talking about what her future plans were. Mrs. Ramos indicates that she was moving back up to northern California as soon as possible to get away from this area and its bad memories. She promised to let him know where exactly she moves to, and promises to send him her new phone number. After a few more moments, she exits the vehicle and heads back into the church. Gene starts his car and heads home.

Entering his apartment, he sees the message light on his phone blinking and checks it out. The caller was Amelia. She was reminding Gene of his meeting tomorrow morning with Dr. Allen, and she also wanted Gene to know that she had scheduled his Bar Examination for Friday morning at City Hall. So, it seemed as if everything positive was working for him. He worried about his meeting with Dr Allen, but was very anxious to finally be able to take the California Bar Exam. With that in mind, he sits down and begins reviewing several law books. After an hour, Gene was very confident in his overall knowledge of law and was positive he could pass that test.

CHAPTER 7; *True Reality Sets In*

Sitting at his police station's information desk, Gene answers a few telephone calls and handles a couple of walk in inquiries. As he was about to take his lunch break, he is summoned to Captain Mitchell's office.

Gene gets up and hurries to the Captain's office to see what he wanted. He knocks and is instructed to enter. Upon doing so, Gene is shocked to see his old partner George sitting in one of the chairs. Stopping to look at George, Captain Mitchell says, "Gene, something serious has happened and George here thinks that maybe you can help. It seems that earlier this evening while shopping at the Del Amo Fashion Center, George's thirteen year old niece was either kidnapped or she ran away. His brother and sister-in-law are panicked and they immediately called George when their daughter did not meet them at the pre-determined time and place. Being a policeman, they hoped that he would be able to help them find her. Now, before we get into why you are here, let me say the young girl has never had any problems with her parents before. She is a good student and it is highly unlikely that she would have run away. So, we truly fear she was kidnapped. When George heard this, he too agreed that his niece, Megan, would not have run away. So, he has come here and asked me if I could release you from your duties here tonight and allow you to accompany him in order to search for her. George has clearly said to me he thinks your special powers and ability to see things might help expedite the search."

Gene is stymied by the request and responds, "Well of course I am willing to help. But, finding people isn't anything I have ever done before. I have no idea how to begin or what to look for. Plus, it seems odd that George who was afraid to partner with me, now suddenly thinks I am somehow 'special.' His comments to everyone else around here about how crazy I am, because of the weird things I claimed to see and feel, seems odd that he would now seeks my help. I sensed that he didn't believe in my powers at all."

"Gene, there is no doubt that your claims scared me to death. And, to be honest, I am still scared. But, if any of it may be true, I plead with you to overlook those comments I made and come with me. Even if you cannot help, I feel it is worth the effort to try. I fear the worst has happened to her, and who knows what some pervert is doing to her right now. I am sorry for what I did to you and I realize why you may hate me. But please come with me and see what you can do to help find Megan. Please. Do it for her, not for me," begs George.

Looking at Captain Mitchell, Gene says, "I will go with George if it is agreeable with you sir. I certainly do not know what I can do, but I am willing to try."

Nodding his approval, Captain Mitchell says, "Go, do what you can. Take whatever time you need and good luck."

Gene and George get up. George thanks Gene and Captain Mitchell. The two men then head to George's cruiser. Once inside, Gene says, "I do not know what to do first, but I have this odd desire to hold onto something of Megan's. Let's first go to her house and get something she recently either wore or carried."

George agrees and heads to his brother's home. As they drive, they are silent. Neither man knows what to say to the other. George is embarrassed and is afraid to say anything. Gene is angry and fears if he says anything it would cause a serious argument. For twenty minutes the two men sit side by side totally silent. Reaching the brother's home, George parks and invites Gene to join him inside. The two exit the car, walk to the front door and George knocks.

Opening the door, George's brother asks, "What have you found, is there any news of Megan?"

George introduces Gene to his brother Ray. The two shake hands. George then says, "Ray, you have often heard me speak of Gene. He and I were partners for several years. About eleven months ago Gene was shot in the head when we responded to a call. While he was in the hospital, they discovered that the bullet wound stimulated a new part of Gene's brain, causing him to experience an increase to his psychic abilities. Now, it is possible those abilities may aid us in finding Megan. What we need from you right now is either an article of clothing Megan recently wore or something she has handled a lot."

Bewildered at George's comments Ray isn't sure about this and like his brother he has never believed in such stuff before. However, since he respects George, he thinks and says, "Well, yes. Megan's back pack is right here and it contains a lot of her personal items. Will that do?"

Gene speaks up and says, "Yes, that would be perfect. Please can we have it and we will bring it back to you this evening."

Handing the back pack to Gene, George thanks his brother and says they will do their best to find Megan as soon as possible. Heading to their car, getting in, Gene immediately begins going through her back pack. He feels everything and closes his eyes. Not knowing what to expect, he is surprised when he begins to actually see images flashing through his mind. They are quick but definitely sights of kids at school and crowds of students walking around. He continues to touch everything and the back pack itself. He opens his eyes, turns to George and says, "George, it is really weird, but I actually can see images of kids doing things at school, and as if I am following them, I see this back pack on the back of a girl with long blonde hair. Does Megan have blonde hair?"

Startled, George immediately says, "Yes, she is definitely a blonde and her hair is really long. Are you telling me you can see her? Where is she?"

Gene answers by saying, "No, I cannot see her now, but I did see images of her when she was wearing this back pack and using the items in it. But those were images of her prior to her going missing. I think in order to find her now, I would need something from her while or after she was abducted. I need to see what she saw. So, if I could find something personal that she held, it might help to identify who took her, and maybe show me where she was taken."

George is silent for a moment and than says, "Back at the station, forensics picked up a sweater and a school book found on the ground close to where we think Megan might have been. It was not shown to her parents, so we are not sure if it was hers or not. But, if it is hers, maybe we can get it from them and see what you can sense." George then turns his vehicle and heads back to the station. Arriving there in less than fifteen minutes, the two men head to the forensics department. George asks the sergeant in control of evidence if they could see the items. The man obliges and George hands the sweater and book to Gene.

Gene takes the sweater and holds it tight, turning it over and over with his eyes closed. He then also holds the book along with the sweater. He tries hard to see something but nothing was happening.

George stands by looking and waiting as the sergeant asks George what Gene was doing. Not wanting to disturb Gene's concentration, George puts up his right hand to indicate to the sergeant to wait and be quiet.

Suddenly, Gene sees a very bright light go off in his head and he jerks backwards almost falling to the floor. Images are being seen of a man grabbing a long haired blonde girl and pushing her into his van. As he drives away, in Gene's mind he sees the license plate and shouts out the number. He says it over and over, and George grabs a pencil and paper from the sergeant and writes it down.

George watches as Gene drops the sweater and book, as he is obviously physically exhausted. With sweat pouring down his face, Gene looks to George and says, "I saw her. I saw the man, and the van they drove away in. I think I saw the license number too. The man was big, with long shaggy hair and a bushy beard. He was maybe in his late thirties or early forties. The van was a dirty white Dodge. God, I cannot believe all of this. I would never have expected to be able to see such stuff. When I have seen people on television do that, I always thought it was fake. But I truly did see those things."

George immediately goes to their communications center and has the plates Gene shouted out run. Instantly a name, address and warrants appear. The van was a 1981 Dodge. He returns to Gene and says, come on partner, I have his name and address. As they get into their police car, Gene radios for back up and gives the name and address of where they were going. Within twenty minutes they are at the address. The white van was in the driveway and one light was on in the back of the house. Quietly they exit their vehicle and wait for assistance. Soon two more units arrive, and the home is quickly surrounded. Standing at the front door, George is so excited that without announcing himself as a police officer, he simply kicks it in. He quickly goes from one empty room to another until he kicks open the door in the back of the house where the light was on.

When the door flies open, the exact same man Gene described is standing there, right in front of George, totally naked. And, directly behind him lying on the bed, also naked, and tied up was Megan. She was crying but alive. A dirty rag was crammed into her mouth with duct tape over it, to keep her from screaming. Immediately, George hits the man as hard as he can right between the eyes, knocking him down and out. George starts to jump on him, but Gene grabs him. As two other officers enter the room they have to restrain George from further hitting the man. They are forced to drag him out of the house. Meanwhile, Gene places a blanket over Megan's naked body, and the kidnapper is handcuffed and dragged from the room too.

As she cries, Gene removes her gag and unties her hands and feet. She grabs Gene around the neck and sobs uncontrollably. Gene says, "Megan, you are safe now. Uncle George found you and you're going to be just fine. Please try to relax. An ambulance has been called and they will take you to the hospital for a quick check up. And, your parents will meet you there. Please try to calm down."

Megan cannot let go of Gene. Therefore, he simply sits on the bed's edge and holds her until the ambulance paramedics enter the room and take over.

By the time the abductor is arrested and charged it is late and knowing that George had been taken to the Captain's office to be reprimanded for his violent attack against the kidnapper, Gene knew that it was going to be a long, heated and nasty discussion, so he decides to head on home. He changes out of his uniform, completes his paperwork and leaves.

Early the next morning Amelia wakes Gene up, to tell him Dr. Allen was on the phone and wanted to speak to him. Sleepy and tired he takes the phone and says, "Good morning Dr. Allen, what's up?"

"What's up indeed? I cannot believe the headlines in this morning's paper. Local law enforcement officer has psychic connection to kidnapped girl. Is this for real? It says you touched her clothing and from that had a vision and actually saw the attacker, and the vehicle he drove her away in. Then upon running the license number you saw, you were able to obtain his home address, whereby you and your partner went there and found him and the kidnapped girl. Is that all true," asks Dr. Allen?

Gathering his thoughts and taking a deep breath, Gene asks, "Is all of that in this morning's newspaper? Yes, those facts sound like what happened, but I have to tell you, it surprised me more than anyone. But yes, we did find the girl and we arrested the kidnapper. Now, this event is something I definitely want to discuss with you and Dr. Mendenhall during my appointment today. It was totally out of left field. I had no idea that I could do it, but my ex-partner asked me to try. I did, and within minutes I saw stuff. It was really weird how it evolved."

"Mr. Wilson, this is big. I mean very big. Do you understand how something like that works? It is so very rare. And, I know when we last checked you out with those tests; such a thing back then was not possible. This means you have really evolved and have achieved some level of awareness that most of us can only dream about. Dr Mendenhall is very anxious to meet with you this morning, please do not be late. Please get here as close to 10:30 am as you can," begs the doctor.

Thinking about it Gene becomes scared. If he has evolved more, does that mean he won't stop evolving? He then asks, "Dr. Allen, this seems to me to be a bad sign. It would appear that I am getting worse. What can happen to me? Will it kill me?"

"Calm down Mr. Wilson. This is not proof of anything. All it proves is that whatever gift you have, it is gaining in positive power. Now, just think about it. What you did last night was a good thing. Maybe it is a sign of how your powers can be focused on helping people. Please do not be worried. Dr. Mendenhall will perform more tests when you get here and he can better explain what is happening. So, we will see you soon, Ok? Just be open minded and we can talk about everything as much as you want," explains Dr. Allen.

Gene agrees to be on time and in his heart, he cannot help but worry about this so called gift. Yes, it worked well last night but, he fears it is a sign he is still increasing his psychic abilities and he will not be able to control it. If it keeps expanding in capacity, then what? Will it eventually kill him? He feels like it is taking him over and he will have no way to keep from turning into some sort of a freak.

"What was that call all about," asks, Amelia?

Gene looks at her and is fearful to tell her what he is worried about. He then says, "Well, my dear, it seems your boyfriend had a psychic event last night, which led my fellow police officers to a home where a missing girl was being held. We found her through my mental capabilities, as I actually saw the man who kidnapped her and the license number of the vehicle he drover her away in. We ran the number, it matched what I saw and we went to his house and found the man and the girl. We saved her and arrested him. That was Dr. Allen on the phone and she says the story is in this morning's newspaper. They are anxious to see me in order to do more tests. I agree what happened last night was good, but what if this 'gift' is growing inside of me. What will happen to me when it takes over my whole brain and body?"

Surprised at his comments, Amelia says, "Gene that's wonderful news. What could you possibly be worried about? Your gift can be used all over the world to help find missing people. That would mean fame and money for you. What is there to worry about sweetheart?"

"No, you don't understand. What if this is only happening because the psychic thing is growing out of control in my head and it won't ever stop? It could easily cripple or kill me. Sure if it stopped, that might be good. But, I fear it will not. And, if that's so, what will eventually happen to me," asks Gene?

Amelia is also concerned and says, "Well, wouldn't the doctors you are going to see be able to determine what is happening? I would think they can tell what is going on by your motor skills and psychic aptitude tests they are administering to you."

"Yes, you would think they could, but so far they haven't been able to determine anything. I really do not think their tests are that accurate. Last time I visited them, they said I was still growing in my abilities, but they couldn't predict how long it would continue to grow. I guess I will just have to see what they say today. Hopefully, today they will be able to know something more definite," says Gene.

Looking at her wrist watch, Amelia says, "Oh I am late for work. I must go." She then leans over and kisses Gene and quickly leaves the apartment.

Watching Amelia heading to her car he realizes what a fine woman she was and how he hopes his life will settle down, allowing him to become a good lawyer at a prestigious firm somewhere and then be able to eventually marry Amelia and have a beautiful family. As she drives away, Gene heads for the shower. He shaves, dresses and then heads to Dr. Allen's office.

Arriving right at 10:30 am, he is greeted by Dr. Allen's receptionist and is told the two doctors would be right with him. Within minutes the door opens and Dr. Allen invites him into her office. Inside Dr Mendenhall is reading some reports and looks up as Gene enters the room.

"Hello Mr. Wilson. It is really nice to see you again. I read earlier this morning of your wonderful involvement in the capture of that kidnapper last night. Isn't it wonderful the little girl was unharmed and you found that man before he could do anything to her? Please tell me in your own words exactly how it all unfolded, which allowed you to see the license number on his van, as well as his physical appearance," asks Dr. Mendenhall.

As Dr. Mendenhall says that, Dr. Allen hands Gene the morning paper and for the first time he reads the article. Looking up at the doctors, he says, "Well, surprisingly enough, the account in this paper is quite accurate. I wonder who told them? But, to be honest, I sure wished they had not. Now, I can only imagine the jokes that I will have to endure at work." Gene then goes on to describe in detail the entire bazaar event, leaving out nothing. The doctors listen intently, asking many questions as he speaks.

Dr. Mendenhall is defiantly impressed and immediately says, "Mr. Wilson, scientists and other medical people who have made a life out of studying the brain still know very little about its real ability and functionality. For example, how it heals itself is the biggest mystery. It wasn't long ago that neurology scientists felt that when the brain was damaged, it was irreversible. But, that isn't so. They now know that the brain can heal itself. And, when examples like you occur, it proves that the brain can also grow in capacity and ability. It use to be that only when patients had tumors were they capable of such increased brain activity. However, as we know now, you do not have a tumor and your stimulus was caused from a trauma, a gunshot wound to the head. It is so mystifying to see what is happening with you."

"Well it might be mystical to you doctor, but to me it is plain scary. I am seeing and experiencing things daily that you only read about in science fiction books. Yet, what is happening to me is real. What do I do, and why is it happening," asks Gene?

Dr. Mendenhall easily senses Gene's concerns and knows how scared he is over this new power. He decides to step into a doctor's roll and try to explain in layman's terms how the brain works. He begins, "Mr. Wilson, let me begin this visit by explaining the basics about how the brain works, and then maybe by knowing some facts you can understand what is happening to you. First of all, I am sure you understand that the brain has several sectors to it, and each part controls various body and motor functions. In fact, there are three different lobes. They are the cerebellum, the Pons and the Medulla Prolongate, which are all connected to the Spinal Cord. The cerebrum is the largest part of the human brain. It ties into the cortex which is the conduit that receives and interprets sensory information that initiates movement, analyzes information and controls the humans reasoning powers. Now, on a physical level, the human brain consists of four principal parts; the brain stem, diencephalons, cerebrum and the cerebellum. And, even though all four are important, the cerebellum is what we are most interested in, when it comes to you. It contains billions of neurons, which is the most developed area of the brain. On a psychic and spiritual level, the crown chakra (one of the brain's seven major energy centers) directs energy through the cerebellum downward causing a divine intelligence development. This causes the power of the mind to increase. This enables you to reach a more spiritual level which causes you to use more of your brain's power than most other people. When that occurs, two types of genes are developed. One is a master gene and the other is a telepathic or telekinetic gene. And, if you do have both of these genes, which I believe you now do, this is what creates your psychic powers. And, with time, these powers increase. In fact, they increase in three stages, called hierarchies. The first stage is simple. It is just awareness of things around you, much like you described your 'shadow people' to be. But, to reach stage two, it requires more external stimulus for heightened complex senses to be activated. And, you seeing the two Nancy women you encountered and her future auto accident meets that stage requirement. And, stage three is where the most phenomenally powerful psychic energy is developed. And, I am suspecting that stage three is the stage you are now entering. Actually, it is my opinion, as well as other scientists that once you enter the third level, that allows you to actually read minds. And, I feel a form of mind reading is what you experienced when you found that young woman last night. By touching her personal belongings you could feel her energy, which directed you to be able to link mentally with her, allowing you to literally read her thoughts and see what she saw. Through her, you saw the man's face who grabbed her, you saw the vehicle she was taken away in and somewhere before entering it, she must have seen his license plate, which you also picked up on. To me, that explains it completely. Now, of course that is only my opinion, but it makes a lot of sense and explains how you saw what you did."

Gene listens intently and actually does understand a lot of what Dr. Mendenhall was explaining. He then looks at the doctor and asks, "So, you are saying I have reached a plain where I can actually read the minds of others? Is that what you think?"

Dr. Allen jumps in to answer and says, "Mr. Wilson, it isn't something that can or will always work. Megan's heightened fear and physical duress made her more emotionally susceptible to someone being able to find her by reading her thoughts. In that state of conscientiousness, her mind was open to the possibility of it being read by you or any other clairvoyant. Of course she didn't know that, but it is the mental state she was in. I think Dr. Mendenhall will agree that any person in such a heightened emotion state is a much easier recipient than say someone else who would be calm and relaxed. They would be much more difficult to read. Yet, in some cases, you can reach into a calm person's mind, much as you did when you were able to read Dr. Mendenhall's mind as he tested you. Obviously, you correctly described most of the hidden pictures and other items he tested you with, because through his thoughts you saw what they were.

Gene listens to the two doctors and partially does understand what they think he may be going through. He then asks, "So, given this newest thing about me finding Megan, am I to take it that you are saying that my psychic powers and abilities have stopped, or are they still increasing?"

Dr Mendenhall looks at Gene and then Dr. Allen and says, "Well to be honest, I do not think you could have done what you did last night if they were not increasing. But, you need to understand that all brain injuries are different. Some heal quickly while others do not. So, trying to determine how far you will progress with these special skills before it finally stops is impossible to determine. But, I know you are worried about it continuing on until you are totally overwhelmed by it. And, I just have to say, in my professional opinion, that will not happen. Now, if you have no other questions, may I begin administering you more tests?"

Gene shrugs his shoulders and says, "Sure, whatever you want is fine with me. That is why I came here."

After a series of new tests are completed, Gene is asked to wait in Dr. Allen's personal office while the two doctors confer with one another. After about fifteen minutes the two doctors enter her office and sit down. Dr Mendenhall says, "Well Mr. Wilson, there is no doubt that your psychic powers have increased from our last meeting. Your responses to all of my tests prove that. It is very surprising to say the least, but I still have no reason to believe they will not stop within time. Yet, it is safe to tell you that we are now entering uncharted waters, as I can find no information anywhere to support the fact or know why your senses are continuing to increase. You are a miracle for sure, and we just do not know what to expect. I still fully believe that this phenomenon will cease and it could happen at any time. So, please try not to be too concerned. But please understand, we need to continue monitoring your progress. So, before you leave today, lets set our next appointment date."

Gene becomes very depressed over hearing this news. He then asks, "So, in your two opinions, how much has my powers increased since my last visit?"

The two doctors look at one another and then Dr. Mendenhall says, "It is my opinion Mr. Wilson, that your powers have increased at least fifty percent, maybe a little more."

Gene is at a total loss. He just sits there for a few moments. He is definitely worried and then says, "And, you say I shouldn't worry? I would say I have a lot to worry about. As depression and desperation consume him, Gene stands up, looks aimlessly at both doctors and leaves the office without saying more or even scheduling his next appointment.

While walking towards the hospital parking lot, Gene's mind is so preoccupied that he doesn't see anyone or anything in the hospital corridor. As he is about to exit the hospital, someone grabs his shoulder and stops him. Looking around he sees George's brother, Ray.

Looking at Gene, Ray says, "Oh Officer Wilson, I want to take this opportunity to thank you. I cannot tell you how much we all appreciated what you did for my little girl. You saved my little girl. After the ambulance brought her here last night, the doctors decided to keep her here overnight because of her delirious actions and erratic behavior. They said it was also a good opportunity for them, because it would allow them enough time to thoroughly examine her physically, as well as her mental state. And, that was an excellent decision, as this morning she is almost back to normal. This morning she has calmed down a lot and earlier was even able to discuss her captor's actions with the detectives that are handling the case. She was able to provide them with accurate descriptions of everything that happened. She also told me how you covered up her naked body and then stayed with her until the paramedics arrived. All I can say on behalf of my family is thank you. We will forever be in your debt. You no doubt saved Megan's life and you have to be something that only God could have created to help people like her. You are a saint for sure, as there is no other way to describe what you are able to do. God bless you Mr. Wilson."

Gene eventually listens to what Ray is saying and slowly gets his mind out of his fears and into what Ray is saying. He does recount the events of last night and admits to himself how strange it was to find her and how he saw what led them to the captor. And, for saving Megan he does feel good. Might what Ray is saying be true? Is what happened last night the work of God? Might this be happening to him for a positive reason? Maybe he was chosen to help lost and captive people. Could that be the answer? Maybe that is why in the hospital he saw what he believed Heaven and Hell truly looked like."

Smiling at Gene, Ray has a hold of Gene's right hand so tightly he continues to shake it, until Gene has to actually force him to let go. Gene smiles at Ray as he begins to leave and says, "When Megan is well enough Ray, I would love to stop by and check in on her. Would that be Ok with you?"

Ray has a broad smile on his face from ear to ear and responds to Gene's comment by saying, "Oh yes sir, we would love to see you anytime. Maybe we can invite you for dinner or something one evening?"

Gene smiles to himself as he heads to his car. As he walks he discovers that he is suddenly no longer afraid or worried about dying. Is it possible that he truly was chosen to do God's work? Maybe everything that he has experienced was for good reasons. He even wonders to himself if saving Megan's life alone was possibly the purpose of all his discomfort? He concludes that since she is alive, everything he has endured makes it all worth while. Is it possible that his actions last night were predestined and he is here for the good of others? Might his meeting the two Nancy women be a similar explanation?

Driving home, Gene's mind is whirling around over so many issues. He recalls the shadow people and how they once helped him save George's life. How he encountered the two Nancy women and tried to save the second one. He wonders if his encounter with Mrs. Ramos and the entity that is haunting her at her old house was because of his powers. Can all of these things be tied to his increasing psychic powers that are continuing to develop?

Pulling up in front of his apartment Gene sees Amelia's car and knows she is home. Anxious to see her he rushes inside. He encounters her on the phone and soon discovers that she was confirming his law test of Friday morning at 8:00 am. When she gets off the phone, they hug, and Gene tells her everything that has happened this day, including the fact that he fears that his powers are continuing to increase. He then tells her about Ray stopping him at the hospital where Megan was held overnight and his comments about his powers being something God gave him for the good of others. Looking at Amelia he asks, "Honey, in your opinion, is that at all a plausible explanation?" He tells her how George's brother Ray made him think that if nothing else good happens; maybe by saving Megan's life, it makes it all worth while. Could all of this which is happening to him be for a greater good? He tells Amelia how depressed and distraught he was at first when he heard the two doctors tell him how his powers had substantially increased. Yet, when Ray found him, his comments definitely helped him to understand why it might be occurring and it caused him to instantly feel better.

Amelia is rather shocked and then says, "Gene, there is no way any of us can know the true answer to that question. But, I think we need to live life knowing that if your powers continue to increase, it is for a specific reason. And, whatever that reason is, there is no doubt you saved that little girl's life. And, who is to say there won't be more, just like her that will need your help?"

Gene looks at his watch and says, "Well, it is time I get ready for work. Given what has happened, I am sure I am in for a rash of crap tonight. Those guys love to make fun of the little things. So, Megan's story will be grounds for a lot of jokes and belly laughs. I sure hope I pass the bar exam tomorrow, so I can find a better job at a good law firm. It would really be nice to get away from police work and especially those people at the station. They all mean well, but they can be so damn hurtful just to make themselves feel better. But, not to worry, I will just endure their wrath one more time tonight and take their comments in stride." Gene then turns, goes into shower and shave before heading to work.

While driving to the station he becomes a little nervous over the ribbing he is sure to be subjected to. He knows those guys and he anticipates he will hear for the next eight hours, all the jokes that he will be the butt of. Pulling into the police employee's parking lot he notices that it is more full than normal. He wonders what was going on. He concludes that there must be some type of seminar or special tactical training going on. Yet, if that was so, why wasn't he invited. He thinks that maybe given his performance last night, his Captain was not going to allow him to stay until he is hired by a law firm. He assumes the news media covering his actions last night may have been an embarrassment to the police department. And, he knows how the department hates negative publicity.

Gene parks and exits his car. He walks into the police locker room. There he quickly puts on his uniform. As he dresses, he thinks to himself how quiet it was. Usually there is a lot of horseplay and loud talking going on. But tonight, it was extremely quiet. In any case, he walks the short distance to his office work area and opens the door and is immediately greeted by a room crammed full of on and off duty personnel. As he closes the door, in unison everyone begins clapping and singing, "For He is a Jolly Good Policeman, that everyone here respects." Hearing that, Gene is completely stunned. He is totally at odds over what is happening. Is it a joke? Or are these people being serious? As the singing stops and the clapping dies down, Captain Mitchell steps forward and extends his right arm and shakes Gene's hand.

"Gene, the men and women here and I all want to congratulate you on what you did for little Megan last night. I admit, when George asked me for your help, I thought it was totally a waste of time. But, I also saw it as a way for you and George to mend the fences, so I was all for it. But, you can imagine my utter surprise when I was told you led them right to the Perp. I was blown away. Then, this morning after reading the paper about what you did and how it all happened, and as I was forced to reprimand George for his conduct last night in attacking the Perp, it was obvious that we were both shocked over your abilities. Yet, there was no denying it now, that they truly exist. And, after my admonishment, before George left my office he asked me if it would be Ok with me if he gathered a few people in here tonight to greet you. I of course said yes. However, let me say this, when word went out about this gathering everyone wanted to be here to share in this moment with you and to congratulate your actions," explains the Captain.

Gene is speechless. He expected an evening of hazing, but has unexpectedly received this wonderful praise instead. As he is about to speak up, George exits from behind the large crowd and walks over to Gene. Putting his arms around Gene he hugs him tightly and says with tears in his eyes, "Partner, I was so wrong in what I thought and believed about you all this time. Yet, when my niece went missing, you were the first person I thought of. I said to myself, if there was any chance you really could see shadow people or predict future events; maybe you could help me find Megan. I admit, when I asked the Captain to lend you to me, in all honesty, I really felt it was useless. But, there was definitely nothing to loose. And, thank God I did. You saved her, and only you could have done it." As he finishes saying that, the room roars again in applause.

After a few minutes of rowdy applause and handshaking, Captain Mitchell raises his hands high in the air, lets out a shrill whistle to get everyone's attention and shouts out, "Ladies and Gentlemen, there is work to be done tonight and sadly those of us on duty need to get with it. So, please say your good-byes and lets get busy." After saying that he motions for Gene to join him in his office. But, before Gene can follow the Captain into his office, George comes over to him.

George places his arm around Gene's shoulder again and says, "Partner, I cannot tell you how sorry I am that I disrespected you the way I did. I was wrong and you were right. But you need to know that at the time, I just couldn't accept this 'ghost' thing that you claimed to be experiencing. I tried my best to understand, but I simply just wanted to make it go away in my mind. And, the stupid way I handled it by getting a new partner was pure childish, to say the least. But, you need to know that I always loved you like a brother and now that you have proven me wrong, all I can say is how I wish you the very best. I hear you are taking the California Bar Exam tomorrow, and I want you to know that I will pray to God you do well. Oh, and thanks again for saving my niece." As he says that he hugs Gene, turns away and departs for his patrol duty, before Gene can respond.

Watching George leave, all the animosity that Gene had recently built up inside over how George treated him totally vanishes. He watches George until he is out of sight and then goes to the Captain's office.

Knocking on the Captain's door, Gene enters when he hears him say, "Come in."

Looking at Gene, the Captain is actually speechless for a few moments, and motions for Gene to sit down. After a few seconds Captain Mitchell says, "Gene, that was quite a showing of respect out there tonight, wouldn't you say? I know how bad you felt when George asked for a new partner and I understand that. But, you must also understand, I completely supported him, when he explained about the things you had been telling him. Yet, knowing you for as long as I have, I also knew you were being up front with him in how you truly felt. I was worried about your mental state and decided that I had better keep my eye closely on you. At the same time, I was happy to accept you into my night watch support program here. But, after what you accomplished last night, there is no doubt that you are everything you say you are, and you definitely got the final laugh. I take my hat off to you sir. I do not believe that anyone will ever think about you again in the same way. In fact, with your proven talents, who is to say what new opportunities may lay ahead for you? I can only wonder how far you will go in the field of law and maybe you can even specialize in helping various police departments in resolving some of their crimes? I am proud of you Gene and very happy I had a chance to know and work with you. So, what are your plans now?"

"Well sir, tomorrow I must go to the Ontario Convention Center to take the long awaited California Bar Exam. Several months ago I paid my $556.00 general application fee, so all that is left now is for me to show up and take the test. The exam begins at 8:30 am and ends at 5:00 pm. Obviously, I hope to finish sooner, but it is tough, and that much time affords me the luxury of being able to go back over every question as many times as I need to in order to be sure I have answered everything as best as I can," explains Gene.

Listening to Gene's comments the Captain asks, "So, when you finish taking the test, how long will it be before you will know your exam results?"

Gene quickly responds, "Well, that is truly the hard part Captain. It normally takes a little over six months to receive the results back in the mail. And, I really don't know how people cope with such a long waiting period. I am normally a very impatient person anyway, so having to wait that long will be the hardest part of the whole thing that is for sure."

Smiling, the Captain responds, "Well, as I said before, please feel free to continue doing your job here with us while you wait or until you locate a good law firm to work for. And, maybe during the daytime you can make a few personal visits to those law firms you have been interested in. I rather imagine with the news coverage you just received, that might even open a few doors for you?"

Thinking about that comment, Gene says, "Well, to be honest sir, I think I would rather no one knew about my psychic abilities, as it would likely scare people off, or just cause them not to take me seriously. I know I will be a good lawyer without those skills. I simply want to find a good job where I can use my legal knowledge, and skills, not my psychic abilities."

Looking at Gene, the Captain smiles and says, "I understand. Make it on your knowledge of the law and show them what a good litigator you will be. Is there a special area of law you would like to practice?"

Gene quickly responds by saying, "Oh yes. I want to learn to be a criminal lawyer. Given my police background and knowledge of the procedures we follow, defending a bad guy would be right up my alley. Or, better yet, defending an innocent person charged with a crime would be even more satisfying."

Standing up, the Captain extends his right arm, which causes Gene to stand up to shake his hand. The Captain then says, "Gene, I wish you the best of luck tomorrow, and I sincerely hope you find what you are looking for. And, if you take until 5:00 pm to finish, come in as late as you want."

Gene thanks him. Returning to his desk, he sits down and immediately sees his message light blinking. Checking it, he finds a voice mail from Gloria Ramos asking him to call her back. Fearful for her safety, he cannot help but to wonder how she knew where to reach him? Gene picks up his phone and dials her number. It rings for a long time, when suddenly she answers.

"Hello," says Mrs. Ramos.

Gene listens for a moment and then says, "Mrs. Ramos, this is Gene Wilson. I am returning your call. What can I do for you?"

At first she does not respond, and Gene senses fear in her silence. Then, almost hesitantly she says, "Sir, it found me again. It is here in my new apartment right now and I fear it wants to kill me. Can you help me?"

Knowing that he cannot physically respond to her request, he, states, "Mrs. Ramos, I personally cannot come there myself right now, but I can have one of our police cars dispatched to you? Possibly, I can even get my former partner, Officer Newton who we spoke of earlier to go. He is now a believer, and I am sure he would be anxious to help you. Would that be all right with you?

Reluctantly, she says, "Well, I guess so. But, are you sure you cannot come? I trust you so much and I know you can help me fight this thing. I don't know if anyone else can deal with it like you can. However, I do need help. So, whatever you think is best is Ok with me. I'm scared to death Mr. Wilson. This thing is here right now and it wants to harm me, I know it."

Gene gets her address and assures her someone will be dispatched quickly and she should remain outside her home until a unit arrives. She agrees, and he hangs up. He then calls the police dispatcher and tells about the call for help he had just received. He explains that it was an elderly woman he knew and she claimed an intruder had broken into her home. He then asks if Officer George Newton and his partner could be dispatched to handle the call, since George knew the woman. If so, he then also asked to have Officer Newton call him before arriving at the home. The dispatcher agrees and the call to George's car is made.

Gene returns to the paper work on his desk and within two minutes his phone rings. Answering, Gene says, "This is Officer Wilson, how may I help you?"

"Gene, it's George. What's up? I just got a B & E call but the dispatcher asked that I call you before responding. What's going on," asks George?

"George, do you remember the woman and her grandson we took to Father Kelley, the night she claimed an evil spirit was in her home," asks Gene?

Immediately recalling the event, George responds to Gene's question by indicating that of course he did remember.

"George, your call here is from the same woman. As you know she was forced to abandon her house, because she claimed that the same entity actually tried to harm her and her daughter there again. Also, you need to know, that the Catholic Church believes that entity is what killed Father Kelley the very next day when he went to her home to try and exorcise the entity out of her house. So, she now says the same entity has somehow located her at her new address and it is once again trying to harm her. If I could go myself, I would. But I am suspended from patrol work, So, I thought of you. Maybe you can handle the thing, or at the least get her away from there and into a safe house? Please understand, I do believe her and I fear there is some danger involved in encountering that entity. So, promise me that you will be very careful. Please call me if there is any problem. Ok," asks Gene?

George thinks about Gene's comments. And, now knowing that Gene definitely knows about such things, he immediately recalls how that thing knocked him down. He responds to Gene by saying, "I understand Gene. I promise we will be careful. And, if I run into any trouble I will call you immediately. So, please promise me that you will remain by your phone."

Gene quickly says, "I'll be here George. Don't worry. But be careful. If it is the same entity we ran into at her house before, there is no doubt it is dangerous and it can't be hurt by bullets. So, if you encounter it, or anything like it, get the hell out of there."

About thirty minutes later Gene needs to go to the restroom. He quickly leaves his desk. Entering the men's restroom, he finds that the lights were off. Turning them on at the wall, Gene instantly turns and is shocked to be standing face to face with three of the shadow people. Since he had not encountered them since he was taken off of patrol, he is shocked to see them there. What could they possibly want here in the men's room?

Looking straight at the three shadow figures, he hears them through mental telepathy say, "George is in mortal danger. Only you can help him. There is no time, you need to go now, or it will be too late." Then as always, they disappear immediately after communicating with him.

Desperately looking around, Gene yells out, "Where did you go, what do you mean? What kind of danger is George in?" He then concludes he had to go now and meet George at Mrs. Ramos house. He knew it could be dangerous as the shadow people's warnings have always proven to be correct. So, if George needed his help he had to go. Departing the restroom, he runs to the Captain's office. Knocking on his door, he is invited in. He quickly explains how he suddenly felt George was in trouble and only his presence at the response call would save him.

Completely unsure of what Gene was trying to explain, the Captain could see from his face he was scared and seriously believed in what he was saying. Also, knowing his psychic gift he doesn't question him. He just says, "Go, if that's what you think you must do, go now."

Without responding to the Captain's comments Gene darts from his office. Returning to his desk, he retrieves Mrs. Ramos's address. Knowing the street she lived on, he was sure he could find the apartment. He grabs his coat and runs out of the office and gets into his car. As he drives he prays he can reach George in time. Within fifteen minutes he finds the address. He sees George's police car at the curb and Mrs. Ramos standing near it. She tells Gene that the two officers entered her residence several minutes ago and nothing has been heard from inside since they went in.

Gene tells Mrs. Ramos to remain outside. He then bolts through the front door and immediately begins calling out to George, but there is no response from anyone. Gene moves from room to room looking and calling out, but he finds nothing. Then upon entering the kitchen, standing right in front of him, as if waiting for him is the beast. Its huge head with the grotesque smile is just standing and looking at him. However, as he looks back at this thing, it is somewhat different in appearance, as he sees it now has curled Ram shaped horns protruding from both sides of its head, which were not there before. Yet, otherwise it was definitely the same entity he first encountered at Mrs. Ramos previous home. Gene immediately yells at it, asking where George and his partner were. The entity just stands there and smiles, showing Gene its long, ugly teeth, with the wild drool running down its hideous mouth. Then it laughs out loud and begins moving towards Gene. As it does that, Gene closes his eyes and out loud prays, "Oh God please help me. Stop this beast and let me save my fellow officers." Opening his eyes the beast had stopped and was just standing there looking at him. Again he yells at it, demanding to know where the two policemen were. Then, as he says that, out from behind the kitchen table comes one police officer that Gene did not know. Obviously it was George's partner.

The man stands up and says, "Thank God you arrived. He hit George in the back bedroom so hard he knocked him out. He then turned and came after me. I ran until I heard you coming into the house. Your shouts distracted it, and it stopped chasing me. When that happened, I hid in back of this table and chairs. I feared it was going to kill me."

Gene looks at the man and says, "Go outside right now and stay with the woman. I will deal with this thing. I have no reason to fear it, because it is a coward."

Without hesitation the officer immediately runs past Gene and from the room outside to where Mrs. Ramos was waiting. Turning to the entity Gene says, "You don't scare me you creature from Hell. You are nothing.

All of your powers are obtained from the fears of women and children. You are nothing, and I command you to go back to where you came from. Tell Satan we know what you are and we are not afraid of him or you. And, he had better not bother to send any more despicable, ugly things like you to earth to scare this woman again. You are a failure here in every way possible. And, I will be sure that the world knows about you and your existence. So, go now, get out of here and leave this woman and everyone else alone. If you do not go now, I will stay here and pray to God and the Heavens right here and right now to destroy your miserable existence. And, you know I have the powers needed to do it."

As if it was truly listening to Gene, he could see from the surprised look on its face it was actually afraid of him. Gene knew it was thinking about what he was saying. He stares at the entity and as if it was being commanded by a superior force, it suddenly disappears while Gene watches it. Once it was gone, Gene immediately runs to the back of the house and finds the bedroom where George was laying. As he feels for a pulse, Gene takes George's portable radio from his coat and calls dispatch for an ambulance. Gene then sits with George until the paramedics arrive.

As the ambulance crew enters the room, they immediately begin to examine George and quickly load him onto a gurney. Taking him out to their ambulance they quickly head to Little Company of Mary Hospital in San Pedro.

Gene instructs George's partner to finish his report and return to the police station to check in with Captain Mitchell. He then turns to Mrs. Ramos and says, "I truly believe the beast is gone. I ordered it out of here and it appears it did leave. But let me give you my private phone number to my cell phone, and please feel free to call me anytime. If it does return, I will be back here as quickly as I can. But, I sincerely think it has left for good."

Looking at Gene with tears in her eyes Mrs. Ramos says, "Thank God for you Mr. Wilson. You are my savior that is for sure. I will pray for you tonight and you will always be in my thoughts." She then hugs Gene and returns to her apartment.

Gene then gets into his car and drives towards the hospital. As he drives he wonders why he was not afraid of that demon. Why did he so calmly stand up to it like he did? Thinking about its strength, it could easily have killed him with one slap to the head. So, why didn't it? Why did it leave? It was strange for sure. As he arrives at the hospital he parks and heads to the emergency room entrance.

Inside, he approaches the front desk. He identifies himself and asks for information on George Newton's condition. The receptionist looks at her computer, but does not find anything that indicated that George had been admitted. She then says, "It is possible that he is still being tended to and nothing has yet been entered in the computer." She then suggests that Gene take a seat and she would go look for George and come back to let him know what was happening.

Gene waits about twenty minutes when a physician approaches him and introduces himself as Dr. Russell, the emergency room's attending physician that was on duty when George arrived. He sits down next to Gene and begins discussing George's condition. He explains how he had suffered a concussion from the blow to the head and his left shoulder was dislocated from the fall he took when he was hit. He explained that nothing was life threatening, but he was sedated and would be asleep through the night. He suggested that Gene return tomorrow if he needed a statement from him. Gene thanks the doctor, the two men shake hands and Gene gets up and leaves.

Returning to the police station Gene heads to Captain Mitchell's office and proceeds to explain George's condition. He then asks if George's partner had spoken to him as he instructed him to do.

The Captain looks at Gene and says, "Yes, Officer Cruz did come in. He was quite shook up and told me a very bazaar story. In fact, I have to wonder if he was in shock or what? He spoke of demons chasing him and other weird activities. He said the demon hit George and knocked him out."

Gene wants to handle the issue lightheartedly and not make anything weird out of the circumstances. He therefore begins by saying, "Yes, I just left the hospital. It seems George has suffered a concussion and a dislocated left shoulder. However, nothing is life threatening and he will be able to be questioned tomorrow." He then ends his comments without expanding on the demon comment.

The Captain smiles and says, "Well, that is good news. I will send two officers over tomorrow to debrief him. But, you too will need to talk to them about what actually happened tonight. So, how much truth is there in this demon comment that Officer Orlando Cruz kept mentioning?"

Gene is very afraid to say what truly happened, but obviously George will and Officer Cruz already has. So, maybe he should tell the Captain exactly what happened. He therefore smiles, looks at the Captain straight in the eyes and says, "Captain, I know what I am about to tell you will sound utterly absurd and no one in their right mind will believe any of it, but I assure it did happen. Yet, you know things about me that others don't know, and if I tell you what happened, I assure you it is the truth." Gene then starts at the beginning with the first call he and George responded to at Mrs. Ramos's home. He explains what they encountered. He then tells him about taking the woman and her grandson to the Catholic Church to spend the night. He describes how Father Kelley died the very next day in that house, as he was performing a cleansing. He tells the Captain about his dream of the demon killing him. Then, he explains his meeting with the new priest at the Catholic Church and how he claimed nothing unnatural happened to Father Kelley. Gene comments on how he sensed that they were not telling him everything they knew, but also felt that Mrs. Ramos would likely know the truth and freely tell him. So, Gene explains how he found and met with her. He explains how she told him why she moved out of her house. He then describes how Mrs. Ramos called him earlier tonight and told him the beast was back. He tells the Captain why he suggested George responded to the call, because he had already encountered the entity, and would likely not laugh at Mrs. Ramos claims. Gene does not mention the shadow people telling him that George was in danger.

Looking at Gene the Captain shakes his head and says, "Yes, you are right. That is totally unbelievable. I know the detectives who speak to George tomorrow will assume he is hallucinating, or just out of his mind if he says the same thing. Yet, you are right. I do know you and I understand your fear of people making fun of you and not believing what you say really went down. I cannot say with any certainty that I believe your story either. But, knowing you as I do, I am not going to say it isn't true either. Let me sleep on it and tomorrow I will decide how to handle the incident report."

Gene looks at his watch and notices that it was past his shift time and it would be best if he headed on home to get some rest. He then stands, bids his boss good night and goes back to his desk to clean it up. He then changes out of his uniform and drives home.

Early the next morning Amelia wakes Gene and reminds him of his bar exam that morning at 8:30 am. He quickly showers, shaves and dresses, and is on the road heading to his exam destination by 7:00 am. Before going, Amelia wishes him good luck and kisses him good bye.

Arriving at the convention center at 8:10 am. the parking lot was already filling up. He parks his car and quickly goes inside to check in.

Taking his seat the exam starts at 8:30 am. Gene carefully reads every question and answers them to the best of his ability. By 3:40 pm. he had finished the exam and double checked each answer very carefully. Looking around very few people had already finished and turned in their tests. However, Gene felt good about his answers and saw no reason to worry any more about it. He gets up, hands in his test and departs for home.

As he drives home, strangely the test he just took was not on his mind, but instead it was the issues surrounding his demonic encounter yesterday that was. Why was he not afraid of that beast and why did it appear to obey his commands to leave? Can there be some connection with his growing psychic powers and how he handled his encounter? Might his insight and powers be something other entities can detect? Might the beast have sensed his abilities and maybe it was not able to cope with him? Whatever the reason, it was something he couldn't get out of his mind.

Exiting the 110 Freeway, at Torrance Blvd., Gene approaches what appears to be a serious three car collision that had just happened. Pulling over he removes some flares from the trunk of his vehicle and upon lighting them he places four around the involved vehicles. He also uses his cell phone to call 911, seeking local police and medical assistance. Approaching the first car he finds a woman stuck behind her steering wheel, trapped between it and the air bag. He quickly deflates the bag and asks the woman to remain in the car while he checked the other two vehicles.

Gene identifies himself as a police officer and immediately begins directing traffic and giving aid to the injured people. It appears as if one vehicle, a pickup truck ran the red light at the intersection of Vermont and Torrance Blvd., and sideswiped the other two automobiles. Checking on the driver of that truck, it was obvious he was impaired by either drugs or alcohol. Getting the man out of the vehicle he places him in the back seat of his personal vehicle. Then turning to the second vehicle damaged, both the driver and the passenger appeared to be hurt, as both women were bleeding from head injuries, and were not coherent. Gene stays with them until the paramedics arrive.

Soon, two Torrance Police cars arrive and Gene identifies himself as a LAPD Officer. The two officers take over and place the truck driver in the back of a police unit. Then, Gene gives a statement about what he saw and did. Gene is asked to wait in his vehicle while the ambulances take care of the injured.

Sitting in his vehicle as he watches the paramedic's working, directly behind him, out of sight of everyone, two shadow people begin coming up behind him and are looking into the passenger side of his window, causing Gene to quickly turn and see them. When Gene looks, one figure tells Gene that there was an infant on the floor of the third vehicle and it was not breathing. Hearing this, Gene immediately darts from his vehicle and heads to the one vehicle where the baby was suppose to be. He immediately begins looking in the back seat area. Upon moving away some jackets that had fallen on the floor, sure enough he finds a baby seat with the infant strapped in it. He yells to an ambulance attendant who sees the child in Gene's arms and runs to help. Taking over for Gene the paramedic runs with the infant to the ambulance where he immediately assesses the child's condition and applies oxygen to it.

One Torrance policeman who witnessed what Gene had done goes over to him to first congratulate him but then to also ask what caused him to look in the vehicle's rear section in the first place?

Gene thinks a minute then says, "Well, when I first checked on that vehicle the woman driving kept turning around to the back, but said nothing before she passed out. Thinking about her action, I just decided to check the back once again myself before the ambulances departed. And, thank God I did, because the infant was back there and not breathing."

The policeman looks at Gene and says, "Well, that was an excellent call on your part. You are to be commended Officer Wilson."

When the last injured victim is taken away, Gene is released and thanked for his heroic efforts and both Torrance Policemen shake his hand and take his business card for their accident report.

Continuing on home, Gene wonders about the shadow people. Will they always be there when danger is present? Where do they come from? Might they be angels? What explanation is there for them to make themselves known to Gene? It is all so strange, that is for sure. By the time Gene reaches his home, it was time to get ready for work. Amelia was home waiting for Gene and follows him around the house as he showers and shaves. Anxious to hear about the bar exam, Gene tells her everything and how positive he felt about the exam results.

Amelia is pleased to hear that and says, "Well Gene, if you did well, then you are one step closer to becoming a lawyer. Are you excited? Where will you apply and what types of law are you really interested in practicing?"

Gene smiles at Amelia and says, "I have no idea as to any of that. Yet, if I had a choice, I would like to be a criminal lawyer, given my police background. But, to be honest, I think I would be happy anywhere, as long as I am working a normal nine to five job, five days a week. I can't tell you how sick I am of working the late shift, night after night these past years. And, now that I have turned in my resignation, I am really happy to think of the prospects of finding a normal job sooner than later."

After Gene says that, Amelia responds and says, "Yes, being able to spend a normal day and night together, plus weekends will be great. I am so anxious for that to happen."

Listening to her comment, Gene kisses her and says he has to be getting to work. Going to his vehicle, he drives to the station. Pulling into a parking space he looks around and for the first time, truly feels good about his future, and seriously acknowledges to himself how anxious he was to begin a new life as a lawyer. Gene sits there a few moments, then exits his car and enters the locker room. He changes into his uniform and reports to his desk, wondering what this night's events will be.

The first three hours are uneventful and Gene handles the paper work and speaks to a few walk in individuals who need direction in finding someone who had been arrested. Then, just as he was about to break for lunch Captain Mitchell calls him to his office. Entering, the Captain invites Gene to sit down. He explains how he thought about everything he told him the night before. He even explains how earlier today he visited George in the hospital. He then comments on how he and the other two officers had maintained basically the same story. Therefore, it was not likely a fabrication. He then reaches into his desk and pulls out a piece of paper and hands it to Gene. He says, "Please read this and tell me what you think, please."

Gene sees that it was the police incident report of last night's activities at Mrs. Ramos home, which led to the hospitalization of George. Gene reads it and is surprised to see it was very accurate, right down to the description of the beast. Gene hands it back to the Captain and says, "Well, I am sure the brass will be calling you up to their offices to see if you have gone crazy sir. Yes, it is accurate, but, knowing how we all work around here, it will definitely raise an eyebrow or two. I have to take my hat off to you, and admire your boldness."

Taking the report back from Gene, the Captain says, "Yes, I am sure it will be discussed. But, to put anything else in the report would not be accurate, and if more should come of this encounter, it is best to disclose everything right upfront that you three officers claimed happened. After all, it isn't my words it is what you three guys claimed to have encounter. And, there is no denying that George is in the hospital for some reason.

So, I just file it and sit back and wait for the repercussion and fall out to happen."

Gene smiles at his answers and asks, "So, is there anything else you need from me Captain? I was just about to go to lunch."

Thinking about it, the Captain asks, "Yes, I was wondering how you felt you did on the bar exam? Wasn't that today?"

"Oh, thanks for asking sir. To be honest, I think I did well. I was done before most of the others, and all of the questions seemed to be subjects I was familiar with. But, who knows for sure? All I can do now is wait and see what the results are," explains Gene.

The Captain then opens his desk drawer and takes out a slip of paper and hands it to Gene. On it was written the name of a man and his phone number. The Captain says, "That is the name of a good friend of mine who happens to be a partner in a very prominent law firm in Torrance. They do mostly criminal law, and when I had dinner with him and his wife last night, I spoke of you to him and he immediately recalled the Megan article. He asked me to have you call him. He says they are looking for a new, aggressive lawyer and maybe you would fit the bill?"

Excitedly, Gene looks at the paper and quickly folds it and places it in his shirt pocket, and says, "Wow, thank you Captain. I will definitely call him tomorrow. This is great." Gene then departs the Captain's office and takes his lunch break.

CHAPTER 8; *A New Beginning for a Hero*

Early the next morning Amelia is up and getting ready for work. As she readies herself Gene wakes up and comments to her how beautiful she looked. He then tells her about the possible job interview that the Captain arranged.

Smiling at Gene, Amelia says, "Oh honey that is wonderful news. When are you going to call the man?"

Sitting up in bed, Gene stretches and responds, "Well, I thought I would call today around 10:00 am. I want to talk to him early, in case he wants to see me today. Then, I thought afterwards that I would head on over to the hospital and see how George is doing. But, everything hinges on if and when the lawyer wants to see me."

"Well, good luck sweetheart. Please call me at school and let me know how the phone conversation went and whether or not you are going to see him today or not. Will you promise? Meanwhile, I will be praying for you to have a good interview," comments Amelia.

Watching Amelia from the window, Gene watches her drive away. As she does, he thinks to himself how lucky he was to have Amelia in his life. And, as her car fades away, his mind then begins recounting everything that has happened over the past couple of days. In fact, he doesn't know what to make of it. So much so quick, from finding Megan, to facing that demon, then actually taking his bar exam and now getting this potential job interview. It is all so strange in some respects. Maybe it's a sign that something good is about to happen to him. Sitting there thinking about it all, he wonders if some how his new psychic abilities are playing into any of this? While he ponders the answer his phone rings. Answering, he says, "Hello."At first the line is quiet then a sudden shrill scream is heard in the distance and the line goes dead. Within seconds, it rings again. This time the voice on the other end shouts out, "Mr. Wilson, I need help, please help me."

Listening to the cry for help, he is taken by surprise but then responds, "Who is this, what's wrong?"

Again there is a long pause. Yet he can hear commotion and movement in the background as if items are being tossed about and people are scurrying around. Then, someone picks up the phone again and says, "Mr. Wilson, this is Gloria Ramos, and the beast is back and it is trying to kill me. Please, can you come here now and help us?"

Taken by surprise and as fear sets in he knows she wouldn't be calling him if she was not desperate. He therefore says, "Yes, Mrs. Ramos, I'm on my way. Just go outside, get away from it and I'll be right over." Gene quickly dresses and heads to Mrs. Ramos home.

Arriving at Mrs. Ramos home in about fifteen minutes, he immediately sees that she was not waiting outside as he had asked. He gets out of his vehicle, approaches the front door of her unit, knocks but there is no answer. He tries opening the door, but it was locked. It was also very quiet inside. He calls out and asks, "Mrs. Ramos, are you Ok? Please open the door." He waits, but nothing happens. No sounds of any kind are heard. He then tries looking into the front room windows but inside, everything appears fine. He walks around to the rear of her unit and immediately sees that the back door was standing wide open. Walking around for a better look, he walks up onto the rear porch, looks in, sees nothing, then enters and is standing in the kitchen. He sees that all of her dining room chairs are tipped over. Cabinet doors are open and some dishes are broken and lying on the floor. He cautiously begins looking for her by searching each room, but nothing or nobody is found. He then stops in the hallway and calls out again and asks, "Mrs. Ramos, are you here?"

Gene stands there for several seconds and does not hear anything. The silence is deafening. He gets chills all over his body. He puts a chair upright and closes his eyes as he holds on to it and tries to see in his mind what might have happened. In seconds he sees an image of Mrs. Ramos running through her house and looking back over her shoulder. She runs from the living room through the hallway and into the kitchen. She stops at the counter, in desperation she looks up, opens the cupboard drawers and begins grabbing items in them, throwing plates, pots and pans at something. However, he cannot see who or what it is that is chasing her. Then, the image goes dark, and he no longer senses what happened after that. He tries to hold on to the chair, but there is nothing in his psychic mind being created by the chair's touch. Perplexed, he wanders through the kitchen and picks up other items. Nothing happens. He begins wondering if maybe his psychic powers are fading away. Maybe his ability to see such things have left him? Gene continues on his quest to pickup items that she obviously handled, but nothing more is seen or sensed. Then, as he was about to exit the house, he reaches for the door knob to close the door when suddenly the image of Mrs. Ramos being tossed out of her back door is very clear, just as if he was watching a movie. He sees something that looks like the entity he had encountered before, but this one is taller, wider and darker in color and has larger horns protruding from its head. It literally has red eyes, large fang like teeth and it has grabbed Mrs. Ramos around her neck with one hand and her right leg with the other. It then hurls her out of the back door, causing her to land very hard on her left side in the back yard. As the beast moves towards her, she crawls into one of the unit's garage door's and slams it shut. The image then fades away and no more visions are seen.

Gene approaches the man door on the side of the garage he thinks she entered. Looking at the door, he instantly notices that there are two large, deep and long scratch marks on its surface facing outwards, just as if a wild animal had clawed at it trying to gain entrance. Cautiously he reaches for the door knob and finds it to be locked. He gently knocks on the door, but there is no answer from anyone inside. He goes over to the single wide roll up car door and tries opening it. He realizes that it obviously was connected to an electric garage door opener, which was holding it down. He peers into the garage through the man door's glass window in its upper section. Looking inside, it was dark, but he could make out the shape of Mrs. Ramos's vehicle inside. Wondering what to do, he decides he needed to get in there to see if she might be inside. Putting his shoulder to the door he forces it open. Rushing inside, he looks around, and sees nothing by the vehicle. He unhooks the electric garage door by releasing the chain drive, which allows him to manually lift up the door. Upon doing that, the garage becomes better illuminated and he is able to easily look everywhere. Nothing is seen on the floor and it did not appear that the beast followed her in there as there was no mess anywhere. He then begins looking in the car. He tries opening the doors, but they are all locked. He looks inside and sees nothing in the front seat. Then, looking in the rear, something was definitely down on the rear floor, between the front and back seat. Gene knocks on the door glass, but there is no activity from inside. Again he knocks, but this time harder and louder. He calls out to Mrs. Ramos. Yet, there is no movement or activity from inside the vehicle. Not sure of what was on the floor he is hesitant to break a window to gain entrance. He then moves around the car to the other side. Looking in, there he sees inside due to a better angle and it definitely appeared to be someone lying on the vehicle's floor. Looking around he finds a large rock outside next to the sidewalk. He picks it up, returns to the vehicle and breaks the rear left door window. Glass falls down inside the vehicle. Gene reaches in and turns the back door handle and opens the door. He now sees that it was definitely a person. Touching the body he rolls it over and discovers it to be Mrs. Ramos. Lifting her head he tries to wake her. He feels for a pulse but there was none. Lifting here higher up he tries to shake her, but there is still no movement. He again feels her pulse and cannot find one. He puts his head to her nose and does not hear any breathing. Was she dead? Gene darts out of the garage and into the house. He picks up the phone and calls 911. He identifies himself as a police officer and requests an ambulance and police backup. He returns to the vehicle to wait for help.

Within a few minutes he hears sirens and soon two police cars, an ambulance and a Los Angeles Fire Department Paramedic unit is at the home. He runs to the front, identifies himself and leads everyone to Mrs. Ramos. The paramedics look at Mrs. Ramos, and quickly inform Gene that she was dead.

One police unit assumes jurisdiction and begins questioning Gene about the details of her death. Gene tells them she called him earlier asking for help as she said an intruder was in her house. Gene describes how he could not reach her by knocking on the front door, causing him to walk around to the rear of the unit where he found the back door standing wide open. He describes the mess he observed inside and how he checked the garage and broke into it and the vehicle. He says, there was no movement from Mrs. Ramos which is why he called 911. Soon, the yard is full of crime scene investigators who again question Gene over what happened. He is there for almost three hours, and unable to depart until approximately 3:30 pm. As he gets into his vehicle to return home, he is mystified over how Mrs. Ramos died. He observed no injuries to her and wonders if maybe she might have had a heart attack. Or, did the beast some how kill her like it did Father Kelley? As he drives, he begins to feel the beast had to have done something to her. In all of his comments to police and investigators, he never mentioned anything about the demon, as he knew what they would think. Yet, maybe he should tell someone and given what he already knows, Captain Mitchell might be the right person to talk to when he goes to work. As he parks his car, and enters his apartment he sees his phone's message light blinking. Checking his message, he finds a message from a John Wagner, of the law firm written on the paper Captain Mitchell had given him. The message left a number and asked that Gene call him.

Realizing how late it was and how upset he was about Mrs. Ramos, Gene decides to wait until tomorrow to return the call. Considering the lateness of the day he showers and decides to go to work early, hoping that he would have extra time to speak with Captain Mitchell before his shift begins. Arriving at the police station an hour early, he goes directly to the Captain's office. He sees Captain Mitchell sitting at his desk. He knocks and is invited in.

Looking up, Captain Mitchell says, "Good evening Gene, what brings you in so early?"

Entering the office, Gene closes the Captain's door and approaches his desk. Looking at the him Gene says, "Captain, I am here to report what I think was a murder. Today, I responded to a cry for help from a woman who I have know for some time and who is the same woman George was responding to when he was injured. Anyway, I went to help her this morning and being unable to find her, I eventually broke into her garage and automobile and found her dead body in the rear seat of her vehicle. I did not elaborate on what I though may have happened when speaking to the police investigators that responded, nor the criminal investigation team. But, I'm here to tell you I believe that demon we all saw killed her." Gene then proceeds to explain in detail everything that happened. He also recounts the first response he and George made, and Mrs. Ramos subsequent comments about being followed to her new apartment by the entity.

Captain Mitchell listens intently trying to understand everything Gene was saying. He then looks at Gene and says, "Well, if that is so, I think you were wise not to say anything. I agree they all may have thought you were nuts. I say, for now lets keep this between the two of us. Let's wait for the autopsy results. Then, depending on what killed her, we can decide then what action to take. Do you agree?"

Gene thinks about that and says, "Yes sir, I do agree. Besides, what good would it do her family to know what I believe happened? I just needed to vent my frustration and you were the only person I felt I could be honest with."

The Captain then asks if he had met with Mr. Wagner yet, saying he was sure he would want to interview Gene as soon as possible.

Gene responds that when he returned home he did have a phone message to call Mr. Wagner, but he explained how upset he was at the time and it just wasn't something he wanted to do at that moment considering how late in the day it was. However, he explains that he intends to call him the first thing in the morning.

The Captain agrees with Gene, but again urges him to call Mr. Wagner early, because he was sure he would want to meet him as soon as possible. He then looks at his watch and comments that it was close to their shift change, and Gene had better go get into his uniform.

Gene smiles, gets up, and says, "Thank you for listening to me and not laughing. I don't know what you might really be thinking, but I truly believe in what I said." Gene then turns and exits the office. He heads directly to his locker where he changes into his uniform and goes to his desk to begin that night's work.

The entire night passes slowly and with no crazy calls or interruptions. He makes notes of everything that occurred with Mrs. Ramos. He tries to figure out how the beast could have gotten into her locked garage and car to get to her. He then wonders if it somehow touched her before she entered the garage and set in motion its deadly desires. It was obviously something he would never know the answer to. He then wonders if the beast was attached to Mrs. Ramos or was it now in her new apartment awaiting new tenants? Should he investigate her place again? Should he warn the new tenants when they move in? Yet, who would believe him? Besides, it had to have followed her from her old residence to this new one. So, it must have been after her and now that she is gone, maybe it will be too. He decides not to do anything more, thinking it may be best to just forget it all.

Early the next morning Gene wakes up as Amelia was getting ready for work. He gets out of bed because he wanted to talk with her about Mrs. Ramos. Finding her in the bathroom, they hug and kiss. Gene then tells Amelia of Mrs. Ramos call and his finding her dead. He describes what she said to him and tells her how the house was all messy. He tells her of his visions and what he thinks happened. He also tells her what he told the Captain, and how he said nothing to the officers at the scene.

Amelia is saddened over Mrs. Ramos death, recalling how she was the one who originally introduced her to Gene. She also was very close to her daughter as they attended school together. She asks, "Why would anything want to harm that kind and gentle woman? She was such a nice and sincere lady. Why would this thing harm her?"

Gene shakes his head no, indicating he didn't know the answers to any of her questions. He looks at Amelia and takes her in his arms and says, "Honey, I do not understand any of it either. In fact, I truly thought that I had chased it away from her and it was gone. And, maybe I did, because in my visions, when I saw it this last time, this beast was bigger and somewhat different. It may have been a different demon all together, I just don't know. But why anything would want to harm her is the mystery. It may relate to her past paranormal encounters. Or, it may have something to do with her religion and connection to Father Kelley and his attempt to exorcise the demon out of her first house. I just can't say. But, I decided last night not to dwell on it anymore, as it could definitely drive me crazy, trying to figure out all the answers."

Amelia is very upset and says, "I must call her daughter today and see if I can do anything to help. In school, we were very close and what has happened is terrible."

Gene hugs her again and then says, "Oh, by the way, I had a call from that lawyer, John Wagner. He wants me to call him this morning and Captain Mitchell thinks he is really interested in hiring me. So, I will let you know what happens after I call him."

Trying to work up a smile Amelia says, "That is great news dear, but I had better be getting ready for work. Yes, please call me if you hear anything." She then returns to the bathroom sink and begins applying her makeup.

Gene turns away and leaves Amelia to get herself ready. He goes into the kitchen where he prepares himself a cup of coffee. Sitting down, he reads the morning paper and waits for Amelia to finish.

Before leaving, Amelia enters the kitchen, they hug and she wishes him good luck on his interview. Taking her purse and car keys she kisses Gene and leaves the apartment.

After an hour, Gene has finished the paper and looks at the clock on the wall. It was approximately 10:15 am. and a proper time to call Mr. Wagner. Picking up the phone he dials the number. A receptionist answers and transfers his call to Mr. Wagner. Answering his phone, John Wagner says, "Good morning, this is John Wagner, how can I help you."

Gene introduces himself and explains why he was calling.

Immediately, Mr. Wagoner says, "Oh yes Gene, thank you for calling. I hear you just took the bar exam. How do you think you did?"

Gene goes on to describe the exam's length and tells Mr. Wagner how he finished early but felt pretty good about it, indicating he was confident that he passed it.

Happy to hear Gene's comments, Mr. Wagner says, "Well, as you may know Gene, your Captain has told me a lot about you, and as I am sure he told you, we are looking to hire a new lawyer who we can train to do criminal work." He then goes on to explain the firms specialties, the number of partners in the firm and what each partner was trained to do. He discussed how long they had all been together. He then asks Gene what type of law he was hoping to specialize in?

Quickly Gene says, "Well sir, I was thinking that since I had a police background, criminal law would be the most rewarding and interesting. So, what you are describing sounds very appealing."

After about fifteen more minutes of conversation Mr. Wagner asks Gene when he could visit his office in order to discuss the opportunity in more detail. Gene responds back that anytime in the morning or afternoon was good for him. With that, an appointment was set for 1:30 pm that afternoon.

Hanging up, Gene sits there just thinking about a career as a criminal lawyer. And, he liked Mr. Wagoner's mannerisms and was very eager to meet with him to discuss a possible opportunity with his firm and to see how he might like working with them.

He then picks up the phone and calls Amelia to tell her of the conversation and meeting time. She listened intently and was pleased with Gene's obvious enthusiasm and pending meeting. She then says, "Well, I have all the confidence in the world in you. And, I also sense that you two will like one another. So, I hope he offers you something you will like. Good luck sweetheart. Please call me again after your meeting."

Gene smiles to himself realizing how nice it was that Amelia was so supportive of him. He thinks to himself how lucky he was to have met her. He then responds to her request by saying, "Yes, just as soon as I finish my interview, I will call you."

Gene then hurries around his apartment getting ready for his meeting. By noon he is cleaned up, dressed and ready to go. He sits down for a moment to compose himself and figure out what exactly to say during the interview. He turns on the television to kill time until 1:00 pm. He then gets up, goes to his vehicle and drives the fifteen minutes to Mr. Wagoner's office. Exiting his vehicle, he locks it, and takes the elevator to the eighth floor. Seeing the law firm's name on the door, he opens it and is greeted by a pleasant receptionist. Telling her he has a 1:30 pm appointment with Mr. Wagoner, he is invited to sit in their lobby and she will let Mr. Wagner know that he was there.

Gene sits in a comfortable couch and begins thumbing through the magazines lying around. As he is looking at one magazine, a large hand is thrust down in front of him. Looking up he sees a tall, well dressed gentleman in his mid fifties.

The man says, "Gene, I am John Wagoner, how are you? Please come with me to my office."

Gene shakes the man's hand and follows him into a very plush and well appointed office. He is asked to take a seat and the two men sit on a couch where Gene is offered coffee or a soft drink. Trying to maintain a totally business like atmosphere, Gene graciously declines any beverage. John then jumps right in, asking Gene to talk about himself and his police career. Gene begins with his completing the L.A. Police Academy, and goes on to discusses his many years as a patrol officer. He talks about how he put himself through college and law school. He finishes up with his description of taking of the bar exam.

John Wagoner sits and listens with great interest, taking a few notes and smiling as Gene speaks of his many police encounters. Gene is careful not to mention his gun shot wound or his subsequent psychic powers.

John looks at Gene and says, "Well, sir, it seems like you definitely have the background we are looking for and I can tell you up front, I like your demeanor and the way you presented yourself. If I had a crystal ball, I would bet that over time you will make a fine criminal lawyer. However, I am curious, as you have said nothing about your psychic powers that Captain Mitchell has spoken of. I understand that you recently found a kidnapped child and have had other similar encounters. If that is true, it would be interesting to hear some facts about that."

Gene is hesitant to speak of it at all, for fear he will sound foolish and maybe diminish his chances of getting hired. Taking a pause, he starts out by explaining his gun shot wound to the head. He then describes how a portion of his brain must have been stimulated by the bullet as that is what the doctors think is responsible for what he sees. He discusses how he found Megan and how he knew what happened to Mrs. Ramos. He then says, "I hope what I am experiencing will only be temporary, as my doctors feel that once the brain damage is fully healed, I may revert back to my old self, but no one knows anything for sure. I am told there is no precedence for what I am experiencing."

John listens with interest and definitely was impressed with what he heard. He then replies by saying, "Well, Gene, if it were me that was experiencing those things, I think I would not wish for it to end. Who can say why such gifts are bestowed on people. It just could be that you will end up helping others and being a positive factor to society. I think it should be looked at as a good thing."

Partially relieved by his positive comments, Gene says, "Well, you may be right, but it is all so new, I am careful to discuss it with anyone, let alone a potential employer."

Smiling, John says, "Yes, I understand that. So, speaking of employment, how would you like a tour of the office and maybe take some time to sit and speak with my two partners?"

The two get up and John shows Gene around the entire office. When they finish, John knocks on a door and they go in to meet one partner.

Two hours later John and Gene are back in John's office, where Gene is anxious to see what John has in mind. John sits back in his chair and looks at Gene. He then says, "Well, you have now seen it all and met the staff as well as my two partners. Assuming you pass the bar, what would you think about working here?"

Quickly gathering his wits Gene says, "John I am very impressed and I feel very comfortable here. Everyone is friendly and professional, I would be extremely please to be a part of your firm."

John smiles and says, "Yes, we all liked you too and feel you would fit right in. So, here is what I propose." John makes Gene a good offer with the promise of allowing him to work with the firm's best lawyers and to allow him to assist in as many cases as necessary to get him properly trained. He quotes his starting salary and suggests he begins in two weeks. He further explains that it wasn't necessary for him to have his law license in order to aid the other lawyers. However, he would need to attend court and assist in the lead lawyers cases by being available to research any added information that may be necessary .

Gene eagerly and quickly accepts John's offer and says, "I cannot tell you how anxious I am to be here, and above all get a chance to work with so many top notch attorneys. I will tell my Captain tonight that I am leaving in two weeks. And, I promise that I will be here early that first Monday morning after my two week notice is up. The two shake hands and Gene quickly exits the office in order to call Amelia and tell her the good news.

Once in his automobile, Gene quickly takes out his cell phone and calls Amelia. He tells her everything and as he expected she is very pleased and excited for him. He then says, "I will tell Captain Mitchell tonight that I am accepting a position with his friend John Wagoner.

Getting ready for work Gene realizes how nervous he suddenly was. Knowing that he had been a police officer for a long time, and now he is suddenly quitting a job he has thoroughly enjoyed for many years seemed so strange. Yet, when he thinks about a new career as a criminal lawyer, that too was very exciting for him. After all, that is what he had been planning on doing for many years and was the subject of many of his and George's conversations as they were on patrol.

Gene dresses and gets into his car to leave for work. While driving, his mind begins thinking back over the past year or so. He recalls his head wound, which caused his psychic powers. He then recalls his involvement with Mrs. Ramos and her demons. Finally, he wonders about his ability to find little Megan. It was all so different for him now. He then wonders if when he and George first encountered Mr. Balsam, the ghost spirit in San Pedro, might that have been the beginning of his new life? Could that event be what set in motion everything else that subsequently has happened to him?

Pulling into his parking space, Gene goes in, changes into his uniform and immediately looks for Captain Mitchell.

Knocking on his door, the Captain asks Gene to enter. "Good evening Gene. How are you and what can I do for you?"

Smiling, Gene says, "Well sir, it is good news. I was offered a position today by your friend John Wagoner. I begin in two weeks. So, I guess I need to offer my resignation."

Standing up, the Captain smiles and extends his arm and shakes Gene's hand and responds, "Congratulations counselor, I am sorry to be loosing a good police officer, but given all of your hard work and your long-term desire to become a lawyer, I think you have made a wise decision. John and his partners are fine people and I think you will enjoy working with them and you will learn a lot. So, please take a few minutes and go back to your desk and type me out you letter of resignation. I will then process it accordingly. And, of course it goes without saying that I wish you all the best."

Gene smiles and says, "Captain, without your referral to Mr. Wagoner, none of this would have ever happened. I will forever be in your debt. I appreciate you thinking enough of me to recommend me to your friend. Thanks so very much."

The Captain just smiles at Gene's comments and then says, "It was my pleasure Gene. I have always respected you and I know you will be a fine asset for them. And, giving John your name was the least I could do for you."

The two then part and Gene returns to his desk. After about an hour with only a few telephone interruptions, his resignation letter is finished. He places it into an envelope, writes the Captains name on it and then hand carries it to his office. Looking through his door he sees that the Captain was out. Entering, he places it on top of his desk and returns to his duties.

About ten minutes before lunch time, his phone rings. Answering it he is pleased to hear George on the other line.

"Hello my friend. How are you feeling? I was intending on coming over to see you tomorrow. Is everything Ok with you," asks Gene?

For a second or two George is silent. He then responds by saying, "Gene, I am healing just fine. However, I am having such weird dreams, it scares me. I was wondering if after your injury you too had bad dreams. They are so vivid and yet they are about things I have no understanding of. If you are coming over tomorrow, can we talk about them? I really would appreciate your take on them and maybe you can give me some advice."

Gene knows exactly what George was talking about. He remembers his own vivid dreams about Heaven and Hell, then dying in a rest home unattended. He also recalls how he once explained it all to George after he was back to work and on patrol. Obviously, George didn't recall any of those discussions. But, knowing what he was likely going through, for sure he would like to help him. He responds by saying, "George, I will be out to see you about 2:00 pm. tomorrow. I suggest you write down as much as you can remember about your dreams. It will help, as it gives me a starting point. And, I would be happy to help you in anyway I can. I will see you tomorrow."

Hanging up the phone he thinks to himself how different George sounded. He was communicating, but it was somehow not the typical conversation the two normally had. Deciding it was likely nothing, his mind shifts gears and the fact that he was quitting the force was suddenly really beginning to set in. He has been a policeman for a long time, and now it is almost over. Becoming a little scared he silently prays to himself that he has made the right decision. He knows his friends and colleagues will definitely support him, and for the first time ever, he will be working a regular 9 to 5 job, with his weekend free. That alone was a huge improvement over his current life style. Actually being home on weekends where he and Amelia can spend quality time together will be great. Plus, once he is licensed and able to work alone, his income should increase substantially. Yet, he admits he will miss the police work and the thrill of patrol and being around his longtime friends.

The rest of the night passes uneventfully. While driving home he becomes more excited over his new job prospect. Arriving home, he finds that Amelia is already asleep. Gene enters the bedroom and sits in a side chair next to their bed and watches her sleep. He thinks to himself how beautiful she was and what a wonderful woman she is. He knows that going forward his life will be very different as a lawyer. He fantasizes about them getting married and raising a family. He thinks to himself, the difference in their religious views was really no longer important to him and he would allow Amelia to decide how to raise the children, religion wise.

CHAPTER 9; *A Time to Establish New Goals:*

Gene wakes up around 10:00 am. He makes himself a pot of coffee and sits down and watches the morning news on television. As he watches, he sees a story about a man who shot four police officers in a restaurant that Gene and George often ate at in San Pedro. The man then turned his gun on himself after being found in his home a short time later. It was all so senseless and totally unexplainable. What makes people go crazy and kill for no reason? How sick must that man have been? And, he thinks how it could just as easily have been him and George sitting there. He then reminisces about other similar situations that have occurred over his police career. He recalls several other similar stories and senseless killings that happened in Los Angeles while he was a patrol officer. The more he thinks about it, the more he is certain that he has made the right choice in leaving the department.

Later that day as Gene enters Little Company of Mary Hospital in San Pedro, he walks up to the receptionist and asks what room George was in. After a few minutes he finds George's room. Pushing open the door he sees George lying in bed watching the television. When George notices his old friend, he appears genuinely happy to see him. Gene reaches his bedside and shakes George's hand. The two smile at one another and then Gene asks, "So, old buddy how are you? When are you getting out of here and going back to work? You have been here now for almost a week."

George smiles and responds, "Yes I feel good. I think I am ready to hit the bricks. I do not know why they are keeping me here so long. I feel like it is all a waste of time as there are serious things I could be doing and people to protect."

Gene then asks if he remembered what happened to him at Mrs. Ramos house? Upon being asked that question, George's face takes on a completely different appearance. He lowers his voice and says, "Gene, it was something from Hell. It wanted to kill me and my partner. What was it? Do you know what it really was?"

Gene looks George directly in both eyes and says, "I don't know how much you have been told, but you need to know that Mrs. Ramos was killed by that thing days after it knocked you down. And, I can assure you, it was most definitely something from Hell. I seriously believe it was a demonic entity. And, I also think it was not the same one we originally encountered that hurt you. Its head was different, with two larger horns perturbing out of it. Plus, it was larger all over than the other one. But, there is no doubting what so ever that it was evil and it definitely had a specific purpose in being there. I can only assume God himself stepped in and saved us all. I really can't explain more. All I know is that Mrs. Ramos was a wonderful person and she didn't deserve to die like that. She was a fine lady. Her funeral was terribly sad and there were more than a hundred mourners at the cemetery grave site service when they laid her to rest."

George is stunned. It was obvious from the look on his face that he didn't know about her death. He looks at Gene and says, "How did that thing kill her? I made her wait out front for you. I assumed she would be safe. She survived all of the other attacks. So, why was this one after her? She never hurt them or did anything to provoke them, ever. Why her? I feel so bad. And, it makes me wonder why it didn't kill me. Certainly it had the chance to do so, once I was on the floor and knocked out I was an easy target."

Gene realizes how upset George truly is and tries to think of a sound answer. Thinking before answering he finally says, "George, I believer that thing and its predecessors were always after Mrs. Ramos. She was their goal and it was only her they were targeting. Why? I just do not know. Maybe they wanted her because of her intense religious beliefs. Maybe they wanted a chance to capture her soul. I just don't know. But I think it is safe to say you were not their target and consequently they didn't want you. I don't know exactly how she died, but let me tell you, I was the one who found her. Somehow that thing got her while she was locked insider her garage and in the backseat of her locked vehicle hiding from it."

Absolutely confused and saddened over the news of Mrs. Ramos's death, George lies back in his bed, stares at the ceiling for the longest time, and says nothing. Obviously in deep thought. After about two minutes he then raises up, looks at Gene and says, "You know, her death might be what is contributing to my terrible dreams. I didn't realize it before, because I didn't know she had died. But, she is in all of my dreams. And, every time, without exception, she is the one that is warning me about that entity, saying that it is coming for me. Every night it is the same dream she is standing next to my bed, bent over me, only a few inches from my face. In my ear she shouts out for me to be careful as that thing wants me. Do you think it could be a real warning Gene? In death, can she be coming back here every night to warn me, or is it just a dumb dream I am having?"

Stunned at hearing this, Gene is careful not to dismiss the event as simply a bad dream. The fact she was in those dreams may truly be a serious warning and certainly not something to put off or dismiss as just a bad dream. Thinking about it all Gene says, "George, what is occurring here might be real, or it might be a combination of your medication and uneasiness over being cooped up here in this hospital. I think we need to know more. I want some time to think about this and I want to find out what we can do if it is a real warning. I will do some researching tonight while I am at work. I will then try to come up with some answers or at least some recommendations. In fact, I will call you later tonight before you go to sleep and we can talk about it more." Gene then makes a few notes and bids George good-bye.

As Gene walks to his car he thinks about everything George told him. He then stops at a nurses station and begins asking them questions about George's health, medications he is taking and why he had not yet been discharged. Waiting to get some answers, a young nurse comes out from a room behind the counter and asks Gene what he wanted. He shows the woman his badge and introduces himself. He then portraits his interest in George as if he was conducting an official investigation.

The nurse responds by saying, "Officer Wilson, we have had to undergo several of these investigations ever since Officer Newton was brought in here. I do not understand why you are all so concerned about his injury and what caused it. The fact is, he is still here because the hospital psychiatrist is worried over his nightly dreams and his claims to be visited by strange entities. He claims almost every night that an evil being is harassing him. Yes, the doctors do try to medicate him, but nothing seems to help him rest. His shoulder injury is healing nicely, and the blow to the head he sustained when he fell is also improving. Yet, the doctors all think the blow to the head is what is causing his nightmares and inability to sleep.

So, I think if you need more specific information, it would be best for you to talk to one of Mr. Newton's doctors."

Gene tries to coordinate in his mind everything George told him, vs. what the nurse is saying. She claimed that he has hellish nightmares every night, where George says the dreams were only warnings and never said how bad they were. And, why is a psychiatrist involved in George's care? What is going on? Gene cannot make any sense of it. Certainly a dislocated shoulder and bump on the head shouldn't require this much hospital care. As to the nurse's suggestion that he speak to one of George's doctors, Gene asks, "How would I go about speaking to one of his doctors? Maybe the psychiatrist would be best, is it possible to speak with that person?"

The nurse immediately picks up the phone and calls someone. Putting it down she looks at Gene and says, "Dr. Read will be here in a moment. If you would like to take a seat and wait, I am sure he will not be that long."

Gene turns, sees a small waiting area and sits down. About five minutes later an older man with gray hair approaches him from behind. He looks at Gene and says, "Hello, I am Dr. William Read, is there something I can do for you sir?"

Immediately standing up to greet and respond to Dr. Read, Gene says, "Yes doctor. I am interested in talking to you about your patient George Newton. I am with the LAPD and he and I use to be partners. I was at the call where George was injured, but I am worried for him, seeing how long he is here. It would seem to me that his injuries are minor in nature and he might be better off getting out of here and back to his own apartment. I know George and given what this young nurse is telling me it sounds like there is some sort of mental problem occurring with him. Is that why he hasn't been discharged yet?"

The doctor looks at Gene and invites him to return with him to his office where they can talk in private. They walk a while and are soon inside, where Dr. Read invites Gene to sit down. He then takes out a note pad and says, "Mr. Wilson, maybe you can help me. Yes, Mr. Newton's physical injuries have mostly healed. He did sustain a minor concussion when he fell, but that too is healing. Yet, every night his mannerisms and actions are getting worse. At first, he complained of bad dreams. However, that has now escalated into a real bout of hysteria, followed by screaming nightmares. He flails his arms in the air, yells out obscenities, and orders mysterious entities to leave him alone. And, at first when confronted by our night time nursing staff, as they would monitor him, he often struck out and hit them. He knocked one woman to the floor, all while he was asleep. It has gotten so bad, that now only men orderlies are able to contend with his vicious acts. It is a serious concern for me as there's no way I can attest to the fact that he is fit to go home, let alone return to work. He is dangerous and definitely a very disturbed man. So, is there any information that you can give me or any ideas why he acts out or behaves this way?"

Gene is at a loss to explain any of it. He thinks about the problem and then explains to Dr. Read about the last call they were on together, when George was injured. He leaves out the details of the demon, but says, "Doctor, the woman he was there to protect was killed a couple of days later. I just told him a few minutes ago, and he was shocked at hearing that and then said she was one of the entities that haunt his nightly dreams. However, as he described his dreams to me, he never said anything about acting out like what you are now describing. I really can't explain any of it. But, if you want, I can come in here tomorrow night, as I am off work. Maybe if I sit with George, I can see for myself what you are saying. Or, better yet, maybe I can even help him."

Dr. Read thinks about Gene's offer and responds, "Well, I do not know what you might be able to accomplish and being untrained, I also doubt that you can help him. But, if you want to stay by his side, I see no harm in that. If nothing else, maybe you can calm him down before he goes to sleep. So, let's plan on your coming here around 8:30 pm."

Gene nods in agreement. He then gets up, shakes the doctor's hand and says, "Fine, I will see you tomorrow night." Gene then exits his office and begins walking to his vehicle. As he strolls down the hospital corridors, a very strange feeling begins to overcome him. He stops and looks around. He realizes that he is suddenly having trouble breathing and he is getting dizzy. He worries that maybe he is having a heart attack. Quickly looking for a chair to sit down on, he sees one outside the room to his left. Sitting there a few moments he begins to feel better, and as he does, a vision of the shadow people pop into his head. What did it mean? This has never happened before. Is it a sign that they tying to contact him?

Sitting there he suddenly hears a noise coming from the room he is sitting in front of. Standing up, he looks through the open door and immediately sees the familiar sight of the shadow people. They are all standing around a bed and looking down at the occupant. As he approaches the bed, he sees a person in it that looks exactly like George. The shadow people are all around him. And, as he approaches the bed he hears the shadow people screaming to him that George was in danger. Then, suddenly the shadow people disappear as does the image of the person lying in the bed. Looking around, he sees the room was now empty. What did it all mean? Why didn't the shadow people tell him exactly what the danger was? It was very strange. In the past they always had a verbal warning for him that in turn allowed him to quickly deal with the problem. Now, there were no such instructions. And, what type of danger is George in?

Once the visitation ends, Gene feels fine again. Was the dizzy feeling caused by the shadow people trying to get his attention? Leaving the hospital Gene is very perplexed by the day's events and has a worried feeling in his heart that something bad was about to happen to George. As he drives home he tries to sort out the message. He recalls what George said and then Dr. Reads analysis of George's outbursts. Both descriptions are very different stories. If he is having serious nightmares, maybe he doesn't even know it? Maybe he is only thinking it is Mrs. Ramos in his dreams. Yet, maybe it is that demon that is appearing to him who is making itself look like Mrs. Ramos. Or, maybe Mrs. Ramos is actually appearing to him to warn him of the demon that may be coming? Could that be the message the shadow people were trying to show him? All in all, it is very unclear. Maybe tomorrow he can witness for himself what is happening and if that demon is at the heart of George's bad dreams, possibly he can confront it and chase it away?

Later that evening as Gene sits at his desk and begins his shift; he picks up his phone and calls George. It was early enough that George should still be awake. They talk about different things and then about Gene's new job. George is excited for him. Then, finally Gene says, "George, I want you to know I met Dr. Read after I left your room this afternoon. He says you are healing fine, but he gave me some startling information about the degree of your nightmares. He described them being much more physical and deeper in nature than what you described to me. He even said while you are asleep you become violent with nurses and orderlies. So, considering what you think is happening and what the doctor says is occurring, there appears to be a big difference of opinions. So, if you don't mind, I would like to visit you tomorrow night, as I am off then, and maybe I could sit with you until you fall asleep. Then, when you are sleeping I can try to read your thoughts and know better what you are experiencing. I fear if we don't do something like that; it may be a long time before you get out of there. What do you think?"

George is surprised by what he hears, but since he now knows that Gene has special powers, he doesn't hesitate, and responds, "Sure, I think that is a great idea. Come early and we can watch a little TV together."

Gene ends the conversation by agreeing to be there about 8:30 pm tomorrow and they can visit more. He then asks George if he needs anything.

George says yes there is one thing I need. He then asks for Gene to bring along a beautiful woman for him, but if that isn't possible, then he would have to settle for his company. They both then say goodnight and hang up.

As the night passes, very few calls come in. Gene breaks for lunch and returns to complete his shift. Driving home he is still in a quandary over what to do about the warning from the shadow people. What did it mean?

Up early the next morning, Amelia is still getting ready for work. He goes into the kitchen and pours himself a cup of coffee and stares out the window as he thinks about George. As he is thinking about George, Amelia comes up behind him and kisses Gene on the neck. Momentarily startled, he spills a little coffee down the front of his robe. Quickly turning, Amelia smiles and expresses her apologies for scaring him.

Looking at Amelia Gene explains how he visited George yesterday and then spoke to his doctor. He tells her that apparently he is experiencing wild dreams and he isn't going to be discharged from the hospital until he has gotten over them. He goes on to explain how he is going there that evening to sit with him for awhile and see if he can help him once he falls asleep.

Amelia smiles and says, "You're a good friend for sure. And, I hope you can help George. But, promise me you will be careful. You know how dangerous trying to get into someone's mind can be. So, be careful."

Gene sips his coffee and responds, "Yes, I will. But, I cannot help him unless I can figure out exactly what's happening to him. I'll pray that tonight I can accomplish that."

As the afternoon rolls along, Gene spends most of the day on the computer. He Google's Demons, Shadow People, dreams, psychics and other paranormal topics to see if he can read and learn about anything that will aid him in trying to accomplish his goals tonight. He learns a lot and finds that there are basically five types of dreaming;

Dream Telepathy
Precognition
Mutual Dreaming
Lucid Dreaming
Out of Body Experiencing Dreaming

Yet, in reading about each one he learned more, but there was really nothing specific that would help him in what he needed to know in order to accomplish his goal once George went to sleep.

At 8:00 pm. Gene dresses and gets into his car and heads to the hospital. He enters the lobby and goes directly to Dr. Read's office. Finding his office empty, he seeks out a nurse and asks if the doctor was in. When informed that Dr. Read had already gone home, he tells the nurse what he and Dr. Read had discussed and agreed to, indicating that he will be sitting with George to try to assess his dreams and help him to overcome his problems.

The nurse looks at Gene rather oddly and asks, "Are you a doctor? Otherwise, if you are not, how is it that you believe you can help Mr. Newton?"

Sheepishly, Gene explains his ESP and psychic abilities. He then mentions the event that occurred when he found the kidnapped daughter of George's brother.

Immediately, the nurse recalled reading about the story of him finding Megan through his psychic powers, which causes her to change her attitude. She then eagerly accompanies Gene to George's room. Inside she visits with George and Gene for a while and then excuses herself after inquiring whether or not either one of them needed anything from her. Listening to her offer, Gene thinks about that and subsequently asks for, and receives a note book and pen, which he figured that he would use to document that evenings events.

Settling in, Gene and George discuss Gene's new job offer and the firm he will be working for. George is happy for Gene and seriously hopes he will enjoy his new career. They then discuss the police department and George's future plans. George tells Gene how much he enjoys being a patrol officer and how anxious he was to get back to work. He then suggests that occasionally Gene should spend an evening with him doing a ride-along. He comments that since Gene is going to specialize in criminal law, it might benefit him by staying in touch with the department's day to day street patrol. To that suggestion, Gene agrees and says he would enjoy it.

He went further on to say likely a Friday or Saturday evening ride would be the busiest and best time for him to accompany George and his partner.

After a couple more hours of visiting and reminiscing about past ventures together, George begins to get tired. Gene suggests they turn off the lights and George should try to sleep. As both become quiet, in the darkened room Gene sits back in his chair and tries to figure out what he will do once George is truly asleep. He wonders if he touched his hand lightly, might that allow him to see what he was dreaming. He knew he couldn't disturb him, and he feared a physical touch might do that. Therefore, he decides that first he would touch his pajama cuff and see how that went. Then if that didn't work, his hand would be next.

Thinking about his choices, suddenly George says something that he believes is directed to him. Leaning in closer in order to hear him, he suddenly realizes that George was asleep and speaking in a foreign language. It was not Spanish and definitely not English. So, what was it? Listening closely, George appears to be fluent in whatever it was he is speaking and it is very rapid as well. In all the years he has known George, never did he indicate that he knew any other languages. And, if he did, it seemed very odd that Gene didn't know about it. Touching George's pajama sleeve, Gene hopes that will help him to possibly see into George's dream and understand better what was happening. Taking a hold of his pajama cuff on his right arm, Gene closes his eyes and concentrates on entering George's thoughts. After about two minutes flashes of light almost blind him, and he begins to hear muffled sounds of what could be masses of people screaming. He immediately equated it to the sounds he experienced when he had the vision of Hell, when he was in the hospital with his own head injury. Suddenly, he senses something very evil, and it seems to be emerging from George's mind and coming out and towards him. As this happens, the entity begins calling out Gene's name. In his mind, Gene clearly hears the entity calling to him and he mentally responds by asking who it is and what it wanted. As he finishes asking those questions, he is suddenly disconnected from George's thoughts and the entity calling him ceases its attempt to contact him. Gene then opens his eyes and sees nothing, but he feels George moving around very rapidly, mostly in an up and down motion.

Gene tries once more to make contact with George's dream, he places both hands on George's shoulders and tries to hold him down. However, he is unable to reconnect with those thoughts he previously felt. Then, the lights in the room suddenly come on causing Gene to turn around and look towards the room's door where the light switch is. Standing there with his hand on the light switch was Dr. Read.

The two stare at one another for a few seconds when Dr Read says, "Sorry to have startled you Mr. Wilson, but I feared for your safety. I was standing just outside this door as Mr. Newton began muttering. I stayed to see what you might do and accomplish. I found your entire effort to be very amazing."

Letting go of George's shoulders, Gene straightens up and walks over towards the doctor. He then asks, "Do you have any idea what language he was speaking? I never heard him speak it before. I just assumed he only knew English and maybe a little Spanish."

Immediately Dr. Read says, "Yes, he was speaking ancient Latin. It was very pronounced and he was calling out for Satan to help him. The call was coming from his mouth, but it was something else deep inside of Mr. Newton that was seeking Satan's help. I have never witnessed anything like that before. It definitely was real on his part, as that language is not taught or spoken anywhere in this world today. I studied it back in college, but the Latin used today is very different. So, I am sure it is safe to say, your friend was possessed by something that knew the language, as there is no doubt he would have ever learned it on his own, since it isn't taught anywhere now a days. Otherwise, I have no logical explanation as to how or why he could be speaking such a dead language."

Gene asks Dr. Read to step outside of George's room. Agreeing, the two men do so and Gene walks the doctor over to a lounge area where there are seats for waiting friends of patients to sit at. Sitting down, Gene immediately begins telling Dr. Read everything. He starts with his head injury. He describes seeing what he believed Heaven and Hell looked like. He then explains his encounter with the woman in the hospital and later seeing her ghost. He explains how he and George went to a traffic accident the following day and discovered the same woman again, and how everything from the first encounter happened all over again to her. He explains how he began seeing shadow people and how they saved him and George from harm a couple of times. He explains how doctor Allen and Mendenhall discovered his psychic abilities, noting that those abilities were continuing to increase without any sign of stabilizing. He explains how scared he is but does find it fascinating to be able to read other people's emotional thoughts and even track kidnapped people by holding their discarded clothing. He specifically mentions George's niece Megan. He also describes how he found the entities at the late Mrs. Ramos home and how he thought he had chased them away from her house. He then tells how George was injured while trying to help Mrs. Ramos the last time she called for help. He continues by explaining how George was knocked down by one of the entities, causing him to now wonder if maybe somehow that evil entity he thought he had chased away may have entered George's soul while he was down on the ground. He describes to the doctor how it felt when he touched George's pajama cuff tonight. He says he definitely felt something evil calling to him from inside George's body. Finally, he explains to Dr. Read how after leaving his office yesterday he encountered more shadow people in an empty room, where upon entering, it appeared George was in that bed and the shadow people were hovering over him, Yet, upon a closer investigation there was no patient at all in that bed and the shadow people immediately left the area.

Dr. Read listens with intense interest. He comments about reading about a policeman who through psychic skills located an abducted little girl and freed her from her captive. He admits that he didn't know that Gene was that person, and comments how pleased he is to have met him. But, he also explains how he had never believed in ghosts or psychic paranormal events before. Yet, he admits that what he just observed tonight in George's room as Gene made contact with his dreaming world, certainly appeared to be genuine and proof that something unusual was happening to George. He then says, "Mr. Wilson, if such a thing is possible, meaning true demonic possession, how can we deal with it? How can we help Mr. Newton to get rid of this entity?"

Gene smiles at hearing the doctor's confession and acknowledgment of his capabilities. He thinks about it and says, "I'm not certain that I can do anything, but I would like to try to exorcise that demon out of George if at all possible. I have never done anything like that before, but for some unknown reason I feel as though I have the ability to do that. Short of that happening, if I can't succeed, we will need to get a qualified Catholic priest in here to perform a real exorcism.

Dr. Read is somewhat worried about trying anything like an exorcism, causing him to say, "Given my medical training, such things like that seem so unlikely and unreal. Yet, I admit I do not know everything there is to know about the human body. And, it does appear from what I saw tonight that it is likely Mr. Newton does have something controlling him from within. So, given that scenario, I am ready to provide my assistance anytime you say."

Gene smiles at the doctor's comments and says, "Ok, I suggest we do it now. Let's go to his room right now and I'll make contact with him. Hopefully, I will be able to see what we are dealing with. If I am successful, maybe I can chase it away."

Apprehensive over Gene's claims, Dr. Read has nothing better to offer so he nods in agreement and reluctantly goes with Gene back to George's room. Inside, Dr. Read asks, "Is there anything I can do to help you?"

Considering the doctor's question, Gene responds, "To be honest doctor, this is a one man experiment. I think it would be best if you would just sit and watch me. You will know pretty quickly if it is working. And, if it is, or you see anything bad beginning to happen, you will need to pull me back into this world by grabbing me and waking me up as fast as possible. I think if you can do that, everything will work just fine."

Thinking about that, Dr. Read asks, "How exactly will I know if anything bad is happening in your head? I may not see anything externally that tells me to intercede. What do you suggest I use as a measurement tool to detect a problem?"

Gene has no idea how to answer the doctors question, so he says, "Doctor Read, I think if I am in trouble it will be evident to you. If you will just listen to my conversation, I think you will know what is going on most of the time. So, I trust you will not have any difficulties."

Gene then approaches George who is still sleeping. Now, he is no longer flailing around and appears to be peacefully asleep. Carefully and gently Gene touches his shoulders. Gene closes his eyes and concentrates rather strongly on trying to enter his dream. After about three minutes, visions begin entering Gene's mind. At first it is nonsense and has no meaning. Then, suddenly this image of a demon with horns and sharp teeth are right in his face. It was as if the thing sensed Gene's intrusion and as if on each side of a window the entity went right up to Gene's face and looked him squarely in the eyes. Staring at Gene, first it snorts, and then orders Gene to leave. Gene responds mentally by saying a resounding, 'NO' and proceeds to order the beast out of George's body. Surprised by Gene's insistence the entity merely smiles and proceeds to yell back at Gene. Gene commands the beast to depart George's body in God's name. He keeps ordering this over and over until the beast gets tired of hearing this and simply turns and leaves Gene's view. Gene has no idea where it went, but he still feels its presence even though it cannot be seen anywhere.

Gene attempts to call out to the beast, but it refuses to respond and eventually Gene's connection to George's dream ends. Opening his eyes and turning to Dr. Read, Gene says, "I couldn't do anything. I saw it and ordered it out but it just ignored me and then vanished. However, it didn't leave George because I continued to feel its anger and hatred of me. And, I do not know of anything more that I can do."

Dr. Read listens with interest and then says, "Well, I heard no words coming from you, so I cannot say what transpired, but maybe there are more conventional ways to deal with that thing. Is it possible that a Catholic priest might be successful? If your friend truly is possessed, I have heard they are the experts in that sort of thing.

Just as the doctor finishes his comments, George wakes up. Seeing both men close to him he asks what was happening and why were they there?

Looking at one another Dr. Read says to Gene, "Shall you tell him or should I. I really think he needs to know. And, maybe he has some insight and can help us."

Gene nods in agreement. He then turns to George and tells him what they believe is wrong with him and what Gene had just tried to do.

Dr. Read then adds, "Mr. Newton, as you know I have been watching over you ever since you were admitted here. And, I will admit, I am, or I should say was, a nonbeliever in such things. But, I have to admit; your friend here has convinced me otherwise and now I truly concur with his diagnosis. So, is there anything you can remember or recall that you might be able to tell us that will be helpful?"

George looks at both men with a look of disbelief on his face. He then says, "I can't understand how you two have come to such a conclusion. I feel fine and I'm not acting possessed. I just need to get out of here and be able to go back to work. Please stop trying to find things wrong with me, in order to keep me confined to this bed."

"George, you have known me a long time and you know I have never lied to you. You also know how my psychic powers work. And, if I tell you something like what I just did, you know that I am telling you what I truly believe is a fact. Also, Dr. Read has no reason to lie to you. He is a professional, and he too wants what is best for you. So, you must understand there is an issue here and we have to find a way to correct it," says Gene.

George looks at both men and says, "Yes, I know you two are not fooling me. I believe you're doing and saying what you believe is true. But, if what you say is fact, why don't I feel it inside of me? I would think it would be obvious to me that I was possessed, if what you say exists is really there."

Gene looks at George and says, "Look, I know what I saw and experienced. Also, it is reported that when you sleep you are a different person. It's likely that when you are awake, it has no power or control over you. Or, maybe it simply elects not to force you to do anything during your waking time. I certainly can't answer the majority of your questions, but you have to believe me when I say you are definitely possessed and we need to get that thing out of you. Meanwhile, Dr. Read here can't release you to go back to work until he knows that you are well. So, if you really want to go home, work with us. We are thinking that bringing in an expert like a Catholic priest might be our best bet. I just failed when I tried to chase it away, so it is obvious, I am not competent enough to do it. So, what do you say, will you work with us?"

George is definitely confused. He doesn't believe their claim at all, but knows Gene well enough to know he isn't lying to him either. Also, it appears that Dr. Read believes too and will not discharge him until he is convinced that he is well. Therefore, with no other way to go, he responds, "Gentlemen, do what you must. I'll do everything you ask and cooperate one-hundred percent with you. And, what ever it is you think you must do, lets do it."

Gene smiles and says, "Good. I will go tomorrow to see Father Sanchez, the new priest at Father Kelley's church. I doubt that he can help, but maybe he will know someone that can. Meanwhile, hang in here my friend and I'll be back in touch with you both tomorrow."

Early the next morning Gene meets with Father Sanchez and tells him what he and Dr. Read were thinking about for George. He candidly explains how he felt George was possessed by a demon and inquired how they could locate a priest with exorcism experience. Father Sanchez being young and inexperienced in such matters was not prepared to give Gene any names to contact. Instead, he said he would have to confer with his church's higher sources. He said he would make the appropriate inquiries that day, but did not know what the outcome would be. Gene thanks the father and excuses himself, with the assurance he would be contacted by Father Sanchez later in the afternoon.

While walking to his vehicle his cell phone rings. It was Dr. Read. Out of breath, he explains that George had gone berserk and had to be strapped down in his bed to protect him from hurting himself or others. Apparently when he woke this morning he was openly possessed and began ranting and destroying furniture. His demands made no senses and it took six orderlies to subdue him securely into his bed. The doctor asks if he had any luck with finding a priest. He then asked Gene to come on over so they could discuss the entire event?

Gene tells Dr. Read that he would come immediately and asked that no one approach or speak to George, as it will only cause him to become more agitated. He then hangs up and gets into his vehicle and hurries to the hospital. As he drives he wonders what he can do. Is this now a total possession? And if it is, how could he do anything to save his friend's life?

Arriving at the hospital Gene runs to Dr. Read's office. Entering, Dr. Read explains how George was discovered out of control and describes how it took six orderlies to subdue him. He then asks Gene if he thinks the demon is responsible.

Gene indicates that for George to have such strength, is proof that something abnormal was happening and a possession made the most sense. He then asks to be taken to George's room.

Dr. Read warns Gene that George may be hostile and to be careful when he sees him. Entering the room, George is in his bed, shackled down with restraints that are on each wrist and ankle. Seeing Gene, George appears to act normal. Gene pulls up a chair and sits next to him. Looking at Gene, George is quiet and looks normal.

Gene sits there looking at George and asks, "George, how do you feel? Are you able to talk with me? Why did you destroy all of that furniture?" He then waits for a response but George does not respond. Gene then stands up, and begins to walk away. Just as he does that, George starts yelling and pulling at his restraints.

"Who are you to hog-tie me like this? Don't you know who I am and what I will do to all of you? I am not to be messed with and especially from humans like you," says George. Then just as fast as he got angry he suddenly calms down again.

Watching all of this happen, Gene is now convinced more than ever that George has some demonic spirit in him that is causing these outbreaks. Turning back to face George, Gene asks, "Who am I speaking to? Who is controlling George's body? What is your name and what do you want? Speak to me and do it now, I command you to speak."

For a moment there is no reply and then coolly and clearly George says, "My name is Apollyon, I am the 'king' of all demons. And it is I who controls this human and there is nothing you or your God can do to stop me. I will use this body as I see fit. And, when I am done and it is no longer useful to me, I will destroy this human. And only when that happens will I move on. So, try whatever you want and do your bidding, but the great Apollyon answers to no human." It then becomes silent and Gene turns and exits the room.

Standing in the door outside of the room Dr. Read was listening. Once Gene was outside he asks, "Was that for real? What was it? What are we dealing with? And, if it is what it says it is, how can we help Mr. Newton?"

Gene is perplexed over what he just experienced and thinks it is important to verify the name that was given to see if it is a real demonic name. He thinks if he can prove that there really is a demon named Apollyon that might confirm that George is possessed. Therefore, turning to Dr. Read he asks if he can use his computer in his office to see if he can 'Google' the term Demon Names and try and see if such a demonic entity exists. If it does, Gene thinks that would be proof that George is possessed, as he knows George could never have come up with such a name on his own.

Dr. Read agrees and the two immediately depart for the doctor's office. Entering the room, Gene is invited to sit down at his computer. Gene immediately brings up 'Google' and enters the topic; Demon Names. Within seconds several options are shown. Opening the most likely page, sure enough there was a demon named Apollyon. And, just as it claimed when it spoke to Gene, it was noted as being the King of all Demons. For Gene this was proof of George's possession.

Dr. Read asks what Gene found? Turning the computer monitor to one side so the doctor could read the information, Gene points to the name Apollyon. Upon seeing the name in print, the doctor is shocked and looks at Gene and says, "Oh my God, he is possessed. He has to be. So, what do we do now?"

Gene agrees with the comment that George was possessed and that given the demons plan to stay inside of George until he dies, it makes Gene very scared and anxious to figure out what to do. Checking the website further, Gene finds a section on exorcisms and begins reading it. He sees the section describing the fact that there are actually Demon Hunters, who go after demons and actually try to destroy them. Gene reads everything thoroughly. He then turns to the doctor and says, "I think I need to try again to make contact with Apollyon. I can't just wait to find a Catholic Priest who will help us. I went to the church this morning and hit a dead end. So, it isn't likely that we can count on them. Maybe I can try to reach into George's memory and see what I might be able to find, in order to fight Apollyon. Otherwise, I just don't know what else to do."

Fearful of Gene doing anything Dr. Read asks, "Do you really think doing anything more is wise? You already went after that beast once and it definitely wasn't afraid of you, causing your efforts to fail. And, what if upon your contacting it, the demon jumps from Mr. Newton into you? How can you guard against something like that happening? I really think we need to give this a lot of serious thought and explore all of our options before doing any more to get it out of your friend."

Gene listens to Dr. Read and agrees with him that it will be dangerous, but considering the entities intentions, he sees no way out of trying again to chase it out of George. He therefore responds by saying, "Yes, you have valid concerns, as I agree it will be dangerous. But, I fear if I don't, that thing will kill George. It so much as told me that. Plus, reading some of the events described by the Demon Hunter article I read in that 'Googled' page, it had some good suggestions that maybe I can use to help me and protect George. So, if you can help me find some items, I would really appreciate it."

Hesitantly Dr. Read says, "Well, I understand your feelings and I am more than willing to help any way I can, so what items do you need?

"Well, what I need are some items from the hospital's chapel. I want a couple of crucifix's and some holly water. Also, if there might be a picture of Jesus we could get that would be great. Do you think we could borrow any of those items," asks Gene?

Thinking about it, it occurs to Dr. Read that Father Nelson, the hospital's chapel residing priest may be of some assistance. He is in his seventies and has been a head priest at many churches. Turning to Gene he says, "Father Nelson may be around here somewhere, and maybe he would be willing to help us. He has been a priest for many years. So, it might be possible that he can aid you. Let's go find him."

Hearing that comment Gene smiles and says, "Why didn't we think of that before? I should have known that a priest was on site and assigned to the hospital's chapel? After all this is a Catholic hospital. Yes, let's find him."

The two men head to the chapel. Entering, there is no one there. Gene looks around and sees everything on the wall that he had hoped to borrow. Before he can remove anything, an elderly man enters through a rear door, wearing a black robe like outfit where Gene immediately sees a priest collar under it. It has to be Father Nelson. The priest approaches both Gene and Dr. Read. He introduces himself and assumes the two men were there for grief counseling. Upon the completion of the introductions Dr. Read explains that he was on staff there as a psychiatry doctor and Gene was a policeman who was there trying to help a sick friend. He asks the priest if they could take a moment of his time and explain what they needed. He of course agrees and the three men sit down and begin talking.

Looking at the priest Gene begins by explaining to the priest how he suffered a head injury and that somehow that event stimulated parts of his brain that had been dormant, allowing him to see and experience things others can't. He goes on to discuss his friend's injury and explains how they had encountered at least two different demons and how George is currently possessed by one. He also explains how he was wishing to borrow some items from the chapel in order to try and exorcise the demon out of George.

Dr. Read then adds the information about Gene finding the kidnapped little girl and how earlier that day he made contact with the evil entity inside of George. He tries to explain to the priest how Gene's claims of psychic abilities are real and he is not making any jokes about what he believes is happening to George and what he wishes to do.

Listening intently to the two men, Father Nelson thinks about what is being said and tries to decide how credible the story was. After a few moments he says, "Well, yes you are more than welcome to borrow anything you want. However, let me make a suggestion. As you can see, I am an older man and I can assure you that there is very little I have not witnessed over my career as a priest. And, yes, I have witnessed possessions and in fact I have even aided in exorcisms. Therefore, it may be best for you to allow me to be the lead in this effort and ask that you assist me. I have to tell you, what you are wishing to do is not easily done. Often, the demon is stronger in resolve and will prevail, but not always. So, if I can be of any assistance, please feel free to let me do what I can."

After hearing his offer, Gene knows the priest is likely a better choice given his background with such things and immediately says, "Father Nelson, I would be proud to aid you. I am more than willing to let someone of your experience take on the lead. What can I do to help?"

Thinking about it, he stands up, looks around the chapel and begins removing items from the wall that have religious significance. He hands two crucifixes to Gene. He also takes down a picture of Jesus and fills three bottles with holly water. He then says, "These items are good and all that we will likely need. However, before we begin, I would like to visit your friend and see for myself how he acts. The worst thing we could do is to perform an exorcism on a person who is not possessed, but simply mentally challenge

Dr. Read interjects and says, "I understand and agree. But let me tell you that I have been treating Mr. Newton for a couple of weeks now and it has only been these past two days that he has begun acting possessed while fully awake. In the beginning, it was his terrible nightly dreams that were his problem. But suddenly he has become very physical when awake and I fear he would be definitely abusive if not restrained. That is why I ordered him to be shackled to his bed. So, be careful, and I will be at your side while you examine him. If he gets too out of control, I will be forced to sedate him."

Father Nelson listens with interest and then says, "Exorcisms are an ancient method of chasing demons from the souls of good Christians. The exorcist job is to simply expel evil spirits out of possessed individuals by calling upon either Jesus or the power of Christ to rid evil spirits from a humans body in his name, per 10:1; Matthew, 10:8; Mark and 6:7; Luke. According to the Catholic Encyclopedia article of exorcism, Jesus points to his ability as a sign of his messiah ship and empowers his followers to do the same.

Dr. Read understands what is being said, but wants to be sure Father Nelson is capable of doing what he says he can do and asks the father, "Given the seriousness of any exorcism, how can you know if or what the chances are that you will be successful. And, why is it that Catholics are empowered to this? Why do you not see other religious groups attempt exorcisms?"

Smiling at Dr. Read's comments, Father Nelson says, "Well, to be honest sir, many other religious orders do perform exorcisms. I have known of Jewish, Hindus, Buddhists, Zen's, Lutherans, Methodists, Pentecostals and Anglicanism's all successfully performing exorcisms. I guess the Catholic approach is likely the most rigid and contains far more exorcism rituals than any other religious group. Hence, that is likely the reason the Catholic religion is normally the one that most often comes to mind when such an involvement is needed. But, I think too, given the age of our religious order, we have likely been doing it a lot longer than any other group, and with that said, we likely have had greater success, as well."

Gene is anxious to begin and asks Father Nelson if he is ready to see George? Picking up his necessary items he looks at Gene and says, "Show me the way my son. It is time we began."

Quickly arriving at George's room, Gene turns to Father Nelson and says, "This is it. He is inside, and securely strapped to his bed. So, what do you want me to do?"

Father Nelson says, "First I need to go in alone. He doesn't know me and I want to assess his true personality. If he is secured, I have no fear of being harmed, but I must ascertain whether he is truly possessed or just mentally ill. So, please wait out here, and stay out of sight. When I complete my exam, I will come back out and we can then decide what to do next." Father Nelson puts all of his tools and holly water down on the floor. Straightens his uniform and opens George's door.

George immediately spots the man and within seconds sees his Catholic collar. As he approaches George, it was obvious the sight of the priest greatly upset George. His eyes are wild and drool runs down both sides of his mouth. Loud howling and growling sounds begin coming from deep within George. The priest approaches George and he is doing everything he can to get loose and attack the priest. "I am here to help you my son. Please calm down and talk to me." As Father Nelson says that, George lunges forward and tries to bite the priest. Standing and looking at George, Father Nelson still isn't sure what to make of his reaction. Certainly the man was not friendly, but he needs more proof to know he is truly possessed.

George looks at the priest with wide open and hostile eyes. He wants to break loose and attack the man. As hard as he pulls and flails around, he cannot get untied. Then, the priest places his hand on George's forehead. The priest's hand is burnt. Quickly pulling his hand away George lets out an evil laugh and then says, "Get away from me you pitiful little man. I have no need for your help. Nor, do I want or ask for your help. Leave me be and get out of here." The sound of George's voice was coming deep from within his stomach, and as he speaks it was almost a hallow echoing type of sound that was resonating inside of him.

Looking closer, the priest liens over to see into George's face, Father Nelson can easily see the hatred in his eyes. Taking a chair he pulls it up beside George and sits down. This obviously agitates George even more. The priest than asks, "Who are you? What is you name? Why are you hiding inside of this man's body?"

For a few minutes there is no response, but the whole time George is silent, the priest just sits there and stares at him, watching as he tries to get away and escape from his bondage. But he cannot do either. As the priest gets even closer, he can smell George's breathe. It is rancid, smelling very much like rotten eggs or sulfur. The priest knows these odors are associated with demonic possession. So assuming that he has a legitimate demonic entity here that he needs to deal with, he wants desperately for it to communicate with him, so he will know for sure.

Pulling his head back, in an almost snake like striking position George looks the priest squarely in the eyes and says in a hallow bellowing type of voice, "My name is Apollyon, I am the king of all demons and I have taken this humans body and there is nothing you can do about it. So, get out of here. And, if you don't, I will kill this mortal, here and now. Believe me, I mean what I say."

Now, finally the priest is completely sure that he is dealing with a true possession, Father Nelson stands up and says, "Apollyon, I am going to remove you from this man and there is nothing you or your master can do to stop me. Our Lord Jesus Christ and the father of all creation empowers me and you have no way to stop me. If you are smart you will leave now, or when I finish with you the only thing you will be king of is the rats that are running all around in Hell." He then gets up and exits George's room.

Outside, Dr. Read and Gene were standing and watching what was happening through the glass window in George's door. As the priest exits the room, he asks both Dr. Read and Gene to join him in the waiting room. Sitting down there, the priest says, "There is no doubt about Mr. Newton's possession. It is serious and there is no doubt that this demon will kill him if I cannot chase him out. And, I have to tell you, it isn't going to be an easy job. So, I will need the aid of both of you gentlemen. It will also be dangerous. There is no telling where that entity will go, if I am able to chase him out of Mr. Newton. So, we must watch everyone as we proceed. If anyone of us sees anything odd about himself or one of us, you need to speak up immediately. And, I will need a few more minutes to go and gather more items that we will need to fight that thing. Please wait here and I'll be right back. Oh, please do not go into Mr. Newton's room or even get close to that door. I'll be back in about five minutes.

As they watch the priest depart, Gene says to Dr. Read, "Wow, I can see now that there is no way I could have chased that thing out of George. Obviously, God was watching over him, when he led us to Father Nelson. He does seem knowledgeable. And, he seems to be confident. Watching him go head to head with that thing was intense. I know I couldn't have done it. The two men talk about the exorcism in general and each wonders what part they will be playing in the fight.

And as promised within five minutes the priest is back. He has a box full of bibles and two very large crucifixes and two small ones. He hands the two small ones to both Gene and Dr. Read and instructs them to place each crucifixes around their necks. He says it was for their own safety. The priest then sprinkles holy water over the heads of both men, and at the same time says a short prayer. As he does that he takes out six bibles. He opens them to separate chapters and places markers in each one. He then returns them back in the box opened to the separate chapters he wishes to read from. In addition to the crucifixes and bibles he also has two large pictures of Jesus. All were items that had hung on the chapel wall.

Gene watches and then asks, "Is this all of what you are going to need to do the job Father Nelson? It is a lot of stuff, but I wonder if it is enough to really help George?"

Father Nelson looks at both men and says, "Gentlemen, there is no guaranty that anything will work. But, the best shot I think we have is using these items quickly when we get into his room. Hopefully, I can overpower the beast with religion and the word of God. But, I agree, it could all be useless stuff. So, are you two ready to follow me in his room? I need one of you on each side. Take these four bottles of holly water and as I speak and pray, slowly sprinkling the holy water on him. Please, don't ask any more questions of me now, let's just get started? The three enter George's room and Dr. Read and Gene take their place on each side of George's bed. As they enter, George is looking all around. Obviously trying to size up what was about to happen and wondering what his resolve would be.

When everyone is in place, the priest lays one large crucifix directly on George's stomach. He then takes the first bible from his box and begins reading from it. After a few words he turns it upside down with the book open and places it face down on George's chest, just below the crucifix. As the bible touches him, George begins bellowing out as if he was in pain. Again and again Father Nelson picks up a bible and reads various chapters and then places the book on George's torso. In Between his reading of the bible he is constantly chanting the *Lord's Prayer.* Slowly, more bibles and crucifixes are placed on top of George; eventually covering his entire upper torso. As he does this, Father Nelson curses the demon as he orders it out of George. The holly water is also being applied constantly by Gene and Dr. Read. George continues to scream in pain each time the water touches him. Father Nelson then places the two portraits of Jesus on each of George's legs. Again he yells out in pain. As all of this occurs, Father Nelson is constantly praying while ordering the demon Apollyon out of George's body.

They continue doing this for at least an hour. They all become tired, but no one wants to stop. As they continue, Father Nelson picks up one bible after another off of George and reads different chapters, and when done returns it to George's stomach. He also moves the pictures of Christ from his legs to his head and then to his feet. Each time, George bellows in pain. Going to their last bottle of holly water the priest instructs both men to begin saying the *Lords Prayer* out loud, over and over as they sprinkle water on George. Constant screams and sounds of pain continue coming from George. With each reading of the bible Father Nelson becomes more loud and demanding. He is now yelling at Apollyon to depart George. After another hour of this ritual, George suddenly stops yelling and bellowing and his body suddenly goes limp. By now, Gene and Dr. Read are very tired too and would very much like to rest. Putting his hands in the air, Father Nelson signals both men to stop. As the three stand there looking down at George, a shallow whisper is heard coming from his mouth, which is immediately followed by a loud swishing noise that is heard rushing past the men, towards the room's door. Suddenly, George's room door opens and slams shut on its own, just as if the entity had left the room.

"Gene, what is happening to me? Who is this? What are you doing? What is going on," asks George?

Looking down at George, they see his sheets are soaked in sweat, but he now seemed more relaxed. Father Nelson removes the items from his head and body. Looking at him the priest asks, "Who are you? Do you know your name?"

Not looking at the priest, George looks directly at Gene and asks, "What do you mean who am I? Gene, you know me. What's going on here?"

Father Nelson reaches down and turns George's head toward him. He then says, Mr. Newton, you were possessed by a demonic entity. It controlled you and your every action. Do you recall that event? Do you know whether or not that thing is still inside of you?"

Sweating profusely George is worn out. He looks at Gene, Father Nelson and then Dr. Read. As if asking everyone, he says, "What in the

Hell are you people talking about? I don't remember anything, I don't believe you either. Help me Gene, please help me."

Looking at Father Nelson, Gene asks, "Can it be over? Is it possible you won? He is acting normal and is no longer in pain from our work. What do you think?"

Father Nelson responds by saying, "It might just be fooling us. Demons are very tricky. It might just be its way of resting. But, I cannot say for sure. I would love to believe it is gone, but we need to be cautious. Definitely we cannot untie him yet. Not until we know for sure that the demonic beast is gone. Let's take a break and let Mr. Newton rest. We can come back later and then see what happens. The three men leave George's room, without any further comment to him.

Once outside, Father Nelson says, "Let's stay here and watch him through this window in his door. He cannot see us, but we can watch him. If the beast is still in him, it won't take long to see how he acts, when it thinks we are gone. It seems to me it left to quickly, especially given how arrogant it was when I first entered Mr. Newton's room. I just do not believe it gave up and left that easily."

Gene asks Father Nelson about the sound they heard and the door opening and closing. He asks if that was the demon leaving George's body.

Dr. Read echoes that same question also wanting to know what it was.

Father Nelson shakes his head and says, "Gentlemen, it may have been the demon leaving or it might have been a hoax designed to fool us. Let's just wait and see."

For the next thirty minutes the three men take turns watching George's behavior, but nothing happens that causes them to believe he isn't telling the truth. He lays there and actually cries and appears to be feeling sorry for himself. As Father Nelson watches, he tells Dr. Read and Gene to wait outside while he goes back inside to interview Mr. Newton. Opening the door, George looks at the priest and this time does not appear to be angry at seeing his white collar. But, he did seem to be perplexed as to why he was tied up. Walking over to George the two talk and Father Nelson tries to smell his breath. Now, he notices that the sulfur odor was gone and George was not angry at his presence. Maybe the beast was gone. But, the priest knows that it definitely could be a ruse. He wants to believe that George is back to his former self, but he knows how deceitful demonic spirits are. He then begins a religious discussion with George. He had learned earlier from Gene that George was a Catholic and as such should know a few facts about the church. As Father Nelson questions him, George responds the way any normal Catholic would. Finally, George asks the priest if he could see his friend Gene. He also pleads with the priest to untie him. Father Nelson responds by saying, "Sir, I am hopeful that you are who and what you say you are. But, I cannot condone letting you free without knowing for certain the beast is gone. But, I will allow Gene to come in and talk with you, if that will help."

Father Nelson turns and exits the room. Outside, he tells Gene that his friend wants to talk to him. He also says he cannot tell for certain if the beast was truly gone, so he warns Gene to be careful and definitely do not undo his restraints. He tells Gene to be cautious, and says, "Try to engage him in conversations that you control and know the answer to. Test his memory and try to see if there is anything wrong with what he says or remembers."

Gene then enters George's room. Walking over to his bed he sits down on the chair next to him. George seems normal in all respects and as Gene can see he appeared happy to see Gene. Sitting down, Gene asks, "So, how are you feeling George?"

George then asks Gene, "What is happening to me? Why am I being chained down like a prisoner? Have I done something wrong?"

Gene smiles at his friend and begins telling him again about everything that has happened. He begins by describing his vicious attacks upon the nurses who first attended to him and then of his being subdued by hospital orderlies after destroying furniture. George looks at Gene as if he was nuts and in total disbelief. Gene goes on to describe how he first treated Father Nelson and their subsequent efforts to exorcise the demon named Apollyon out of him. Gene says, "George, I was so scared for your well being, that I was going to come in here and try to save you myself. But fortunately Dr. Read and I met Father Nelson and after telling him your story, he offered to help. And frankly, I am happy he did. I know now that there is no way I could have done the things he did. So, tell me how you feel and do you remember anything about being possessed?"

George says, "Partner, I do not recall anything, let alone being possessed. I certainly have no memory of anything you have said. But, if I did do what you claim I did, then thank you for helping me. All I want now is to go home and get some sleep in my own bed. I am so tired and weak; I doubt that I could even feed myself right now. Please let me sleep.

I want to feel better and maybe tomorrow we can talk more. Is that all right with you?"

Gene smiles at George and says, "Certainly that is fine. I will see you tomorrow. Go ahead and get some sleep. That will be good for you." Gene exits the room. Outside he tells Father Nelson and Dr. Read what George said. He also explains that George seemed to be his old self, and he saw no sign of the demon in him.

Father Nelson listens and considering what they had all gone through, he suggests they too go on home. He says, "If that demon is gone, good. But, somehow I just cannot believe it left so easily. In any case, by tomorrow when George is rested, we can better tell what his true condition is. I have to be here early in the morning for chapel business, so I will come back here tomorrow and check on him and see what I can detect. If you two look me up later, I'll tell you what I think his condition is."

Nodding in agreement, Gene and Dr. Read leave the priest and go to Dr. Read's office. There, they discuss what transpired and what their next steps should be. Gene agrees to meet Dr. Read in his office at 10:00 am. tomorrow. He then gets up and departs the hospital.

Driving home Gene considers how fortunate it was for him and Dr. Read to have found Father Nelson. He knows after watching him perform his exorcism that he could never have done what he did. And, if George is now truly free of that demon, Father Nelson is the sole reason why. Gene also decides it would be helpful for him to chronologically list out in a binder the entire events of George's possession and how he was exorcised. He decides that he will do that just as soon as he gets home.

Arriving home he finds Amelia already there and busy preparing dinner. As he approaches her in the kitchen, she hears him coming in and turns to greet him. They kiss and Gene begins telling her about his day and all of the events associated with George's exorcism. He tells her how good Father Nelson was and how hard they worked at trying to help George. He says, "I have to think finding Father Nelson was not only lucky but maybe pre-ordained. I know I could not have done what he did and I would have likely failed all around. And, in my opinion, George is now free from that Demon. But, we will know that for sure tomorrow, as I need to meet everyone at 10:00 am. in Dr. Read's office.

Listening intently, Amelia doesn't know what to say. She is shocked to hear Gene's comments and tells him how brave he was to assist the priest. They then change the subject and begin discussing Gene's new job and how nice their life will be once he begins. They both agree that a normal day job with weekends off will be an excellent beginning in promoting their relationship.

Early the next morning Gene wakes up before Amelia departs for work. He dresses, makes himself breakfast and reads the morning paper before departing for Dr. Read's office. At 9:30 am. he gets in his car and heads to the hospital. Arriving a little early he goes to see George. Looking in his room he sees George in bed and still shackled. He decides not to go inside and heads to Dr. Read's office.

As he knocks on Dr. Read's door, he hears a "Come in." Gene enters and sees Dr. Read at his desk reading something. Entering, Dr. Read looks up and says, "Good morning Mr. Wilson. Please take a seat."

Sitting down Gene asks if he had spoken to the priest yet today. To that question Dr. Read replies that he had, and in the priests opinion George was no longer possessed. However, he mentioned that he felt it best to keep him shackled to his bed until mid morning when he would look in on him again and decide for sure if he was free of the demon. The two men sit and talk about the exorcism and how the overall event unfolded and how they both perceived its affects.

Dr. Read says, "The whole thing was something I never expected to see. I never believed in those things before. And, hearing how you saw those 'shadow' people hovering over your friend, warning you as to the danger he was in, was also something extraordinary. It really forces one to think about life differently. It is obvious that there is so much more that occurs after death and it also appears that maybe there really is some sort of a hereafter. Obviously, what we are taught or learn through normal academic channels is not the entire story."

Gene smiles at hearing that and responds, "Dr. Read, I cannot explain how my mind has opened up since I was shot and experienced my new psychic visions and powers. It tells me that the human brain is so intricate and capable of so much more than what we normally encounter. And, if that is so, then it stands to reason there is also so much more to life and death than what mortal humans realize. I have come to believe we are all here today and who knows where we go after death?"

The two talk more on spirits, demons and other mysterious events and experiences. Dr. Read is truly interested and wants to know more. After about an hour Gene tells the doctor everything he had done and experienced. To that, Dr. Read is truly impressed and enlightened. Concluding his conversation, Gene then gets up and bids Dr. Read farewell and departs his office.

Gene then heads to George's room and sees that George was there and awake watching television. Entering, George was happy to see Gene.

Looking at Gene, George says, "Well, it's about time you came in to visit me. Where have you been? And, when are they going to remove these restraints?"

Gene explains to George what the priest had done and that they simply needed to be sure he was now normal. He tells George that the priest will return soon and then the restraints would be removed. The two talk a little longer and Gene looks at his watch and tells George he had to be going.

George makes Gene promise to stay in touch and once he becomes a lawyer not to forget his old friend. He again invites Gene to ride along on patrol with him sometimes if he gets bored sitting behind a desk. Then, as Gene begins to leave, George says, "Hey buddy, thanks for everything you have done for me. I can't tell you how much it all means to me."

Gene smiles and says, "It was my pleasure George, and I will definitely stay in touch with you. Also, thanks for the kind comments and offer to ride along. And, when I have the spare time I will call you. That would be fun. Meanwhile, you need to get out of here and back on the beat. Lying around here isn't good for you and I know the Captain sure misses you." Gene then reaches down and pats George on his right shoulder, smiles at him and slowly leaves his room. Heading towards his vehicle, he thinks how great it was that George was back to his old self and how good it was that demon was gone. He again wonders what would have happened if they had not found Father Nelson. Gene once again admits to himself that there was no way he could have done what Father Nelson did. And, if that was the case, where would George be today? What would eventually happen to him? Gene is truly thankful and knows this was one more chapter to the bazaar experiences of his new life. Reaching the parking lot, Gene finds his car and drives home.

CHAPTER 10; *New Beginnings:*

On Gene's last day as a police officer, he arrives at work early, not knowing what if any plans Captain Mitchell may have for him, he enters the locker room to get dressed for the last time. Gene puts on his uniform and heads to his desk. As he sits down he sees a hand written note from Captain Mitchell lying on his desk asking Gene to come to his office. Standing and looking around Gene sees no one close by, but he is certain the Captain will do something special for his final night of employment.

Knocking on Captain Mitchell's door, he hears him say, "Enter." Opening the door, he is asked to sit. Captain Mitchell is gracious and tells Gene how much he will be missed. However, he is also told how happy the Captain was that Gene was going on to such a prestigious law firm and how he knows it will be better for him and that he is making the right decision. He then hands Gene a folder containing a few pieces of paper and tells him they need filling out and signing. He explains that they were separation papers and standard procedures for all departing staff members. He also reminds Gene that upon leaving tonight he had to turn in his badge and identification card.

Gene assures the Captain that he would do everything needed and also tells his boss how he will be missing the police force, its people and the thrill of the work that he has enjoyed for so long.

Captain Mitchell smiles at hearing that and tells Gene again how he would be missed and that his ethics over the years was exemplary. He then stands, extends his hand and the two men shake a final time.

As Gene begins to exit the office, he turns and asks, "Captain, have you heard anything from George Newton? Is he close to returning back to work?"

Captain Mitchell looks at Gene and says, "Yes, I spoke with George just today. He is out of the hospital, resting fine and will be released to return to work next Monday. You should call him, I am sure he would like to hear form you."

Smiling at hearing that, Gene says, "That is great news." He then exits the captain's office and returns to his desk where he begins completing the paperwork he was given. As he works he fields only a few telephone calls and answers two questions from walk-in citizens that came to the station seeking information. Time passes quickly and soon it is his lunch time. Gene gets up, grabs his lunch sack and goes to the station's lunch room for his break. As he opens the door, standing there waiting for him is a room full of people who were there to say good-bye and wish him good luck. The Captain was there too, along with many of his fellow police officers that he had worked with over the past several years. Also, standing in the back of the crowd more or less hiding, was George. As Gene spots him, George waves and smiles, and then begins working his way through the large crowd and comes forward.

Gene watches as his friend moves towards him, George stops directly in front of him and says, "Partner, to be honest, back when we were together, I really never expected you to become a lawyer. I never expected you to leave the force, let alone take the bar exam. But, obviously I was wrong. And, on behalf of everyone in this room, I want you to know how much we will all miss you and how much we wish you the very best. I know you will be good at your new career and I'll bet very successful."

When George finishes his speech, Captain Mitchell comes forward and is carrying a big white cake. Setting it down on a table he says, "Gene, what George says is very much felt by us all. And, I too want you to know how much the department has enjoyed your dedication and how you will definitely be missed." He then hands Gene a card, which was signed by everyone. On it, the slogan simply says Congratulations and Good Luck. The Captain then suggests Gene cut his cake, so everyone on duty could get a piece and then go back to work.

Surprised and slightly embarrassed, Gene cuts the cake in many small pieces and places them on the little paper plates that the Captain had handed him. Quickly, everyone comes forth to grab a piece of cake and shake his hand. They then take their cake and for those working, they quickly return to their duty stations. George sits down next to Gene at a table once the captain and the crowd departed. He begins talking as Gene eats his lunch.

Looking at Gene, George says, "Partner, I know when I asked for a new partner a few months ago, you were hurt and upset. And, I truly am sorry for doing that. But, to be honest, you scared the shit out of me with your claims of psychic powers and all. I just wasn't ready to hear that kind of stuff. And it seemed to me that ever since we encountered that ghost, in San Pedro you seemed to have change. It was something I couldn't deal with. Then when you got shot and began claiming to have psychic powers, you really scared me. So, I felt we needed to split up, for my own peace of mind. The first night on patrol with my new partner, it was hell. I knew immediately that I had made a big mistake. But, I also knew it was too late to undo what I had done, and I would have to live with my decision. But, when my niece went missing, I saw that as a way of us making up and my getting back on your good side. And, to be honest, I never dreamed you would really be helpful. I simply wanted you to know how much I missed you and needed your help. So, you can imagine my shock when you so quickly found her and the bastard that had abducted her. Believe me; from there on, I knew you were the real deal. But, when you recently told me I had been possessed by that demon that got inside me while I was at Mrs. Ramos's house that scared me to death too. And, to your credit, I know you saved me in that instance as well. So, let me just say, I will never, not believe you again. And, I want you to know, I will always be there for you. I owe you so much more than I can ever repay, if you ever need anything, please do not hesitate to contact me."

Gene smiles and says, "Thanks George. Yes, I was hurt when you didn't want me anymore as a partner, but I understood that it was because of my beliefs and comments, and I soon got over it. I realized how stupid my comments must have sounded. So, I sucked it up and took the desk job the Captain offered me. Yet, when you asked for my help to find your niece, I truly was pleased, because I felt that I could contribute some of my talents to helping find her. But, I have to admit that I was as shocked as anyone when I discovered how easy it was for me to find Megan. I was happy and for the first time, I saw what my new powers were worth and could do. But when you became possessed, I truly wanted to help you, but didn't know how. You must understand that it was Father Nelson who did all the work, not me. I was just there for support."

"Your support was good and I know you would have done what you could if the priest had not been found. Yet, you need to know that just being there and explaining everything to me afterwards is what I meant by helping me. I was so much more relaxed after talking to you. And, you made me understand what all I had gone through," says George. George then looks at his watch and says, "Well, it is late and I had best be getting home. Please stay in touch, and again, I wish you the best of luck at your new career." George then stands and the two men hug, as Gene watches George leave.

Sitting at his desk Gene reflects on his career as a police officer. He recalls his many high and low moments. His being shot and the subsequent side affects from that event. He also considers all the good men and women he has known and worked with. He knows he will miss the work but he also knows his new career will also be rewarding.

At the end of his shift he removes his badge and takes his identification card from his wallet. He goes to the Captain's office to turn them in, but he is not there. Entering, he leaves his badge , I.D. card and completed paperwork on his desk. He then goes to his locker, cleans it out and removes the pad lock. As he leaves he feels sad knowing a historical and important part of his life has ended. He reaches his vehicle and drives home.

Waking early the next morning, Amelia is still getting ready for work. He gets up, kisses her good morning and tells her of last night's little good-bye party.

Looking at him Amelia says, "Well honey, this coming Monday begins the first day of your new career. And, I know you will fit in quickly and you will enjoy the work. Plus, it will be normal hours and weekends off. We can spend a whole lot more time together from now on. That will be wonderful. And, by the way, I have something for you." She then hands Gene a letter from the State of California, Department of licensing.

Nervously, Gene looks at the envelope, knowing it could be the results of his bar exam. Yet, he didn't expect it this soon, as he was told it could take up to six months to arrive. Holding it up to the light he can't see anything. Hesitantly, he opens the envelope and instantly sees that it was indeed his confirmation and official notification that he had passed the California State Bar Exam. He shows it to Amelia and the two hug and kiss. Gene is totally happy and tells Amelia how he didn't expect this response for a few more months.

"I never doubted that you would pass honey. I do and have always had the utmost confidence in you. In fact, I don't know why you worried about it at all," comments Amelia.

Continually looking at the letter, he responds to Amelia by saying, "Well, I have confidence in me too, but it was a long difficult test and with all that was on my mind on that day, anything could have happened. But,

I am really happy now. The best part is, I can tell Mr. Wagner I passed and maybe he can assign me some real work. However, I cannot consider myself a lawyer until I actually receive my certificate. But, nevertheless, I am sure my new employer will be happy over hearing the news. In fact, I think I will call him today."

Amelia smiles and says, "Yes, it is good news that is for sure, and what better way to begin your new job. When will you actually get your lawyers license?"

Gene isn't sure about that but assumes it isn't quick. He therefore says, "I'll bet another ninety to one hundred and twenty days at least. This notification was faster than normal, so who knows?"

Getting her purse, Amelia kisses Gene and wishes him a happy day. She says that since it was Friday, they should plan a good dinner tonight at a fancy restaurant and celebrate all of their good fortune. She then leaves for work.

Watching her leave Gene thinks about everything and agrees that he has had extremely good fortune in passing the Bar Exam and finding what he thinks will be an exciting new career. After he finishes breakfast he sits down and calls John Wagner. When he is informed of the passing of his test, John invites Gene to join him and his partners for lunch. He agrees, hangs up and gets ready for the meeting.

At 1 pm. Gene arrives at the restaurant and enters. Obviously early, he is the first person there. As he sits in the waiting area he soon sees John walking towards the restaurant entry with a man and a woman. Entering, he sees Gene and approaches him. They shake hands.

Entering the restaurant, John says, "Gene I would like to introduce you to Carol Lowry and Mark Smyth. They are both lawyers in our firm and I wanted them to meet you. That is because on Monday you will be helping Carol and Mark to obtain facts for a new case we just got that is right up your alley."

Gene looks at John and isn't sure what he is referring to when he says right up his alley. Might it be as a policeman, or maybe a psychic? He therefore, smiles and asks, "And what alley are you referring to John?"

John quickly responds and says, "Gene, both Carol and Mark are aware of your 'special' talents. They also know about your history as a police officer. But what we are asking you to assist them in is with a new case we just obtained, where a fortune teller has asked us to defend her in court because she is being sued by a woman who asked for, and was told her fortune in a San Pedro Restaurant. The fortune teller is employed there to mingle with guests and tell people's fortunes. Our client is being sued for telling this woman her fortune in front of her employer, fiancé and other friends who were dining together. Apparently our client told the woman of her past and actually tied her to the Salem Witch Trials of the late 1600s. The fortune teller apparently said she was originally one of the beheaded witches and then went on to describe in detail what all she had done to them and why she was executed. The woman claims this has caused her irreparable harm at work, making her the butt of every sick joke that can come up, but more importantly, listening to this, her fiancé has broken off their engagement. What we want you to do is to get into the details of what was said. Meet with the fortune teller. Assess her credibility and maybe if necessary actually study the events of those trials to see if any credible evidence can be uncovered and useful to defend her with."

Shaking his head, Gene says, "Well that does sound interesting. I have never met a fortune teller or had my fortune told before. But on the surface, to tell someone what apparently our client did, seems to be a bit too much information. I can see how this is inflammatory. To be honest, I would much rather prosecute the fortune teller than defend her. But, of course I am here to do whatever you ask of me, and it will be interesting to work on it, to say the least."

Stepping in to defend the woman Carol says, "I agree, she was out of line to say what she did. But according to her, the woman asked if she could see into a person's past and especially tell her about past lives. So, being honest our client obliged her."

Mark then says, "I am not sure, but I think the woman was pleased with what she heard until the fall out occurred. At the time of the reading, the fortune teller was given a sizable tip and no one said she was out of line then. In fact the fortune teller said everyone laughed, including the woman."

John then says, "Gene, you will find that no case is ever black or white. As a litigator our challenges are to dig in, find all the facts, apply logic and make decisions based on what the evidence shows us. It is very much like being a policeman. Do what is right and never make up your mind until you know all the facts."

Gene listens and admits to himself now that he heard more, he can easily see where our client could be innocent. He therefore says, "Yes, I see everyone's point. And, I will do all I can to uncover all the facts for you."

They continue lunch by discussing each person's background and Gene explains his story. Everyone is extremely interested in what Gene had experienced and each lawyer tells him how anxious they were to work with him and see how he handles the paranormal events of this newest case.

Gene and Amelia enjoy a nice weekend and are amazed how fun it is to be off for two contiguous days together. They dine out, go dancing and enjoy their freedom. Also going to bed together at a decent time is a whole new experience and one they know they will truly enjoy.

Monday morning, they both wake up and get out of bed at 6:00 am. They shower, get ready and leave for work. Gene enters the building of his new job at 7:45 am. Upon entering, he is greeted by John Wagner, who shows Gene to his new office. Once there, he is given a packet of new employment forms to complete. By 9:00 am. he returns the paper work to the human resource representative and then joins John, Carol and Mark in John's office to discuss the fortune teller case. Gene says he would Google fortune telling and the Salem Witch trials to try and learn more about the issues. Meanwhile, Carol and Mark will research case histories to see if there are any past rulings that they can use to help the woman. John feels comfortable that all is being done to address and provide the woman a good defense. John does say, "Gene, when you feel that you are adequately informed, I would like for you to invite Greta Andrews to our office so you three can meet and assess her attitude and overall credibility."

Each person then goes to his or her office to begin doing what was needed. Gene goes to his new office and Google's fortune telling, and the witch trials. In his fortune telling research he finds a lot of information on the subject. He is surprised to find that there are many types of fortune telling and many methods in which it is practiced. Surprisingly, every country also has different methods used to arrive at the same conclusion. He is amazed how popular the service is. One method Gene discovers is called 'reading' or 'spiritual consulting.' This method claims to make direct contact with the dead, which the practitioner uses to transmit past and future events to their clients. He reviews 34 different fortune telling methods. Some cause him to chuckle to himself over what he thinks are stupid practices. However, two methods are also interesting. One is what you normally associate with fortune telling, which is palm reading. That method discusses how the practitioner reads the hand lines and ridges to make predictions. The second is called Necromancy. This is a method which puts the practitioner in direct contact with the dead or spirits. As he studies the other 32 methods, he sees nothing that could be used to explain his client's ability to see the past or make the type of comments she did.

As the day goes on, Gene is interrupted from his research many times for different reasons. However, when he finally is able to study the Salem Witch Trials, he is amazed at what he discovers. Some of the trials actually took place in several towns and villages in Massachusetts and not solely in Salem. It appears that the height of the trials was around 1692, but they did continue on for a few more years. Surprisingly these were legitimate trials conducted in real courts, by lawyers and judges. He sees that more than 150 people were arrested and imprisoned. Yet, he can only find where about 30 were hung or beheaded. And, most victims were women. What appeared to be the underlying motive of many of these acquisitions by friends and neighbors of the accused, were mostly based on the fact that the accuser wanted to reclaim or buy the land the accused owned. And, in many cases, widowed women were their prime target. Also, it appeared that the laws at that time allowed property to default back to the former owner if the accused was guilty. Surprisingly, the names of many of the accused were also noted along with their conviction dates and reason for being accused in the first place. Gene can easily see how their client could have reviewed the same information and noted down some of the names in order to attach them to a customer during her reading.

Upon concluding his investigation, Gene e-mails, John, Carol and Mark to inform them of his findings and denotes his concern about what the client may have done if she too Googled and found the same information. About 4:00 pm. John responds to his e-mail and invites Carol, Mark and Gene to come to his office to discuss Gene's findings.

In John's office, Gene explains to the group how their client could have looked up names of victims of the Salem Witch trials and used them to tell her customers that they were either reincarnated or related to those specific people. He also describes the very few types of methods she could have used to truly see what she claimed she saw. The concluding suggestion from John was to get Greta Andrews into the office and have Gene lead the meeting and discuss with her how she actually saw the names of the person she claims the victim was linked to. John also suggests that once they meet maybe Gene's own psychic abilities might let him know with more surety how credible she truly was. He indicates that he will have his secretary make contact with Greta and set a meeting as soon as possible and then they would be notified of the day and time it is set for. Carol, Mark and Gene agree and return to their offices.

Three days later, Greta Andrews arrives and asks to meet with Gene. Gene quickly invites Carol and Mark into his office, and then has the front desk receptionist escort Ms. Andrews to his office. Upon entering, Gene stands and extends his hand to greet her. At the same time he introduces himself. The very moment their hands touch, Ms. Andrews and Gene simultaneously experience a very strange and totally new experience. Since both were psychics, each one immediately sees directly into the others mind. It was like an electrical shock between them that causes each to instantly recoil and quickly pull back their hands. Looking at Ms. Andrews, Gene says, "Wow that was certainly something. I have never experienced anything like that before, nor did I see it coming."

Ms. Andrews shakes her head in the affirmative and says, "Yes, me too. I have never experienced anything like that before either. It was strange but stimulating. I can only assume that you too are psychic."

Gene then explains to Carol and Mark what the two had just experienced. He then goes on to introduce himself and the other two lawyers to Ms. Andrews.

Carol says, "Yes, that was a strange handshake for sure, I was wondering what happened that caused you two to pull back so sharply. It was a very strange sight for two people meeting for the first time to do."

Mark smiles and says, "Yes it was different. I guess that says a lot about being psychic and how you two could see into each others thoughts. Maybe if we all could do that it would save a lot of time and money by shortening these types of meetings."

Gene begins by discussing Greta's case and asks her to tell the group in her own words exactly what happened. After listening to her and everyone asking questions, Gene asks if she has ever had such an in depth look into anyone's past prior to the one that she is being sued over?

Shaking her head no, Greta says, "No, such a thing has never happened to me before or since. It was really strange, but holding her hand and reading her palm, these strange visions of old England began coming to me. I mentally began seeing buildings and signs on them that I could read and they actually told me I was viewing the Salem Witch Trial in old Massachusetts. And, I then suddenly saw this woman being on trial and heard the name she was being called. It was weird, I admit. But, because it was so vivid, I automatically told her what I saw before I realized what I said. I immediately knew I should not have told her that, but by then it was too late. She looked at me rather curiously, and then shrugged it off. I assumed at the time that she was fine with it. And, as I left her table, I was given a very nice tip for the reading. So, when I was served with this lawsuit three weeks later, I was dumbfounded."

Listening intently, Gene responds by saying, "Well, what is done is done. And, whether or not what you said was believed by her or not isn't really the issue. It seems to me what occurred afterwards is the basis for her claims and anger. Suddenly, she now wants to retaliate for some reason."

Carol then adds, "If she was so upset over your comments, she should have said so then and there. And, the fact that jokes were made later on is ridiculous. Plus, if her fiancé dumped her, I'll bet anything it had nothing to do with his hearing that she was a reincarnated witch. I cannot see how any of this will have any standing in a courtroom."

Mark then adds his comments and says, "All of your arguments are valid. However, if this case went to a jury, there is no telling how it would play out. The plaintiff could play on their sympathy and cry enough, that there is no telling how Greta would do."

Gene suggests that the three lawyers meet tomorrow and come up with some ideas how to proceed. He tells Greta that they will call her afterwards and go over their ideas with her.

Greta gets up, shakes Carol and Mark's hands but not Gene. They smile at one another and nod their heads as if to say, yes, I agree, it is too much to go through again.

After she leaves, Gene tells Carol and Mark what he felt and saw as he shook hands with Greta. He said he never experienced anything like it before. He says it was like seeing and feeling an electrical charge and bright lights instantly passing through them both. He also tells them that there was no doubt she was a clairvoyant and it was possible that her explanation over what happened and how she saw the Witch Trials is exactly what did occur. Then, looking at his watch he sees it was 5:45 pm, and time to be going home. They all depart Gene's office, confirming that they would meet again Monday morning at 10:00 am, to discuss the case in more detail.

Arriving at his home, Amelia was already there and changed into nice clothes. He enters, they hug and Gene comments on how good she looked.

Before Gene can relax, Amelia says, "Before I forget, Dr. Allen called and said Dr Mendenhall will be in town next Tuesday and he has a special kind of test for you to do. He was hoping you might be able to come to Dr. Allen's office around 11:00 am?"

Gene is happy to hear that, as he was anxious to talk to them about his experience with Greta. He knows it was something totally new and maybe they would have some kind of medical explanation. He responds to

Amelia by saying, "Good. Today something rather strange occurred and I am anxious to tell them about it."

With a lot of interest Amelia asks what had happened and why he wants to discuss it with the two doctors.

Gene smiles and says, "Look, let me change into something more casual and while we are out having dinner, I will tell you all about it. And, seeing how nice you are dressed, I do assume that you want to go out, since it is the end of my first full week of work at my new job."

Smiling at Gene, Amelia says, "Yes dear, I do want to go out. And, I would really like to find somewhere that we can dance and celebrate a little. In fact, I know a great place in Torrance. Good food, live band, and a little dance floor. Maybe we can go there?"

Upon entering the restaurant, they are escorted to a booth and quickly order a round of drinks while they look over the menu. Seeing on the menu that Prime Rib was the restaurant's specialty they both decide to have that. As they sit and enjoy the evening, Gene explains the case he was assigned to and how today he met the client and what happened when he shook her hand. He described it as very odd and says he really wants to discuss the event with Dr. Mendenhall.

The night passes slowly. They enjoy their meal and dance until 2:00 am. Heading home, Gene realizes how much he is enjoying his new job, with normal working hours that allows him to be with Amelia like this. It was certainly all that he had anticipated. He also realizes that he didn't even miss his old police work, which surprised him.

Monday morning Gene and Amelia are both up by 6:00 am. After dressing for work they sit around their small kitchen table and drink coffee and discuss the weekend. Both say how great it is for them to be on the same working schedule. By 8:00 am. they both are at their respective jobs and ready to begin a new week.

Gene e-mails John to let him know he has a doctors appointment Tuesday at 11:00 am. He doesn't go into details but says he will be out of the office from 10:30 am. until after lunch. He then begins working on the Greta Andrews case. He documents his file with the results of their first meeting and how that went. He comments about their hand shake and how he sensed she was a legitimate psychic and it was very possible she did see what she claimed to have seen. He then contacts Carol and Mark to see if they had the time to meet and discuss their next steps.

Within fifteen minutes they are all in Gene's office discussing what they should do. Carol recommends they make a list of the most serious questions in the suit and find good answers to each questions. She volunteers to do the work. Gene and Mark agree and decide to wait for her questions before proceeding further.

During the morning John comes to Gene's office in order to question him about his Tuesday doctor meeting. He was concerned that something may be wrong. Gene explains to John how he has been going through a battery of tests to determine whether his psychic powers are increasing or decreasing. He says one doctor that he is to meet with has apparently developed a new test he wants to administer to him. He then tells John about the strange hand shake he and Greta experienced.

John is seriously impressed with Gene's overall skills and tells Gene so. He even wonders out loud whether or not it made any sense for the firm to market those psychic abilities. He says there might be money to be made helping people find lost persons or objects. He comments that there may be groups who have needs for psychic people. He tells Gene that if he didn't mind, he would like to explore with his partners what options might be available to their firm, in using Gene's special abilities.

Gene sees no reason not to go along with John's idea and so indicates. He says that he can be available whenever they need him. After hearing that, John smiles, nods his head affirmatively and then stands up and reaches out to shake Gene's hand to finalize the agreement. As he does this he says, "Thank you." And, just as it occurred with Greta, the moment the two men clasp hands, Gene experiences a flash of light and instantly sees things as if he was inside of John looking out of his eyes at past events. It was as if he was in his head, seeing things. As John leaves, it was obvious he did not sense the same thing Gene did. But most distinctly, he did have visions of John's memories and saw quick glimpses of where John had been and what he did. Yet, they were so quick he couldn't make any sense of what was seen. However, Gene now wonders why this happened. At least with Greta it was two physics touching, which may have been an explainable event. But with John, he has no psychic powers, and is normal. Was this a new phenomenon that is beginning to occur? Is this a sign of his ever increasing powers growing even more? Gene is suddenly scared. Is he growing at such a rate he will soon be incapacitated by his growing psychic powers? Gene is now very eager to meet with Dr. Mendenhall to see what he thinks is happening to him.

Sitting in his office worrying over his newest problem, his phone rings. When he answers it, he is surprised to hear Captain Mitchell on the other end asking how he was doing and how the new job was. Gene eagerly tells his former boss how much fun it was to have a normal work week, and how good the job itself was. He then asks how he was.

"Gene, I am happy to hear you are happy and doing well. But, the real purpose of my call is to seek your help in finding another missing child," explains the Captain. He goes on to tell Gene how an eight year old girl was abducted from her grade school at lunch time today and the parents are frantic and the police have no leads, except for the lunch box and sweater the child dropped when she was abducted. He asks if Gene could come to the station and see if he can gather any information from those items?

Looking at his watch he sees that it was almost 2:00 pm. He thinks he wasn't that far and he definitely wanted to help. He therefore says, "Captain, let me check with John and see if it is Ok with him for me to do that. Assuming it is, I will be there in twenty minutes. Upon hanging up Gene calls John on the intercom and explains the situation and receives permission to go help the police.

Arriving at the police station Gene goes directly to the Captain's office. There, he is invited in and asked to sit down. Without any preliminary discussion, the captain hands Gene the child's items and Gene immediately starts to touch and hold them. Suddenly, flashes of scenes run through his mind. He sees the school, kids playing and a large, dirty man standing off under a big tree looking at whomever he is watching. He sees the man grabbing the child's arm and dragging them off. He drags the child around the corner and down the street. The child is pulling away and screaming as she resists the pulling. Yet, no one sees what is happening and no one comes to the child's aid. Then, the man turns and pulls the child into a nearby home, which is only one block from the school. He sees the house very clearly and then as the door closes, his vision stops. Gene opens his eyes and tells the Captain everything he saw.

The Captain actually has tears in his eyes as he says, "Gene, please show us where the house is. I will drive you myself, right now. I will also request backup of three other units. Please, let's go now."

As the Captain asks that of him, he is already holstering his weapon and grabbing his bullet proof vest. Gene stands and then follows the Captain out into his squad car. As they drive towards the school the Captain is silent.

Looking over at him Gene asks, "So Captain, are you going to tell me who this child is and why you are so emotionally involved? Also, your shift doesn't start yet for several more hours, causing me to wonder why you are here and so involved in this abduction. Is this child related to you?"

Turning towards Gene he says, "Yes, it is my granddaughter, my daughter's only child. Her name is Janie Russell. She is so precious and I am scared to death. I thought of you the first thing after my daughter called me at 1:00 pm. this afternoon and said Janie did not return to class after her lunch break. Then, when her books and lunch pale were found, we knew something bad had happened to her. Oh dear God I pray she is still alive."

As they approach the school, Gene closes his eyes and directs the captain and three squad cars directly to the house he saw in his mind.

Converging on the house, one group covers the rear, one goes to each side and one at the front door. After pounding on the door and identifying themselves, no one comes out. The Captain directs two officers to knock in the front door. Instantly, the front door is opened by a large battering ram. The two officers and the Captain enter the house. Gene is asked to wait outside.

While the officers search the house, gun fire is heard after about three minutes. Gene is afraid that someone other than the kidnapper was injured. And, just as he was about to go inside and see for himself, Captain Mitchell walks out the front door. And, in his arms is the child. The Captain opens the back door of his vehicle and places the crying child inside. The child doesn't want to let go of grandpa. As he puts her down she screams as the Captain returns to the house.

Gene walks over to the child and tries to calm her. She appears fine physically, but is totally emotionally uncontrollable. Gene talks to the child and assures her she is safe. He explains how grandpa had to go inside to arrest the bad man. After a few more minutes she quiets down, and snuggles down into the rear of the police car.

Calming the child, sirens are heard and soon an ambulance is on scene. Hurrying outside, Captain Mitchell exits the house ahead of everyone else. He immediately goes over to his granddaughter and sees that she was now asleep. Gene explains how he calmed the child and how she fell fast asleep.

"Gene, I cannot tell you how much I appreciate your help. You are a miracle for sure. I recall George's emotions when you found his niece. Now, I can fully relate to his elation. When you think of what that monster in their was planning on doing to my granddaughter, it is impossible to hold your emotions in check. We already had our weapons out as we slowly went from room to room looking for them. But in the rear bedroom, just as we were about to open the door, he exited holding a shotgun. I immediately dropped him. We called the ambulance, but, there is no doubt he was dead the second he hit the ground. So, it is over and I will forever be in your debt. Thank you from the bottom of my heart," explains the Captain.

Gene too is very emotional and responds, "I am pleased to have so easily been able to help. I have to wonder if this new psychic thing I am experiencing has happened for some purpose. Maybe it is God's way to make me a useful person.

The Captain motions for one of the other officers to come over. When he does he says, "Please take Gene back to the station so he can get his car and go on home. I will need to remain here while the shooting is investigated and IAD officially designates this as a good killing. I have asked the ambulance crew to also check on my granddaughter before they depart. Then when we are through here I will take Janie home before I go on to work tonight. The Captain then extends his hand to shake Gene's hand. Somewhat dubious, Gene reciprocates. And, as before, the minute he does so, he sees the shooting through the Captains eyes. Absolutely shocked, he sees the man coming out with his hands over his head and high in the air. Yes, a shotgun was in one hand but he was definitely giving up. Yet, the Captain immediately aims his revolver and puts a bullet directly between the man's eyes. Shocked at the Captains actions he worries over what the other two officers will say. He highly respects the Captain, but this was an act of revenge and considering how he admonished George for hitting the kidnapper of his niece, this is far worse. As the two end the hand shake, Gene turns and follows the officer to his cruiser. All the way back to the station he wonders what to do or what if he is questioned? What would he say? Obviously his psychic insight would not be admissible evidence if the Captain faces charges. But, what would he say, if questioned. Gene knows the kidnapper was an evil man and now he is one less pedophile to worry about.

Back at the station, Gene exits the car and thanks the officer for the ride. Getting into his car he drives home. As he drives he calls his office to speak to John. Once on the phone, Gene explains how they found little Janie.

John is elated. He says, "Gene that is excellent work. I am sure we can find a specialty area for you to work in. Oh, I am so proud of you. See you in the morning."

Arriving home, Amelia is not yet there. Sitting down, Gene turns on his television and watches the 5:00 pm news. As he sits there, suddenly there is a story describing the coverage of finding little Janie. The news crews had obviously arrived moments after he left. His picture is prominently displayed and captioned 'A Hero, Among Us.' Then there is an interview with Captain Mitchell, explaining how he was forced to shoot the kidnapper. He goes on to talk about Gene and his exceptional psychic powers which led to their finding his granddaughter. The coverage is long and Gene cannot help but be a little embarrassed. As the story coverage ends, Amelia walks into the house. Smiling they hug as he tells her of his day's events.

Amelia is proud of Gene and tells him so. She knows now that his psychic powers are proving to be a positive thing. She tells Gene how she believes that God obviously chose him to bestow this power on him. She says, over time, he will become a saint, and a very famous person.

Listening to her, Gene smiles and takes Amelia's hand and squeezes it. He then says, "Sweetheart, if I could be as good and as positive of a thinker as you are, that would be all that I would ever want. But, to be truthful, I fear my gift is a curse, not something necessarily good." He then goes on to tell her how he now sees into every persons mind as he shakes their hands. He explains how hard it is to be objective when he sees the truth. He goes on to describe what he saw when he shook Captain Mitchell's hand and how it showed that the Captain murdered the kidnapper. Gene comments on how his powers are definitely increasing, causing him to fear it will soon overpower him totally and possibly cause him to go crazy or even die.

Amelia is concerned over Gene's comments and says he needs to be totally frank with the two doctors tomorrow. She even wonders if there is medication that he can take to stop his powers from increasing. She makes Gene promise to ask them that question. The two then settle in and watch television after Amelia prepares dinner.

The next morning as Gene enters his office, he immediately sees newspapers of the previous day's events lying all over his desk. Sitting down he begins reading a couple of the articles when John enters his office.

Smiling at Gene, John says, "Boy that was really something. It was excellent work. And, just think, we own you. I can see big things for you in the future here Gene. I am not sure yet exactly how we cash in on this, but somehow we will. I already spoke to my partners and they too agree that you need to head a special department, based solely on you psychic abilities. Think about it and lets talk later this afternoon as to what you think might work. Meanwhile, I told Carol and Mark you were off of the Andrews case. I want you to concentrate on this new idea and figure out how we can capitalize on your abilities." John smiles, then gets up and departs Gene's office.

At 10:50 am. Gene enters Dr. Allen's office. He is greeted by her receptionist who congratulates him on finding little Janie. She then asks him to sit and she will tell Dr. Allen he was there. Within a few minutes Dr. Allen emerges from her office and invites Gene in. He gets up and Dr. Allen immediately extends her hand to shake his. Again as the two touch, Gene sees into her history and quickly puts the images he sees into his memory. Inside, he shakes hands with Dr. Mendenhall and the same thing happens. Definitely his psychic abilities were growing and with each handshake the images become more vivid and understandable. Sitting down he waits for their comments.

Dr. Allen is the first to say how surprised she was over his ability to find kidnapped children and see where they are.

Dr. Mendenhall echoes her comments and asks, "So, Gene, are these abilities to see where lost people are, increasing or was it always something you could do after the head injury?"

Gene begins by telling them this last event was the second time he found a child. The first time was a little harder but yesterday was fast and easy. He then immediately goes into his visions he now has when he shakes people's hands. He even comments on what he saw when he shook each of their hands.

Extremely shocked at hearing this, Dr. Mendenhall asks how long this has been occurring and does it happen to everyone he shakes hands with?

Gene quickly responds by explaining that the first time it occurred was three days ago with a client who was also a psychic. He then says, since then it is occurring with everyone. In fact, he describes shaking hands with Captain Mitchell after he found Janie and he vividly saw him shoot the kidnapper. He says, it is something he cannot control or stop. He describes in detail what he saw when he shook both Dr. Allen and his hand. And, his visions were vivid and were what each doctor had experienced earlier that day.

Dr. Mendenhall says, "That is incredible. I have to say, this wasn't anything I would have anticipated. But, I did bring along a new test I think will aid me in assessing your growth. Are you willing to try to do it?"

Gene indicates yes, that was why he was there.

Dr. Mendenhall gets up and retrieves a box full of miscellaneous items. He sets it down in front of Gene and says, "In this box are specific items that have history associated with each one. I do not want to tell you what that history is, but I want you to touch each item, and you tell me what each one is and what occurred to make them special. So, if you have no questions, please begin whenever you want."

Gene leans forward and takes the first item out of the box, which was a gold colored woman's purse. He touches it all over and closes his eyes. He opens them, looks at both doctors and says, "This belonged to an elderly Asian woman. She crossed a street in a big city and a local yellow taxi cab ran her down, just as she stepped right in front of the vehicle. The driver had no time to stop." To that Dr Mendenhall says nothing, but writes something on a pad of paper. The next item was a small red sweater. He picks it up and does the same thing. Soon, he looks at the two doctors and says, "That is strange, because all I see is a large German Sheppard dog wearing this sweater." Again, Dr. Mendenhall says nothing but continues writing on his pad. Gene does this three more times and tells them what he observes. The final item is a light yellow woman's jacket. He touches it and quickly responds, "This belongs to Dr. Allen. I see her wearing it as she goes to dinner."

Dr. Mendenhall looks at Dr. Allen and then at Gene, and then says, "I cannot explain it, but you were 100% accurate. Every item you described was exactly correct. I was sure the red sweater would baffle you, as I put it on my own dog over the weekend. But there is no denying your psychic abilities have skyrocketed. You are definitely in the upper percentile of any psychic I have ever examined or studied."

Looking at him Gene asks, "So, when will it stop? Or, will it continue until it kills me? I am scared to death that these powers will consume me. What can I do? Is there any medicine I can take to stop it? What is your professional opinion?"

Dr. Mendenhall thinks about his questions and concerns and replies, "No, there is no medicine to stop it. I agree it looks like it might continue to increase in power. But honestly, I cannot see how it could harm you. My fear is that your abilities will grow at such a rate that your everyday life will become boring to you. As your psychic abilities increase, so does your I.Q. In fact while you are here, lets test your I.Q. to see what level you are at. I know when you were originally here with that gun shot wound we tested you and you were normal. So let's administer that same test now. It is quick and it will be extremely helpful."

Gene agrees and is given forty questions to answer. He quickly finishes and Dr. Allen grades the test. She then shows it to Dr. Mendenhall. He takes the test and goes over to Gene and says, "Gene, when you were here before you tested at about 109 which is average. Today you scored a 150. That is above the Genius level, which is 140. I have never seen anything like it before. You are moving into uncharted water. There is no telling how far you will go, or how great your powers will become. I simply do not know what to say. I also am at a loss to explain it. There are special institutions where they can research your growth and maybe predict what is happening. But frankly, I doubt that you would want to attend them, as you would be bored to death. So, I recommend that the best thing we do for you now, is to stay in touch with one another and we continue testing you. I would say we should meet at least every ninety days. What do you think?"

"Well, it is a scary for sure. What I originally feared would happen is now becoming a reality. I see no hope for me to ever enjoy a good and normal life. What can I expect? How can I plan anything," asks Gene?

Dr. Allen responds and says, "Gene, seriously, we do not sense anything that is happening to you is life threatening. You are simply evolving mentally. There is no reason you won't live a long and happy life. Do everything you would normally want to do. Don't let this thing cause you to worry extensively and make you an invalid. You are strong, healthy and I assume except for this, happy. You are now a lawyer, making good money and every so often you save a life. What more can an individual want? Just live your life as you want."

Dr. Mendenhall says, "I agree, there is nothing disabling about what is happening to you. In fact, with a growing I.Q. you can do more than the average person. Forget what you are afraid of here, live life to the fullest."

Gene tries to listen and take their advice but he is so consumed with worry he cannot. He then gets up and says he will see them in ninety days. He then departs Dr. Allen's office. As he drives he tries to accept their advice. He wants desperately to be normal. He knows his gift has saved two lives, and for that he sees some good. But, it isn't stopping there. He fears the worst. He tries to think happy thoughts and suddenly he has an idea. Looking around as he drives he spots a jewelry store. Stopping, he exits his vehicle and enters the store. He is quickly waited on by a sales lady. He asks to see wedding and engagement rings. Looking over the selection, he picks a set and becomes very anxious to give them to Amelia as soon as he goes home tonight.

Sitting in his office he constantly opens the jewelry box to admire his purchase. Thinking about marrying Amelia does make him happy. He thinks that if only she says yes, it would be wonderful. As he looks at the ring, John enters his office. Quickly putting the box in his desk drawer the two talk about his doctor's visit and then the possibility of creating a special business where the law firm can best use Gene's skills. Gene does not tell John of his increasing psychic abilities or of his increase in I.Q. he simply does not want to get into that with John.

After John leaves, Gene checks his messages and sees one from Amelia. Calling her she was anxious to know what happened at the doctor's office. To that Gene says, "Look honey, lets go out to dinner tonight and I will explain it all to you then. How does that sound?"

Immediately responding, Amelia says, "Oh that would be wonderful. Do you have some place special in mind?"

Laughing to himself he realizes that if he is going to spring the question on Amelia tonight, it had best be a special place. He therefore responds to her by saying, "Yes, I want it to be special. Let me think about it and I will surprise you when I get home. Ok?"

Amelia snickers to herself and says, "What ever you say Gene, I know that you will find us a good place to eat. So, I will see you tonight. Goodbye."

Gene hangs up and thinks about where to go. As he does this Carol enters his office and asks if he has time to discuss the Andrews case? Gene agrees and the two begin talking. Carol asks, "So, in your opinion Gene, do you believe Greta is truly a credible psychic? And, in saying that can you state with any certainty that she really did see the past, which she is claiming she did?"

Gene thinks about Carol's comments and replies, "Well, there is no doubt that she has psychic abilities. Shaking her hand proved that to me. But to say with an absolute commitment that she saw the actual Salem Witch Trials is impossible for me to say. She easily may have seen them. But, I have no way to prove that. So, I think you have to go with your 'gut' reaction. And, for me that is yes, I believe her. And, since we are defending her, I think believing her is easier than not believing what she claims. What are you thinking anyway?"

Carol then explains how she wanted to respond to the lawsuit and what her defense methods would be.

Gene listens and agrees completely with what Carol's plans on how best to proceed.

CHAPTER 11; *The True Meaning of Life:*

At the end of the day Gene looks at his watch and decides it was time to go. He also suddenly knows where he wants to take Amelia for dinner. He gets up, and begins the drive home. Along the way he sees a street vendor selling flowers and decides to buy Amelia some roses. Entering the house Amelia is there and already dressed and eager for the evening's dinner. Seeing the flowers she is instantly pleased and takes them and places them in a vase with water.

Hugging Gene she says, "Oh, sweetheart, thank you. The flowers are beautiful. But, I have to wonder why you bought them? It isn't my birthday or any special day. But, it was a very nice surprise. So, where is it that we are going to eat?"

Gene smiles as he tells Amelia where they were going to eat, saying he thought a nice dinner at the Redondo Beach Pier would be enjoyable. He then says, "And after dinner, if you want, we can walk around the pier and see what everyone else is doing."

While eating dinner, Gene waits for the right moment to show Amelia the ring. Meanwhile, he discusses the findings of Dr. Mendenhall. He explains how worried he was and wants Amelia to know everything. He figures she needs to understand his fears and concerns. And, if she agreed, that needed to be taken into consideration if they were to be married. Soon, a waiter checks in on them and Gene asks him to bring them a bottle of their best Champaign.

Hearing that, Amelia asks what he was doing. She says, "That will be expensive and I see no reason for such a thing. A modest glass of wine would be just fine." She then sits quietly and waits for Gene's explanation. However, he says nothing.

A few moments more the waiter is back at their table, showing the Champaign bottle to Gene. He looks at it and says, "Yes, please poor us a glass full sir." Upon doing so, Gene reaches into his jacket side pocket and places the box on the table in front of Amelia.

Shocked at his ordering Champaign, she sees the box and literally has no idea what it was. She looks down at it and asks, "What is this?"

Gene looks her in the eyes and says, "This is why I ordered the Champaign, open it and tell me what you think."

Picking up the ring box, Amelia opens it and her eyes widen as she looks at Gene and asks, "Is this an engagement and wedding ring? Are you asking me to marry you?"

Gene smiles at her and says, "Yes I am."

Amelia immediately leaps up from her chair and hugs Gene. She is so excited that she can barely contain herself. People around them are watching her and wondering what caused her sudden actions. Then in a loud voice she says, "Yes I will, and oh I love you so much." She then shows the people around them what Gene had just given her, and they all immediately applauded, and verbally say congratulations.

Gene then smiles and asks, "So, do you still think the Champagne was unnecessary?"

After dinner they stroll around the pier for about an hour and watch people fishing while also looking into the many shops that were still open. Happy, they both enjoy the moment as Amelia cannot stop looking at her ring. After about an hour they get into their car and drive home. Along the way, Amelia asks Gene when he first decided to ask her to marry him.

Gene smiles and says, "Well believe it or not, the first time I laid eyes on you at school is when I decided you were for me. You were so beautiful and smart, I knew instantly that you were all I could ever hope for. But, not until I really passed the bar exam did I feel I could truly ask you anything. However, I also have to say this psychic thing worries me to no end and I am constantly thinking about it taking over my body."

Amelia lays her head on Gene's shoulder as they drive and says, "I too was attracted to you when we first met. Yet, your question about ghosts made me worry about your overall mental condition. I wasn't sure if you were joking or if you were serious. And, being a policeman was not the type of man I could ever see myself with. That was even more the case given your shift hours and lack of weekends off. In fact, I was surprised to find myself agreeing to move in with you at all, because I feared we would never have any quality time together."

Pulling into their apartment, as they are getting out Gene says, "Yes, I know that was bad. Not being able to spend time together was and is very important. In fact, it was my desire to be with you that forced me into taking the bar exam. If you hadn't come into my life, I am sure George and I would still be patrolling together."

As they enter their apartment, Gene sees the message light on the phone blinking. Checking the message he finds a call for Amelia from a Leticia Perez, asking Amelia to call her when she came home. The caller sounded a bit desperate indicating that it didn't matter what time it was when they got in. Gene asks, "Who is this woman, I have never heard you mention her before."

Amelia picks up the phone, and while dialing, she explains that Leticia is Gloria Ramos daughter. I believe you met her the first time you visited Mrs. Ramos in San Pedro.

Calling the number, a voice answers. "Hello."

Amelia asks, "Is this Leticia? This is Amelia. I am returning your call."

"Oh Amelia, thank you so very much for calling me back. I hope you don't mind, but I got your phone number from your mother. Look, something very bad is happening here and I need help and do not know where to turn. My baby is being scratched by something I cannot see. It scares me and I am at my wits end. My husband is scared too and whatever it is, it is most definitely evil. Two nights ago it pushed Carlos down the stairs which go up to our bedroom. Fortunately, he was able to grab the hand rail and stop himself from falling all the way down, as it could have killed him. Is Gene there or can you ask him if he could possibly help us?"

Amelia is shocked and says, "Yes Gene is here. Please wait a moment." Turning to Gene who was there going through the mail, Amelia says, "Honey, Leticia is being bothered by something she cannot see. It is scratching her baby and it has pushed her husband down the stairs. Can you talk to her and maybe offer some help?"

Taking the phone Gene says, "Hello Leticia, this is Gene. Please explain to me what you are encountering?" As she describes what they had experienced, Gene wonders if somehow her mother's demon may now be attached to her. Or, is it possible this family has an unfriendly ghost in their house, similar to the first one her mother documented in their San Pedro house. It was too bazaar.

Leticia answers Gene's questions and has no real idea what they were encountering. When her mother's house was being haunted, Leticia was young and was not fully aware of everything that happened. But, this new set of events scares her very much. She is afraid for everyone's safety and doesn't know what to do or who to turn to.

Gene tells her he will do what he can. He gets her address and tells her he will come over before noon tomorrow and see what he can detect. Writing down her address he is shocked to see that she lives at 666 Sixth St. He immediately knows sixes are a demonic sign which could explain the attraction to that address. Gene thinks about it and decides the best thing to do is tell John in the morning about the call and seek his permission to go see the woman.

When he finishes the call to Leticia, Amelia asks Gene what he was going to do. She says that she and Leticia had been friends since grade school.

Gene explains that he will go see her in the morning and see if he can detect what is there and whether or not it can be chased away. He tries to explain the significance of the sixes. He explains it is a demonic symbol. Gene says, "In the Book of Revelation of the New Testament, in sections 13:18, 666 is known as the number to call out the beast. It is also assumed to be the code name for the Roman Emperor Nero." But, he also says that he has heard it used to describe Satan himself. He continues by saying, "It is just interesting that they live at 666, 6th St. Whether it has any significance or not, he could not say."

Given the lateness of the evening the two decide to call it a night and go to bed. They lie there together in each other's arms for a long time. They plan their wedding and decide that June would be a good time to get married. Gene then suggests a honeymoon cruise down through Mexico to what is referred to as the Mexican Rivera. He explained it was a seven day cruise and they stop at three cities. He feels it would be a nice trip. Amelia thinks that sounded great to her and soon falls asleep dreaming of that event.

Up early the next morning, they both get ready for work and depart their apartment around 7:30 am. Gene gets to his office and checks his e-mails. He then places a call to John. Not yet in, he leaves a message asking John to call him.

About twenty minutes later John calls and Gene explains his need to visit Leticia. He explains that he has done similar cleansing before and he thinks he may be able to help the woman. He also comments that if they are wishing to establish a paranormal unit in their law firm, this might be exactly what they would be looking at doing.

John quickly says, "Gene, go for it. But, is it safe for you to be doing this kind of thing alone? And, would you mind if I went with you just to see what such a visit is like?"

Gene responds by saying, "Sure, come along. You might find it interesting. It would give you a better insight as to what kind of issues I am dealing with. Let's leave by 10:00 am. I will call the woman and tell her we will be there around 10:30 am.

Arriving at the address, Gene parks and he and John get out of the car. Knocking on the front door, Leticia quickly answers the door. Gene introduces Leticia to John and asks if they can come inside. Sitting in her living room, she again explains everything that has been happening. After a few minutes Gene says, "Well, I think the first thing to do is start in your child's bedroom. Let me see whether or not I can feel anything paranormal in there. He tells John to stay behind him and not touch anything. The two are then escorted to the daughter's room.

Gene asks Leticia to wait outside of the room. He enters with John close behind. He walks around with his eyes closed. Sensing nothing, he takes a pillow from the child's bed. Immediately, flashes of light penetrate his head and he sees weird images, of which none appeared human. They were more like shadows of animals, walking on all four. After doing this for a few minutes he tells John they need to go out of the room. There, he asks Leticia where her daughter was? She escorts Gene and John upstairs into her bedroom where the child was sleeping. He asks if he could pickup the child for a few moments. Doing so, again visions come to him. But again, he cannot make out what he sees. Placing the child back down on the bed he wanders around the room trying to sense anything.

Gene looks at John and Leticia and suggests they all go down to the kitchen and see what they might find in there. Then, just as they depart the bedroom, John receives a hard shove by an unknown force. He starts to trip down the stairs, but Gene grabs his arm and stops him from going down on his knees.

Absolutely startled, John looks at Gene and asks what had just happened? He says, "Something pushed me from behind. I felt its hands on me. It was as though someone was behind me and pushed me. And, it was very forceful."

Leticia quickly says, "Yes, that is exactly what happened to my husband. He said he felt strong hands pushing him down. It has to be the same entity."

John is definitely shaken and follows Gene downstairs. Once down there he quickly sits on the couch. Gene looks at John, smiles and asks, "Still happy you came with me boss? I think the fun stuff is still yet to come. Would you prefer to wait here while I meander through the rest of the house to see what I can find?"

John just sits there as he shakes his head yes.

Gene then turns and heads into the kitchen. Walking around and touching various items, nothing comes into his vision. He sits momentarily at the breakfast counter and verbally asks, "So, who is here? Why are you bothering this family and what do you want?"

He waits and at first nothing happens. Then as he was just about to get up, an empty glass on the counter is immediately hurled at him. Hitting his shoulder it falls to the ground and breaks. Looking around Gene says, "You coward, show yourself. Let me see your ugly face. Why are you here?"

He sits back down and waits. Like before, nothing occurs. Growing tired of waiting, he starts to leave. When he stands up, he too is pushed from behind causing him to lunge forward and hit the sink and counter top. Turning around to face the direction the push came from he says, "Coward. You are afraid to show yourself to me, aren't you? You cannot go face to face with me because you know you are weak. If you are a demon, you're a sorry example of one, that is for sure. And you are also very weak. But, if you are a ghost, you must have been a serious weakling in life. I command you to show your ugly self to me. Let me see the coward that I am dealing with. Still nothing happens.

Gene then goes back out into the living room. John and Leticia are sitting there talking. Gene looks at then and says, "Well, it pushed me and through a water glass at me which shattered on the floor, but it wouldn't show itself to me. I seriously don't know what it is that we are dealing with. It is dangerous, as it or others pushed both John and I. But, if I cannot make direct contact with it, I do not know what else I can do."

Leticia asks, "Do you think it will harm my child? I know it has been inflicting scratch marks on her arms and legs. Then it pushed my husband. What does it want from us?"

Gene is definitely perplexed. He is at a loss of what to say or suggest. He does believe the entity to be dangerous. He therefore says, "Leticia, I think if you and your family had somewhere else to live, you should go.

One thing that worries me is you address. It is three sixes. And, that is a bad sign all by itself. Those three numbers together are believed to be an invitation to the beast. Plus, the address is on 6th Street. It may have nothing to do with any of this, yet it cannot be ignored. If you can stay with relatives for a few days, maybe I can come back here and try again in the early morning hours, when such entities are more active. Maybe I can see if anything can be determined. Otherwise, I just do not know what else to do."

Leticia looks at Gene and John and says, "Well, yes, we could stay with my brother. He lives close by and maybe we could stay in his spare room. I will need to call him and see what he says. Is there a chance this thing will follow us over to his house?"

Gene reluctantly says, "Yes, it could. If it is tied to you directly it definitely could follow you. On the other hand, if it is tied to this house then it won't go. Once you are there you will quickly know if anything is around you. The question is, you need to be up front with your brother, as his family could also be at risk too, if you go there and it does go with you, those people could be subject to its attacks and activity just like you are here."

Gene could tell Leticia was seriously troubled and was at a loss of what to do or where to go. She was desperate and yet Gene felt helpless in being able to help her. With her mom, the beast made itself known to him by facing him, and he was able to communicate and chase it away. But in this case, he doesn't know what to do since he doesn't know what he is dealing with. Looking at Leticia he says, "You know we were successful on one occasion of sending your mother to stay at her church with your son while we dealt with the entity that was in her house. The entity did not follow her to the church and maybe you could ask your local parish if you too could stay there until this thing is dealt with. Maybe it would workout better than staying with your brother. In any case, that is my recommendation."

Leticia tries to be brave but it was difficult since she was worried for the safety of her family. She didn't know who to call at her church or whether or not anyone would put her and her family up for a night or two. She says, "I will call them now. Would you mind waiting until after I speak with them? I just feel safer with you two men here."

Gene agrees and says they will do anything she wants to help her feel safe. So, the two men sit in the living room while she goes upstairs to check on her daughter and get the churches phone number. About two minutes after she leaves a loud scream is heard coming from her bedroom.

Bolting up the stairs, with John right behind him, Gene throws open the door, and there standing directly in front of him is the most grotesque thing he has ever seen. Standing at well over seven foot tall was this goulash looking, hairy beast with horns, long pointed ears, large fangs, beat red eyes and brownish red fur. And, instead of human feet it had hooves. This was like nothing Gene had ever encountered before. And, in the beasts arms was the little girl who apparently was still sound asleep.

Leticia is crying uncontrollably and John is hiding behind the bedroom door. Trying to use all of his psychic powers to make contact with the entity, in a calm and almost sedated manner, Gene slowly approaches the beast and calmly asked for it to hand the child to him. As if protecting it from danger the beast pulls the infant into its stinking, hairy body even tighter.

Gene stands there and says, "Come on Lucifer, you don't want to hurt this child. It is way to young for its soul to be of any value to you. Here, hand me the child, I can give it to its mother. Then you and I can talk."

Reluctantly the beast finally does as Gene asks, but instead of handing him the child he tosses her to Gene. Quickly reaching high in the air to catch the child he almost drops her. But he does catch her, and quickly hands her to Leticia. As he does that he tells her and John to immediately go down stairs. With the room empty accept for John and the beast, Gene inquires why it was there and what it wanted. At first it didn't talk. Then it says something rather odd. It barely speaks audibly but it whispers, "I don't know why I am here. I was sent here and I am here to wait for my orders."

Gene looks at it and staring it directly in the eyes he says forcibly, "You must depart this home and never return. I am a servant of God and through me he commands you to depart and never return. He commands Satin to depart and never return to this family, do you understand?"

As Gene says that, the beast raises both of its arms and lunges towards Gene with its mouth wide open as if it was going to devour him. Its fangs penetrate Gene's right arm while thrusting its long hairy arms around Gene's body. However, as it does this, it suddenly dissolves, and disappears, appearing to obey and leave. Waiting to see if it returns, it doesn't. After a few minutes of quiet and not feeling its presence, Gene walks down stairs and meets up with Leticia and John.

Quickly Leticia says, "You are bleeding and your shirt is torn. Are you Ok? Let me clean you up."

John is now at a total loss of what to say or think. Eventually he says, "Gene, what we saw could no way have been real. It was awful. It was worse than any horror movie I ever saw. And, it had a terrible odor. Where did it come from and where did it go? How could you have stood up to anything like that?"

By this time Leticia is back with cold rags and bandages. His right arm was bleeding and his shirt sleeve was soaked in blood. As he removes his shirt, he finds the gash was not all that bad. But, it did require a larger bandage. Quickly Leticia cleans out the wound with hydrogen peroxide and then bandages his arm.

While she worked on him, Gene explains what happened after they left. He tells Leticia that the room felt cleansed and he thinks the beast has gone. He says, "At first I thought the thing was going to eat my head off. It pounced towards me with its huge mouth wide open. Then, after clawing me, it just disappeared. That is why I think it is gone. So, what do you want us to do? We can still take you to the church to stay if you want, but I really do not sense it being here any longer. Now, it or another one can return, but if it was going to linger, I don't think it would have disappeared like it did. I truly do think you are safe. But you decide."

Leticia looks at Gene and says, "Gene you are my hero. If you think it is gone, I will take that to heart. And, if it returns, then we can leave at that time. But, I do not want to leave right away, because if it is still here, it will think it won. This is my house and it isn't welcome here. Thank you so very much. I don't know what I would have done without your help."

Driving back to the office both men are quiet for a long time. Then, John speaks up and says, "Gene, even seeing it for myself, I cannot believe it. What we encountered had to be something directly from Hell. I have to admit, I never truly believed in a Heaven or a Hell before. Yet, with that thing showing itself to us like it did, that is proof enough for me that Hell exists. And, if it does, then it would stand to reason that Heaven does too. Wow, it is all so weird. You know, no one will ever believe what we saw and what you did. Just to think about it is so crazy. Damned, you are one good advocate for making others believe in the paranormal. Thanks for letting me go along with you. My life has certainly changed after encountering that thing."

Gene thinks about what John told him and says, "John, there are a lot of things in this world we know nothing about. But, after going through what I have since my gun shot wound, nothing I encounter anymore surprises me. Yet, if I were you and had never seen anything like that beast before, I too would be scared, confused and worried. I think that is perfectly normal." As Gene says that he pulls into the attorney's parking lot. John gets out and tells Gene to take off the rest of the day and that he would see him in the morning. He also indicates if that wound to his arm needs more tending, he should go see a doctor and have it looked at.

Heading home Gene sees that it was only 3:45 pm. He decides when he gets home he will call George to tell him about he and Amelia's wedding plans. He thinks George should be his best man. He also thinks about the entity they confronted this day. He recalls being scared when it lunged at him. He thinks how really strange it was to go away like it did. Why did it leave so easily?

Gene pulls into his apartment parking garage. He exits and goes into his apartment. Taking a beer from his refrigerator, he sits down and dials George's home phone. Within seconds George answers.

"Hello," says George.

In response Gene says, "Hello my friend, how are you? Gene here, what is happening?"

George is happy to hear Gene's voice and immediately asks how his job was going? He congratulates him on finding the Captain's Granddaughter. He then wants to know what he is doing at the law firm. He is so excited he doesn't know what to ask first.

Gene interrupts George and tells him about his pending marriage to Amelia and how much he wants his old partner to be his best man.

George is elated and immediately indicates how honored he would be to do it. He inquires about a date and time.

Gene responds that the wedding will be in June, but the date, time and place is still undetermined. He says over the next week or so all of their plans will be finalized and he will let him know the specifics as soon as possible. The two then spend about a half an hour talking about what each other was doing. Gene was happy to hear how well George was doing and that he was back to work and enjoying himself. When he thinks about his friend being possessed, he is so grateful that they found Father Nelson. Otherwise there is no telling where George would be today.

Upon hanging up, Gene relaxes with a glass of beer and sits down to watch television. Recounting his luck earlier that day, he thanks God for protecting him and aiding in the chasing away of that demon. He then wonders how John was coping with what he went through and saw. He knows it was so bazaar and something he was glade John had a chance to witness. This way, going forward, John will always believe him when he tells of his encountering something. And, if they can actually develop a law business specializing in his areas of expertise, maybe it will all be worth the pain and worry he has gone through. Before long, Amelia is home. Gene immediately tells her of his day. He describes the demon he encountered and shows her the place where it bit him. He also describes his conversation with George. He says, "Amelia, George was genuinely happy to hear of our pending marriage and when I asked him to be my best man he was over the wall elated. He also said how good his life was now that he was back to work and enjoying it. So, I am happy for him, considering what all he went through, he is a lucky man."

Amelia is more concerned over Gene's arm injury. She says, "Let me look at that wound. Who bandaged it and did you use any disinfectant? Let me redo the bandage." She quickly gets up, goes into the bathroom and returns with gauze and tape. Plus, she too also has with her a big bottle of Hydrogen Peroxide. Sitting down next to Gene, she gently removes the old bandage. It was a deep wound, but it appeared not to be that serious. As she removes the bandage, she notices a fowl odor coming from the wound and there was even a feeling of a heavy breeze shooting past her at the same moment.

Looking at Gene she asks, "What is that odor? It smells somewhat like sulfur. And, did you feel that breeze shoot by when I removed the bandage? It was weird."

Gene looks at Amelia and says, "I didn't smell anything at Leticia's house when she bandaged my arm. But, yes, it does stink now. And, yes I did sense a breeze when you removed the old bandage. I think it is all really weird, that's for sure."

Thinking about Gene's comment, Amelia assumes everything will be fine once she rinses the wound out with the Hydrogen Peroxide. Blotting it dry she adds a few dabs of iodine into the cut and then places a large gauze patch over the wound and securely tapes it down. She then stands up and says, "Well, I really need to clean myself up now, so I am going to put this stuff away and grab a quick shower. When I get out, I will make us a nice dinner. So, sit here and enjoy your beer and T.V., and I'll be right back.

Gene turns the T.V. channel control to the local news station and follows a story about an armed robbery at a San Pedro liquor store. He knows exactly where the store was, as he and George had responded to the same call there several times in the past. Relaxing, he suddenly hears

Amelia screaming from the shower. Leaping up from the couch, he enters the bathroom and there lying naked on the floor huddled around the sink was Amelia. She was crying uncontrollably. Going over to her he squats down, puts his arm around her and asks what happened. He first assumes that maybe the hot water turned instantly cold. But what she explains sends chills down his spine.

Looking up at Gene as if she was a child she says, "Something was in the shower with me. It began rubbing my back gently and then reached around and touched both of my breasts. At first I thought it was you. But when I turned around to see you, there was nothing there. And, when I screamed, the shower door immediately opened and whatever it was got out. Look, over there, see those wet spots on the floor. It has to be its foot prints. I was so scared; it was like nothing I ever experienced before. It also stunk very badly. Gene what was it?"

Gene immediately recalls the sulfur odor coming from his damaged right arm and the breeze swishing buy her. Is it remotely possible that the demon he thought he had chased away this morning from Leticia's house, somehow took refuge inside his wound, and came home with him from that other place? Could the beast now be in his own home? Oh, what a terrible thought. Yet, he knows this wasn't something Amelia would make up or joke about. Plus, there were watery feet prints on the bathroom floor.

Gene helps Amelia to her feet, and grabs a towel for her to dry off with. He than escorts her into their bedroom and waits while she dresses. Sitting on the edge of their bed, Amelia approached Gene and asks again, what was it in there with me? It was not my imagination.

Looking into her eyes Gene says, "Sweetheart, I fear that the beast I chased away this morning is now here in our home. I need to walk around and see if I pickup on anything. I don't know what else to make of it. I have never had anything attach itself to me before or follow me home."

Looking at Gene, Amelia asks, "Gene might it be a ghost? Maybe one was at that house along with that demon. Maybe it liked you and attached itself to you. Or, could a ghost just be out wandering around and looking for a new place to haunt? They saw our house and decide it looked good?"

Gene knows that neither scenario was very likely. He was betting on it being the demon that bit him. He responds by saying, "Honey, when you smelled that sulfur odor, it was a definite sign of a demon's presence. That is their odor. So, my best bet is that thing somehow got into my wound as

I was being bandaged and when you changed the bandage, it exited. And, it is now here, amongst us.

Grabbing his arm Amelia asks, "So, what are we going do now? I don't want to stay here knowing that thing is lurking around here and watching us?"

Gene immediately agrees. He then says, "I don't want you staying here either or be exposed to it's actions. So, grab a few clothes and I'll follow you over to your mother or sisters house. I am sure in a day or two, I can make contact with it and get it out of here. Then, I will call you to come back home. And, everything will be as it was before. Ok?"

Nodding in agreement, Amelia grabs Gene's hand as she pulls him back into the bedroom. Obviously, she didn't want to be alone in there packing her clothes. She then instructs Gene to follow her over to her sister's house.

Outside, each get into their own car and Gene follows Amelia to her sister's Torrance house. Arriving, Gene gets out and the two knock on her door. Soon, Amelia's sister's two little girls answer the door. Seeing their aunt, they scream with joy and immediately hug her around the waist. That is followed by Amelia's sister coming to the door and greeting the two visitors. Inside, Amelia explains why she was there. The sister being familiar with haunting events of course believes them. Amelia takes her clothes into the spare bedroom and lays down her suitcase.

Gene then invites everyone to join him at a local pizza house where he offers to buy pizza. However, since the sister and her kids had already eaten, they decline. Amelia and Gene then go to the restaurant themselves and split a pizza. While they wait, they discuss the demon. Gene explains how he intends to deal with it. He assures Amelia, he would get it out of their house very quickly.

After eating, Gene returns Amelia to her sister's home. He then goes home. Entering, he sense the beasts presences. He walks around the house from room to room and invites it to show itself, but nothing happens. Finally, it was getting late and Gene is becoming tired. He quickly undresses and crawls into bed. Lying there he wonders if the beast will make its presence known. It doesn't take long before noises and pounding begin occurring. Lights all over the house go on and off. Laying there Gene now knows how other people who were trying to seek his help felt. Finally the sounds, flashing lights and other interruptions were too much to deal with. Gene gets up, puts on his robe and again begins walking through his house. As he walks he yells out for the beast to make itself visible and talk to him. Gene slowly walks from room to room. Yet, nothing appears and all the previous sounds and lights going off and on ceases. Finally, in his kitchen he sits at the counter and says, "You ugly drooling son of the Devil, show yourself. You are afraid to let me see you, because you are so hideous and ugly. I don't blame you, as there isn't likely anything so hideous in this world. But, you came to me, and now you are hiding. If you came here, you must have wanted something from me. My girlfriend is gone as she feared you. I told her there was nothing to fear, because you are a coward. But, she wanted to go somewhere away in order to be away from you. My question is why would anything as revolting as you try to touch a beautiful human woman. I am sure you are a freak and even a female animal would be disgusted by your touch."

As Gene says that, a loud howl is heard, which sounded as if it was coming from something standing right next to his right ear? Then, that sound is followed by a violent shaking of the kitchen refrigerator.

At first Gene fears the beast will tip the refrigerator over as it was moving it around very hard. Therefore, in order not to incense the entity any more he says nothing, hoping that in silence it would soon stop. Once it stops, Gene waits a few moments and then says, "Is that the best you can do? As big and strong as you are, why waste your energy on such dumb things. Again, I demand that you show your ugly self to me. I need a good laugh. I really want to see you before I send you back to Hell."

Sitting there, not a sound is heard. He waits about thirty minutes and even drinks a beer while he waits. Yet, the beast is totally silent. Getting sleepy and bored with the entities antics he once again goes to bed and falls immediately asleep. Waking at 6:00 am., Gene lies in bed a while looking around the room. It is so quiet you can hear street noise outside. Gene wonders if the beast might have left last night? Maybe his comments scared it back to Hell? But if it is still there, for sure tonight he needs to force it to show itself. Gene gets up, showers and readies for work. As nothing more occurs. And, the more he thought about it, he wonders if the entity left?

Later in the afternoon at work George calls. The two talk and George says he wants to stop by tonight and have a beer or two with Gene and discuss the wedding. He tells Gene that it was his day off and a good time to visit him. Gene agrees and tells him he would be home around 7:00 pm. They agree to meet then.

Gene knows he needs to try and call out the demon, if it was still there, which he needed to accomplish before George arrives. As the day ends, Gene hurries home. Entering the house he sees a message light blinking on his phone. He checks it and it was Amelia, asking Gene to call her.

Gene immediately calls and speaks to her. She wanted to know when she could come home? Gene relays the events of last evening and comments that maybe the beast had already fled. He tells Amelia he would call her later tonight after George leaves and he has had time to look more for the beast.

Gene begins walking around the house calling to the entity. He hears, sees and smells nothing. It was as if it was truly gone. How could that be? He was sure nothing he said last night was that scary. Why would it have left? Yet, the entire house felt friendly and warm. Gene goes into his bedroom and changes into casual clothing and gets a beer and watches the news on T.V. At approximately 7:10 pm., George arrives. He immediately heads to the kitchen and gets himself a beer from the refrigerator. The two sit and visit for a while. Eventually, Gene tells George that he was getting tired and needed to go to bed. He also wanted to call Amelia and tell her it appeared safe to come home tomorrow.

George finishes his last beer and indicates he needs to use the bathroom. Gene just smiles and points down the hall to indicate where the bathroom was located.

Finishing his last beer too, Gene begins to wonder why George was taking so long in the bathroom, when he suddenly hears a loud crash coming from there. He immediately gets up to go check on his friend. Knocking on the door, George immediately opens it and says he fell down. Exiting the bathroom George has a strange look on his face. As George makes his way around Gene, he throws open the front door and leaves without saying anything. No good-bye or see you later, nothing. Gene watches as George makes his way to his car and slowly drives away.

In all the years he has known George he never saw him get drunk on two beers before. It was very unlike him. And, why was he suddenly acting so strange? What was the noise in the bathroom? He knows he appeared fine when he went into the bathroom, so did he do or take something while he was in there that caused his strange behavior? Gene decides to go into the bathroom to see if he could smell anything that would explain George's actions. Watching George drive away, he prays that he would get home safely. After checking the bathroom and finding nothing, Gene sits down and calls Amelia to tell her it appeared that it was now safe to return home tomorrow as he no longer sensed the beasts presence.

After coming back home, Gene and Amelia have no problems or issues as the beast was indeed gone. Gene marvels over how easy it apparently was now for him to chase these entities away. And, if the firm does eventually establish a separate paranormal department someday for him to operate, maybe these were some of the things that he could specialize in, along with locating missing persons and other items.

CHAPTER 12; *A Vision of Things to Come:*

As Gene settles into his new job, he quickly realizes how much he truly enjoys the daily challenges he encounters while working with his company's clientèle on their various legal issues. He also recognizes how different this new career is from his former job as a police officer. The excitement of corporate law is like nothing he had ever imagined before. And, knowing that he is being groomed to become a criminal litigator is exactly what he had dreamed of while attending law school. Plus, there was still on going discussions among the firms partners about establishing a separate department where Gene could utilize his proven psychic powers to help people. All of which are opportunities that are so different from what he use to do, he marvels over the good fortune he has encountered. He firmly believes that over time he will not only be able to do many interesting things here, but at some point in time he hopes that he may also have the opportunity to become a partner in the firm.

Working closely with his company's top legal minds to learn all he could, Gene feels that he is getting close to being ready to work independently and with his own clientèle. Everyday he enjoys all of the new things he encounters and anxiously looks forward to the next day where he knows that he will be learning even more. Unlike the routine day to day responsibilities of being a police officer, being a litigator was much more challenging and very rewarding, which truly excites him. And, the proof of his improving skill level was evident in how quickly he was grasping what he was being taught, and also by the growing respect afforded him by his fellow colleagues.

One of Gene's more endearing skills and something his colleagues liked and respected was his ability to quickly assess and address many of the difficult issues that could suddenly occur. As a police officer, one of the many responsibilities and skills that are quickly developed was the necessity of being alert and able to quickly respond to dangerous situations that could arise at any time. Over the years as a police officer, Gene's aptitude for addressing such situations became very strong, which allowed him to be able to quickly deal with most job related issues. However, something new to Gene and an event that he was not prepared for occurs on a day when he suddenly cannot control his mental emotions. For some reason, his thought process was out of control, causing him great stress and an inability to concentrate on any company issue. He is suddenly experiencing strange mental images which makes it impossible for him to concentrate on anything. His thought process is completely interrupted by images swirling around inside of his head. Feeling very fatigued early in the morning, he acknowledges to himself that his mind was just not capable of concentrating on his work. Gene assumes that his problem must be related to a lack of rest, which causes him to anxiously look forward to going home and relaxing. As the day passes, Gene tries to avoid his colleagues and staying away from engaging in any serious conversations with anyone. As he works through the day, he tends to mundane issues within his own office. Then, at 5:00 pm, he cleans off his desk and leaves work. As he drives home he tries to figure out what had happened to him this day, but he cannot concentrate on even that question. All he feels are the constantly evolving strange images that fill his head. He tries to tell himself how much he loved his job and how he wishes he would have worked harder in law school to finish quicker, but his mind is out of control. He decides to drive carefully and get home as safely as possible since he even has difficulty concentrating on the traffic.

Arriving home, he goes inside where he finds Amelia standing in the kitchen. Smiling at her he walks over and kisses her on the cheek. Then, as they often did, they sit on the couch where each one tells the other about their day at work. Gene begins by explaining his strange day and how wild and vivid images continually filled his mind, making work impossible. He explains how tired he was all day and how he thinks maybe he is not getting enough rest.

Amelia sits next to Gene as she listens to his description of the days events. Looking over at him, she says, "Yes, you do look very tired. You not only have dark circles under your eyes, you look rather haggard as well. Maybe after dinner you should just consider going to bed for an early night's sleep."

Gene listens to Amelia's suggestion and responds, "Yes, maybe you are right. I have a lot to do tomorrow at work, and I need to be alert and able to concentrate on the meetings we have scheduled."

After dinner, per Amelia's suggestion Gene gets up, kisses her good night and goes to bed, and immediately falls asleep. But, it proves not to be a restful sleep, as he brain will not shut down, causing him to immediately begin mentally reliving all of his past psychic experiences he has encountered, beginning when as a police officer, he and his partner saw a man sitting in his pickup truck in front of his own home in San Pedro pushing the vehicle directly in front of him. He recalls how they investigated that event by interviewing the man, and later how shocked they were when they found out while interviewing the man's wife, that the man (her husband) had actually died one year earlier that very night, after being run down by a drunk driver, driving the very vehicle that the man was pushing away. He recounts how that event totally changed his overall perception of life and death, causing him to actively pursue answers about ghostly activities and the paranormal world. He then recounts how after receiving the gun shot wound to the head, he began experiencing growing psychic powers, which continued increasing to a point that he was eventually able to see and communicate with various unearthly entities, as well as what he now calls the shadow people. Lying there, he begins tossing and turning uncontrollably while visions of many events fill his head. Soon, his dreams become even more bazaar. He soon sees images of his former partner, George Newton, whose actions in his dreams were totally inconsistent with reality. George's strange activities eventually consume Gene's entire dreams. His partner's speech and movement were also totally different. And, he was even sensing erratic behavior from George while he was driving his police car as he patrolled the streets of San Pedro.

Waking up in a sweat, he sits up and looks around his darkened bedroom. Reaching over to his left he feels Amelia sleeping besides him. Getting out of bed he enters the bathroom to get a glass of water. As he stands there sweating, he wonders why earlier today and now tonight he was experiencing such weird and restless dreams and thoughts. He wonders if this is being caused by his constantly increasing psychic powers.

He knows up until now he has never experienced anything like this before, which now causes him to worry that something bad was beginning to happen to him. And, maybe these strange images he is suddenly seeing are signs of what may plague him from now on. And, if that was the case, he fears that he will be totally unable to perform even the simplest of jobs at the law firm.

Going back to bed he looks at his alarm clock on his night stand and sees that it was already 3:00 am. He knows that he has got to get some rest in order to actively participate in the various meetings he has scheduled. As he lies back down he tries to think of pleasant things, hoping he could fall soundly asleep for the next three and a half hours. Unfortunately as he lies there his mind once again begins drifting in and out of a state of unrest and all of the same strange dreams once again fill his head and those same unexplainable images and activities begin repeating themselves over and over again.

At 6:30 am his alarm clock goes off and he and Amelia wake up. Turning to him, Amelia immediately says, "Boy, what a terrible night I had. I was constantly being woken up by your continuously loud talking and constant twisting and turning throughout the entire night. And, since you have never done that before, I have to wonder what is suddenly wrong with you?"

Sitting up, Gene responds by saying, "Honey, I'm very sorry, but I was in a terrible state all of last night. My mind was so busy, and constantly filled with bad dreams. It was worse than yesterday at work. I actually relived everything that I have gone through since being shot in the head. And, on top of that, I had the strangest dreams about George. In my dreams, his actions and behavior were completely out of character and totally inconsistent with the reality of his duties. I cannot understand what is wrong with me, nor what is causing these things. But, I'm sorry for disturbing you. I assumed that I was the only one suffering from what I was seeing."

Getting up they both get ready for work. Amelia is the first to depart. Gene then leaves about ten minutes later. As he drives to his office, his mind still continues to relive everything he went through during the night. Those thoughts make it impossible for him to concentrate on anything else. He even wonders if maybe he should call Dr, Allen today and make an appointment with her, hoping that she might be able to help with his dilemma.

Arriving at the underground parking garage where he worked, he parks and exits his vehicle. He takes the elevator to his office. Entering, he is greeted by the surrounding staff. Yet, as he walks to his office he is barely aware of their presence and totally unable to hear their comments that were directed to him, as his mind was now totally engaged with the images and thoughts of last night.

The day passes slowly as Gene goes from one meeting to another, continually in a fog and unable to participate in anything being discussed. Whenever he did try to participate in any conversation; his mind simply could not concentrate on what was being discussed. After his final meeting, Gene looks at his watch and sees that it was almost 4:00 pm. In desperation he picks up the phone and calls Dr. Allen's office.

When Dr. Allen's receptionist answers, he immediately asks to speak with her. With in a few seconds, Dr. Allen answers the call.

Gene says, "Dr. Allen, this is Gene Wilson. I am sorry to be calling you so late in the day, but something weird is happening to me and I need your help." He briefly describes what has been happening and wonders if she had time to see him today.

Listening intently Dr. Allen says, Sure Mr. Wilson, can you come over right now?"

Smiling to himself upon hearing her invitation, he quickly responds, "Yes I can. I will be there in fifteen minutes." He then thanks her and hangs up the phone.

Arriving at the doctor's office, he enters and finds that the receptionist had already gone home for the evening. Looking around he decides to take a seat and wait in her outer office. Soon, Dr. Allen emerges from her office, seeing Gene sitting there, she invites him in and asks him to take a seat on her couch.

Sitting down, he begins by explaining his dreams last night and how he had never experienced anything like that before. He goes on to describe how his mind just wouldn't let go of what was occurring. He also explains how he saw his former police partner and how strange his actions were while on patrol. He continues by telling her how all through today, last night and the day before at work, his mind could not engage in anything productive because of the images and visions he was experiencing. He comments on his inability to perform any of his normal daily responsibilities because of that.

Dr. Allen listens with great interest, and then says, "Well, that is definitely strange. Usually when we dream, we forget about them during our waking hours." She then asks more questions, and is especially interested in knowing more about the strange activities he saw as it related to his former partner. She wanted to know specifically what was so different that made Gene worry about him.

Gene thinks about the question for a moment and then says, "I can't accurately or completely describe to you everything that I saw, but basically in my dreams George was very rigid in his posture and mannerisms. He was also very aloof, as he never once spoke to his partner who was sitting the whole time right next to him. In fact, during my entire dream, he never spoke at all. But, it was his physical movement that was so strange. It was more or less like he was in a trance and unable to control his own body, or perform his job responsibilities. I could see him on patrol, yet he was not acting like a policeman. He was doing strange activities and driving his cruiser very fast and dangerously. Strangely enough, I even sensed that he had disconnected his police radio and severed all contact with his command center. It was all so weird. I don't know why I would envision him that way, but it is how I truly saw him in my dreams last night."

Thinking about Gene's answers, Dr. Allen concludes that he was definitely stressed out and needed a good nights rest. She decides that strong sleeping pills would allow him to do that. Thinking that sleep would free him from the visions and strange events running through his head that plagued him all night long, she gets up, goes into her storage room, searches her inventory and finds what she was looking for. Retrieving a small sample packet that some sales person had given her, she hands the medicine to Gene and instructs him to take both pills around 9:00 pm. She also says he must be truly sleepy before he goes to bed.

Standing up, Gene takes the package and says, "Thank you Dr. Allen. I appreciate you making the time this evening to see me and listen to my problem. However, there is something that I have been worrying about since last night, which is seriously bothering me. Ever since these sudden visions and weird dreams have occurred, I have to wonder if it is being caused by my increasing psychic abilities. Is it possible that they have now grown totally out of control, and these events are being caused by that affect? Is, what I am now experiencing a sign of the way my life will be from now on?"

Listening to his question Dr. Allen admits to herself that she really had no answer for him, as his psychic abilities and growth patterns were subjects that were way out of her area of expertise. However, knowing that she had to calm him, she responds by saying, "No, even if your powers are growing, it is unlikely that your sleep cycle would be affected. I think whatever is causing these dreams is purely self motivated. So, take those two pills as I have instructed tonight and hopefully they will cause you to sleep very soundly, and tomorrow you will be just fine. But, if they do not help you, please call me first thing in the morning and I will call Dr. Mendenhall and seek his advice.

Placing the pills in his pocket, they shake hands and Gene departs her office. Driving home he hopes that what she said was right and he truly prays that the pills would work and allow him a good night's sleep. He admits to himself that after talking with her he does feel a little better. He acknowledges how good it is to obtain professional advise, which gives him some peace of mind.

Arriving home, Gene finds Amelia busy cooking dinner. They hug and kiss and she asks why he was so late, Amelia tells Gene she was worried about him, given his state of mind this morning.

Gene explains to Amelia that he had another really bad day at work and he went to see Dr. Allen, hoping that she could help him. He explains the discussion they had and shows her the sleeping pills she gave him. He tells her how he hoped they would allow him to get a good night's rest.

After dinner the two sit on the couch and discuss various issues, but the conversation always came back to Gene's dreams and his comments about how disturbed he has been. He tells her how he can't help but to worry that his psychic powers are growing out of control and maybe this new agony is what his life will be like from now on.

Amelia listens to him with great interest and concern, but of course does not have any answers. She says, "If Dr. Allen said that was not possible, I really think you should listen to her. But, maybe it would be helpful if you spoke to Dr. Mendenhall and see what he thinks. He is the senior psychologist of the two and he has always been right in his analysis and rational over the growth of your powers and abilities. So, if anyone would know the answer to your concern, I would think he would."

Gene agrees that Dr. Mendenhall would be a good source to talk with. But, for now, he decides to take his two pills. After doing so, he and Amelia sit down on the couch to watch a little television. And, within thirty minutes Gene starts nodding off.

Looking over at him, Amelia nudges Gene and says, "I think those pills are beginning to work. I suggest you go on to bed before you fall asleep sitting here, because if you do, there is surely no way that I can carry you to bed."

To that suggestion Gene gets up and goes to bed. Sleep immediately consumes him. For several hours he sleeps soundly. Then, early in the morning he wakes up needing to use the restroom. He looks at the alarm clock and notes that is was again 3:00 am. Going into the bathroom, he turns on the light and is immediately shocked to see three shadow people standing by the sink just staring at him.

As they stare, they say nothing. Yet, they definitely appeared to be real. Reaching out to them he asks, "Do you have a message for me?" But, they say nothing and only watch his every move. He senses that they wanted to speak, but for some reason do not. Gene continues to wait for some sort of response, but none is forthcoming. Asking his question again, this time as they look at him and then simply dissolve into thin air and disappear.

Back in bed Gene's mind is once again wide awake. He wonders if the shadow people were really there or was it just his imagination? If they were really there did it mean that something bad will happen to him? But, if that was so, why didn't they communicate with him? Eventually sleep begins to take over and he falls fast asleep. At 6:30 am, his alarm goes off and wakes him up. He immediately recalls seeing the shadow people in the bathroom earlier this morning. Looking around his bedroom he sees nothing. So, was what he saw real or not? Looking over at Amelia he sees that she is still sleeping. Knowing they both needed to get up he gently wakes her.

Sitting up, Amelia looks at Gene, rubs her eyes and asks, "So, sweetheart how did you sleep last night?"

Not sure how to respond to her question Gene decides the best way is is to say, "I slept just fine. I woke up at 3:00 am to use the bathroom, but I quickly fell back to sleep when I returned to bed. So, whatever bothered me before, must have been something unnatural and nothing for us to worry about." He decides not to mention his seeing the shadow people.

Later that day at work, Gene feels good and rested. All goes well. Early on he had concluded that he had only dreamed that he saw the shadow people, because if they were real, they would have surly said something to him, as in the past they always had. Then, while Gene is at his desk reading a legal brief, his phone rings. Picking it up he says, "Gene Wilson here, how can I help you?"

The caller says, "Hello Mr. Wilson, this is Dr. Allen. I was just wondering about you and was anxious to find out how you slept last night. And, did anything else happen that I need to know about?"

Gene explains that he had a good nights sleep and that he felt much better today. He jokingly says, "But, I did dream that when I woke up during the night to use the bathroom, my old buddies the shadow people were in there waiting for me. But, they never spoke and were totally silent. Unlike their usual actions, they did not give me any messages or warning about things that are about to happen. Then, as I questioned them more about their silence, they simply disappeared. So, when I woke up this morning, I concluded that they were only a fragment of my imagination and were never really there."

Dr. Allen listens with great interest and responds, "Well, I am very happy the pills worked and you got a good night's rest. But, knowing about the relationship that you have with those shadow people, I have to wonder why you dreamed that they were in your bathroom in the first place? Maybe, it was a psychic vision of something in the future. Possibly they will soon appear and warn you about something that is going to happen. I guess we will just have to wait and see. In any case, if you need my help or have any other issues, please feel free to call me at any time."

Gene responds by saying, "Thank you Dr. Allen. Seeing you yesterday was very helpful and I appreciate everything that you and Dr. Mendenhall have done for me. However, after sleeping soundly last night, I feel much better now and think that all of my prior visions and disturbing dreams were just an anomaly and nothing to really worry about. I seriously think going forward I will be just fine".

After Dr. Allen ends her conversation with Gene, she decides to call Dr. Mendenhall to discuss all of Gene's actions with him. As the two talk, she tells him everything that Gene said to her, including the detailed visions of seeing his former partner acting so oddly and about all the other strange dreams and visions he had. She also tells him how he dreamed about seeing his shadow people and how he later dismissed it as only a dream, since they never communicated with him.

Dr. Mendenhall finds the whole scenario very interesting and says, "Cathy, let me tell you something. In my opinion, if his psychic powers are indeed increasing, they could very easily be responsible for his wild and vivid dreams. And, knowing his relationship with those shadow people, such a vision could surly be a precursor to his interacting with them very soon. In fact, if you will recall, once when he and his partner were responding to a disturbing the peace complaint, those shadow people warned him of pending danger, and that warning saved his partner's life. So, it could easily be a sign of something bad that is about to happen. Also, his seeing his partner acting so oddly is very likely a vision into the future where his partner will do something that he has no control over and it could be dangerous for Gene. Therefore, it may be that his psychic abilities are trying to warn him of pending problems and because of his lack of experience he cannot understand those signals. It is now possible whether he is awake or asleep his powers are at work. I believe whatever he senses is important. It is possible that everything he dreams about now is real. It very well might have been a view into the future. At this point, we cannot just dismiss those dreams and visions as simply a restless night. And, if his powers are increasing, I do not think anything is occurring simply by chance. It could easily mean that messages are coming to him whether he is awake or asleep. So, if that is the case, we need to find out what they are and what it all means. He also needs to be able to understand for himself what is happening so that he can learn and deal with it. I recommend that you and I meet with him again as soon as possible. Besides, it is time for us to measure his psychic progress again anyway. Therefore, please call him and set a quick meeting so we can discuss everything with him.

Dr. Allen responds by saying that when she met with Gene, he did ask her whether or not she thought his growing psychic powers could be causing those nightmares and visions, to which she responded that she did not think so. However, after listening and understanding what these new comments are, she knows that the information she gave him was wrong, as she fully agrees that they definitely do need to help Gene. She then promises to call him today to schedule a meeting.

Dr. Mendenhall then says, "Actually I am happy you didn't say yes to his question, as it would definitely have scared him. Your response was best, and together we can discuss it with him at our meeting." He goes on to tell her not to say anything about the dreams when she schedules the meeting. He suggests that she simply let Gene think it is just a regular meeting to measure his growing psychic powers.

Upon hanging up, Dr. Allen calls Gene's house. There being no answer, she leaves a message on his voice mail, saying, "Hello Mr. Wilson. This is Dr. Allen. In speaking with Dr. Mendenhall this evening, he reminded me that it was time for all of us to meet again in order to reassess you psychic powers. Therefore, when you get this message, could you please call me so we can set a time and place to meet?" She then leaves her private home phone number for him to call.

Later that evening, Amelia and Gene are enjoying a nice dinner at a restaurant located on the ocean's edge at one of San Pedro's finer locations. Given Gene's good day without his bad dreams and visions, he felt a little night out at a fancy restaurant would be appropriate. As he and Amelia relax in the restaurant's outdoor patio, they enjoy a bottle of wine while watching a spectacular evening sunset. Eventually seeing the time, they reluctantly pay their tab and begin their drive home.

Upon entering their house, Gene sees the light on the telephone blinking, indicating that he had two messages. Checking the first message he hears Dr. Allen's comments and request. Writing down her phone number, he tells Amelia of the requested meeting and how it looked like he would soon be able to ask Dr. Mendenhall all of his question.

Amelia responds by saying, "Yes, I really think the timing is good and a follow up meeting is likely needed. And, when he explains the facts to you, I am sure you will be relieved and much happier."

Gene then checks the second message and is surprised to hear the voice of his old boss, Captain Mitchell, who says, "Gene, this is Captain Mitchell. We have a problem that we would really like your help with. Again, we have another abducted child. In fact, the child and her parents are good friends of George Newton's. So if you could call me tomorrow and let me know if you can help, I will have George come by and pick you up." The Captain then leaves his cell phone number for Gene to call.

Amelia smiles to herself knowing that searching for a missing child was something Gene was very good at, since this will be his third opportunity to help in that endeavor. She also knows that if he is successful and finds the child unharmed, it will greatly benefit him in his position at the law firm. She thinks if Gene can find her quickly and she is safe, just like he did with Megan and Janie, that may accelerate the firm's decision to establish that new department for Gene to run. Amelia knows that with enough positive press exposure, the demand for Gene's help will be very strong from people seeking help.

CHAPTER 13; *The Meaning Behind Gene's Nightmares are Discovered:*

Waking up at 6:30 am the following day, Gene feels remarkably rested. He smiles to himself knowing that he has had two good nights of sleep and no bad dreams or visions. He is very appreciative. As he and Amelia get out of bed and prepare for work, he recalls the two messages and Captain Mitchell's plea for help. He goes over to the phone and listens to the messages again and makes sure that he has both numbers, He then places the numbers in his jacket pocket.

Amelia is excited for Gene because she know that a successful search will help his reputation and be a positive event for his future at the law firm. They both get ready for work, prior to departing, she says, "Honey, there is no doubt that your company will allow you to take off and help the police. And, there is also no doubt that this will be a very good day for you. But, I want you to promise me that you will be careful. Remember you are no longer a policeman. So, do not let George lead you into anything dangerous or harmful. Also, I hope your powers are so strong today that you quickly find that child and bring her home safe." To that, they kiss, and say good-bye as Amelia departs for work.

At work Gene seeks out his boss John Wagner. Finding him, he quickly explains everything to him, just as the Captain had asked. He also explains that the child was well know to his former partner, George Newton. Further explaining that George was ready to come and get him and the two would meet the child's parents and then go off together to search for the little girl.

John is extremely pleased to have the opportunity for his firm to help. He says, "Gene, this is exactly what we need for you to do, if we are actually going to move forward with that new paranormal division, which will allow you to outsource your abilities for such endeavors. And, if you can be successful and quickly find the child as you did in the past, the media's attention will be all over the story and it will be very good for you and our firm. Absolutely, we can let you off to meet with your old partner and go find that child. Call Mitchell right now and tell him you are totally available and that our firm completely supports your efforts 100%.

Gene smiles at John and comments, "Thanks boss. I knew you would say yes, but of course I needed official approval before calling Captain Mitchell."

Gene then gets up and returns to his office. Once there, he searches his jacket pocket and finds the two phone numbers. The first call is to Captain Mitchell. Dialing the number, only a few seconds passes when the phone is answered.

Captain Mitchell doesn't even say hello. Instead he says, "Gene is that you?"

Laughing to himself, Gene responds, "Yes Captain it is. I am very impressed at finding out what a sophisticated cell phone you have. One which denotes who is calling. I had no idea the city would equip you with such an expensive piece of equipment."

The Captain laughs and says, "Yes, my new phone does show who is calling. And just between you and me, I find it really handy when I get unsolicited sales calls. When that occurs, I just hang up on them. But, knowing John Wagner and how anxious he is to get positive media coverage for his firm, I had no doubt that he would loan you to us."

Gene responds by saying, "Yes, you are right about that. In fact, I am yours for as long as you need me. So, what is the plan?"

Happy to hear Gene's eagerness the Captain says, "Ok, the first thing I want is for you and George to go to the parents house so that you can talk with them. Get all the facts. Hold the kids clothes or anything else you need to get a vision of where the child is being held. Then together, you and George will go on and search for her. I am placing my entire squad room on alert if you need more officers or backup. Also, if you need any technical help, I will provide everything I can. So, when will you be ready to get started? George is standing by and very anxious to come and get you."

Gene replies that he is ready to go right now. He hangs up knowing that his old partner is on his way.

Gene then decides to call Dr. Allen. This time she was out, so he leaves a brief message about his being out of the office all day aiding the police in locating another abducted child. He goes on to tell her to set a meeting as soon as possible and he will be there no matter what.

Gene then leans back in his chair and admits to himself how much he was looking forward to visiting and riding with George once again. Momentarily, he recalls how strange he acted when he last saw him, after drinking two beers and going into the bathroom at Gene's house. He thinks about how strange it was that he just walked out of the bathroom and left without saying anything. He certainly hopes he is well now and assumes that George likely became ill, as he didn't have that much to drink. As he thinks about George, he recalls the many nights that the two patrolled together. He recalls the numerous jokes each man played on the other. He remembers the many calls they went on, including the one where he got shot, and how George stayed by his side the whole time waiting for an ambulance.

As Gene reminisces it suddenly occurs to him how the gun shot wound totally changed his life. He knows that since becoming psychic, he now believes there is definitely a Heaven and a Hell. In fact, he now believes that God himself directed that bullet into his brain in an area where it would cause Gene to experience growing psychic powers. An act that has already led to his finding and saving three lives, including George. And, if he is able to continue saving lives, then all of his pain and suffering was well worth it. He thinks that if his law firm does start a new paranormal division to help people with their problems and aid in locating missing people, that in itself is proof of God's intervention and something he wanted.

Gene then recalls his recent bad dreams and visions and especially those images about George. He admits that he can't see what good such things were for him, as obviously it was caused by fatigue and an overactive imagination. He knows how dedicated George is as a policeman. He knows he is a joker, but on the job he is very serious. Therefore, to see him acting so oddly as if he was possessed was really mystifying.

While thinking about all of his good fortune and those crazy dreams, his office phone rings. Answering it, the receptionist in the front lobby tells him that a policeman was downstairs waiting for him and he said his name was George.

Leaving his office, going down stairs, he opens and exits through the front door. He immediately sees a police car parked at the curb. Inside, he also sees his old partner George behind the wheel. Opening the passenger door and getting in, he says, "Ok partner, I'm ready, lets hit it."

When George pulls away from the curb, Gene expects a response, but none is forthcoming. All George does is drive fast and heads towards San Pedro. In his haste to get into George's vehicle, unseen but standing by the office building's front door were four shadow people, watching as Gene and George drive away.

After about twenty minutes of silence between them, Gene finally asks, "So, what is the story on the missing little girl? How long have you known her and her parents? What do they think happened to her? What is her name?"

George remains silent while he drives faster and stares only straight ahead. He soon enters Palos Verdes Drive South, which is a bluff road overlooking the ocean. The road also contains a lot of curves and many bumpy spots due to the constant shifting of the land.

Looking over at George, Gene says, "Partner, your driving way too fast for this curvy road. If you're not careful, we could easily go over the edge and wind up in the the ocean below. Slow down, we will get there in plenty of time to talk with the parents and then go find the child. I know you are worried about the child, as Captain Mitchell said you were close friends of her parents."

There is still no response from George, and he does not slow down. And, considering he has not said anything since Gene got into the car, Gene worries that there may be something else wrong with him. Maybe what he saw the other day when George so suddenly left his house after being in the bathroom, was proof that he went in there and took some type of dope. Maybe he is still taking dope and it was affecting his mental capacity.

Gene says again more forcefully, "Dammit George, you are driving to fast. You are going to kill us both if you do not slow down. Answer me, what is your problem?

Slowly turning his head towards Gene, he is now driving and not looking at the road at all, which is really scaring Gene. Finally, George speaks. His voice is loud and almost hollow sounding. He says, "So you think I am ugly and hideous? Well, I wonder how beautiful you will look when your face is splattered all over the rocks from the ocean below? Sure, now you are afraid. But you were not fearful of me when you chased after the great Apollyon, the king of all demons and drove me out of this man's body, a few weeks ago. You were not afraid of me when you thought I had entered your house to torment you and you girlfriend. And, you were so stupid to think I actually got chased off by you and left. The fact is, I got into you through that bite, just so I could travel with you to your home for one reason. And, that was to complete my mission, which was and still is to take this man's soul with me to Hell. I waited in your bathroom for two days knowing he would eventually visit you and come in there. And, when he did, I had him. I took over his body which is why we quickly departed your house. I did not want you to know what had happened. I knew this man was weak and I stupidly left him when that priest used your God and his tools to get to me. The moment I left him, I knew it was wrong. My master was very angry with me. I returned to that old lady Ramos's daughters house because I knew she would seek your help and I could get to this man through you. I knew that was my best way to reclaim this man's body."

Gene asks, "So, why am I here? Why are you doing this to me? I will never give up my soul to you, as God is my savior, and I belong to him for ever. Also, what about the missing child we are suppose to be helping? We need to find her"

The entity looks again at Gene and says, "You fool, there is no missing child. I lied to your friend the Captain. And, like a fool he believed me. I knew he would seek your help. That was my way to get you here. I knew your pride wouldn't allow you to turn away from helping a child. I wanted to get you alone so that I could treat you like you did me. Now, doing away with you is my personal reward. Plus, look at all the people that will miss you. They too might be susceptible to my charms. I'll even bet your Amelia would offer up her soul to me quickly just to have the ability of seeing you again. Your colleagues at work and at your former police job, some of them may be weak too. You are here because you offended me and my master said this was how I could redeem myself in his eyes."

As Gene is looking at Apollyon, George's face suddenly changes completely. Now it is the demons head on George's body. It is ugly and repulsive. Wild drool is running down its mouth. Upon changing to its real self, it begins laughing uncontrollably and yells to Satan to take him and George into his family. His eyes are a vivid red and almost glowing.

Sitting there, the vision of the shadow people in his bathroom the other night had to be real and it had to have been a warning to him of pending danger. It had to be their way of trying to help him. But, if only they would have been more specific and spoken up, he wouldn't be here. He also realizes how obvious it was that all of those bad dreams and visions were really warnings too. He especially now realizes how the actions he saw about George with his strange and erratic movements was exactly how he is now. Obviously, they were all clues of George's possession by Apollyon . Why did he not recognize them for what they were? Gene bows his head and begins praying out loud. He hopes some how God can still save him.

The demon looks over at Gene upon hearing his prayers and laughs uncontrollable, as he says, "You fool, nothing can save you from what is about to happen, As you mortals often say, payback is a bitch, and let me add, it is also so much fun too." As he says that the demon quickly turns the car right, hitting a guardrail straight on. The velocity of the vehicle's speed propels it into the air and over the embankment, heading nose first straight down, crashing into the rocky beach and surf below. Upon impact, the vehicle immediately explodes into a ball of fire and smoke.

Immediately, several cars who witnessed the event stop at the site of the impact. Cell phones in hand they all immediately use them to call 911, to report a police car crash and the obvious death of all occupants.

EPILOGUE

While Amelia sits home waiting for Gene to return, she is watching the television news channel at 11:00 pm. Half awake, she debates whether or not to go to bed. She assumes the reason Gene is so late is that he likely had good luck in finding the missing child, figuring if he wasn't having any luck he would have already been home. And, since he is becoming somewhat popular with the news agencies over his finding those two previously kidnapped children, Amelia is kind of expecting to see some news coverage on T.V. about his success.

Half way nodding off she is awakened by the report of a police car driving over a cliff in the Palos Verdes Peninsula, crashing down the cliff and exploding on impact. The story relates how observers saw the police car traveling at high speeds on P.V. Drive South without its red lights on, when it suddenly turned right smashing the guardrail and flew in the air, zooming to its death one hundred yards below. The story was sketchy and unable to give any description or names of who was in the car or what may have caused the vehicle to run over the embankment.

Amelia is immediately panicked. How can she get more information? Who might she call? She knows that Gene had George's cell phone number somewhere and she begins looking for it. Finding his personal phone directory on top of their dresser she sees several names. She locates George's and dials the number. There is no answer. She then finds the number to Captain Mitchell and calls that number. It too went unanswered. Then, just as she is looking for anyone else to call, there is a knock at her front door. Immediately going to open it, there stood Captain Mitchell and a female police officer. Staring at them she begins crying, as she knows the only reason they were there this time of night was to give her news that she didn't want to hear.

As Amelia looks at them, Captain Mitchell asks if they could come in.

Without responding she opens the door and goes over and sits down on the couch. She then says, "I just saw a story of a police car flying off of P.V. Drive South and down into the rocks below where it exploded. Please don't tell me that was Gene and George."

Sitting next to Amelia, the two officers are momentarily quiet. She could easily see how distraught they were. Then, Captain Mitchell speaks up and says, "Yes Amelia, it was George and Gene. I cannot say at this time what happened, or why they turned into the guardrail. But, what I can say is the alleged kidnapping of that child turned out to be bogus. I only found that out this afternoon, long after George had picked up Gene. I tried several times to contact George's car, but there was never any response. I then dispatched several officers to look for them. I do not know why they were even on Palos Verdes Drive South. The address for the alleged missing child was nowhere close to that area. It is a complete mystery to me. When Gene and I spoke this morning, he was eager to see his old partner, and we thought nothing of George's offer to pickup Gene. And, assuming George knew the people personally I figured he was simply anxious to find the child."

Amelia is crying uncontrollably and tries to make sense of it. She manages to stop crying long enough to ask, "If there was no kidnapping who made the false report? Wouldn't George have called the parents himself to verify what had happened. Certainly he would not have gone looking for that child without first talking to the parents?"

"Yes, that is a good question and one we have tried to figure out. When we contacted the family, they confirmed that they knew George, but they had not seen him in several weeks. We also spoke to Sarah, the supposedly missing child. She too said she had not seen George in a long time. So, the whole thing is one big mystery," explains the Captain.

The female police officer introduces herself as Officer Cynthia Jones and explains that she came along because she had heard a lot about her and Gene from George, who she had been dating for several months. She says, "When I heard about the crash, I told the Captain that I wanted to meet you and maybe together everyone could figure out why and how something like this could have happened. I was very fond of George, but these past couple of days he treated me very coldly. His nature was to be quiet, but last night when I stopped by his apartment to chat before he went to work, he was totally a different person. I just sensed something was definitely wrong with him."

The Captain then says, "Yes, his partner called me this morning at home and said how different he thought he was too. He said in the past they communicated a lot while on patrol. Yet, last night he never spoke one word to him all night. Later, he also detected that he had turned off his radio to the command center, which was obviously what he did again tonight. It was all so unlike him. I was really hoping you might have had some conversation with Gene that may lead us to a possible answer."

Amelia is in such a shock over Gene's death that their problem with George was really unimportant to her at that moment. All she wanted was for them to leave, so she could grieve alone. As she is about to say something, a noise is heard coming from behind them. Turning around to see what it was, all three see a three ring binder lying on the floor opened up.

Amelia gets up, picks it up and notes that it must have somehow fallen out of their small bookcase. But she wonders how could that of happened? There was nothing visible that would explain why it just fell out of the bookshelf. She looks inside the binder and finds that it was open at the exact spot which denoted in Gene's own hand writing the entire account of Gene's experiences in helping Father Nelson perform an exorcism on George, and how he became possessed in the first place by a demon that they later learned called itself Apollyon. It described everything that occurred during the entire exorcism, and it noted how the demon was chased out of George. Handing the binder to Captain Mitchell, she says, "Maybe this will explain the mystery. It contains some rather startling facts about George."

Quickly looking through the binder, Captain Mitchell becomes emotionally choked up as he knows this book didn't just fall out of the bookshelf by accident. He knows it was deliberately made available to them by something paranormal. And, it contained valuable information that would easily explain why George was acting so odd, if somehow he became possessed again by the same demonic entity. Looking around the room and up to the ceiling, the Captain says, "Thank you Gene, God bless you and rest in peace."